DEATH BY CHOICE

DEATH BY CHOICE

Masahiko Shimada

Translated by Meredith McKinney

THAMES RIVER PRESS

Death By Choice

THAMES RIVER PRESS
An imprint of Wimbledon Publishing Company Limited (WPC)
Another imprint of WPC is Anthem Press (www.anthempress.com)

First published in the United Kingdom in 2013 by
THAMES RIVER PRESS
75-76 Blackfriars Road
London SE1 8HA

www.thamesriverpress.com

Original title: Jiyu shikei
Copyright © Masahiko Shimada 2003
Originally published in Japan by SHUEISHA, Tokyo
English translation copyright © Meredith McKinney 2013

ISBN 978-0-85728-247-7

Cover design by Laura Carless.

This title is also available as an eBook.

This book has been selected by the Japanese Literature Publishing Project
(JLPP), an initiative of the Agency for Cultural Affairs of Japan.

CONTENTS

FRIDAY

Somewhere over Tokyo

You are hereby sentenced to Death by Choice. From now on, this form of execution replaces this country's customary Death by Hanging. You have the honor of being the first criminal to be executed by this means. You should make haste to decide your chosen means of execution and execution date, and to personally carry out the aforesaid execution. For the next two weeks the weather should be fine, and all those involved are able to be at your disposal.

You have got to be joking, thought the traveller, his head bowed before the judge's sentence. The "courtroom" was exactly like the little *oden* restaurant he dropped into a couple of times a month, and a haze of steam obscured the faces of both the public prosecutor and the lawyers. The judge who had delivered his sentence of Death by Choice was riding piggyback on a woman in a denim skirt. In fact, there was no getting around it: the judge was actually a baby. So what did this baby think it was up to, treating him in this high-handed fashion? The traveller felt half inclined to retaliate with a bit of sarcasm, but he felt constrained by the presence of the woman and held his tongue. He somehow felt he knew her, but he couldn't put his finger on who she was. He'd met her quite a while ago; that much he was certain of. As for this smart-arse baby, he'd never laid eyes on him before. Babies were absolutely anonymous creatures to him. Whoever it might be, it was only someone's baby as far as he was concerned. He guessed this particular baby must plan on being a judge some time around the mid-twenty-first century. But why did this poor traveller have to find himself being sentenced by a baby?

1

"Mumma! Milky!" the baby shouted suddenly. The woman carrying him on her back brought down her gavel with a thud, upon which the traveller was summarily ejected from the courtroom.

He found that the aeroplane had taken off, and had already levelled out. The traveller always grew drowsy just before takeoff. That gavel hitting the desk had actually been the sound of a baby's bottle hitting the floor, fallen from the hand of the young mother in the seat across the aisle from him.

Fresh from his dream, the traveller had the feeling that the baby judge had somehow resembled his dead father. Come to think of it, the woman carrying him seemed to be one of his classmates from middle school days.

He examined the mother and baby across the aisle out of the corner of his eye. The baby gazed back at him. "Abama oodleoodle," it remarked. "Eh?" said the traveller, caught off guard. The mother, becoming aware that her little darling was talking to some unknown man, murmured, "Yes dear, I'll give you your milky now sweetheart," throwing the man a tense, warning smile as she did so. In an attempt to dispel her fears, he responded by relaxing his frown and attempting to entertain the baby by blowing out his cheeks and crossing his eyes. Breathing noisily through its nose as it sucked away at the bottle clutched in its hands, the baby glared back. It looked as if it was about to give him a stern piece of its mind. The traveller gave a little sigh, and settled back to flip through the magazine from the seat pocket in front of him. The baby sighed too. From then on, the traveller found their eyes meeting again and again. Whenever their gaze locked, the baby would try to engage him in conversation. It seemed to be speaking in words that only the dream world could make sense of. Unfortunately, however, the traveller knew neither the grammar nor the pronunciation of dream language, and it didn't look like the mother could interpret for him either. From time to time, the baby sighed, and gave a derisive snort of laughter. The traveller too had once been a baby. More than thirty years ago it was now. He had no way of recalling the sort of things he'd thought as a baby, but it seemed to him the world of time had been different back then. Yesterday and tomorrow had been all jumbled up together, a year would pass in the space of a day, and he could slip easily in and out of past and future lives – that was the kind of dream world he imagined he'd inhabited as an infant.

Sure, it would be enough to make anyone snort with derision, or heave a sigh or two, if a man turned into a baby and looked back over his own life.

Dreams were the sort of thing that seemed at first glance to have some meaning, but in fact you could interpret them any way you wanted. With the one he'd just had, though, he'd certainly feel a lot better if he treated it as completely meaningless. Being able to interpret dreams any way you wanted meant in effect that you could rewrite them as much as you liked. In the hands of someone who had a way with words, a nightmare could become a harbinger of good luck, while a pleasant dream might turn out to be simply the flip side of harsh reality. Dreams get used according to the needs of the moment. If something's preying on your mind, take a look at your dreams and you'll discover what it is. If the future's weighing on you, ask your dreams for the answer. It will help you prepare yourself, if nothing else.

The traveller had never been psychoanalysed. Nor did he have any particular worries. He never remembered his dreams. Trying to recall them only made you feel anxious, after all. As to the question of where he came from and where he'd go when he died, well the answer had always been perfectly clear. The fact was, there was nothing he could do about it. What his dreams told him was: you yourself are quite meaningless.

On a sudden impulse, the traveller had just been to visit the grave of his father, who had died four years ago. His father's name was inscribed on a gravestone in Dazaifu, his birthplace. At the age of sixteen he'd left Kyushu for Tokyo in search of fame or fortune, and for the following forty years he'd moved from one suburb of Tokyo to another, working virtually without a break all that time. He'd gone to his final rest still dreaming of returning home in triumph. He'd requested that he be buried back home in the family tomb, but there were no longer any family members left in Dazaifu to look after the ancestors, just the lonely grave. The priest in charge of the cemetery had intended to make the plot over to another family, and this new addition foiled his plans. The traveller and his mother had also come up with a plan to move the grave to a new site in the suburbs of Tokyo so that they could look after it, but his father had stuck to his guns. I may have nothing else in the world to call my own, he declared, but that grave is home and I want to go back there. Nothing had gone his way in life, thought his son, so the least they could do was follow his wishes in death.

It was four years since he'd visited the ancestral grave, and it was an overgrown wilderness. The traveller weeded it, cleaned up the gravestone with a scrubbing brush, and placed fresh flowers and sake before it. As he worked, he had to smile. What on earth had his father been thinking to want to come back to his birthplace, even if it was as a corpse? Did he believe that the soul should return to its place of origin? Or was it that forty years after he'd left home, forty long years of Rip Van Winkle existence, he still wanted to go to his eternal rest in the bosom of his ancestors?

His father had gone through life a good-natured dupe, too spendthrift ever to make his fortune and too gullible ever to make his mark on the world. And his son had quite a lot in common with him. His father had named him Yoshio, "good man," and his own foolish good nature had come down to the boy. Yoshio Kita was thus at the mercy of genes that inclined him to serve others. In reaction, he longed to try a life devoted to the impulse of the moment, to follow his instincts, to give way to explosive emotions.

Since about the age of thirteen, Yoshio Kita had developed a tendency to despair of the future, and from time to time he had the recurring thought that he may as well just throw it all in and die. Nevertheless, he'd made it this far without putting the idea into action, just mooching along through an uneventful life, relying on his own good nature to get him by. But, as sometimes happens, he suddenly became possessed by the idea.

Still, when he came to think of it, dying wasn't all that easy. That French philosopher who died of an autoimmune disease had advocated the idea of suicide as a death as pleasant as making love to your sweetheart in some hotel room. But he had actually latched onto the idea after his visit to Japan. Here in Japan, suicide had traditionally been a matter of form, without necessarily any need for a motive or a reason or a crime to justify it. It was the same for the mourners who saw you off to the other world – they mourned you according to custom, without feeling they had to get to the bottom of just why you killed yourself. Sure, there were people who enjoyed tossing round ideas about death and suicide, but then they weren't the ones who did it. They stayed alive, which meant they got to say whatever they liked about it. They could bewail its absurdity or investigate its true nature all they liked. But the dead are mute. The living can choose to take that silence as ironic or see it as some kind of joke if they want. Nevertheless, the person who dies gets to choose his own death. That's essentially what suicide's been about in Japan all along. You may be forced to commit suicide by society or other people, but the act itself is completely meaningless. What's without any meaning can sometimes make people laugh. And since the dead can't laugh, the living have to make up for it by getting the joke he intended and laughing for him. How ironic it would be for the poor guy if they didn't get it!

There's a story about the comic storyteller who liked to make his audience groan by being intentionally unfunny. Apparently, as he lay in the hospital bed about to breathe his last, he stretched out his hand toward the family members gathered round him. But when his wife and children went to seize it, he waved them feebly away.

"No, no," he said, "I'm after money."

There he is, about to die at any moment, surrounded by people weeping at this parting from their beloved husband and father, and he goes and makes a tired old gag like that. This was the man who liked to scandalize his audiences as a matter of principle. That was his art, his very essence, so even on his deathbed he was still at it. People found this moving. Even at the very doors of heaven or bound for hell, they said, it looks like he couldn't resist one more stab at getting a laugh.

This way of dying is revered in Japan, you might say. It sticks in people's memory. The one dying and the ones seeing him off are both essentially following the old traditions.

In the airport restroom, Yoshio Kita threw away the Boston bag he'd been carrying, and emerged empty-handed. The bag held a change of clothes, a couple of magazines, and a packet of Dazaifu rice cakes. There was no need to carry any of this stuff around any more now.

Swaying along in the carriage of the monorail into the city, he pondered where to start, but his mind was a complete blank, and nothing came to him. Finally, as he arrived at the last stop in Hamamatsucho, he came up with a few ideas – he'd withdraw money from the bank, he'd indulge in luxury and debauchery, and he'd do something for the world and humanity. He had 1,116,715 yen in his bank account. It was quite a hefty amount to take out all at once, and he may well want to make some purchases on the credit card, so he settled for withdrawing 300,000 yen, which he divided up and stuffed into his pockets.

Not Just Your Average Guy – A Sermon

OK, he thought to himself as he stepped out into the main street, let's use my remaining time on earth meaningfully and efficiently. He set about trying to hail a cab, but not a single one that passed him had a "vacant" light posted. Not a good start. But as he was standing there, eyes peeled for cabs, he was startled to catch a sudden glimpse of a figure out of the corner of his eye. Just two yards back down the road, a middle-aged man, of medium height and medium weight, in a grey three-button suit, was standing with an innocent air, trying to sneak in ahead of him to nab the first vacant cab. He looked like he'd only just managed to haul his heavy-looking aluminium briefcase as far as the street and was anxious to get to his next destination by the shortest possible route as soon as he'd caught his breath. In short, he looked like the sort of guy a policeman would immediately be inclined to ask a few questions. Kita simply wanted to be somewhere else – anywhere else, he'd decide where once the wheels were rolling – and had no reason to compete with this fellow, but on the other hand he didn't want his adventures to get off on the wrong foot. And so, keeping a careful check on the man's back, he moved five yards down ahead of him, and stood there squirming about with his hand raised like an elementary school student with the right answer, trying to draw attention to himself, as if to say to the world "I got here first." The man, however, ignored him completely. He just moved himself two yards down beyond Kita. There he slipped a cigarette into his mouth and set about searching for his lighter, slapping his pockets up and down both sides of his suit, then glanced at his watch, and even clucked his tongue in mild impatience. A taxi drew in, its indicator flashing. The middle-aged man turned to Kita. "Got a light?" he said. Kita pretended not to hear him. Determined to be heard, the man went on, "It's difficult to catch a cab right now, so why don't you join me and we can ride together?" No longer able to ignore him, Kita asked, "Where are you going?"

Guys off to the cycle races might share a cab, but Kita didn't think this was the sort of town where two men completely unknown to each other could nonchalantly just hop in together like that. As for himself, of course, he was quite prepared. If the guy turned out to be a murderer, he'd simply resign himself to the fact that his fate had caught up with him. But wasn't the other man at all concerned whether he himself might be a killer?

The taxi was sitting idling beside them with the door open. The other man climbed in, hugging his case, and beckoned Kita to get in after him. He hadn't even asked where Kita was going, probably to forestall any refusal. So this was his justification for sneaking in ahead for a cab – he'd simply planned to share it, eh? Kita settled down beside him without a word, annoyed that he was tacitly allowing the man to get away with his tactic. The man gave a destination to the driver, then turned to Kita. "What about you?" he asked. "That'll do fine," Kita said casually. His old teacher would have told him not to let things sweep him passively along like this, to assert himself. Too bad, though. The other guy was too pushy to resist.

The taxi set off for downtown Shibuya. Shibuya's actually not a bad idea, he thought, immediately setting about justifying having let himself be swept along by events. A good place to relax what goes on above the neck, and liven things up below the waist. After all, I'm going to die in a week's time, so why not go easy on the resentment and hatred side of life? He found himself feeling more magnanimous and openhearted than he had in years.

The cab radio was tuned to the news broadcast. The announcer's even, detached style of reading had a way of making any murder, air raid, terrorist bomb attack, robbery, or collapse of the share market sound like a matter of no personal concern. After all, things were all going all right as far as you yourself were concerned, so you could get a mild kick out of tales of terrorist attack, or feel happy that you weren't among the victims of a murderer, without ever registering despair or hope or indulging in self-reflection as you listened. Sure, there were moments when you felt envy, but five minutes later it was gone.

"Another convenience store robbery, eh? There's been a lot of that lately. Never out of a job in that line of work – and pretty easy work in Japan at that, with all those drink machines packed full of money standing around on the streets."

The man was holding forth with the aim of getting Kita and the driver to chime in.

"Those vending machines are real moneyboxes, aren't they?" said the driver, with a trace of a northern accent. He seemed to relish talk. At times when he had no passenger, he'd probably amuse himself by talking back to the radio announcer as if they were on air together.

"Japan's a dangerous place these days, that's for sure. There are plenty who'll understand you when you talk, mind you, but nowadays we've got a lot of foreign types who can't follow a word you say. Get mixed up with those guys and bang, you're done for. We cab drivers who got to work with our backs to folks are always feeling danger right behind us."

"So what would you do if I turned out to be a robber?" murmured the man, tapping a finger against his aluminium case.

"Stop the bad jokes, won't you?" responded the driver.

"Well there you are saying you're always sensing danger behind you, aren't you?"

"Ah well," said the driver with a laugh. "Your life's in my hands, after all."

"OK, you got me there. But when you think about it, the guy that robbed that store will be listening to the news somewhere right now, won't he? What's he going to feel when he sees his own image caught on security cameras, if he's watching the TV news?"

The man now turned to Kita. "I'll bet you go to convenience stores quite a lot," he said meaningfully.

Oh, Kita realized at last, so there's been news of a store robbery has there?

"I sometimes go to them to buy dinner. And students go to read magazines, labourers go to buy drinks, gangsters go to buy ice or cat food, office girls go to buy a quick stew or some cookies."

"OK. I wasn't really asking what you went for. Me, I go to use their bathrooms from time to time. Sorry, I should have introduced myself."

The man abruptly held out a name card. "Heita Yashiro, Executive Director, Thanatos Movie Productions," Kita read. Checking the man's face again, he had the impression it was shining with eager curiosity.

"I don't have a name card."

"Free men like you don't need name cards or luggage I guess. It's good to have your hands free for everything that comes along. Your own self is the biggest piece of baggage you own. Still, you can't get on with the job if you leave yourself behind, can you? What's your name, by the way?"

Kita had had no intention of indulging in mutual introductions. On the other hand, he wasn't prepared to be the butt of this busybody's suspicions, so he said, "Yoshio Kita." The man then wanted to know what characters he wrote his name with, so Kita found himself having to write his name in the man's notebook. The man stared hard at what he'd written and seemed about to speak, so Kita cut in quickly.

"Is that a camera you've got in that case?"

Yashiro nodded as though he'd been waiting for the question. "I'll get anything on film," he said.

"You're talking adult videos and stuff like that?"

"Porn, news, documentaries, personal stories… like I say, anything. I shoot whatever there is to shoot."

"And what do you do with it?"

"I sell it. There are video cameras all over the world now. The world's full of peepholes wherever you care to look. And there are people who can't wait to be peeped on, what's more."

"So I guess that means you're pretty busy."

"My problem is I spend my life being busy and never making much money at it. The competition's fierce. But everyone wants to believe these days that whatever's on camera's got to be the truth. That's what keeps me doing it."

"You're a man of conviction in your work, then."

Kita couldn't bring himself to simply let the man know he had no interest in what he did for a living. He kept up the flow of casual responses while he waited for the man to realize there was no point in talking.

"Conviction's an important thing, you know. There's a big difference between someone with conviction and someone without it. Your customer is moved by your conviction, see. Even a criminal, he'll find supporters just so long as he's got good strong convictions."

"Do you have anything to do with crime yourself?"

"Good God no. Do I look like that sort of guy?"

Kita shrank at the sudden roughness in Yashiro's voice, and said softly, keeping a wary eye on him as he spoke, "Well, no, but you can't always judge by appearances, can you?"

After a moment's pause, Yashiro let out a rather forced chuckle.

"True enough, true enough. It's the guy who wears a nice-guy mask who'll turn around and commit the most cold-blooded crime. That's the kind of perfectly average face you get the feeling you've seen somewhere before. It's the same with evil these days, you don't even notice it any more. It happens absolutely naturally. But the good, well that's often artificial. If you shoot real evil on camera, you can't really tell what it is you're seeing. But good comes across real pretty. It's made itself up to look great, see. Same as a naked woman. But real good's a thing you don't even notice. That's why you won't catch it on camera. That's what I want to shoot."

Kita could see what Yashiro was saying. He nodded with a sigh. "I'm a serious guy too, though I don't put on any solemn airs," he said. It wasn't just a joke or some kind of excuse; in his own way he meant it. But he wondered if it would make sense to his sermonizing companion.

Heading up Dôgenzaka, just after the traffic lights Yashiro announced he'd stop there. He asked Kita whether he was going on, so Kita said this was fine with him too. He sat back and waited for Yashiro to pay and get out. When he proffered a couple of notes as his share of the fare, Yashiro waved them away, then glanced at his watch.

"Well then, what do you say to a cold beer?" Yashiro pointed towards a drinking place that had just opened its doors.

Kita hesitated. There was no reason why he should keep this man company, but on the other hand he couldn't think how to excuse himself.

"Sorry, but would you mind carrying the camera for me?" Yashiro continued. "My neck's kinda sore." And so Kita found himself acting as porter, and following Yashiro in. The place was completely empty. They sat at the counter, and as the cook was busy writing up the day's menu on the blackboard before them, Yashiro set about ordering. He asked for one dish after another – flounder sashimi, deep-fried tofu, salted squid, boiled potato and mincemeat, and finally beer.

Well, thought Kita, it wouldn't matter if he put off carrying out his plan until he'd had two or three beers and evening had come. His impulses would be able to flow unchecked with alcohol and darkness on his side, after all. But was Heita Yashiro the right companion to give him the boost he needed? A company director is generally the kind of guy who's brimming with self-confidence, who can dupe you all too easily. They put all the failures down to the other guy, and the successes down to their own foresight. Kita had worked for three directors in his life, and it was due to his own foresight that he'd managed to leave the company before it folded. He couldn't claim to have been lucky exactly, but he did manage to get through it all without giving in to despair. He'd managed this by telling himself this was what happened to everyone else too. Gangsters, office girls, students, housewives, directors, labourers, foreigners – they all felt the same hopelessness, he told himself. It soothed him. Sure there must be labourers who wondered where the joy was in having to slave away on the roads under a broiling midsummer sun, but after ten bottles of beer they'd have forgotten all about their problems. A student who failed to get a job at the end of his studies would feel pretty depressed about the future, but he could always comfort a friend who was even worse off than him. Kita believed his own limited experience had taught him how to come to terms with despair. He also had a fair understanding of how to deal with the despair of others. You listened to their woes with warmth and concern. The death of a relative, the death of a child, a friend's betrayal, a broken heart, illness – if you'd had a similar experience yourself, you could exchange stories at least. A kind of bartering on the troubles market. Then in the end you could both laugh together, united by your sorrows. That laughter was the special prerogative of people in that situation, the reward for having managed to produce some sort of comfort and friendship from the dregs of despair.

He'd done all this from time to time, but now he found he'd somehow grown sick of getting along so well with despair. He'd begun to feel that even that special humour that despair breeds was kind of empty. It was in fact quite scary to cross over to the far shore and leave despair behind, and Kita was disturbingly aware of feeling himself tumbling into the muddy depths of his own unconscious. Perhaps Yashiro intuited this, or perhaps it was just a passing remark, but as he wiped his face with the warm towel provided by the establishment, Yashiro said, "You're a weird sort of guy, I must say."

"I don't mean that negatively," he went on. "Hey, I make my living with the camera after all, and I'm used to relying on my own intuition. I'm pretty good at guessing right. I can at least look at a face and guess whether this is just an average guy or not."

"I'm an average guy."

"Anyone who says that about themselves has got to be weird."

Kita twisted his head around and smiled. "Sure enough, we're not going to get along, are we? It was a funny kind of meeting," he said.

At this, Yashiro brought his prying face up so close that Kita could feel his breath, and said, "Look here. I'm not letting on what's on my mind, you know."

When Kita failed to take the bait, Yashiro tried to call his bluff. "You looked away just then, you know. See, you can't meet my eyes."

"Well anyone would want to look away if they were being stared at by your goggly deep-sea fish eyes."

"Deep-sea fish eyes, that's a good one," Yashiro said jauntily, backing off, and he offered to pour Kita another beer. "Hey, companionship on the journey, kindness in life, as the saying goes. Let's treat this like a once-in-a-lifetime chance, hey? They say that's what keeps two people connected into the next life, after all."

People who like proverbs and sermonizing will talk just the same whoever they're speaking to. They probably talk the same way to themselves too. Yashiro opened his notebook and stared at the page where Kita had written his name. "Yoshio Kita, eh?" he murmured.

"I've gone pretty deeply into the science of names," he said, "and yours is a really fine one, I must say. You're a good man and full of joy, these characters say, right? You can sense the way your parents felt when they gave you this. Mind you, you'll often find someone betrays the meaning of their name. All you have to do is just change your way of thinking a bit, and you'd have the life your name suggests, mind you."

"I'd prefer you not to go messing about with my name please."

"Oh come on, don't be like that. If you don't like it I'll happily apologise. No, the fact is, I can't help being interested in you. Besides, you're a handsome guy."

Yashiro seemed about to add, "I could be looking at my younger self." Kita felt quite sickened. He clenched his stomach muscles to control himself.

"I can just tell. You've taken the sins of the world on yourself. But you don't let on, do you? No, you sit there pretending nothing's going on, and worrying about what crazy thing the other guy might suddenly spring on you. How old are you, by the way? You'd be around twenty-five I'd say. You can still pull the girls. Older ones, younger ones. Once you're past fifty you don't want older ones, you know. But at your age, you'll still find some good women even fifteen years older. Life can change for you if you go around with a mature woman. And you can hang out with a girl in her teens without having to pay for the pleasure too. Boy, I envy you."

"I've no idea what you're envying."

"Sure you do. You go at it hammer and tongs while you're young and still have the books balance out in the end. Go ahead and have the time of your life, no regrets, that's my advice."

Did he really look like someone who wanted to be preached at like this? Surely all this amounted to a form of sexual harassment. An embarrassing memory from his high school years began to surface in his mind like a dead fish. Riding the train to school, he'd regularly had his bottom fondled by a middle-aged man with gold-rimmed spectacles who reeked of nicotine. The man had greying hair parted in the middle and pasted down with pomade, and always carried a briefcase tucked under his arm. He had the habit of sniffing his own fingers. He'd rub his fingers against Kita's dusty school uniform, then greedily devour the faint scent left on his fingertips. He was never deterred by rush hour platform crowds or packed carriages. He'd push his way through the polite commuters, in dedicated pursuit of the bottom he was after, then press up close behind and use the train's swaying to let his hand caress the bottom of his chosen darling as he thrust his half-erect penis against him. Young Kita had changed carriages to escape him, and taken later trains or earlier ones, but the man had always sniffed him out and was already there in wait for him, grinning. Kita had agonized over the problem. It was shameful enough for a girl to come out and accuse a man of feeling her up, but far worse for a boy to go looking for help because some parasitic middle-aged guy was getting off on your backside. But one day he finally made up his mind. He borrowed from the school's Flower Arranging Club a little metal plate covered in spikes, used for pinning flowers in place at the bottom of vases, and bound it firmly onto his palm with a bandage. Then he lured the guy over. It turned out to be a more powerful weapon than he'd anticipated. "Urgh!" said the guy, giving a quick groan. Then, clutching his briefcase to his crotch, he scuttled off in defeat, glaring bitterly up at the gloating Kita.

There was something about Yashiro that reminded him of this guy. Whenever he spoke he touched Kita's shoulder, or grabbed his arm, breathing heavily at him. Was he after Kita's ass too? Or maybe he just liked being physical. True, men in Korea or Pakistan often went round together arm in arm or hand in hand. Brazilians and Russians went so far as to kiss each other. Maybe this was just their way of swapping unhappy stories and forging comfort and friendship between them.

Kita turned to face Yashiro, and asked with calculated bluntness, "Are you gay?" Beer in hand, Yashiro froze, his mouth open. Bingo, thought Kita, suppressing a grin and glaring at him.

"Well, I guess that's one way to see things," Yashiro replied with an innocent air. "If that's what you're after."

"Are you crazy? No way!"

"Well in that case, don't try to come on to me."

"I'm not coming on to you. I was just a bit worried, so I thought I'd check."

"What's the point of worrying over stupid stuff like that? Anything's possible in this world, after all."

"What do you mean by that?"

"If some guy told you he'd kill you if you refused, you'd sleep with him, wouldn't you?"

Kita was about to indignantly deny he'd do any such thing, but Yashiro silenced him and went on, "What I mean is, you won't achieve anything in life unless you can act as resolutely as that." He'd neatly shifted the conversation back to sermonizing again.

"By the way, what are you doing right now?"

Kita didn't feel inclined to let Yashiro in on the answer to that. The fact was, he was planning to commit suicide. Round about next Friday. He'd made the final decision the evening before last. There was still a week to go before Friday. After all, the world had been created in seven days with one off for rest, so he calculated most things could surely be achieved in the same amount of time. There must be all sorts of things he wanted to do before he died. But when he settled down to really put his mind to the question, all he could think of was the usual stuff – sleeping with two gorgeous girls at once, spending all his money on delicious food in a three-day orgy of eating, doing something so monstrous it would make everyone gape, that sort of thing. He ended up simply depressed by the obvious poverty of his imagination. With a certain amount of courage and money he could do all that anyway, without the excuse of dying. Mind you, though, most people usually indulged such delusions by reading popular novels and comics, or watching television, and hardly ever so much as dreamed of being the star of the action themselves.

But come to think of it, they weren't planning on suicide, were they?

This was a pretty convincing rationale, but Kita still felt somehow cheated. The usual order of things was that first of all you decided to die. Next came the plan to do all you could before you killed yourself. Even if your dreams of debauchery were impossible, there was no need to despair. You still got to die. In other words, it didn't matter if you did nothing, and simply died without any particular motive. You'd be hard put for an answer if asked why you were killing yourself, of course. The simple fact was, you were doing it because you wanted to die.

When Kita remained mute, Yashiro pushed the sashimi and potato mincemeat dishes over towards him, and said quietly, "You should eat." Suddenly, with the aroma of deep fry oil, Kita found his old teacher's voice echoing in his head.

"Choose your own pace of life."

Well he was half taking her advice at least, by choosing to die at his own pace, Kita told himself. There was no need to be afraid of other people's prying questions, no one could change his mind about dying in a week's time. Suddenly he laughed.

"Actually," he said, "I was planning on throwing everything to the winds even before your advice. But it's no good simply deciding. I haven't had any experience, so I'm not quite sure just how to go about it."

"Ah yes, I can see that would be so. The most important question is, what do you want to do? Is it sex you're after?"

"Among other things."

"Murder? You must have someone you'd like to murder."

"I don't like murder. And I don't have anyone I want to kill."

"You've got money?"

"Not a whole lot…"

"Are you prepared to go to jail?"

"No, I don't think that will be necessary."

Yashiro seemed a little downcast by this news. "I see," he murmured. He shovelled in the deep fried tofu, then went on with his mouth full, "Well anyway. You're after a huge shot of adrenaline, hey? If you don't have that, you could suddenly find yourself dead, after all. I really let my hair down when I was young, but I survived thanks to my nerves."

"Oh I don't mind if I die."

Startled, Yashiro looked him up and down from head to toe, then took a swig of beer and, in a low, menacing voice, asked, "Why?"

"I'm planning to kill myself next Friday, thanks."

"Thanks? Are you asking me to do something?"

"No, nothing. Well, I'll be off now."

"Hold on a minute. You've made me suddenly sad, telling me you're going to kill yourself."

"We've only just met. You'll soon get over it."

Kita got to his feet, but Yashiro seized his arm. He went through the motions of pondering something, then he suddenly declared in a low voice, "Let me introduce you to a great girl – Mitsuyo Kusakari, the porn star who took the world by storm five years ago. You must remember her? She's working in my office these days. She's the kinda girl who likes sex more than money. How about it? You'd like her to give you a good time, eh? Look at this."

Yashiro produced a piece of paper with the contact number for the former porn star. "I'll do the talking," he added.

"How much?" Kita asked.

"Depends on the guy, but a token amount will do," Yashiro replied. He was assuming Kita was talking about payment for the porn star's services, so Kita reframed the question.

"I mean, what do I owe you for the beer?"

Yashiro shook his head, and instead of answering he launched into a bizarre business discussion.

"You know, it's a poor show to just commit suicide. Can't you come up with a kind of suicide that's some benefit to others? There's no shortage of folks like you that want to kill themselves these days, But the fact is, you just die a dog's death as far as the world's concerned. Every life's got to have a certain worth to it. It's too bad to go handing it over for nothing. Think of the people out there who'd be grateful for your life. That's the reality. But you just need to use your head a bit and you can sell that life of yours for quite a bit. Life insurance, now there's a profession that talks in terms of how much a life's worth."

"You're telling me to take out life insurance before I die?"

"Now don't go being petty-minded and putting me down as someone who's after your life insurance. But hey, let me give you some money. You'll need it so as you don't leave any regrets behind when you die. And in return, like, how about letting me in on things?" Watching Kita carefully, Yashiro tapped his aluminium case.

"If you're suggesting shooting a record of me going through the whole process of committing suicide, you're wasting your time."

Yashiro made a great show of hanging his head despondently, as if to say that Kita had caught him out there. "Too bad!" he murmured.

Then he immediately perked up again, and pulled out his wallet. "Not that I'm forcing you or anything," he remarked with a smile, as he thrust thirty thousand yen into Kita's coat pocket.

"Hey, what're you up to?"

Kita hated the idea of any money tied up with someone else's schemes finding its way into his pocket even for an instant, and he shoved the notes back almost violently. Instantly, Yashiro's face grew grave. Gazing up at him earnestly from under his brows, he whispered in a surprisingly gentle voice, "You must accept people's goodwill with gratitude."

"Not if it's a deposit or advance I won't. I don't intend to let myself become a spectacle."

"You've got me wrong. There's no need to feel any obligation just because you've accepted thirty thousand yen, you know. This is my funeral offering, see. It's a bit odd to be giving it to you before you die, I'll admit, but you could get yourself something good to eat with it."

Kita simply wasn't up to parrying this with some smart joke, so he decided to accept the money meekly. He bowed his head deeply in thanks, and attempted to leave, but Yashiro only increased his urgent attempts to detain this prospective suicide. "Just one more minute," he said, opening his case. He produced a Polaroid camera, and quickly caught a snap of Kita's bewildered face. Then he called over the man behind the counter to take a photo of both of them to remember the occasion by. He kept back the first photograph of Kita, and handed him the other together with the camera. "You'll see a different world if you look through the viewfinder," he said. "Sorry to burden you, but do take it."

"Thank you for everything. May I go now?" said Kita.

Yashiro gave him a parting wave. "Be seeing you," he smirked, with the apparent implication that he planned to meet Kita again soon.

He was the sort of guy that Kita suspected had had to do with prospective suicides before. He seemed to know how to deal with them, to have some special knowhow. The funeral money, the gift…did he mean for Kita to use this camera to record his final week? He'd taken the funeral money, so maybe he had to return the favour somehow. But why should someone who's planning to die have to distract himself with this sort of thing? This Heita Yashiro fellow was no ordinary guy. Kita realized he'd been putty in the man's hands ever since the moment the guy had tried to steal a taxi on him. Everything Yashiro said and did had a peculiar persuasive power to it – he couldn't resist him, even though he was aware there was something odd going on. He was insolent, but at the same time oddly polite. He came on strong with the moralizing sermons and proverbs, but on the other hand he made no attempt to talk Kita out of suicide. Maybe he'd just been part of the evening's entertainment for Yashiro, a tasty morsel to snack on over a beer? He'd believed Tokyo was full of nothing but simple folks, but no sooner did he make the decision to kill himself than up had popped this bizarre fellow. Anyway, Kita told himself as he set off down the hill, let's do something positive and get him out of my mind.

Dinner's Ready

Kita counted up how many meals he had left before next Friday. Even allowing for the full three meals a day, he made it only twenty-two. He suddenly felt somehow bereft and sorrowful. At any rate, he decided, he'd set off to find himself a place where he could warm his heart and his belly. He was reasonably hungry, but he felt what he needed was the kind of food that satisfied the heart as much as the stomach, and that would relieve him of this empty sadness that had overtaken him. Up until now, Kita had only ever been interested in filling his belly, and had been content to eat just about any rubbish. He was on a different wavelength from the types who worried themselves about chemical food additives, and took special pains over which brand of sake or miso to use, or the precise thickness of dough in a piece of pasta or a meat dumpling. Although all food probably did have an appropriate season and a particular taste, as well as different effects on the body. The reason why labourers liked to eat offal roasted in salt after a day's work, after all, was because their body needed energy and salt. Yoga practitioners didn't eat onion or chives because these dulled the lower half of the body. Well then, what kind of food was good for getting rid of the blues?

Ice cream? Potato chips? Oolong tea and rice balls? These were all things he often ate. Kita realized suddenly that he was a guy who'd lived his life on convenience shop meals and fast food. People who don't worry over food have strong stomachs. Still, it certainly wouldn't do to die with heartburn. If there was one time in your life when you should cleanse your body, it was surely before death. There was no need to be stingy about food, of course. The reason why he hadn't eaten any of the dishes at the drinking place just now was because he was planning on cleansing his body with something a bit tastier, but here he was thirty minutes later, still puzzling over what to eat. There were all sorts of things he'd like to have, but then he only had twenty-two more meals. He mustn't eat just any stupid thing, he decided. He wouldn't go for the usual packed meal from a convenience store, for instance, or a hamburger.

He'd wandered into the Maruyamacho love hotel area, and as he went up and down the hilly roads he passed seven couples walking along in search of the best place to have sex. He momentarily met the eyes of several lovers who were strolling along discussing the pros and cons of various establishments – this one didn't have karaoke, that one offered a free bag of toiletries like they do in airplanes, another allowed extended stays for the same price. One couple he locked eyes with was a pair of high school girls, another was a bald cameraman sporting a moustache and round sunglasses with a tall girl on his arm. It was dinnertime, but quite a few of the hotels had red lamps indicating the rooms were full. In these parts, people had sex the way they had a cup of tea or a meal.

Sure they might come back to a hotel later, but what Kita was interested in right now was someone to eat with. On his own, his feet naturally set off in the direction of a convenience store or a curry house or noodle stand. He intended to give this habit up, so he stepped into a telephone booth with the idea of starting by getting in touch with the porn star that Yashiro had told him about. He dialled the number on the piece of paper, and after two rings her voice came on the phone. "Er, I've just—" Kita began, when she cut him off.

"You're quick," she said in a high-pitched voice. "It's only fifteen minutes since I heard from Yashiro."

Kita asked her to show him somewhere to eat, with the offer to treat her to anything she wanted there. Mitsuyo giggled flirtatiously into the receiver. "Hey, let's party!"

There was a jazz coffee shop in a street leading from Maruyamacho into Hyakkendana, she said. She'd meet him there. He sat down obediently on one of its wooden benches to sip a tequila and wait. He didn't recognise the piece they were playing, but it was a combination of a rush of wild sax, accompanied by trumpet and piano. A man was sitting alone in a dim corner, jiggling his hand and feet in time to the music, like someone on the verge of having some kind of fit. He looked like it would cheer him up to have someone there with him, beating out the rhythm together, but he was used to this lonesome feeling of not quite knowing what to do with his own body. Normally, Kita would have dismissed him as one of those gloomy, slightly weird types, but tonight he felt as if they were in the same boat.

Come to think of it, there'd been someone just like this guy back when he was in college. He hailed from somewhere like Oita down in Kyushu, a shabby fellow who talked in a low, monotonous voice. But he had amazing powers of concentration, and he could get right inside a piece of music. What his name now? Nikaido was the family name, maybe, and his other name was something like those rough spirits they drink down in Kyushu, Shochu or something of the sort. He was a fan of classical music. He used to listen to Dvorak and Tchaikovsky on his Walkman, conducting with his hand, although he'd get a bit embarrassed at being caught doing it. Next door to the jazz coffee shop where Kita was sitting there was one called Lion that played the classics. He imagined Nikaido sitting there with a bowl of green tea, eagerly awaiting the Bruckner's fifth symphony he'd put in a request for. As soon as Knappersbusch's performance began, he'd be deep inside wartime Vienna.

Where was he and what was he up to now? Kita wondered.

He hadn't known Nikaido that well, but now he tried imagining a likely scenario for him in the present. He'd have joined some respectable company, and be striving earnestly to increase the pieces he could conduct. If he did hang out in Lion, maybe Kita would run into him on the third day. Even if he realized Kita was there, he wouldn't greet him – he'd just sit there with his eyes closed and go on conducting. In amongst his repertoire he must have a few funeral marches and requiems. Maybe he conducted them for the dead occasionally. When he passed on, Kita thought, he'd rather like to have Nikaido conduct something for him too.

Through the pauses in the music, a bittersweet scent of perfume sidled into his nostrils. Before his eyes stood a woman, wearing an expression that suggested she was about to burst into laughter. "Miss Kusakari?" he asked, and she sat down beside him with a simpering little laugh.

"I hear you want to kill yourself."

She moved right in without going through the conversational formalities. Kita was annoyed. He'd have a stern word to that Yashiro about this. "I'd rather you didn't spread the news, thanks," he replied.

"Oh come on, what's the problem? You're not the only one, after all. I know someone who's failed to kill herself four times – she's normally perfectly cheerful. I'll introduce you if you like."

"I'm not looking for anyone to share the experience with, thanks. Anyway, what would you like to eat?"

"Mmm, I guess I'm in the mood for Chinese today. But we wouldn't be able to order many dishes with just the two of us, would we? Come on, let's call in some others."

"Whatever you like," replied Kita, whereupon Mitsuyo informed him with a shamefaced little pout that she'd already invited them. It was a good thing she was so well prepared. Kita was eager to get on with things.

Mitsuyo's friends turned up at the Chinese restaurant in Udagawacho, three women and two men. All seven of them settled themselves around the big circular table. Without pausing a moment to establish who they were and how they were connected, they all broke into various conversations together, glancing occasionally in Kita's direction to check whether he seemed to be enjoying himself. They ordered a large number of dishes – assorted hors d'oeuvres, fish fin and crab soup, abalone in cream, whole carp dressed with thick starchy sauce, beef sautéed with chives, Dongpo pork, fried rice with seafood, prawns in chilli sauce, tofu and bamboo shoots in a black soy sauce, noodles with mustard greens, Xiaolongbao, fried rice with fish and vegetables, and almond jelly.

Kita seemed to be the oldest among them. The youngest-looking was a lad of sixteen or seventeen, and his appetite was quite intimidating. He didn't have a spare ounce of flesh on him, however. His face was childlike, and smooth and white as a boiled egg. Mitsuyo referred to him as Calpis. In reply, he referred to her with casual deference by her first name, in a voice still hoarse from having only just broken. Kita later learned they were cousins.

"Why are you called Calpis?" Kita asked him casually. "That's the name of a milky soft drink, right?" All four girls promptly burst into laughter.

Calpis was a shy lad who seldom spoke, just ate, and occasionally nodded to others with a face innocent of any wrongdoing. But the other man both ate a lot and talked a lot. He wasn't as good-looking as Calpis, but his dexterous way of seeing to the needs of the girls with talk and attention was a great hit. Still, they sometimes ignored him. Whenever this happened he looked hugely put out, and did his best to get in on their conversation at every opportunity with a constant flow of "Why?" or "I see," or "Really?" As if this wasn't annoying enough, his cell phone would ring every half hour or so. The girls called him Daikichi. Daikichi was obviously senior to Calpis in the way they related. As for the girls, one by the name of Takako was Calpis's girlfriend, while another, who they called Poo, a girl barely five feet high with a thirty-six-inch bust, evidently worked part-time in the same place as Takako did. Then there was a rather unassuming girl who lurked in the background, who had the name Zombie. This was apparently the girl of the four failed suicide attempts that Mitsuyo had mentioned, who was usually so cheerful. She was fine-boned and her voice was frail, but she looked at people with a calm gaze.

It seemed odd to Kita to find himself in among this bunch of people, but it was only for tonight, he told himself, so he sat letting the conversation flow on around him, watching and comparing faces.

Daikichi: I went along to one of those cheap Osho restaurants that do Chinese dumplings the other day, and ordered up a great big dish of noodle stew. Usually those Chanpon stews cost around seven hundred yen, yeah? But this one was only three sixty!

Poo: Wow, that's cheap!

Daikichi: Usually you get lots of shellfish in Chanpon, but this one had pork and bean sprouts and meat dumplings and all sorts of things. It was kinda fun fishing around in it to see what you pulled out. There was even some fried chicken in there. It had tooth marks in it.

Takako: What? You mean to say they topped it up with other people's leftovers?

Poo: Cheap can be pretty nasty.

Takako: Good thing there weren't any cigarette butts, at least.

Daikichi: You hear of gangsters bringing along a cockroach and popping it in the food they're eating, you know.

Poo: Yeah, one did that in the bar where I work. Hey, he says, what kinda place is this? You put cockroaches in the food here or something? Trying to make trouble.

Daikichi: To hell with 'em. They must breed the things at home.

Zombie: I never saw a cockroach till I came to Tokyo. We never had them in Hokkaido.

Daikichi: That so? You get them in *ramen* noodle shops, I heard.

Takako: Talking of *ramen*, I heard there are lots of Iranians that just love pork. They can't believe how delicious it is, apparently.

Daikichi: But Moslems aren't allowed to eat pork, surely?

Poo: Yeah, but the more you're not supposed to eat something the more you want to eat it, see? Like me, whenever I'm on a diet I dream of ice cream.

Daikichi: I wonder if there's some religion where you're not allowed to eat cucumbers or aubergines.

Mitsuyo: Some girls just go all wet as soon as they see a cucumber or one of those long aubergines. And there are guys who come just looking at an oyster or a shellfish, or *konyaku* jelly.

Calpis: Not me!

Daikichi: But when you want a shit you always get a hard-on, don't you?

Takako: Hey come on guys, we're eating!

Calpis: Well it's not that I...hey, you're having me on. And anyway, who was it who dropped all his spare cash in Kinshicho the other day?

Mitsuyo: Daikichi! You may not be a hit with the girls, but that doesn't mean you should go living it up in cabarets you know.

Daikichi: Well if that's how you're going to be, come on and scout me for one of your movies then. You promised you'd use me as the male star in one of those clips of yours, didn't you?

Mitsuyo: Hey, what do you think of Poo?

Poo: Eh? I'm an out and out people hater, you know.

Zombie: Oh wow, you guys are all really living hard, aren't you?

Takako: Seems like there's something wrong with living hard.

Zombie: You don't want me around?

Takako: I didn't say that. You were behind Mitsuyo in the same high school, weren't you Zombie?

Zombie: Yeah. I wrote to her when I saw her in one of her videos. And she really looked after me when I came to Tokyo.

Daikichi: But you're smart, Zombie. Didn't you do literature or something at Keio University?

Takako: There were lots of really unusual, talented people at Mitsuyo's school.

Zombie: There's also this really sharp-tongued guy who you see on discussion programs, he's from our school too.

Mitsuyo: And there's that actress who used to be in one of those morning drama series on TV a while back, who does whiskey commercials now – she was about five years ahead of me at school. And I heard of another girl about fifteen years older, she attacked the American embassy with a stick of dynamite.

Takako: That's the kind of place Hokkaido is.

Mitsuyo: Whaddya mean?

Takako: I mean there are actresses and critics, and literary types like Zombie, and I guess terrorists… you get a lot of people who throw dynamite at the American embassy up that way?

Mitsuyo: What school were you at?

Takako: I was at a mission school in Yokohama.

Mitsuyo: You mean like Felaccio Girls School? Well then, I guess you'd only find office girls and housewives from there.

Takako: No way. You ever heard of the manga artist Hiyoko Kannazuki?

Zombie: I know her! She did that story about the girl who had one hundred eight disastrous love affairs.

Takako: You read Kannazuki's latest?

Zombie: Sure. The girl starves to death from anorexia.

Daikichi: You could find one or two odd guys who graduated from my school too, if you looked.

Calpis: We had that weird headmaster, didn't we?

Daikichi: Oh yeah, old Jomon. Named after that prehistoric Japanese period. He was really weird.

Poo: What kinda guy was he?

Daikichi: He graduated from the Nakano Military College.

Poo: Eh? What kinda school is that?

Daikichi: The place Onoda went to.

Takako: Onoda? Who's Onoda?

Daikichi: That soldier who didn't know the war had ended and stayed holed up in the jungle in Sumatra for thirty years.

Calpis: It wasn't Sumatra, it was Lubang.

Poo: You mean he went on fighting all by himself for thirty years?

Daikichi: He lived like they did back in the Jomon Period. The Nakano Military College is the kinda place where you're taught to survive anywhere, even in the jungle. Our headmaster was like a Jomon guy too.

Calpis: He used to teach his students weird stuff. Like how to dig a tunnel just with a stick, or how to make a house by cutting down a single tree, or how to get water from grass, or how to tell which herbs and stuff you can eat.

Daikichi: It's called "survival technique". He always said it would come in handy some time.

Mitsuyo: You'll probably find it useful when you turn into tramps on the street.

Zombie: Or when your house is destroyed in an earthquake.

Calpis: But there isn't any jungle round here.

Daikichi: There's grass and trees, at least.

Mitsuyo: "Survival" means knowing how to live all alone without anything, yeah?

Daikichi: You can do that just by using that lovely body of yours, can't you Mitsuyo?

Mitsuyo: And as for you, you're so scruffy you don't know what to do with yourself. Anyway, there are people like Zombie here who don't care about survival. What about you, Kita?"

Twelve eyeballs turned as one to stare at him. Kita hadn't said a word about himself so far. Now their attention turned at last to the fellow who'd been sitting there all along, simply taking in the conversation as it bounced back and forth over the round table. A vague uneasiness hovered in the air – would he suddenly come out with some deep remark under his breath? Would he lose his temper over how boring they were all being?

"Well I don't really understand about life…" Kita protested with a wry little self-deprecating grin.

"Come on now," said Daikichi.

"Kita wants to die, see," Mitsuyo said, looking at him gently, and after the tiniest pause the rest of them nodded gravely. Only Zombie sat looking down at her lap, somehow shy.

"Why do you want to die?" Takako asked, helping Kita to some Lao-chu. "You're still young." Beside her, Poo had tucked her chin in and was gazing earnestly at Kita from under her brows. When their eyes met, for some reason she clapped her hand to her mouth and burst out laughing. When she realized no one else was joining in, she blushed and murmured "Sorry."

"No, no, you can laugh if you like," said Kita. "It's funny enough, after all," and at this everyone obligingly laughed.

"Seems a bit dangerous to me," Poo remarked lightly.

"Now listen, girl," said Takako in a reproving voice.

"What's the danger? I feel like I'm acting perfectly normally," said Kita.

"I mean, once you've decided to die, you can do pretty much anything you want, right?" Poo flapped her hands about to illustrate her point.

"I don't think deciding to die makes you all that free to act. After all, it's tough work dying. You don't have much leeway to think about other things," muttered Zombie. For once, she spoke in a tone of deep conviction. Kita had to take his hat off to her – failing to kill yourself four times was no mean feat. "It's just not that easy to do it at your own pace," she went on. "You've got to have your act together or you get half way and it all fizzles out."

The two of them were cool as cucumbers. You'd think the topic of dying was the thing of the moment.

"And how do you want to die, Kita?" Takako cut in.

"Well I haven't quite decided. What do you think's the best way?" said Kita, falling in with the general tone.

"I'd go for hara kiri myself," said Daikichi.

"What, with that belly of yours?" Mitsuyo shot back mockingly. "You'd better tone up the muscles first."

A sunny laughter filled the table again. Through the hilarity, Calpis shouted, "I'd like to just drop dead suddenly."

"Me too," said Takako.

Poo thought for a moment. "I think I'd go for double suicide with a guy," she said.

"I'm not wild about the idea of dying, myself," Mitsuyo threw in.

Everyone was waiting with interest for what Zombie would say, but she threw everyone completely by ducking the issue and casually remarking, "I wonder what I'll try next time?"

Takako gazed into her eyes with a serious expression, and inquired about suicide methods. At this, Zombie gleefully replied, "I was still in sixth form at elementary school the first time I tried it, so I hadn't done much research on methods. I didn't really think about it, I just jumped into a freezing swimming pool in winter. I thought the shock would stop my heart, but I guess my heart was pretty strong, so all I got from it was a cold."

"Why did you want to kill yourself?"

"When I thought about how I was going to have to leave all my friends when we went off to new schools, suddenly there just didn't seem any point in living."

"Did you write some kind of a will?"

"Uh-huh. I kept a diary back then, and the day before I committed suicide I wrote 'I'm so sorry Mum and Dad, I can't face going on living so I have to go to heaven ahead of you.' But no one believed I'd committed suicide, so afterwards I tore it up and threw it away. Everyone had the idea I'd fallen in by mistake, see. There was a big fuss at the PTA meeting about how the school was negligent over safety, and it just wasn't a situation where it would've felt right to explain I was trying to kill myself."

"You always did have bad timing," Mitsuyo remarked. "So what about the second time?"

"Well that was in third grade at Middle School. I had this good friend, and we used to exchange diaries. When that rock singer Ozaki died she got real depressed, and said a world without Ozaki was like Japan without the emperor, and there was no point being alive. And then she started talking about following him into death like the loyal retainers used to do in the old days. Well of course I already had experience from the time I tried to kill myself when I was twelve, so we started getting excited about dying together, and ended up deciding to hang ourselves in the store room of the school gym. We were just about to put our heads through the noose when the gym teacher walks in naked from the waist up and yells 'Hey you two, what're you doing messing about in here at this hour? Go on home this minute!' so the whole thing went kinda flat for us."

"You gave up, huh? Suicide was just a kind of fooling about."

"But third time lucky in third year high school. I meant business that time. I cut my wrists and there was blood everywhere. It was quite a shock, so I panicked and dialled the 110 emergency number, but they said 'Wrong number miss. Ambulance is 119." Anyhow, the blood was still pouring out and my brand new dress was all red with it, and I was just feeling like I was going to faint from lack of blood when my boyfriend called up. 'Get an ambulance and come quick!' I yelled, and that's the last I remember. Next thing I was in the hospital, and my boyfriend was being grilled by a policeman. He said he was dead scared about what I might come out with when I woke up. We'd had a quarrel, see."

"So how did you explain it? They must've asked what the motive was?" Everyone was listening agog. Zombie simply went on calmly with her story.

"I said I'd just felt it was all kind of pointless somehow, and the policeman really told me off. I only thought that if I said it was disappointment in love, it would've made things tricky for my boyfriend, see. But we split up anyway. He said he didn't want to hang out with a girl who committed suicide at the drop of a hat."

"That was honest of him."

"Really was. And what about the fourth time?" Mitsuyo demanded, urging her on with the story.

"There's more?" muttered Kita, with a wry smile.

"This time I was determined I wouldn't cause anyone trouble and no one would get in my way, so I decided to give my heart an electric shock. I cut the lamp cord, and stuck one end onto my back with sticking plaster and the other between my breasts, and attached it up to a timer I'd bought at the electrical shop and set it to go off and kill me while I was asleep. I thought I'd be so tense I wouldn't be able to sleep, so I drank lots of that stuff you take to avoid motion sickness, and off I went. I left a will on my desk. I was sure the electric current would hit my heart just as dawn broke and I'd die, but I woke up again near noon next day. I just lay there for a while in some kind of stupor, then I finally realized I'd left the plug out of the socket, so I'd failed again."

"You forgot to plug it in before you went to bed?"

"No, I distinctly remembered plugging it in. But I guess I must've pulled it out without knowing. I toss and turn a lot in my sleep."

"And when was that?"

"Last year maybe. When I was twenty-one."

"So you've failed to kill yourself every three years since you were twelve, huh?"

"Yeah, I guess it's just turned out like that."

"So if you keep to pattern, the next time's the year after next."

"I can't wait."

Daikichi and Mitsuyo and Poo all turned to look at each other and grinned. Zombie smiled shyly too. "You're putting a lot of pressure on me with all this anticipating," she said, and she smiled over at Kita as if looking for support. At this, everyone's smiling faces turned to him again, as if waiting for him to add the final word on the subject.

"You did well to get through death four times," said Kita with a straight face. "No matter how you look at it, seems like you're made to survive."

"Mm, could be," Zombie answered, blushing and covering her face with her hands.

His cheeks bulging with fried rice, Daikichi broke in, "But it's a real waste to go using up your luck like that you know. Come on

Zombie, let's go to the races together. If you use up your luck at the races, you'll actually get to die next time, you know."

"Listen Daikichi," Mitsuyo pointed out. "That name of yours already means 'excellent luck' if you think of how it's written. I'd say your name's swallowed all your luck."

Daikichi nodded deeply. "Hisao Daikichi," he commented. "That's me. 'Man of long life and excellent luck.' I was born on New Year's Day, see."

Kita turned to Zombie, and casually asked how her real name was written. "Maybe you've got a name that's unlucky for future suicide attempts," he added. "Let's see what the characters reveal."

"Izumi Mizusawa," she said. "Watery Stream Fountain." The wet connotations struck Kita as just right for her.

The food on the table had largely disappeared by now. Occasional garlicky burps and sighs scented the air. Everyone was in need of a little light exercise after the meal. Kita glanced over at Mitsuyo. Would he be able to share her bed tonight? She sent him back a little smile.

"Death is ridiculous."

Her abrupt remark startled Kita. "Eh?" he said. Gripping Zombie's hand, Mitsuyo went on.

"Here she is, almost died four times, and she's learned nothing. She doesn't understand a thing. You feel a fool for listening to her. It turns you right off any idea of suicide, there's that to be grateful for. Thanks for saving me, Zombie! Now how about saving Kita while you're at it?"

Zombie seemed suddenly uncomfortable. Her eyes skimmed here and there around the room like a couple of flies. The others were grinning vaguely, having no idea what Mitsuyo was really trying to say. It suddenly struck Kita that he wanted to avoid being left alone with Zombie tonight. He agreed that death was ridiculous, and he could see just how bad Zombie's luck was. Whether she managed to kill herself or not, others would only treat it as a farce. This was perfectly clear to him. And… and that's precisely what he couldn't stand. Death isn't absolute. It doesn't even teach you the nature of infinity. Zombie probably knew this, and that's why she was putting it on.

31

"What'll we do next?" Daikichi looked inquiringly at Kita to see how he was feeling. "How about heading off to a karaoke joint and really hitting it? Or maybe you got some other plan?"

Daikichi sure knew how to suck up. Kita picked up the bill that had been placed before him, and stood up. The others all thanked him and set off to follow, assuming there'd be more to the evening. After he'd paid, Kita lined them all up in front of the entrance, and took a commemorative photo with the camera Yashiro had given him.

Walpurgis Night

After they'd done the rounds of a few game centres, shot dead a gang of forty-five, crashed seventeen cars, rescued two stuffed toys, and battled twenty-three combatants into unconsciousness, they polished off three games of bowls, and finally all tumbled into a love hotel that had a pool and karaoke machine.

They weren't wasting a moment. No sooner were they in than they'd flung themselves into a singing competition. They divided up into two mixed sex teams and took turns to sing, using the electronic grading system to see who won. Losing meant taking off an item of clothing – not just the singer but everyone on the team. The plan was that the game would go on until everyone on one team lost all their clothes. Then they'd be flung in the pool. When Kita's turn came, he sang 'Cape Erimo,' but he lost to Zombie's rendition of 'My Way' so he and Calpis had to take off their trousers, while Mitsuyo was already faced with having to remove her bra. The competition was reaching its climax and Calpis had a bulge in his underpants, when Takako refused to take off her skirt and suddenly declared she had to go home before her curfew.

"I'll see you home," cried Calpis, struggling quickly back into the trousers he'd recently taken off, but the crotch was too tight and he couldn't do up the zipper. Everyone laughed.

"What's this? You're off already? Before you've had a swim?" Daikichi stood there feet apart, the mike firmly gripped in his hand.

Then Poo also reached for her skirt, declaring she had to leave. Daikichi clicked his tongue reprovingly. "Why?" he demanded obstinately.

"But my boyfriend's coming back tomorrow. From Mt. Fuji."

"That's tomorrow. You're still free tonight."

"But if we lose one more time I'll have to take off my slip. I'd feel guilty about him."

"You don't know what he's up to at Mt. Fuji, do you?"

"He's on army exercises. He's in the Self Defence Force. I want to be a good girl for him. He's protecting our nation, right? If I serve him well, that means I'm serving the nation, see."

As she spoke, Poo was getting back into her clothes with the speed of a soldier under orders.

"Self Defence Force, eh? Oh well, too bad," sighed Daikichi, without any clear idea of just what was too bad. He gave up trying to hold her back, and turned to Mitsuyo. A chill had descended on the entertainment, and Mitsuyo had also slipped her breasts back into her bra.

"Come on, let's keep hitting it!" Daikichi said to her, tossing back his beer.

"You oughta head down and hit it at Mt. Fuji yourself, Daikichi."

"But they say Self Defence Force guys don't make it with the girls."

"Well *you* certainly wouldn't. But the SDF are pretty cool, you know. They're great when there's an earthquake or a typhoon. If it's a toss-up between an SDF guy and a policeman, I'd take the SDF guy. There are a lot of creepy policemen, and they use dirty tactics. And I've had run-ins with them before. You take good care of that man, Poo."

"Sure thing."

Poo, Calpis, and Takako checked to see they had everything on, then all turned to Kita and thanked him politely. "It's been fun," said Kita. He stayed sitting on the bed to see them off, but for some reason they didn't go straight out. Poo and Takako glanced at each other and grinned. Kita waited, wondering if he ought to say something more.

"Would you have the fare?' said Mitsuyo. The three of them immediately shook their heads as if by agreement, and smiled at him.

Kita realized they were after money. "How much?" he said. Takako said four thousand yen, and Poo asked for six thousand.

"I see," said Kita, "two thousand more if you take off your skirt." Then he followed up by asking how much a taxi cost if you'd taken off your bra.

Takako turned to Poo for confirmation, and held up one finger, indicating a ten thousand yen note. Poo nodded. "And panties is twelve," she said.

Calpis instantly turned to his girlfriend, Takako. "You're talking about selling your body?" he asked.

"Don't be stupid," Takako said, and Poo went on, "Being naked is different from having sex."

"Women have it good, don't they. There's a price on breasts and a price on pubic hair." Daikichi spoke into the echo on the mike.

Mitsuyo seized the mike from him. "There are guys who like guys like you! Five hundred yen a go," she yelled.

"Yuck! I'd rather join the SDF than sell myself to a man."

"Idiot. Selling yourself to the nation's just the same as selling yourself to a man." Mitsuyo knocked Daikichi on the head with the mike. The echo filled the room. Daikichi grabbed the mike back from her, held it to his mouth, and did a skilful imitation of a helicopter, a bazooka and a pistol shot.

"Hey, when did you learn that? Teach me how to do it," said Calpis, in genuine admiration of Daikichi's talents. The praise went to Daikichi's head, and he proceeded to grip the mike and produce a further rendition of a wild battle.

"Hey Daikichi, you look like you're performing fellatio." Zombie had been silent all this while, but now she held her hand to her mouth and giggled.

"No way! Right, I'm off too. I'll head on home on the last train, all on my ownsome." Daikichi flung the mike onto the bed, thrust his fat legs back into his baggy jeans, and slung his sweater round his shoulders.

Kita passed a ten thousand yen note to Poo. "Divide it between you," he said.

"Thanks," said Poo. "Well Kita, let's do it again some time," and she put out her hand. The other three did likewise, adding things like "Stay alive till we meet again, won't you," and "Hope you have a really cool death," and "Give us another meal some time please," and out they went.

The second hand was just a fraction past eleven. During the time it took for the gap to widen to an inch or so, the sudden silence oppressed Kita, thrust by others into the position of being left alone with two women in their underwear. He climbed back into the black wool trousers he'd carefully folded to avoid wrinkles and lay down on the bed. Zombie followed his lead, and reached for her checked wrap-around skirt.

"You going home?" Kita looked from Zombie's face to Mitsuyo's.

"You won't kill yourself tonight, will you? You're just going to sleep, aren't you?" Zombie inquired in a bright, breezy voice.

"Yep, that's the plan. Quite a bit's happened today. That first guy I met was the problem. He goes and spreads the news around, and then he goes and introduces me to Mitsuyo."

"What, you mean that was bad? But you're the one who rang me, remember. I just came along because it was work, you know."

"Don't get me wrong, I'm really glad I met everyone. You in particular, Mitsuyo. And you too, Zombie. That story of the four failed suicide attempts was very useful, thanks."

"I see. You mean, you haven't tried to kill yourself before?" Zombie spoke casually. She wasn't setting herself up as superior.

"Given that I'm going to do it, I don't want to make a mess of it," Kita said meekly.

Zombie nodded deeply. "Good luck," she said encouragingly.

"OK, all those rowdy ones have gone, so why don't we take a bath?" suggested Mitsuyo. Zombie and Kita both assented. All three found themselves looking forward to soaking in a warm spa bath and relaxing. The two girls showed no sign of planning to leave. Did this mean he had to buy them both for the night? Both of them suddenly looked like prostitutes to Kita. Without hesitating, both Zombie and Mitsuyo stripped to nothing, and began by jumping into the pool—though this "pool" was actually about the size of a storage closet. Kita watched them through the transparent synthetic glass screen as they joked about, playing at synchronized swimming together. Mitsuyo waved to him from the water, so Kita took off his clothes, climbed the diving ladder, and plunged in between the two mermaid heads.

The mermaids had pale skin, and appeared considerably slimmer under water than they did on land. Their hair and their public hair rocked gently like waterweed. Their four breasts floated about like jellyfish, flattening, swelling, twisting.

Mitsuyo suggested they have a competition to see who could stay underwater longest. They all sank together. Beneath the surface all was quiet. Breath held, Kita looked at the two pale, meditative faces of the girls, their cheeks bulging like squirrels. From time to time a few bubbles would go dancing up to the surface. The sound seemed to Kita like the mermaids' murmuring voices, chattering on about this and that. The sudden humour of this made Kita suddenly expel his breath in a laugh, and pop out of the water. Mitsuyo and Zombie both poked their faces up after him.

"OK, let's bet something this time," said Mitsuyo breathlessly, looking around for agreement. She apparently assumed she'd be likely to win at holding her breath.

"What will you two bet?" asked Kita. Zombie replied she didn't have anything to bet.

"How about your body?" This development struck Kita as only natural, considering that he was cavorting in the water with two stark naked girls.

"You've got great tits, Mitsuyo, and you've been in films and everything, but I'm pretty much flat-chested, and, well, I've never done it for money before… Poo would've been good. She's prepared to sell herself for her SDF guy, after all."

"She can be full-on once she gets an idea into her head. And she's so rebellious. She's anti-school, anti-society. She really hates the way it's just irresponsible dirty old men who lead our society. Says she sells herself to these lechers and pays what she gets as tribute money to the SDF. It's helping protect the nation, is what she tells herself. It's pretty weird, but the way Poo sees things I guess there's some justice in the idea."

Kita agreed it was pretty weird, but still, he didn't think it was such a bad thing really, to be naive enough to believe you were selling yourself for the sake of the nation, or society, or the disadvantaged. He'd lost that kind of naivety many moons ago. But did it mean that Poo saw him as one of those dirty old men? If that was the case, it would be too bad if he couldn't meet her again before he died and really put on a display of being the lecher. He'd love to be able to help her in her mission of justice.

"OK, let's try this. If I lose, I'll be Kita's secretary for a day. You've got lots of things you want to do before you die, haven't you? I'll help you do them. If there's someone you want to meet, I'll telephone and make the appointment, or if there's a book you want to read or a CD you want to hear, I'll get it for you. How about it?" said Zombie.

"Yeah, great idea." Kita was all for it. In return, he sounded her out on the possibility of buying her one hundred tickets in the Dream Jumbo Lottery. She liked the idea.

"I don't really have anything I long for," said Mitsuyo a little morosely.

"What about betting your own body like we were saying?" said Kita.

Mitsuyo responded that she'd undertake to be Kita's slave for a day if she lost. "You can do a lot more with a slave than you can with a secretary," she added.

"Right. I'll get you three hundred Dream Jumbo tickets, then."

"I'm not interested in lotteries. What I want is for you to promise the same thing, you'll be my slave for a day."

She sure seemed like she'd be a rough master, but hey, why not?

They'd have one go. If Kita stayed under longest, he'd get twenty-four hours with Zombie as his secretary and Mitsuyo as his slave. If he lost to Zombie but won against Mitsuyo, he'd have to buy a hundred lottery tickets but he'd get a slave. If he won against Zombie and lost to Mitsuyo, he'd be a slave with sidekick secretary.

They took a series of deep breaths, calmed themselves, and emptied their mind of thought. When the second hand on the clock moved to upright, they were to all dive together. Five, four, three, two, one. Kita held his breath and sank, checked that his two opponents were down there with him, then closed his eyes.

Occasional bubbles broke the stillness. At last they all signalled to each other that they were at the end of their tether, and all broke surface with a burst of bubbles, barely a moment apart.

The mermaids gasped for air. "God, that was scary!" "I thought I was going to die!" they declared in shaky voices. The first up had been Zombie, next Kita, and last Mitsuyo. Kita found himself slave-with-sidekick.

As they warmed their chilled bodies in the 40°C Jacuzzi tub, the three of them discussed how things should begin. It was already past midnight, so there was no avoiding their various roles. Mitsuyo, whose breathtaking skills had won her the crown, immediately began by ordering a beer and an oil massage after the bath. Kita told his secretary Zombie she needn't do anything until morning. Both the queen and the secretary were exhausted. The secretary curled up on the sofa with a blanket and fell asleep, and the queen began to snore as Kita massaged her. Left to his own devices, Kita became turned on, and found his little feller suddenly standing up. He hesitated to take the prone queen from behind in case she got mad, but there was insubordination in the ranks below, so he slipped on a condom and thrust in his cock. The queen curled away from him for a moment and said, "Don't," but once she'd established that he was wearing a condom she turned lazily over, opened her legs, and let her slave do as he would. Zombie was peeking from under her blanket while Kita used Mitsuyo's body to masturbate. He stretched his hand out beyond the pillow, and turned off the light.

Kita woke to the sound of splashing water. Secretary Zombie was lying in the bottom of the pool. Fearing that she was up to her old suicide tricks again, Kita rushed to the poolside, beat on the transparent screen, and shouted, "Are you alive?"

She was. The now wet Secretary Zombie announced that it was Saturday and enquired what she could begin by doing for him.

"Let's go out somewhere," he replied. First, however, he must learn the opinions of the queen. There was still no sign of Mitsuyo waking. Still wet, Secretary Zombie went over to her and hugged her. "Ergh!" moaned the queen in a pathetic voice, evidently dreaming that a snake was twining itself round her. Her eyes opened. Secretary Zombie leaned close to her ear and whispered, "I was a bit lonely last night. Don't leave me alone too much."

Mitsuyo placed a light kiss on Zombie's lips. "Right," she said, and rose to her feet. "Let's go to the seaside."

At the word from Mitsuyo, both the others hurriedly set about getting things ready. Kita remembered that he had a camera, and took a picture of the two naked girls snuggling up together.

They paid at the desk and stepped outside to find a light rain was falling. Kita had used about one hundred thousand yen the previous evening. The three ten thousand yen notes that Yashiro had given him as funeral money were still in his pocket. Just outside the hotel there happened to be a lottery ticket booth, so he bought thirty thousand yen worth of tickets and presented half each to the secretary and the queen. He tried to give Queen Mitsuyo an extra thirty thousand on the grounds that he'd slept with her the night before, but she shook her head. "No charge," she told him with a smile.

SATURDAY

A Seaside Health Resort

The three of them joined the pleasure-seeking crowds on the train bound for the resort town of Atami. Each sank greedily into a doze inside the carriage, and when they got off at the station an hour later, they were all hungry.

"Atami's famous for its dried fish, isn't it?" said Mitsuyo, so they hopped in a taxi and asked the driver to take them somewhere where they could have some sake and dried fish.

They settled themselves down in the tidy little restaurant and put in an order for a grill of the dried fish they'd selected from the display outside the door, along with various top grade sakes. Dried fish by itself would be pretty boring, they decided, so they added sashimi and seasoned boiled vegetables to the order. They had such a fine time eating and drinking that pretty soon they attracted wry smiles from the other customers and the lady behind the counter.

"Dining in fine style, eh?" A skinny old man remarked in the direction of the three, who had by now settled down to idle the time away around the table. He was sitting alone at the corner of the counter, sipping sake as he picked at a dish of dried mackerel. He had the air of one who was indulging in one of the modest pleasures of old age. "The great thing about dried fish is you can nibble away at 'em like a pauper," he went on. "One of these little things only costs me eighty yen. My great grandfather used to love 'em."

"Wow, so this is a really old restaurant," said Mitsuyo, in response to the old man's monologue. He immediately turned to her, as if he'd been just waiting for someone to talk to.

"When I say 'my great grandfather,' you realize the man I'm referring to is the great gang boss Hatayama the Third, don't you."

What? So the supreme boss of the Hatayama Gang, the biggest gangster organization in Japan, was mad about dried mackerel? It wasn't only Kita who was tickled by this story. Mitsuyo and Zombie also suppressed a smile as they exchanged glances.

"So you used to be a gangster?" asked Mitsuyo in her usual carefree way.

The old man turned his faded eyes to her and stared hard. "I did a lot of wicked things in my youth," he muttered.

Mitsuyo invited him to join them, and poured him some sake. The old man raised his hand to his forehead in a brief gesture of thanks, as sumo wrestlers do before accepting their winnings in the ring, and settled himself down beside Kita.

"You're all down from Tokyo, aren't you? I can tell from the accent."

"And where are you from?"

"Sunpu originally. Village in Tokugawa. These days I'm in an old folks' home in Atami. Death's got a set against me and won't kill me off, so here I am, condemned to a long life."

"What a weirdo," Mitsuyo murmured in a tiny voice, then carefully turned a smile on him and said, "There's someone here who's just the opposite, you know. He's been lured by Death. Right here," and she pointed impudently at Kita. There she went, using him again. Kita waved his hand to tell her not to pursue the subject, but Zombie chipped in, "He says he's going to die by next Friday."

The old man furrowed his brow and turned his gaze on Kita. "Some illness?" he said.

"Well yeah, a kind of illness I guess," Kita replied casually. The old man didn't seem interested. He blew his nose once, then set forth in a long-winded monologue.

"All through my youth I survived all the daredevil antics I got up to. When I gets back in one piece after the war I thinks to meself, here's a bit of luck! Ill weeds grow apace, you know the saying, so I sets out to be an ill weed, and I raised hell I can tell ya. Young folks these days can't raise hell like that, poor things."

"What hell did you raise?"

"Damned if I'm going to go plugging away at some stupid job, I thinks. I'm gonna have fun making money, and use it to debauch meself in fine style. I'm gonna get me a thousand lovers, says I, so out I go and pick up whatever woman comes to hand. Sold off all I got when I left the army, and used the money to hang out in the whorehouses. But I soon got sick of that, so I bought up some girls from the country and set up shop meself. So I was runnin' the joint, and thought I was really somethin' I can tell you, but hey, it always happens eh? Started steppin' on other people's turf, and not paying me dues to the lads, so pretty soon I'd fallen in with the *yakuza*. Ends up I exchange sake cups with the big boss and I'm into the gang. I'd slept with over five hundred girls by that time, but comes a time when you get sick of women. I'll get me a wife and see what it feels like to live a normal life, thinks I, but I'd gotten old, and then along comes the anti-prostitution law. Just my luck not to have a buddy inside the police department, so they nabbed me. And on top o' that, my trusted head clerk made off with the money, and the gambling debts were mountin' up, and the whole thing's goin' ass over tits. And then a woman does the dirty on me. My first wife, she was. A real little worker, always lookin' after people. Five years older than me, never married, but she was born in the downtown area and good with the customers. Ran a little restaurant down in Totsuka, did pretty well out of it too. Didn't waste money. She had a million yen saved up when I married her. Well I quit work for a bit, got the others to do whatever needed doin', hung around waitin' for my lucky break. But then one of the girls went and got pregnant, it was my kid, so things got pretty sticky with the wife, she was really losin' it, and right around then that head clerk that made off with the whorehouse takings gets run to earth down in Kawasaki. The bastard'd set hisself up runnin' a massage parlor in Horinouchi, and he was rakin' it in. I was a hot-headed young fool, I was. Well so I decide on the spot I'm gonna half kill this guy, but I got him on the wrong bit of the head, and didn't just half kill the guy, I went the whole way. Got five years for it. When I gets out, the wife's closed up shop an' disappeared. The girl'd gotten rid of the kid and gone back home. Right, let's start all over again, says I to meself, when I gets a call from the big boss, and he gives me the job of runnin' a billiard joint in the old part of town by the gates of Ise Shrine and trainin' up the retired cops who join the gang. When those guys come in with us they get a real good salary, see."

The old man was feverishly summing up his life to his three young listeners, determined not to let them get a word in edgewise. He was obviously an old hand at talking, and it was easy to sit back and listen, but at this point the owner of the restaurant came over and said firmly, "Come on, Mr Naito, let's leave it at that eh?"

"You'd be sick of hearing it all, but these youngsters don't know the story."

Mr Naito turned an ingratiating smile on the owner, but when this failed to work he sulkily picked up his sake cup, and turned a soulful gaze to Mitsuyo. She poured him a fresh helping of the top grade sake, and waved the bottle in front of his eyes.

"So did you chalk up the thousand lovers?"

In answer to her question, the old man gave a choking laugh, and nodded. "Finally got there just before I turned sixty. Yep, took me forty years."

"And how old are you now?"

"Seventy-six."

"I bet you're past it now."

"No way, I'm still up for it. You've got a nice little body there. If you'd care to spend the night with me tonight, you'd be my one thousand fiftieth."

"I've had enough of dirty old men. I'd advise you to just settle down and await your Maker, at this stage."

But Mitsuyo's scolding went right past him, and he went blithely on with the talk about the thousand lovers.

"I've known girls from all over Japan, y'know. I've tasted 'em all the way through, from Wakkanai in northern Hokkaido to Miyakojima in southern Okinawa. You get the beauties in Akita, Niigata, Amami and Okinawa. My second wife was an Akita wench. Born back in the Taisho era, but she was a tall one even so, five feet six she was. A big girl, but sickly. She went through a lot. They say a beauty dies young, and sure enough, she died at thirty-five. After that I took to the road and had a wandering life all over, north and south, hawkin' this and that. Spent some time doing it rough and sleepin' out. But there's a reason I never gave up goin' after the girls. Women are what bring luck, good luck and bad, so nothin's going ta happen unless you sleep with women, see. I can tell fortunes. Open up yer legs a bit and watch me. I'll see if I can tell you what kinda guys you've been with. I've told the fortune of any number of actresses before – I can tell if they'll sell or not, when their career'll hit the skids, what kinda guy they should marry…"

It seemed there was no end to the old man's boasting, but Kita was in a hurry to move on, so he stood up and went over to pay the bill. They left the premises with the old man's gravelly voice still following them, "Hey, you guys're still young, ya know. I ain't finished talkin' yet."

Down the street, they came across a couple of black Mercedes Benzes parked in front of a shop selling dried fish. A bunch of gangsterish guys with tight punch perms, comb-backs and shaved heads were standing about inside, glaring at the dried fish and buying up big.

"Oh yeah, Hatayama the Third was crazy about dried mackerel, wasn't he?" Kita remarked softly in a reminiscent tone.

"Eh?" said a strapping skinhead.

"The old guy in there says, why not drop in and say hello," said Kita, pointing back to the restaurant they'd just left, and he walked out, with Zombie and Mitsuyo following a little behind, turning back to look at the shop as they left.

"Hey, those scary guys have all gone over to where the old man is," Mitsuyo announced. Kita broke into a run, and grabbed a passing taxi. When the other two were settled in there with him, he asked the driver to take them to some hotel where they could take a rest.

"You don't want to get yourself killed, eh?" laughed the driver.

"Right, he's aiming to die peacefully. Says he wants to pass on without a fight. That's why we want you to take us to some hotel that'll give him some good memories to take to the grave. It'd be even better if it had a beauty spa and a nice big bath for us girls, and great food."

There Mitsuyo went again, telling the whole world his story.

"You're in the grip of nihilism, are you? It's a popular thing these days, nihilism. Especially with youngsters. You don't look exactly young, mind you."

For an instant, the driver locked eyes with Kita in the rear view mirror. His eyes behind their black-rimmed glasses were two horizontal slits. His vacant face nevertheless had a foppish, girlish look to it. It somehow made Kita angry to have a face like this accusing him of nihilism.

"Sensitive kids get too easily attracted by nihilism, you know," the driver went on. "I've got a girl in middle school myself, and I can't bear the thought that she might fall for it without my knowing, and go and kill herself. They do say great souls suffer greatly, you know. But there's no progress without overcoming suffering."

"That's enough of the talk. Just take us to a hotel where we can take a rest," Kita repeated.

"Dangerous stuff, nihilism," the driver muttered balefully. At this, Zombie suddenly gave a cry as though she'd remembered something. On impulse, Kita swung round to look behind him.

"My stocking's got a run in it. Could you stop off at a convenience store?"

For some reason, Kita couldn't shake the feeling that Nothingness was pursuing them in a black Mercedes Benz. He could see how stupid he was being. So his death impulse was because he'd fallen into the grip of nihilism! What a fine explanation that was. If nihilism was one of those viruses that brought on cancer or immune deficiency, and crept into the host cell and killed it off, he'd welcome it with open arms. But nihilism was just nothingness. And nothingness was actually nothing. What a fraud, to use something that was nothing to explain everything! It gave nothingness a kind of bizarre reality. Real nothingness had nothing to do with death. It was just a pure zero floating way off over the edge of infinity. Nihilism was different from giving up. And it was different from the cessation of thought. When people claimed to have a sense of nothingness, they were simply talking about the effects of giving up. The effects of giving up did have a direct connection with death. It wasn't the same thing as the essential connection between nothingness and death, though. There was some obstacle in between them in this case. What you want is to get hold of that obstacle and remove it, so you can merge with pure nothingness. That's how those young girls felt when they got suicidal. And that's what this taxi driver believed too. But despite the fact that humans hate nothingness the way they hate a virus, nothingness has sucked up to the system. It's corrupt. Ever since people discovered nothingness, they've been putting all their vague impulses and fuzzy feelings down to it. The result was that these days nothingness was just another cute commodity on the market. Mickey Mouse and all those other cartoon characters were eyeballing nothingness while they carried on, fought, died, and were resurrected.

The taxi halted in front of a convenience store. The three got out, and scattered among the shelves, breathing in the rich scent of winter *oden* stew simmering on the counter. Zombie picked out a packet of stockings, while Mitsuyo began to browse among the magazines. Kita slipped into his shopping basket two pairs of underwear and socks, one of each to replace the ones he'd been wearing for the last two days, the other set in reserve. As he wandered down the shelves, he scooped up a few other things he noticed that he might need—a bandage, some condoms, a pair of nail clippers—then carried them all to the checkout counter.

"Somehow we don't seem to be keeping up this slave and secretary thing any more, do we?" remarked Mitsuyo, coming up behind him to the checkout counter with some Haagen-Dazs Belgian Chocolate.

"Just give me your orders. You're the queen, remember."

Mitsuyo nodded in agreement with Kita's proposal, but then added with a laugh, "But I've still got a long time to live."

"Yes, I've been slack about being secretary too," Zombie broke in. "Give me something to do please." She was determined to keep to the letter of her promise.

"Hmm. Maybe I'll remember something that needs doing once we're all in a hot spring tub."

The three jumped back into the pseudo-nihilist's taxi cab, and he drove them up to a hotel that towered high on a cliff. As Kita was paying, the driver removed his glasses, fixed his horizontal slits of eyes on Kita's face, and said, "I get the urge to die every week myself. But I've got a family." Was it just Kita's fancy that those slit eyes were gazing at him with envy? Guys who want to die should just get on with it, that way they'd at least be doing their bit for the population problem. Though mind you Kita wasn't convinced that the world's population really needed thinning out. Nor did he think that those folks who talk about the population problem ought to throw themselves into the struggle. The point was probably that it's harder for a guy who loves his family to stay alive for them than to die for the sake of humanity, he decided.

"There's no need to talk about living and dying if you love your family," he said, getting out of the cab and turning to follow the two girls who were headed for the hotel.

The nihilist driver shot back a disgruntled response to his departing back.

"That's what a guy with money would say. It takes money to die too, ya know. You can't die for free in this world."

Kita turned with a heartfelt nod, and replied, "OK, so start saving. Me, I've got together a million yen."

"The family's not going to get far on a million yen after I'm gone."

What a pain the guy was. He didn't have a clue. Kita went back to the pull-in bay, stood up close and said in his ear, "If you've got yourself a million yen, and the energy to more than match it, you've got no worries. You could die just like me if you wanted to, you know. The family would get along just fine. You say you love your family, but I'll bet they love you more. As long as you stay alive you bring in the money, after all. That family of yours will be thinking your life isn't just your own. Just wait a bit, and you'll get to my position. I'm not that old, but I got no wife and no children, and no father or brothers and sisters either. I'm an only child, and my mom lives in a public housing block downtown. She's told me she'll be happy just so long as I do what I want to. You need the family's cooperation to die, see. I'd guess you're a nice guy. That's why you can't get the family to be with you on this."

The cab driver rested his chin on the steering wheel. "Listen buddy," he began, obviously still wanting to keep the conversation going. "No one can stop you dying, huh?"

"Nope, there's no hope. I've made my decision."

"Those two girls couldn't do it?"

"We're not that close."

"Who needs to be close? It's only human kindness to save a guy who looks like he's going to die. It's just coldness to let you do it."

"Hey, you're singing a different song now, aren't you. You were just saying before how you wanted to die yourself."

"Talkin' to you's made me change my mind."

"I'm glad to hear it. Here, have this." Kita held out a five thousand yen note.

"I don't need it," said the driver, making no move to take the money. He drove off, clucking his tongue in disapproval.

Sitting in the hot tub outside the hotel, Oshima Island floating off the coast in a vague mist before him, Kita finally managed to rid himself of the toxins of the old gangster and the nihilist cab driver. Back on the bed in their luxurious room, he drifted into a doze under the hands of the masseuse. After a while he was aware that breathing had grown difficult, and he realized the woman was walking about on his back. On the next bed Zombie was lying flushed and exhausted.

"Hey Kita, isn't there anyone you'd like to meet?"

He paused to think about it, but no one sprang to mind, so he tried out the same question on the masseuse.

"Someone I'd like to meet? I'd like to meet my dead husband again."

"When did he pass away?"

"It'll be seven years now. Cancer."

"What would you like to do if you could see him again?"

She looked bashful for a moment, then said, "I'd like to sleep with him."

Kita nodded silently, and tipped her ten thousand yen. She took it reluctantly, explaining that she'd use it on a pilgrimage to Ise Shrine.

After she'd left, Kita and Zombie were alone together. Mitsuyo was apparently getting a total body beauty treatment.

"There's got to be some famous person you want to meet, Kita. Some famous singer or baseball player?"

"Not really. What about you?"

"If there's someone I want to meet I just go and do it really. There's quite a few novelists I like, so I just go along to some lecture or signing session they give, and go up and ask a question and shake their hand."

"Is that all it takes to satisfy you?"

"Sure. It'll do. I did get a free meal out of someone once."

"That's a special privilege you young girls have. I don't imagine any pop star would bother to meet me."

"Who knows? If you really beg them, they may well go for it. I've managed it. I telephoned Junichiro Nabefuta and begged him to see me, and he didn't bat an eyelid, just told me to go to the Imperial Hotel bar at nine on such and such a day.

"You've slept with Junichiro Nabefuta?"

"Yep. He said I was the three hundred thirteenth."

"I'd die to be able to have sex with stars as easy as that."

"So who'll it be?"

For the last ten years Kita had been a secret fan of Shinobu Yoimachi, and he'd always been comforted by her photos and CDs whenever he felt gloomy. He'd had intimate conversations with her in dreams, even gotten her to clean his ears for him, but still she was no more than a fiction. Her breasts had always been the object of lust for men, but voluptuous as they were, somehow they left you with a D-cup's worth of emptiness.

"I'd love to bury my face in Shinobu Yoimachi's boobs before I die."

Mitsuyo had returned to the room in time to hear this muttered confession. "You're after some pretty high-class boobs there," she said with a laugh.

"D'ya think I could get her?" Kita was beginning to warm to the idea.

"Well with your money you'd probably beat down the competition if they were up for auction, anyway. Shall we have a try? We can try using Yashiro's connections, you know."

At last, Kita was getting the feeling he could spend his remaining time before his execution just as he chose. Mitsuyo quickly rang Yashiro. They talked, and it was arranged that Yashiro would call back.

Kita took Yashiro's return call while the two girls were out taking a walk on the beach.

"Hey there. Having fun?"

Kita wasn't keen on the idea of Yashiro stepping back into the story again, but he had to admit the guy was useful. "So what was the answer?" he asked, getting hastily to the point.

"The production manager suggested a figure of a million. How about it? A million yen just to bury your face in her boobs... I'd say it was a bit steep."

"My budget won't run to that. Couldn't they halve it?"

"That wouldn't be easy, I'd say. It seems she won't do a special deal for just the boobs, you gotta pay the full package rate. If you pay a million, she'll spend the night with you, see. Shinobu's on the way out as a star. She's a third of what you'd pay for the likes of Naomi or Norika. Judging from the way the guy was talking, I'd guess you could beat them down to eight hundred thousand."

"I see. Good. I'll be needing the money for other things yet, see."

"Hey, cool it. Cool it. Mitsuyo's all you need, surely. Her market price is just fifty to a hundred fifty thousand a night, after all."

"Last night was free."

"Wow, that's rare. She must like you. I'd say she wants to give one last warm glow to a guy who's made up his mind to die."

"You're wrong, that's not how it is at all. Well anyway, if that's the deal they're offering then I'm out."

"Wait a moment there, just hold your horses. The guy said if all you wanted was to have a cup of tea with her, it'd be only one hundred thousand. You can negotiate things from there and see how you go. So why not just pay the hundred grand to the manager and at least have tea together?"

Kita took up the offer on the spot. "OK, go ahead then please," he said.

Yashiro seemed to want to continue the conversation, but Kita hung up on him, and set off still wearing his bathrobe to chase down the two girls. As he wove his way through the crowd around the lobby shop, he heard a child sobbing. A boy of around three was plumped down on the floor refusing to move, clutching a big box containing a combination robot. His mother had evidently run out of patience, and simply left him to it.

"You want that?"

At Kita's question the boy tensed up and stopped crying. Still hiccupping up a sob or two, he nodded. Kita slipped a ten thousand yen note from the sleeve of his robe, handed it to the child, and said encouragingly, "You go and hand this over to the lady and buy it yourself." The boy looked bewildered. "Go on," urged Kita, and at this the boy simply nodded, and ran off to the counter holding the robot and the note.

There were kids running all over the place in the lobby. Anxious parents were calling names all around, and in among them Kita heard one he recognized.

Mizuho – that was the name of the woman who'd left him six years ago and gone off and gotten married. Suddenly he found himself wondering just what sort of life she was leading these days. It hadn't worked out between them, but if his plan to die went according to plan, she was the only woman in his life who could've been his wife. But in all these six years he'd never tried to imagine how that phantom life with her might have been. He'd simply done everything he could to forget her. It would be a lie to say he didn't feel anything for her any more. But he knew it only made you miserable to go on yearning for someone, so he'd done his best to tell himself that he'd never had a relationship with her.

Six years ago, Mizuho had chosen to marry a bureaucrat on her father's advice. There would certainly have been calculations about the future involved in her decision – she would have assessed her probable future with the both of them. But Kita had been fool enough not to notice the third party in this triangle until she passed her judgment on him. It embarrassed him to remember how he'd half mistaken as a sign of acceptance that little smile on her face when he brought up the subject of marriage. That was no smile, he told himself, it was a sneer. "Marry you?" it was really saying. "You must be joking."

Ever since, whenever he saw a reproduction of the Mona Lisa, he was sure she was actually mocking people. It made him angry. It was useless to add a moustache to her lip, or rearrange the portrait so her teeth were exposed. He couldn't shake the belief that cruel malice lurked behind that subtle smile.

One day as he was walking around the Shinjuku area, he came across a signboard with a Mona Lisa who had an astonished look on her face. It was actually an advertisement for a shop selling artists' supplies at reduced price, but it made Kita think that he'd like sometime to freeze that little sneering smile of Mizuho's and change it to just this shocked expression. All such thoughts of revenge faded after about six months, however. He fell ill, and during the two months he spent in hospital even his hatred for her disappeared and he finally moved on. It was easier to just tuck his tail between his legs and accept defeat, he decided. He got to thinking that in fact, once this bureaucrat husband of hers had made his mark in the world, Kita would be able to feel pride in the fact that he'd once been in a love triangle with the fellow.

From Mizuho's point of view, he could see he must have been a piece of cake to handle. First off, she announces her parents are making her go through a meeting with a prospective arranged marriage partner; next, it's "Alas, my parents are dead set against me marrying you," declaimed in the tones of a tragic heroine; and finally, all she has to do is round things nicely off with the punch line, "When I'm married I'll still treasure the memories of our time together."

He caught up with Mitsuyo and Zombie enjoying a game of mini golf in a garden overlooking the sea. When they noticed him, they both paraded their matching dresses for him to admire.

"What's with the matching clothes?" he asked, and Mitsuyo replied, "We got them in the hotel boutique shop. On your bill."

"Hot springs resort geishas numbers one and two!" Zombie proclaimed, striking a pose.

"It looks like I'm going to get to meet Shinobu Yoimachi, girls."

"Congratulations, your wish has been granted," said geisha number one. "You're a big boob boy, aren't you Kita," added geisha number two.

"The boobs were too expensive for me, actually. But that's OK. Hey, hot springs resort geisha number two, I've got another favour to ask you. I want news of the girl I split with six years ago. Her name's Mizuho Nishi. Her married name's Higashi. The husband works for the Ministry of Finance."

"So we should check out the address of a Higashi in the Ministry of Finance, right? I know someone in the Ministry of Agriculture, Forestry and Fisheries, so I'll ask him on Monday."

"Please."

Geishas one and two looked at each other with cheerful, easygoing smiles. Those smiling faces were worth ten Mona Lisas.

"My you're a romantic, aren't you Kita? Wanting to meet up one more time with an old sweetheart who's married someone else. She must have been a fine woman. But hey, good women get snapped up by money and status in no time, don't they? You still love her? If you do, the only thing to do is snatch her back."

He felt no hatred for her any more. He'd had no unrealistic thoughts of getting back together with her or being a candidate for adultery. He'd simply done his best to get used to the fact he'd been ditched. Still, there'd been dreams. In those dreams, he'd tried to reconstruct the honeymoon time with Mizuho that had lasted less than two months, or brought her up to his dream flat as she might have been when there was no rival in love and it was only him she cared for. He also used her in his masturbation fantasies. Just for those brief moments, she was his and his alone. So was that some kind of lingering attachment? After all, he'd gone right on secretly cultivating this fantasy relationship after she jilted him. Suddenly, Kita came to himself, and what he realized was that when it came down to it Mizuho Nishi and Shinobu Yoimachi were the same thing, just fantasy women.

They went back to the hotel lobby, and there Kita found the little boy he'd bought the toy for being scolded by his mother.

"Tell me the truth! Where did you get this money?" "A man gave it to me." "What man? There's no such man here. You're lying to me." "But a man gave it to me." The little boy caught sight of Kita. Sure he'd be in for a tongue-lashing, Kita made a dash for the elevator.

His Sixth Last Supper

The evening's meal was Mediterranean style. Abalone salad, a fish terrine with caviar on the side, seafood paella with squid ink, grilled lobster etc., washed down with Dom Perignon and Chablis. Once they were full, there was a karaoke nightclub, followed by the hot spring bath. By the time Kita got back to his room, both the night-time Pacific Ocean outside the window and the chandelier were spinning.

At dawn, he was woken by the tiny squishing sound of mucous membranes rubbing together. The dead television screen opposite mirrored the room behind him, and looking closely he realized that the two naked hot springs resort geishas were locked in an embrace in there. He sat up, intending to go and get in on the action, but the moment he did so his gorge rose, and he turned and vomited into the drawer of his bedside table. His stomach heaved up its contents remorselessly, the bile burning in his throat.

"Hey Kita, you OK?" came Zombie's voice from next door.

"Don't come in here!" he said, and heaved again. When the last spasms were done, he turned on the light and checked the contents of the drawer. Good God, he'd gone and defiled the Bible and the Buddhist sutras with his undigested seafood and wine!

Holding the drawer in his arms, he made for the bathroom. He rescued the Bible and the Sutras from the sea of vomit, rinsed them off under the shower, and wrapped them in a towel. Meanwhile, Zombie had crept over for a peek. She rushed off as if horrified to have witnessed some forbidden sight, to report to Mitsuyo.

"Help! Kita's washing the Bible!"

"Eh? I didn't know that was something you could wash..."

Once in a Lifetime

Kita lay there with a hangover until close to midday. Meanwhile, the two hot springs geishas set off early for a game of tennis. When he finally surfaced, Kita took a bath, then grabbed a taxi with the idea of filling his empty stomach with noodles or something. The driver took him to a noodle restaurant in a made-over old farmhouse. As he sat there, blankly making his way through omelette and grated yam, an old couple arrived and sat down at the same table. They said hello with friendly smiles, which made Kita nervous that he was about to get himself mixed up again with more well-intentioned meddling.

The wife then pointed to the garden of the farmhouse beyond the little lane, and murmured to her husband in a languid undertone, "Look at that lovely house, buried in flowers. So many! Hydrangea, orange blossom, pinks, rose of Sharon, petunias…It reminds me of that poem:

I never thought to see
One speck of dust disturb them,
This bed of endless summer flowers
Where once my love and I
First lay in one another's arms."

"Ah yes, that's in the *Kokinshu*, isn't it. Not 'endless summer flowers,' 'endless summer blooms,' it is."

"What about some sake, darling?"

"Well, why not. It's splendid weather, after all. Let's be daring and have a cup, eh?"

"Soon it will be time for the gardenias and cotton roses to bloom, won't it?"

"Those summer scents are so enchanting."

"I remember Kenji used to love cotton roses."

"Ah yes, how many years is it now since he died? I still feel as if he's alive and could pop in for a visit any time, you know."

"He made enough noise while he was alive, didn't he, but how quiet he is in death."

"Yes, it's a sad truth, that old saying 'silent as the grave.'"

Could they always have such elegant conversations with each other, wondered Kita, casting a furtive glance at this couple who seemed to inhabit a different universe from himself. True, they were speaking Japanese, and sitting at the same table as him, but their words struck him as some imagined poetic ephemera.

They sat there sipping their sake and picking at the side dish of wild vegetables they'd ordered, gazing at the flower-filled garden across the way. Taking them in, Kita's eyes caught the husband's.

"Would you like a cup?" The old man delicately wiped a finger over the rim of his sake cup, and held it out for Kita.

"Thank you so much, but I have a hangover and all I can face is water," Kita replied politely, whereupon the wife remarked in the kind of elegant tone with which she might recite some poem, "Kenji tried to cure both hangovers and cancer with sake, I recall."

"Kenji was doing his best to disinfect his body with alcohol."

The wife smiled soundlessly with her teeth.

"Are you on holiday?" asked Kita.

"Yes. Death's messengers will be coming for us soon enough, so we're spending our remaining time on earth in perpetual travel. We're still in the middle of the journey."

"Really? So you do the pilgrimage to Ise Shrine, and so on?"

"What do you think, darling? Shall we?"

Her husband inclined his head thoughtfully. "Well it's a bit late to hope for salvation at this stage," he said, and he too gave a soundless laugh.

I get it, thought Kita. The post-retirement couple indulging themselves in refined travel. Just then their order of cold noodles arrived, so Kita returned to his own private world of hangover woes. Still, the couple continued to prey on his mind, and his eyes moved between the two as they ate their noodles, and the flowery garden opposite.

The old couple ate as though they'd forgotten what appetite was. This restaurant did a pretty filling tempura noodle dish that seemed to be a particular favourite with the clientele, and the customers who ordered it were gritty, no-nonsense types. But these two had not a trace of grit on them. The way they sat there politely sucking in their noodles, they could have been performing Zen meditation. It took quite some time for a single noodle to pass through their pursed lips. Watching from the sidelines, Kita was beginning to get annoyed. They sucked gently away at their food, sipped the side cup of noodle water as if sunk in meditation, then carefully replaced the throw-away chopsticks in their paper covers, remarked to each other how delicious it had been, and turned once more to look at the flowering garden.

"You must be lonely, all alone like this." The husband was casting a lure in his direction again.

"No, the only problem's the hangover," Kita replied with straightforward frankness.

But the old man wouldn't accept this. "I imagine there's more to it," he said, and soundlessly produced a complicit smile.

"Where will you go after Atami?" Kita asked, resorting to the usual question.

"I'd have loved to climb Mt. Fuji if only the old body would do as it's told a bit more. Maybe we'll head off to Kyoto."

"I'd like to see Okinawa before Death's messengers come for me," his wife cut in.

These messengers kept cropping up in the conversation, so Kita made an attempt to say something in keeping with the tone.

"So the final destination of the trip is Hades, eh?"

It was intended as a joke, but the husband gazed at him levelly and said, "Actually, it's a Fall By The Wayside tour."

The original idea of falling dead by the wayside involved a great deal of poverty and misery, thought Kita, while these two retained an astonishing luxury of time, money, and sense of enjoyment.

"You no longer have a home to go back to, then?"

"We don't."

"Well then, you're the same as me."

"You have nowhere to go back to either?"

"I'm just into the third day of the journey. What about you? How long since you both set out?"

"It's only been a week."

"Really? And how long do you plan on continuing?"

"What do you think, darling?"

"Well," replied the husband, "it's hard to calculate that." He fell into silent thought for a moment, then announced that he'd composed a little verse.

"Selling our swallow's nest
We take flight with the money
To die by the roadside."

The wife added the explanation that they'd sold their house and were using the money to travel, so they could keep on going for a year or even two if they felt so inclined.

"But my husband's determined to fall by the wayside, you see."

"'Fall by the wayside' doesn't have quite the right nuance, perhaps. The fact is, we've decided to simply quietly disappear, without causing anyone any inconvenience."

"I see…" Kita couldn't think what more to say.

"But it must be hard for you, having nowhere to live. We could be of assistance, if you'd like."

"Thank you very much. But I've left a few things undone in Tokyo that I have to go back and attend to."

"What a shame. So you go East and we go West, it seems. We meet only to part once more. But it was very nice to meet you."

"Take care," said Kita, putting out his hand. The old man held it in a feeble grasp. "You too," he said, and watched him leave. Take care and die, was what it amounted to for both sides.

On his way back to the hotel, Kita reflected that he'd made the right decision when he decided on next Friday for his execution date. If he went on not managing to die, day after day, he'd get to be like this old couple and no longer capable of really getting the best out of his last days before the execution date. Their appetite for food and sex had faded, there was no youthfulness, no yearning, not even the strength to really throw around the money they'd made on the sale of their house – all that was left was to pursue their pointless journeying. Maybe by the time you reached that age you were inclined to be attracted by those old wandering poets of yore like Basho or Saigyo, but somehow Kita couldn't imagine himself there.

Still, that pair were intent on achieving their last great undertaking, to disappear and die quietly by the wayside. Once you got beyond a certain level of debility, it was just too much trouble to die. You could no longer die by your own hand, you had to rely on a doctor or a virus to get you there.

While you were young, on the other hand, you could do it under your own power. If something nasty happened, well you could probably finish yourself off that very day. Cancer loves vital young cells. Be it by accident, or illness, or suicide, young people could die all too easily. If an old death was decay, then a young death was more like an explosion.

When he got back to the hotel, geishas one and two, fresh from the bath, took him by both arms and marched him off to the beauty spa, where he was given something called "a roamer therapy," and had his hair cut and his nails done. Looking at his freshly peeled and glowing face in the mirror, Kita thought he didn't look too bad really.

Once out of the three-hour confinement and over his hangover, he went back to their room, looking forward to his next feast. "Here I am," he called, but there was no answer. On the bed, he found a note:

Dear Kita, I'm really sorry to disappear on you without saying goodbye. There's some stuff I just can't get out of back in Tokyo. These last two days have been amazing, a kind of trip to the Dragon King's Palace. You're a great guy, Kita. I really mean it when I say I hate the thought of you dying. Still, it's really cool that you'll meet your death the way you'd visit the Dragon King's Palace. It's a bit on the B class side, with occasional fantastic moments. I'll keep my promise, don't worry. I'll follow through by checking out that Finance Ministry fellow's address and getting that high-class lady to come meet you. But how will we communicate with each other? I'll leave you my cell phone number. I'd love to meet you one more time. This necktie's a present for you — it's so cute, with all those tropical fish swimming around on it. It'd make me happy if you use it when you hang yourself. Finally, from my heart, *merci beaucoup*. From Izumi Mizusawa (aka Zombie).

I hadn't really thought about dying before, but after meeting you I've started wondering if I should do it too. Thanks for all the delicious food. If you feel like making a meal of me again, just give me a call. I'm happy to have sex with you one more time. I mean it this time. The world's full of rotten guys, but I just got the feeling you're really struggling with something. I don't really get it, but anyway, hang in there! Sorry to leave you behind in the beauty spa like this. But I just thought maybe you somehow want to be alone, so I decided to go back to Tokyo a bit early with Zombie. I'm not running away, believe me. I know there's not much you want in life, but if you do want me to do something, feel free to tell me. There's only five days left before Friday, so make sure you really get the best out of them. No regrets, OK? If you want to do something bad, try not to make people hate you for it. I remember there was this thief once called Umegawa Something, who murdered someone he was holding hostage, by shaving off her ears, stripping her naked, and torturing her. They finally shot him dead. Don't you do anything like that, will you? But hey, you're a nice guy, I'm sure you wouldn't. My present to you is a backpack. There's various things inside. Please use all you can before you die. Bye bye. Love, Mitsuyo."

Kita emptied out the backpack. Somehow, she'd managed to assemble a knife, a rope, an enamel cup, an aluminum pan, and some chocolate. Seemed like she was trying to tell him to go hiking.

Now that the two girls were gone, it was so quiet his own breathing began to get on his nerves. It was quite hot, but the room felt chilly. Was this that empty feeling that comes after a good feast? At such times maybe the only thing to do is skulk about in bed. If only someone was there to stand by his pillow and watch over him, hold his hand. He should have employed a partner he could lean on when he needed to.

He was just dozing off when the phone rang. It was Heita Yashiro. The first thing he said was, "Still alive, eh?"

"That Mitsuyo tells me she's gone and left you alone and gone back to Tokyo," he went on. "I really told her off. You all by yourself there?"

"All alone."

"That's bad, that's bad. If someone's not there beside you all the time, you're likely to follow through on your plan and pop right off to the other world."

"You're worried?"

"Sure I'm worried. You're not insured yet, and we never finished discussing that business deal. I'm askin' you."

"Asking what? I'm not interested in the deal, and I'm sure I refused to take out life insurance."

"You oughta get it. Who'd turn down the chance to get money if it's owing you?"

"I wouldn't be getting any money. Nor would you."

"I'm not interested in getting it. But if your mother or your brothers and sisters are still around, surely you should send twenty or thirty million their way? After all, you've done your old Mum quite a bit of wrong to date, haven't you?"

"Too late now, surely. I'm a homeless man these days, after all. Those insurance guys are no fools."

"Something could be managed. You could say you were a live-in employee in my company."

If he left some money to his mother, would that really erase his debts to her? Kita was letting himself be convinced by Yashiro again, and accepting help he'd rather do without. Still, it was hard to take Yashiro's goodwill at face value. Kita was inclined to suspect him of ulterior motives.

"This wouldn't cause my mother any problems, would it?"

"Don't be crazy. You're trying to say it's unfilial to name your mother as the recipient for your life insurance? Now let me tell you just one thing, don't you go letting on to anyone that you'll be committing suicide next week. And if by any chance you've told someone already, make it clear to them it was a joke, right? Hell, it's not the sort of thing most people really mean when they say it, after all."

"I haven't said a word to anyone personally."

"Ah yes, those girls. There's no saying they won't find themselves hard up for something to talk about and use your story as fodder."

"You did the same yourself, if I may say so."

"No, I'm different. Me, I think you should leave some proof of the few decades you've spent on this earth. I just want to help you leave a really vivid memory for all those people who're planning to hang around and grow a bit older in this life. Surely you'd like to be someone that people recall with fondness – 'Oh yeah, that guy called Yoshio Kita. He was a bit odd, wasn't he?' That sort of thing."

"Not particularly."

"You wouldn't like to do one really important thing in this life, to make people remember you fondly as the guy who passed away kind of intentionally?"

"It's not that kind of romantic thing at all."

"Don't knock romance. We men have lofty convictions women know nothing of."

"That so? Well I don't. You're too late."

"Come on, you could put your death off a bit longer."

"No I couldn't. I've made my decision."

"I don't imagine you've promised anyone though, have you?"

"I've promised myself."

"You sure are stubborn for a youngster. OK. You're coming back tomorrow afternoon, right? You get to meet Shinobu Yoimachi at nine tomorrow evening, so drop in at my office before that. I'll take you to the meeting place. I'll have all the insurance papers here ready. Let's have a meal together, eh?"

He wasn't quite sure what was going on, but it seemed like he was going to have to meet Yashiro again. But why was the guy so eager? Was he just having fun, or was this some complex plot to make money? Never mind, why worry? He could break the appointment tomorrow if he chose, after all, Kita told himself. He was about to put the receiver down when he heard Yashiro's voice continuing, "By the way, what are you doing this evening?" He hung up without replying. Immediately, the phone rang again. Kita left the room.

At the hotel's sushi bar he mutely picked away at what was probably his fifth last evening meal. Raw lobster, raw octopus, conger eel, bluefin tuna, bonito, abalone, salmon roe, wrapped up with a miso soup with sea bream. He chuckled when he realized that somehow everything he'd chosen had felicitous associations.

The bar lady looked at his face and remarked on how shiny his skin looked. When he explained he'd just had it scrubbed in the spa she took him for an actor, and asked him to sign a square of poem paper for her. He couldn't be bothered turning her down, so he wrote his name down in careful script. He stared at the remaining blank space for a while, then imitated the old gentleman he'd met at the noodle house by writing a little poem:

> All I know is
> I must fish myself out of
> The bad son soup
> Signed: Yoshio Kita

MONDAY

Don't Tell Mum

By the time he left Atami, Kita had spent three hundred thousand yen. It had taken him two days to spend what he'd normally spend in six weeks. Living sumptuously takes it out of you, though. Even if this decadence suddenly tipped him into insolvency, come what may, it was no big deal. He'd always had the habit of doing things on the cheap, so he couldn't be bothered letting expense worries overshadow things now. Besides, luxury was no doubt an irrational pleasure. What meaning beside irrational pleasure could there be for a guy to choose to drink an eighty thousand yen bottle of French Romanée-Conti wine rather than an eight hundred yen bottle of Chilean? If you were curious about the difference, why not at least try them both? Mind you, if you downed three bottles of each on your own and ended up defiling the Bible with your vomit, it would be all the same anyway. Yes, it was all irrational. A real connoisseur probably would regret nothing even if he drained three bottles of Romanée-Conti then threw the lot up again. Irrationality is the very thing he's after.

So what about himself, wondered Kita? He was still scared of the irrational.

He bought a gift box of assorted dried fish at the station shop, and hopped on the bullet train. He had to be systematic about how he spent his time from now on. Sure, other people's expectations were part of it, but he'd begun to think it would be a waste to idle away his remaining time like that old couple in the noodle house. If he met up with Heita Yashiro again, it would set the clock ticking smartly towards the appointed hour of his death, he decided. The guy was eager to make some money out of Kita's voluntary death. Before long, Kita would become a valuable item for a death merchant. He didn't mind that much. After all, he was the one who got to die, and Yashiro was the businessman who used him. It was only right that their perspective on death should differ. If Kita didn't die, Yashiro wouldn't turn a profit. Kita, on the other hand, couldn't care less about Yashiro's interests. Nevertheless, while Kita was alive, Yashiro could apparently be helpful in all sorts of ways, so why not put himself in his hands for a while? After all, come Friday Kita would be released from all such worldly calculations, and he wouldn't give a damn what happened after that. This was the freedom of the dead.

Still, it was only Monday today, and Kita was still alive. He couldn't go about like he was dead yet. He decided to get himself some new clothes for his remaining days, something cool that he could use as his death clothing as well. He headed for Ginza, Mitsuyo's survival backpack still on his back.

First off, he looked for some shoes that would put a spring in his step for the remaining days. Smooth leather ones would be too slippery. On the other hand, his tread would be too heavy with thick caterpillar-type soles. The best kind would allow him speed lightly towards his destiny. His eye happened to fall on a pair of zebra-striped basket shoes. They had a layer of air in the sole, and he liked the sinewy feel of the tread. He threw away the old shoes that had kindly seen him through until now, and set off right away walking down Ginza mounted on his new "zebras." Just the difference in feeling underfoot gave a lift to his mood. Wherever he might find himself flying away to, these shoes seemed to promise to give him a good strong run-up before takeoff.

He headed for the menswear section of a department store. It was still morning, and there was only a smattering of customers there. He bought a shirt with the same zebra stripes as his shoes, then at the urging of the salesgirl he added a cream jacket to the combination. This went perfectly with the tropical fish necktie that Zombie had given him, and gave him the air of one of those exotic gamblers who showed up in the casinos of Lido or Monte Carlo. The salesgirl added in a pair of mustard-coloured cotton trousers. When he turned up the cuffs over his basket shoes he looked, if not like someone about to commit Death by Choice, at any rate like some neurotic playboy.

Then, adding the backpack to this attire, he was transformed into a vagrant with a touch of good taste. The sensibility revealed itself in the little clank of the aluminium pan at every step he took. Next, box of dried fish in hand, he added in for good measure a huge pair of Infinity sunglasses. Deciding against a hat, he instead bought a bright red umbrella. The whole thing came to eighty-two thousand three hundred yen.

He also popped his head into the basement food hall. His father often used to slip in the department store food halls on his way home from work to catch the closing-time sales, and would buy a cylinder of fish paste or some baby dried sardines, dried fish, or sukiyaki beef. He would just buy whatever was on special offer. Spurred on by his new outfit, Kita decided to follow his dead father's example, and scooped up whatever food his hand fell on. To begin with, he limited himself to dry goods – dried cuttlefish, edible algae, kelp, dried white radish slivers and dried scallops – but before long he found himself on the kind of roll that shopping excitement induces, and he bought a kilo of high-grade Matsuzaka marbled beef, a box of early white peaches, and three skewers of roasted eel. The total set him back twenty thousand yen.

He glanced at his watch and saw it was right on noon. Manoeuvring his great pile of shopping into a taxi, he ordered the driver to take him to Takashima Daira.

There was somewhere he wanted to drop in on before his execution. Anybody in his position would do the same, as the hour of their execution approached. Not because the place was famous for its suicides, but because the woman who had brought him into this world was there. He hadn't done much for her while he was alive, and now he was going to give her further grief by preceding her into the next world. Thus, he wanted to go and humbly express his regret, without putting on any airs about what he was going to do. Most people under sentence of Death by Choice make their way to their mother's sitting room, driven by the same compulsion.

He decided not to talk to the driver. He couldn't take another dose of any contradictory philosophising on life. But there, coming from the car radio in a sleep-inducing murmur, was a voice harping on about that very theme. The road was jammed with traffic. Kita closed his eyes, and did his best to shut out the distracting sound. He began to think of the various things he had to do.

He'd need papers in order to apply for the insurance. He'd better go to the local Ward Office and get an abridged copy of his family register and a document certifying his registered signature seal. He owed money to friends, so he should write a will leaving them an appropriate sum from the insurance money after his death. When would he do that? Where should he leave the will once he'd written it? He'd better ask Yashiro later. Where would he stay tonight? Surely there was no way he'd be spending it with Shinobu Yoimachi.

He stopped off at the Ward Office, then hailed another taxi, and called in on his Mum. Each time he went there, the sitting room seemed to have gotten smaller. His mother didn't seem either delighted or put out by his calling in unexpectedly like this. She just said lightly, "Hi, welcome back. You been somewhere?"

"Not really, I just went down to Atami for a bit."

"Atami, eh? A school trip?"

"What?" said Kita with a laugh, and he sat down. His mother gazed fixedly at the clothes he was wearing and looked as if she was about to say something, but remained silent. Unloading all the food he'd bought item by item and laying it on the table, Kita said, "Put the fresh stuff in the fridge, would you?"

His mother looked dubiously at the meat and peaches, then back to Kita's face. "Who did you get all this from?" she asked.

"I bought it. At a department store."

"I wonder why you've started acting like your father."

"I'll get more and more like him as time passes."

"Don't be in too much of a hurry. You'll be in danger of being mistaken for him."

His mother had this tendency to say really stupid things with a straight face. He hadn't dropped in on her like this more than about once every six months for the last few years, and even then, he'd come along like some guest with a gift for her, just stayed for a meal, and hardly really spoken to her. He guessed she'd be feeling lonely since his father died, but she'd carried on living alone and always put up a brave front, assuring him she didn't want to be a burden on him by moving in together. Most parents would let themselves be overheard murmuring to themselves that they wished their son would hurry up and marry, and give them the blessing of a grandchild. But Kita's mother never said a thing. She chose to act as if it was no problem. Kita was aware of all he owed her, but he too found himself playing dumb, and just keeping an eye on her from a strategic distance.

"You won't have had lunch yet, I guess. I'm just about to have some, so you've come at the right time. I've got some cold rice, so shall we grill some of this dried fish to have with it?"

"Sure. And let's have some eel. How about making miso soup?"

His mother went into the kitchen. Her movements were listless, and quite confused. This mother of his, who used to slip constantly back and forth between kitchen and sitting room so swiftly and efficiently, now seemed to have shrunk as though the air had been let out of her, and had grown sluggish. Her life had been reduced to a painstaking repetition of the tiny day-to-day rituals of life alone in this thirty-year-old sitting room.

He looked in on the bedroom. There was a row of potted plants out on the balcony, pansies and mini tomatoes and so on. There was quite a lot of stuff about considering her solitary life, with tea chests and cardboard boxes crammed into the tiny room. Opening the drawers and top closets, he came across boxes marked "Yoshio's summer clothes" or "Daddy's formal wear". Why did she keep clothing belonging to these two men who had left? What's more, she had carefully kept the set of illustrated reference books that Kita had treasured back when he was a grade schooler. One whole area of the closet was exactly as it had been twenty years ago.

The smell of grilling fish came wafting down the corridor together with his mother's voice. "Food's ready, Yoshio."

On the table was an extra rice dish and plate of fish. "Is someone else coming?" Kita inquired.

"It's your father's portion," his mother said.

She'd never in the past gone through this kind of performance. Perhaps she just wanted to pay her respects to the dead there today?

Kita stirred the miso soup about with his chopsticks. It contained some slivers of the dried white radish, sliced onion leaves, and seaweed flakes. His mother had made this soup without a saucepan. She had just put the stock powder and miso into a bowl, added the reconstituted white radish, then poured boiling water from the kettle over it all and stirred, finally adding the onion leaves and seaweed.

"This was the way to make miso soup that you came up with so that Dad could make it even on his own, wasn't it Mum?"

"That's right. He really liked it."

"I guess you used to make it this way before they ever started selling instant miso soup in packets, eh? It's quite an invention."

"In the days before stock powder, I used to use Ajinomoto. This mackerel's good. So who'd you get the food from?"

"I bought it at Atami. Like I told you."

"What did you go to Atami for? You're not into shoplifting again, are you?"

"Shoplifting dried fish? I'm not a cat, you know."

"You on holiday today?"

"I've taken some time off. Till Friday."

"What'll you do with all that spare time? Planning to get up to some mischief, I'll be bound."

What could she be imagining? The conversation wasn't going too well so far. "Come on, let's stop messing about, eh?" he said, forcing a smile. "You're throwing me off." Then he looked at her face. He hadn't really gotten a good look at her face when he first arrived, but now he saw that his mother's eyes were somehow misty, and when she looked at her son's face, she did so with the kind of straight gaze a child would use. She was close to sixty, so no doubt her eyesight was getting poorer and her field of vision narrowing, but there was something completely innocent about her look. Then there was that bewildered look on her face, as if she wasn't quite catching on.

When he was fourteen, Kita had realized there was no fooling his mother. He'd fallen in with bad friends, and gotten into shoplifting. At the time, he'd felt his survival hinged on his loyalty to these friends. He was balanced precisely on the boundary between the bullies and the bullied, and every action was monitored and judged by the "gang." Ultimately, what it amounted to was that Kita had managed to ensure his own safety by committing a series of deeds encouraged by the gang, but it had not been without pain. He had of course felt guilty when the gang first enticed him into shoplifting, but once he'd complied with their demands, he'd have been branded a traitor if he attempted to pull out again, so he could only do his best to stick with them and not make any blunders.

If I'm going to shoplift, Kita thought, I should go for something cheap at least. He'd also got it into his head that it was somehow less sinful to steal a book than food or clothing or stationery. He was probably simply balancing appetite for food against appetite for learning, judging that it was better to sate the latter. He was in this thing unwillingly, and he wanted at least to be able to make distinctions where he could. In contrast, his friends were only interested in shoplifting for its own sake, and saw greater value in stealing something difficult.

Still, it was amazing how his mother had picked up on his shoplifting. He didn't think he'd been acting particularly guiltily around the sitting room.

He tried asking his mother about it now, as she poked at her dried fish. "How did you know I was shoplifting? Back when I was in second grade, remember?"

"Intuition. Your feelings always show on your face. If you've got anything to hide, you suddenly clam up and lose your appetite. You've been that way since you were little. If you didn't like someone's question, your nose would twitch. You get that honesty from your father. When you were doing that shoplifting you had no appetite at all, did you? You did eat up all the eel, it's true, but you left the rice with the gravy on it. Then you went straight off to your room after dinner. Then there was this book that you wouldn't have been able to buy on your pocket money."

"Oh yeah, that book of Dali's paintings. That was really hard to steal."

"It was a real shock to me. But you gave it up right away, didn't you? You started Zen meditation instead. You must have had a guilty conscience."

"No, actually I was doing it as a kind of sport."

"But that *zazen* gave you a bit more staying power, don't you agree? You had that classmate who committed suicide. Miura, wasn't it? If he'd done some *zazen* he'd still be alive today, instead of going off and killing himself on a passing impulse. Such a pity, when he could've had good things happen in his life. It was a great shame."

Let's change the subject, thought Kita uncomfortably. Still, come to think of it, why was she hauling out this long-gone incident right now?

"I don't care whether it's for sports or whatever, but you should keep up the *zazen*."

"I gave it up long ago."

"How come? You've only just begun."

It was twenty years ago that he'd gone along to the temple in Azabu to do *zazen*. It was exactly twenty years ago that Miura had committed suicide. Had she remembered it through an association with shoplifting leading to the *zazen*?

Could it be possible that she suspected he was planning to kill himself this coming Friday, he wondered a trifle uneasily as he sipped his cold miso soup. The taste of the soup was just as it used to be. He could guarantee that it was made by his mother. Only his mother would be capable of making a soup like this. So it stood to reason it could only be his mother sitting in front of him now, he thought.

His mother seemed to be harbouring some doubts about whether this man was her son or not, as well. There'd been no particular strangeness there when he'd called in four months ago. Of course, there'd never been any hint of a need to reconfirm that they were indeed and undoubtedly mother and son. They just were, without saying so.

No, maybe what was disturbing her so much now was the kind of sharp intuition that came precisely from her being his mother. Did he really look so suspicious?

Whatever, he couldn't stay long. His plan had been to just drop in, have a meal, and leave again. But his mother seemed to find something dubious in the way he was behaving. She drew a deep breath, and finally decided to speak.

"You're very quiet. What are you hiding? You've been acting strange ever since you got here."

Rather than go over the same conversation again, Kita said, "Do I look to you as though I want to die?"

There was no way to guess what his mother was thinking, but she looked like she'd seen through him somehow. Kita pulled a funny face, in an attempt to cover up his thoughts. But his mother barely glanced at him. Eyes down, she murmured, "No, I was just thinking how quickly people age. You must be tired, surely? You seem to have aged six years in three months. Is anything worrying you?"

"I feel like I look about normal for my age really. Surely you haven't forgotten how old I am?"

His mother looked puzzled, and said nothing. She picked up the thermos and topped up the teapot with hot water in an apparent attempt to fill the silence. Then she turned over the two cups that were sitting face down on the tray and, pouring tea by turns into each, she murmured, "I thought you were your father when you first arrived."

"Just walking in out of the next world to say, 'Here I am,' huh? I had a look in the cupboard in there just now and found that collection of our old clothes, Dad's and mine. I even came across those old reference books you bought me when I was a kid."

"Well I can't get things organised properly. There's mountains of stuff I'd like to throw away, but if I just did it without asking, you and Daddy would complain."

"Dad couldn't complain if he wanted to. OK, if you want to keep things Mum, go right ahead. This house is too big for you on your own, after all. Having some junk around won't bother you, I imagine."

"What are you saying!" exclaimed his mother, astonished. "Your father's due back at any moment."

"You're living with a ghost, I see. Good thing ghosts don't take up any room."

His mother made no attempt to smile at the joke. She simply looked as if she couldn't follow his thread. She didn't even seem to recognize that it was a joke. Could it be that she wasn't putting it on, that she really was going senile?

"Dad died four years ago, right?" The only thing for it at this stage, if she really did have the illusion that he was still alive, was to come straight out with it.

"Yes, I guess he did, didn't he? Four years ago already?" His mother turned her empty gaze to left and right, like a puzzled child groping for the answer to a math problem.

"Hey come on, pull yourself together."

"But it's very strange. He came home as usual last night. And when he went out this morning he said he'd be able to come home by three today."

"Where did he go?"

"He said he had something to do in Shibuya."

Shibuya was precisely where Kita was headed next himself. Did she dream it? Or was she still playing out the dream now in her sitting room? Or had the clock inside her head broken, so that the past tense had changed into the present continuous? No wonder she couldn't figure out what was going on, if her son of around twenty suddenly turns up looking thirty-five.

Had living alone done this to her? Was she watching television? Was she communicating with the neighbours? He'd telephoned from time to time, but their only conversation had been of the "How are you?" "Same as usual, thanks" variety. And now this "same as usual" life had somehow become one in which the son had come to announce his self-appointed execution, while the mother had grown senile.

"You haven't been in hospital with some problem like a stroke or a brain tumour or something, have you?"

"Yes."

"When?"

"I forget."

"Why didn't you tell me?"

"I didn't want to worry you."

"You can't live on your own if you go senile, you know."

"If I go senile, you and Daddy will come back and look after me. We'll be able to live here all together just like the old days, won't we?"

"Why are you like this? Go and get some treatment, for heaven's sake. You've got to get a grip on reality again. Dad's dead, OK? And I can't come back home. So I'm begging you… please."

"Please what?"

"Please don't go senile, I'm saying."

Here he was begging his senile mother not to go senile, he thought. He felt like going down on his knees and praying, although he knew prayer wouldn't get his mother's brain back to the active brain it had been fifteen years ago.

"Is it wrong to go senile?"

"Yes, it is."

"I just stay here in the house, you know, I don't bother anyone. What's wrong with it?"

"It's because you stay in the house all the time that you're going senile."

"I go out shopping. If you're worried about me, come back and live here. There you are just messing about, not getting married. I'll bet you don't think about anything much."

"I'll look after you in your old age, Mum."

"I don't need you to. I'll freeze being looked after by such a cold fish of a son. No, I'm the one who'll look after you. You can't do anything on your own, Yoshio. Just when I think you're improving yourself with some *zazen*, you go and give it up—"

"Stop talking about stuff that happened twenty years ago. The problem is how you're going to cope with the present." A fine thing for an intended suicide to say, he heard a little voice saying inside him. Still, he went on berating her.

"When you get up in the morning, check your face in the mirror. Put on a bit of make-up. And go out for walks. Take a good look at the world getting on with things all around. Talk to children whenever you get the chance. Children grow up fast, you know. And keep a constant check on where you are right now and what you're doing. You can do that, can't you?"

Tears began to flow from his mother's misty eyes. She didn't attempt to wipe them away. She sighed, with an expressionless face that registered no particular sadness or pleasure. Maybe her tear ducts just leaked a bit these days.

"What can it be, I wonder? My face looks weird when I look in the mirror, and this area's all changed too – there are all sorts of faces around that I don't know. It's like I'm left behind all alone somehow. Though there's nowhere else to go, mind you."

If his Dad was still alive they could go off on a trip together, have a few quarrels, make up again, drink sake, make love. Maybe while they were in Atami someplace eating dried fish or noodles his father would suddenly declare, "It's splendid weather, darling. Why don't we commit suicide?" If his Dad showed up right now and made such a suggestion, his Mum would probably go off with him with pleasure.

"Right, I'd better be off."

"Where to, dear? You're not staying here the night?"

"There's somewhere I have to go."

"You don't have to go there today, surely?"

"No, I can't put it off."

"You won't be back for months again, I guess. My mind may well be in a worse way by then, you know."

Was she trying emotional blackmail on him? Or was this perhaps her only means of resistance? Probably his presence would be her best form of rehabilitation. If there was someone else around to keep making clear to her that her husband was dead, she'd get the message and scramble back out of the past in panic. It didn't seem like she was having problems with the housework, so things weren't too bad yet, after all.

Maybe, on the other hand, it was better for her senility to grow worse. At least that way she'd have a happy old age. If you're senile, your pleasures halve, but so do your sorrows. If the pleasures and sorrows to come in her life were weighed in the balance, the sorrows were probably greater. This son of hers who'd do her so much good if he stayed around was going to be dying this week, sure, but in his mother's hazy mind he probably wouldn't be dead. Her son would simply turn into a ghostly young man of around twenty who came and went in the house. He and his Dad together could settle back in to become a family for her again. That was a better outcome. If she underwent some kind of half-baked rehabilitation and got her mind back together again, the next thing that loomed in her life was double the sorrow over losing her son, after all. The only way to escape from this was senility.

"I'll be back. Soon. Say hi to Dad for me."

Kita hoisted on his survival backpack and slipped his feet back into the new zebra shoes. Next time he came, he'd be without form or shape, no more than a hint in the air. Nevertheless, thanks to her fine intuition, his mother would no doubt sense her son's presence, and cook him up his favourite croquettes. Though all you would see would be plates of croquettes and chopsticks on the table, Yoshio and his Dad would be there in a corner of her brain, remembering things with an occasional laugh together, smoking, clipping their nails, flipping through the newspaper, and easing out an occasional silent fart.

How Much for Dying?

Kita wandered about for over an hour before he found the address printed on Yashiro's name card. His father was hanging out there in Shibuya too, in fact. It wasn't that he had any intention of conniving with his mother's delusions, he just happened to cross paths with numerous elderly men loitering on street corners. They were the kind of guys who wouldn't be given the time of day in this part of town normally, but for some reason today they all seemed full of a wordless self-confidence.

Close to six in the evening, Kita finally located the block of assorted shops and offices containing the one marked "Thanatos Movie Productions". Across the way was a private hospital, while next door on one side was a grilled meat restaurant and on the other a florists. The first floor of the building held a sake shop. He took the elevator, which stank of raw rubbish, up to the fourth floor, where he emerged into a corridor stacked with piles of videos all the way up both walls, forming a passage just wide enough for a single person to pass. The scent of perfume hung mysteriously in the air. When he knocked on the door at the end, Zombie came out to greet him.

"Well, well, Kita. Long time no see. How've you been?"

Could it really be only twenty-six hours since they'd seen each other last? The sight of her made him oddly nostalgic even.

"You're late, you know. We were getting sick of waiting for you."

Seated on the sofa beyond, Yashiro waved him over. A man in his thirties in a businesslike dark blue suit interrupted what may have been chat or some business discussion to stand and greet Kita, as did a pink-suited woman of around the same age, who was providing smiles and the scent of perfume gratis to all around. Kita immediately sensed from their behaviour that there was business involved for them, and he returned the greeting without enthusiasm.

"Hey Kita, that get-up suits you. Sporty, speedy, cool. Got a whiff of Mexican coriander about it somehow," said Zombie.

Kita sniffed his jacket sleeve. "I can't smell anything," he said.

"What's that backpack for?" Yashiro asked with a serious face. "Something's rattling around in there. Some kind of emergency bag?"

"I thought I'd carry it round with me so I could start sleeping on the streets any time I feel like it," said Kita, saying the first thing that came to him. He lowered the backpack to the floor. The man and woman in their thirties were both nodding. Yashiro introduced him to them. It seemed he'd suddenly become the company's head planning officer. The pair took turns to proffer their name cards to him.

"Organic Transport: Coordinator, Kazuya Koikawa"

"Pacific Insurance Mutual Company, Shibuya Office, Yoshiko Koikawa."

"You're husband and wife?" he asked, raising his eyes from the business cards bearing the same family name, and looking from one to the other.

"No," Yoshiko replied. "Brother and sister."

"We've learned from Mr. Yashiro that you wish to take out life insurance from us," she went on. "Thank you very much."

"I see. No, no, I'm the one to thank you." Kita lowered his head in a slight bow, keeping an eye on Yashiro as he did so. They'd be making quite a loss if they had to pay out the insurance money to his mother a mere four days after he'd taken it out. He planned to apologize to them for it.

When Kita had sat down on the sofa, Yoshiko Koikawa spread out a brochure on the table before him and set about explaining the insurance. She proceeded to talk about how it would give him peace of mind to add a special clause covering the possibility of cancer or Aids, how the version that allowed you to convert the amount into a monthly pension once it had almost reached full term meant that you could plan for your old age, while there was a type that was popular with young people whereby you could take out the money for your own use if you knew you didn't have long to live. Kita listened with only half an ear. There was something more important than all this that he needed to ask.

"What happens if I decide to commit suicide?"

Yoshiko's smile froze into an expression of astonishment, but she quickly pulled herself together. "Don't even think of it," she said.

"Eh?" said Kita.

The explanatory tone returned. "You shouldn't consider suicide. There's no profit in it at all. We do occasionally get young people of this sort among our customers. Someone who asks whether there's a payout if they commit suicide. Actually, accident and suicide are major causes of death in the twenties and thirties. Suicide's the top cause in the forties, maybe because it's a hard time in a lot of lives. My brother and I are about to enter our forties, actually, so we're being very careful. I would guess you're in your mid-thirties, Mr Kita, so that's why the word springs so easily to your lips. I do understand how you feel."

Yoshiko leaned forward on the sofa and gazed at him, as if speaking to a child. He in turn scrutinized her more closely. She had a rather blank face, a bit like a badger and with moles under the eyes to match, and her plump lips seemed to emanate a confidence in her continuing ability to maintain her popularity with men.

"Come on Kita, cut the scary talk," Yashiro chimed in with a laugh, wiping a fine sweat from his forehead. "You're making it sound like this company's giving you a really hard time. Leave the suicide to Zombie here. You can rely on her. She can commit suicide and still stay alive, after all."

"That's right. I'm immortal."

Everyone laughed. Then, the mirth still hovering at the corners of his mouth, Kita asked, "So if you do commit suicide, is there an insurance payout?"

"It's all here in detail in the Contract Guide. The fundamental rule is, if the insured commits suicide within one year of signing the contract, no life insurance can be paid. However, there are cases of payout if the insured was of unsound mind at the time."

So there he had it. No payout if you kill yourself four days later. Kita looked at Yashiro. There was no point in taking out insurance, if that was the case. Yashiro knew this when he arranged for Kita to sign on for life insurance. He was telling Kita to make it look like an accident.

"So you don't get anything from it if you kill yourself, Kita. Better give the idea up." Yashiro stuck out his thumb and sent Kita a warning signal as he spoke. He looked satisfied, however. Kita had just been presented with one good argument for changing his mind about suicide. But Kita was still determined on his plan. He just had to change his tactics a little.

"So what other situations are there where the money doesn't get paid?" This time, Kita thought he ought to find out all the facts.

"Well, I don't imagine this would apply to you Mr Kita, but if for instance you were condemned to death by the courts, that's another example. Or if you died in the course of committing a crime. If, say, you hijacked a plane, or holed up in a bank or hotel with hostages, and got yourself shot in the process. The same applies if you try to kill someone and get killed yourself – the other party's acting in lawful self-defence, and you were asking for it. Certain conditions also apply if you're injured in a war or a terrorist attack. I believe we limit payment to situations in which general damage is relatively limited – if the damage is widespread, there can be more claims than the company's capable of paying, see. If you take out a contract with special conditions attached, I'd also mention that there are conditions related to damage from earthquakes, volcanic eruptions and tsunami. By the way, Mr, Kita, do you drink?"

"Yes, a bit."

"There is no payout if you die in a condition of extreme drunkenness. As in the case of death in a car accident in which you were driving while under the influence or without a licence. Also, I'm sure I don't need to tell you that there's no payout in a situation in which the recipient of the insurance causes the death of the insured."

"That's Kita's Mum in his case, and it's her own son who's the insured, so I don't think we need to worry there. Now if it was me who was either the insured or the recipient, there might be room for suspicion." Yashiro was the first to laugh at his own joke again.

Kita signed the necessary parts of the contract, and inserted his mother's name as recipient. When he'd paid the first instalment with his credit card, Yoshiko urged him to drop in to the medical clinic across the way and get a check-up. For some reason, her brother came along too. "Are you in the insurance business too?" asked Kita.

"Not directly, but she and I do support each other in our work. Mr Yashiro asked me along today, that's why I'm here. I'll explain in more detail after your check-up. The truth is, I'm extremely interested in your state of health. It's kind of my business, you might say."

It's none of your business at all, thought Kita, but he said nothing.

The check-up should have been a simple and straightforward matter, but the doctor took pains to listen with his stethoscope, take his pulse, and even take an X-ray, even though the results would take time to process. He also took a blood sample. It really got to Kita that thanks to Yashiro he was in the ironic position of getting a health check-up four days before his death.

Once the doctor had signed the check-up form, the insurance contract was finalized. "The money will be paid out even if you die in an unexpected accident this evening," Yoshiko told him. Her brother congratulated him on his clean bill of health with innocent delight.

As soon as Kita was back inside the office of Thanatos Movie Productions, Kita inquired about the puzzling line of business of the brother.

"Well, you know about organ transplants, don't you? The official term is 'organic transplant.' We're in the business of organic transport. Our main job is to coordinate the transplant operation. You'll be aware that there are a great many patients these days who need organ transplants. Traditional organ banks can't keep up with demand, so we're doing our best to help increase the supply of available organs. We use our own independent network to find people willing to donate an eye cornea, say, or bone marrow, or a kidney or liver, and organize the transplant for patients who are members of our club. To date, we've been able to coordinate one hundred and twenty-three transplants."

"You're telling me I should donate my organs? But if you take my liver out, I'll die, won't I? If I donate a cornea I'll lose the sight of that eye, surely. And the kidney, now—"

"You have two of them," the brother chipped in with a businesslike smile.

"So has Mr Yashiro here, doesn't he?"

"Oh, mine are getting pretty tired. Your engine's in much better condition than mine."

It really did appear that Yashiro was out to sell Kita's organs. But he couldn't go selling things he was still using. The brother went on with his explanation.

"Naturally, the donation itself would take place only after your death, but we need the donation recorded while you're still alive, you see."

"Sure, I can see that. You can't go stealing organs from dead bodies, after all. Even if the guy's made you a verbal promise, eh?"

"But of course." The brother spread out a brochure. "Over ninety percent of those requesting organ transplants are Japanese, but the majority of donors come from South-East Asia, China, and India. To tell the truth, we encourage people engaged in dangerous work to donate."

In other words, the Japanese are buying Third World organs cheap just like they do with timber and oil and seafood, thought Kita.

Yashiro broke in, "His sister hopes her customers will live as long as possible, while he wants them to die as quick as they can. The younger and healthier the organs the better, after all. And Japanese organs are less of a worry, too. You'd pay more for Japanese organs than Chinese or Indian ones, wouldn't you?"

"All organs donated to us are equally precious."

The brother and sister exchanged a quick glance and an embarrassed if somewhat eerie smile. It was just as Yashiro had said, the two were in the same game from polar positions. Surely they already knew this. Why on earth were they siblings, when it came down to it?

"I get the feeling I'm the only person who's not quite getting all this," Kita remarked, and though it wasn't particularly funny, he laughed.

Yashiro explained. "If you die, what would be the point of burning your healthy organs, after all?"

"Well no one's going to want to eat them, are they? I guess if I was in Tibet or somewhere the vultures would, of course."

"In Japan, there are patients with kidney or liver problems who'll happily use them for you. They may be second-hand, but these folks will take them over and treat them well. You're a very lucky man, you know."

"So you're telling me to sell 'em, that's what you're saying."

"Not without payment, of course. We wouldn't have the nerve to do that. There's nothing that costs you more than something free, as the saying goes. No, the patients want to pay. And you can't go offering them for a bargain, either, like they were bananas or antiques or something. That's why I called in Mr Koikawa here."

Mr Koikawa bowed. "I'm honoured," he said.

To shut Yashiro up, Kita shot him a question. "You're after something, aren't you?"

"We'd like your corneas, liver, and kidneys."

"How much?"

"Well it rather depends on the results of the medical check-up, but I believe we could offer you a total of one million one hundred twenty thousand yen. Just to itemize it—"

"No need to itemize. And I could get the money now?"

"We can finance at time of contract."

"I guess that means I mortgage my organs to borrow the money."

"Precisely."

"The debt's cancelled in return for the organs when I die, right?"

"Correct."

"And if I don't die?"

"No interest for the first month, and from then on three percent a month. We use the same repayment plan as for home loans, so you pay interest accordingly. Of course, it may be that you change your mind at some later point. You can cancel the contract if so, but this will incur an additional charge of ten percent of the original amount borrowed. That's Plan A. In Plan B, we pay the sum for organ donation directly to the recipient of your life insurance, at the time of your death. In that case, there's a big increase in organ price paid. Oh, and I forgot to mention that you need a guarantor if you choose Plan A."

Kita turned to Yoshiko. "I get the feeling there's something more to this," he said ironically.

She responded with a look that said she had nothing to hide. "I also register clients for organ donation you know," she said.

Her brother followed this up with a confession. "I've taken out insurance with my sister as designated recipient, actually."

Was this all supposed to mean they got on well together or something?

"There's nothing suspicious going on," Yashiro said softly.

Well, even if there was, they'd be hiding it from him. He had nothing to gain by doubting them. "OK," he said lightly, "I'll sign.

Mum's going to get fifty million yen from the life insurance, so I'll go with Plan A."

When the brother and sister left the office, bowing constantly as they retreated, Zombie, who had been silently watching the proceedings, said excitedly, "Kita, you've gone and sold your life away! A total of fifty one million, one hundred and twenty thousand yen – wow!"

"Yeah I guess so," said Kita, rubbing his upper lip to cover for his embarrassed pleasure. He suddenly felt like tasting the delights of the nouveau riche. In fact, the amount at his disposal totalled one million six hundred sixty thousand, adding in what was left in his own account. If the blood test and X-ray came up clean, the money would be paid into his bank tomorrow afternoon. He wondered what the real price on the organ market was like. One million one hundred twenty thousand was surely too cheap. If he considered that he wouldn't have earned a single yen without registering, he'd definitely come out ahead in the deal, but on the other hand someone eager for the organs would quite likely add another zero to that sum.

Yashiro, who'd acted as his guarantor, assured him the price was probably pretty normal. He'd taken on joint liability for the handover of Kita's organs. Kita felt he had to clarify just what Yashiro stood to gain and what risks were involved for him in this.

"So I mustn't commit suicide, eh?"

"I wouldn't advise it if you want the money to be paid, no. We need to come up with a plan. Firstly, it has to be an accident. Don't you dare write a will of any sort, now, will you? Next, you can't die from drink driving or a fight. The insurance payout gets lowered. Next, don't try a traffic accident or falling to your death or burning to death. They wouldn't be able to use your organs. I'm requesting this as your guarantor."

"What if my internal organs are damaged?"

"I'd have to shoulder your debts."

"I see. Sorry about that."

"No, it just means you can't damage your organs. And you have to die in what appears to be an accident."

This was a tall order. He'd handicapped himself considerably in that moment he sold over his life, now he came to think of it. He had a few complaints about what Yashiro had let him in for that he needed to air.

"Oh and another thing, don't go anywhere too far away. Everything hangs on an organ's freshness. Do your best to breathe your last in a hospital, please. They need to be flown to the recipient right away for the transplant."

Kita felt his anger rising. Zombie, the suicide specialist, muttered "Life's tough, eh, even when you're trying to get rid of it." She suppressed a smile.

Kita turned to her for advice. "What's the best way to do it?" he asked.

"I should think the best plan would be to be killed by someone," she replied lightly without a moment's thought. "You've got lots of dough, so why don't you hire a killer? I should think Yashiro could introduce you to someone good."

"Sure, sure. It'll cost you five hundred grand with commission included," muttered Yashiro.

Kita was lost for words. This guy might really come up with a killer, it seemed. He decided to have no more to do with him, and set about preparing to leave. Observing him, Yashiro cut in, his voice suddenly cold and quite unlike his previous tone.

"Go to the Moon Palace Hotel bar at nine. Shinobu Yoimachi will meet you there."

"A date with your favourite star, Kita! Go for it, boy! Tomorrow's the assault on Mizuho, right? I've uncovered the address of that Finance Ministry couple. Seems like your Mizuho is enjoying the high life of an upper class suburban lady. She spends her days at home busy with her hobbies. Drop in and disturb her for a while."

Zombie passed Kita a piece of paper containing an address and telephone number.

"Good luck! This really is the last time we'll meet. Let's have sex if we meet in the next world, eh?"

Yashiro stood beside her as she waved Kita goodbye. "Wait a minute," Yashiro broke in, handing Kita a cell phone. "Let me give you this. Keep in touch. I'll give you a call as well, to keep an eye on things."

Kita took the phone without a word and then, preparing to face his difficult sentence of Death by Choice once more, he stepped, a little pigeon-toed, out through the door. That business about the killer was a joke, wasn't it? Unable to dispel a touch of uneasiness, he hurried off down the slope with a sense that he was being followed.

Confession of Faith

"Those guys sell whatever they can lay hands on. They even put a price on what they can't sell. From one day to the next you're sold off like a cow – sirloin here, fillet there," murmured Shinobu with unconcealed distain. She made a blatant gesture with her chin towards the two men in dark suits perched at the counter of the Moon Palace Hotel bar, glancing in her direction from time to time.

Kita had just come from his meeting with the Koikawa siblings, in which he'd sold his life to the sister, and an organ set of corneas, liver, and kidneys to the brother. He was feeling just like a cow at a meat market himself, and her words made him feel suddenly close to her.

"I paid one hundred thousand yen to those guys to have tea with you, you know," he whispered in her ear.

"Eh?" she exclaimed, loud enough to make the other customers turn and look, then quickly brought her hand to her mouth when she realized how loudly she'd spoken.

"Payment in advance."

"Oh God," moaned Shinobu, like a little calf, and then glared from a distance at the two sitting at the counter. "They do a ruthless trade all right. I was just told to go have tea with the son of the programme schedule head."

"It's a million to spend the night with you apparently."

Shinobu sighed. "I'm sorry," she said, bowing her head. When he asked why she felt the need to apologize, she said, "Those guys are…" and made a slicing action with her forefinger down one cheek. Kita looked more closely at the men's profiles, to see if there really were scars there. The faces of both were oddly smooth.

"They must be hard up for money," he remarked sympathetically. Shinobu leaned her head back and laughed.

"Money's all they think about."

Well if you decided to die, you could make forty or fifty million without lifting a finger, thought Kita. Though mind you, there was no guaranteeing whether you could use the money while you were still alive. But here was Shinobu, who could simply lay down her body on some bed for a night, or drink eleven rounds of tea, without selling her cornea and liver and kidneys, and she made someone the same money as Kita just had for his cornea and internal organs. So how much money would change hands if she actually sold her life? Those *yakuza* businessmen over there were keeping a vigilant eye on this prize piece of goods. They were playing the same role as the armed guards of some van transporting gold bullion.

The real Shinobu Yoimachi struck Kita as a rather faded version of the star who had seared herself into his brain four or five years ago. This girl, who he'd only ever seen on television or in photos till this moment, was sitting so close he could pinch or rub her, and talking to him in her real voice. But then why was it that she somehow didn't feel alive? Maybe it was because he'd spent so many years worshipping her surface appearance that he couldn't quite believe she was alive in the same way he was. This voice was indeed the same one that had sung 'Italian George' and 'One Rainy Day,' but he felt as if he was hearing something pre-recorded when she spoke. Her smiling face was just the same as in all those images, but now that she was here in three-dimensional reality, with expressions playing on her face, she looked in fact like some exquisite doll.

The Shinobu Yoimachi that Kita knew was someone without feelings, personality, or past – a flower in a florist's. It was true, of course, that Kita had never smelled the tulip scent of her. He could now smell the herbal scent of her hair, and the French perfume sprayed on her flesh, but still, the real thing just didn't connect with the impression he'd had of her.

When she'd come over to the table where he sat idly waiting, led by one of her guards, and shook hands with him, Kita had found himself asking, "Are you really Shinobu Yoimachi?"

"Actually, I'm a look-alike," she'd replied with mock innocence. They talked a while about her recent performances, and after a while she appeared to revert to some previous bad mood, and began to complain about how she was being "sold off piecemeal."

"My face, my legs, my breasts, my hair – they've all been taken over by others. I think that must be why I don't feel any pain when I get hurt any more. But if you stick a pin in my calf, or give my cheeks a good hard pinch, that hurts. That really makes me sad. I mean, I'm the only one feeling the pain, right? Those guys just make money, they don't feel the pain. And I've got nothing but pain, and not much money."

"Shall we have a drink?"

Kita called the waiter over, and ordered wine and cheese for himself. Shinobu went on talking, without glancing at the menu.

"The fact is, I'm one of those dolls you can dress up. I always have been, ever since I was a child. My Mum used to put me in kimonos, or dress me up like a countess or like a boy, to suit her whim. She sent off applications to little girl contests without telling me, gave me a bit of pocket money and put me up on stage there. By chance I passed an audition for some TV drama, and they coaxed me into singing and I made a hit recording, and my bust was growing bigger and bigger so they started taking heaps of photos of me in swimsuits. I wanted to run and hide whenever I saw a photo of me in a magazine or a poster in the station, smiling in a bikini. Still do. I wonder why all this happened to me? There's no going back, but I'd just love to spend my life in some quiet little corner of the world instead of this. Is that asking too much?"

"You're only twenty-four. Things are only just beginning for you."

"I feel incredibly old already. I feel like my life's growing shorter and shorter, always exposed to these masses of unknown eyes. I was just a kid when I made my debut, but now I'm an old lady. I want to believe I've just gone along unthinkingly, doing what's natural, but actually if I do anything a bit different, the media beats me up, and all these young stars are coming up now and starting to lower my stocks for me, and those guys are getting to think it's about time to play the last trump card."

"What's the last trump card?"

"Nude. They're after a one strike come-from-behind home run on this. Gangsters all think the same way. God, I want to be free! I'd love to wash my hands of all this, maybe do some study. I never studied when I was in high school, I can't even read properly. I've got no clue what's happening out there in the world, but if I take off my clothes, I can make a living. But seems to me something's wrong here. Things shouldn't be this way. Seems to me like God shouldn't allow this sort of thing."

Kita nodded silently, and filled her wineglass. She bobbed her head like a pigeon in thanks, then gulped it noisily down. Maybe she'd mistaken it for juice.

"What God do you believe in?" He'd been amazed to hear the word come from her lips.

"I read the Bible in between jobs. Here, see?" She drew from her bright red handbag a suede-covered pocket-book Bible, and showed it to him. "I go everywhere with it," she said.

Remembering how he'd thrown up on the Bible in the drawer two days earlier, Kita muttered, "A washable Bible would be a good idea."

"The Bible can wash the heart clean," Shinobu said with a nod, then went on, her eyes on Kita's face to see his reaction, "My singing teacher gave it to me. 'Everything's in the Bible,' he told me, 'so just read a little every day.'"

"Is it interesting?"

"I'd say there's no one quite like Jesus. I wish I'd lived two thousand years ago. I might've got to be one of his disciples, who knows?"

"Do you go to church?"

"No, what's the point? Jesus isn't there in church. But he's in the Bible. When I read it, I get the feeling he's going be reborn in our world. Or at any rate, that's what I want to believe. I can't believe in myself, or my Mum. And if I believed in those guys there, who knows what'd become of me. But I feel like if I just believe in Jesus, I'll be saved. He's a superstar, he gives me hope, he's my idol."

Kita felt he hadn't come across such innocence in a long time, and he found himself placing his hand over Shinobu's where it lay on the Bible. She came to herself with a start, and gazed at him with serious eyes, making him feel so awkward that he withdrew his hand again.

"I'm so sorry. What have I been saying? I've just rambled on about myself without thinking. You wouldn't care about any of this, would you Kita?"

"There's no salvation for me I'm afraid."

"That's not true. Actually, when I looked in your eyes I just suddenly wanted to blurt out everything that was in my heart – all my troubles. I don't know why."

"What sort of eyes do I have, I wonder?"

"I can't really express it, but they're completely different from those guys'. Gentle eyes, quiet eyes…"

She might think so, thought Kita, but in fact he was quite unqualified to play the role of counsellor. To hide his embarrassment, he smiled and crossed his gentle right eye and his quiet left one at her. A short silence followed, which he filled by pouring more wine. It suddenly struck him that he'd never seriously prayed to God or Buddha. This was followed by a sudden urge to bludgeon her with something cruel.

"So what exactly has Jesus ever done for you?"

Her right hand on the Bible and her left on the wine glass, Shinobu was stumped for an answer. Her lips opened and closed like a goldfish. Kita followed through with, "Was it Jesus who led you into the performance world, for instance?"

"No way," Shinobu responded in a low, indistinct voice. Then her voice suddenly grew high, and she spoke normally again. "But he may have been testing me, I guess.

"Jesus will do anything for us. Anything to do with the soul. I'm convinced he's protected my soul from being dirtied by money and fame and hatred. I have to throw off my old self as soon as I can, and take on a new self, one that's like Jesus – that's what I believe."

"You'll shed your skin?"

"I must learn to become naked body and soul, atone for my sins, and love my fellow man. My aim is to free myself through the teachings of Jesus."

Why was she confessing her faith to him like this? And why was he moved by it, condemned to self-appointed execution though he was? He'd been planning on spending a much more frivolous, not to say vulgar time with Shinobu than this was turning out to be. Things had gone seriously awry here.

Shinobu had begun to look as though possessed while she was making her confession of faith. The girl who'd sat down beside him in the dimly lit bar thirty minutes earlier had quite disappeared.

Perhaps this possession of hers had something to do with it, but the bar seemed somehow brighter. And that girl who'd seemed like an exquisite doll had now become a real live person no different from himself, with flesh and substance and body heat that he could actually feel.

He took some more cheese, and ordered another glass of wine. Glancing over at the counter, he saw the men collapsed in loud laughter, shoulders shaking, as if they'd just invented the most stupendous joke. With those guys there, he just couldn't get the feeling that he and Shinobu were really alone together. If this hundred thousand yen meeting was going to end in nothing more than this, it amounted to fraud. No sooner had he thought this than Shinobu said "Tell me a little about yourself now, Kita."

"What would you like to know?" He couldn't think of anything really worth saying. He wasn't planning to mention either the fact that he'd just signed away his life plus a set of organs, nor that his self-appointed execution would take place this Friday. Their paths would never cross again. And as for Christ having brought them together – well, it was charming of her to explain mere coincidence in these terms, but things got a bit abstract once a man who was nailed up two thousand years ago came between them like this. It would give him greater comfort to silently worship her round breasts.

"Have you ever thought of suicide, Kita?" As he sat gazing with lowered eyes at Shinobu's breasts, they heaved suddenly with the abrupt question. Kita reeled as if they'd landed him a sudden punch.

"Why ask me that, out of the blue?" Kita sat back.

"I've stopped thinking about suicide since I started reading the Bible."

"You used to think about it?"

"Every night, without fail."

"You've done well to survive, then."

"It was touch and go for a while."

"Was it because of those guys over there?"

"They sell my body. To the big boys over in Nagatacho."

A moment's silence fell over the bar's hum of noise. The customers at surrounding tables had been gazing into space, but their ears were tuned in to this table. For some time now these anonymous people had been taking in the confession pouring forth in Shinobu's clear voice. Their curiosity was focused on the question of the identity of the man she was with. Surely they wouldn't be mistaking him for some Nagatacho politician?

"So which politicians have bought you?" Kita's question was meant for the listening gallery to hear.

The two guys over at the counter rose and came towards their table.

"It's about time to call it to a close, buddy" whispered the smaller one in his ear. His eyes blinked rapidly behind gold-rimmed spectacles. "Miss Yoimachi has another job to go to." The anonymous spies all around resumed their interrupted conversations, poker faced. The bar was filled with a hum of conversation again.

"Go away," said Shinobu. "I want to talk with Kita a bit longer."

The taller of the two leaned over and whispered to her, "Don't go shootin' yer mouth off then." He struck a pose like Michelangelo's David, intended to strike fear into the public gallery, then slowly returned to the counter.

Shinobu bent forward and brought her face so close to Kita that he could feel her breath. "You remember that hardliner politician with the love child, whose legitimate son's an actor?"

"That Minister for Construction?"

"Yeah, him. And that gangster type one who made off with two hundred million from the casino."

"The 'you can bet your life on Kentaro' guy?"

"And…"

"You mean there's more?"

"What's his name Suzuki, the Depillatory to the Treasurer."

"Deputy."

"Yeah, him. I'm a sullied woman, see? I'm a sacrifice to the ruthless urge of those guys to do all the business they like. I was like a corpse till now, as good as dead. These guys and those creeps in Nagatacho, they think I'm just some doll with breasts, they think I've got no brain or soul. Sorry. I guess I must be drunk."

"But why are you telling me all this, when you've only just met me? Surely they make sure you keep your mouth shut?"

"I don't care. I need someone to know the truth, just in case something happens."

"Something?"

Shinobu lowered her voice further. "I may be killed to keep my mouth shut," she murmured, and sent him a meaningful look. "But my plan is to tell the world before I get killed, and then leave it to Jesus to protect me."

The guys at the counter rose to their feet again. His time was up. "Thank you for the precious talk," Kita said, holding out his hand.

"Let's meet again soon, Kita," said Shinobu. "Without those guys."

"Thank you, but I don't really have any time left."

"You don't have to pay another hundred thousand yen. Money shouldn't come into it when two people meet. Please see me again. Next week, even."

"I won't be here any more by next week."

"What do you mean?"

The men stepped between them. The little one bowed to Kita and thanked him, and the taller one followed suit. Kita watched them lead Shinobu away, a crooked smile frozen on his lips. Did she feel a little happier now that she'd used her hour of Cinderella time this evening to get her troubles off her chest? She walked backwards out of the bar still gazing at him, her brow furrowed in a bewildered look, and her lips pouting in the unspoken question, "Why?"

Mass

There was a vacant twin room at the Moon Palace Hotel, so he took it. Handing his backpack to the bellboy, he went up to the room, and no sooner was he inside than he ordered room service – turtle in rice stew, and champagne. As he tucked into what was probably his fourth-last supper, all alone, he savoured the aftertaste of the strange tryst he'd just had with the star.

How to describe her expression as she left the bar? It was like a child being taken back to some awful classroom against her will at the end of playtime. He felt for her. If she'd begged him to run off with her, he might have felt tempted to play the abductor. What did he care that her minders had wicked underground links with politicians, or that they dealt in violence for pleasure? He could have stayed desperately on the run with her till Friday. Or at least he could have given them a good scare, and let her enjoy the thrill of escape and the taste of freedom. But he hadn't had the time to find out how she felt about it, nor the inclination to explain his own situation. It would have cost another nine hundred thousand to bring her up to this room, and he'd be a fool to line their pockets like that. It would be better to conduct a live burial for himself in the park, and distribute the money among a hundred vagrants, passersby, and students, to get them to attend the party.

Having polished off the mild-tasting turtle stew and dry champagne for his simple supper, he got into a tepid bath. All alone in this empty room, his flesh-and-blood self gazed at its own reflection in the mirror.

The hotel mirror wasn't alive, but it still ate people. His stomach had suddenly begun to sag, and bags had formed under his eyes. He'd aged years. Every time he opened the bathroom door or the closet and was abruptly met with his own reflection, he was surprised to see himself there. He had forgotten his own existence completely until he saw himself in the mirror. He'd never experienced the thought, "I think, therefore I am." When he was talking to someone, he was always sucked into their identity, and when he walked in the street he dissolved into it. But the mirror put him unequivocally centre stage. And this mirror self was a sort of other person who was just like himself, a self that was in between self and other.

Well, to start with, anyway. This mirror had reflected back the images of countless anonymous visitors, and the experience had warped it. It wouldn't be long before the mirror gobbled him up and he disappeared. Being reflected in this mirror was as good as not being there at all.

On his own, time slowed and grew stagnant. After eating, taking a bath, and scratching an itch or two, he lay vacantly on the bed for a while, then turned on the television. It was still only eleven. But the television brought him a chance blessing. There on the screen was Shinobu Yoimachi, the girl he'd just left, staring out at him as she brushed her teeth. Maybe it was that kind of role, but she seemed to be brushing away as though ridding herself of some fierce resentment. Then she rinsed, and the star's golden smile reappeared.

Who'd have thought that this girl held the key to a potential political scandal, Kita murmured to himself, and he raised his champagne glass to the screen.

Suddenly the cell phone he'd gotten from Yashiro rang. He was determined to have nothing more to do with the guy, so he ignored it. But whoever was on the other end wasn't going to give up so easily. The phone rang relentlessly on and on until Kita reached the end of his tether and picked it up. He was about to simply cut the guy off, but before he knew it he'd pressed the green button instead.

Maybe his luck had turned at last, for it was Shinobu's voice he heard. "Hi, it's me," he said hastily.

"Sorry for being a bother. I got this number from Yashiro. Where are you right now?"

"I'm in the Moon Palace Hotel."

"What're you doing?"

"Watching television."

"I've just been a bit worried by what you said as I was leaving. When you say you won't be here any more by next week, do you mean you're going away somewhere?"

"That's the plan."

"Where to? Overseas?"

"Kind of, yes."

"You'll be back, won't you?"

"I don't think I'll be able to come back."

"Why not?"

There was no way to explain. The place Kita was heading for this Friday was a one-way trip. He remained silent.

"So we really won't be able to meet ever again?" Shinobu persisted.

"I'm afraid so," he replied.

At this, she let out a little sigh. "Did you have some reason to meet me?" she asked.

Kita had the impression she wasn't going to take some watered-down response for an answer. He'd have to come up with something substantial. He thought for a moment, then muttered, "A dream, I guess."

Everyone becomes decadent to some extent once they reach thirty-five. Jesus apparently preached that we must throw off our old self and take on a new one; well, you can't really take that on board when you're young. Jesus was crucified before he even reached thirty-five, wasn't he? So you could say he never experienced decadence. Even if he did, of course, he had something to believe in. Kita, on the other hand, had just used a fair portion of his savings on realizing the petty dream of trysting with a star.

Shinobu's voice on the other end of the line brought him back. "You mean it was a dream to meet me?"

Kita gave a quiet, simple nod. "If I realized that dream, I'd be able to remember it till the day I died, see."

"I'm just so moved that you think of me like that," Shinobu said, in exactly the voice she'd been using in the television commercial. "Is there anything you'd like me to do for you? You listened to my tale earlier, and paid a hundred thousand for the experience, so I feel I should compensate you somehow."

"Well I'm really happy to hear that. But…"

"Would you meet me again now? Those guys aren't around any more. Shall we go for a drive somewhere? I'll hop in the car and come right over and get you. I'll be there in twenty minutes. Wait for me in the lobby."

Those guys must be taking advantage of this urge of hers to serve others, thought Kita. Of course she should by rights have been suspicious about the motives of a guy who'd pay a hundred thousand to meet her, and be wary of the connections he might have. In fact, though, she was being remarkably honest with him. Kita accepted the invitation. He was inclined to let her purify his heart a little more.

Shinobu arrived outside the Moon Palace Hotel lobby in a yellow Alfa Romeo with a black hood. Kita lowered himself awkwardly into the passenger seat. To ride around with a star driving a sports car with the hood back…he'd had such impossible fantasies in the past, of course, but he'd never dreamt he'd actually do it. It seemed like Shinobu was taking it into her head to fulfil his dreams for him.

"I know nothing about you, Kita, so tell me."

At this, she whipped the engine into a high nasal groan, and began to hurtle along the left bank of the imperial palace moat.

"I've lived a really normal life. I could exchange myself with just about anyone else, really."

"That's not true, Kita. You're different from other people, just like Jesus' disciples were all different from each other."

"Most of the people in this world are pretty much like me."

"You really think so? Most people are all greasy with desire, but I get the feeling that you've cut through all that somehow."

The truth was rather that he'd never been able to find an outlet for his desires. Here he was at last, trying to live the high life, and all he could summon up to show for it was a hangover and a sense of futility. Maybe his desires were lacking cultivation. The high life was actually an exhausting business. He couldn't last beyond three days. He'd love to be able to suddenly feel the kind of sense of fulfilment that led him to praise God, but he never had. He recalled some Olympics, he couldn't remember which, where an athlete who'd just broken the world record in the decathlon sank to his knees, hung his head, slumped down and covered his face with his hands, and wept. Just then he could easily have been mistaken for someone who'd lost. The fact is, when someone is deeply moved, they get the urge to pray. That athlete's mind must have been flooded with light at that moment.

Shinobu gunned her baby Alfa Romeo and snaked through the traffic along the metropolitan expressway, heading for the bay. The bridge was lit up in rainbow colours, and trembled like the strings of a harp. The bridge lights reflected in the water below spread out like the tentacles of a sea anemone, threatening to swallow up all the motor boats, pleasure boats, and barges that floated there. Though the night was late, the sky still emanated a faint grey light, which dappled the bay. On the shore was a park where square-eyed, four-wheeled animals gathered to graze. Couples out for a night drive made their way here to talk of love and – if they reached an agreement – to rub mucous membranes together. Shinobu drew up in the parking area. "Kita," she said in a hushed voice. Maybe she was planning on observing the couples' biological activity, in the spirit of a bird watcher. "You can fulfil your dreams now."

"Eh?" he said. He turned and saw that she'd leaned her seat back down and was lying there face up beside him.

"I'll let you touch, just once."

Kita's heart thundered in his chest. The valley between her breasts, that object of lust for men all over Japan, was peeping from her gaping neckline. The breasts beneath her crimson dress glowed a faint white in the dim light, and a scent of tulips wafted up from them. With the fingertips of his trembling right hand, he touched her, whereupon she took his hand and slid them into the valley. It was a moment of pure bliss. His fingertips ran over her nipple, brushing the faint tulip scent.

"Thank you. Really. Thank you," said Kita, his expression grave, as he bowed his head over and over, until Shinobu giggled.

Chancing to glance at the dashboard, Kita suddenly noticed the Bible Shinobu had shown him in the bar. Wherever she went, it obviously went with her.

"The Bible must serve as a charm against traffic accidents," he said.

"It's a kind of Linus blanket," she said with a laugh.

"I've got one more request." Kita turned meekly to face her again.

"What? What is it?" asked Shinobu, intrigued, as she raised her seat back to sitting position again.

"Could you read me something from the Bible?"

Shinobu didn't speak for a few seconds, then she reached for the book. "Sure," she said in a singsong voice, and began to turn the pages.

I'm moving to some town or village in the next world soon, Kita said inside himself, so I guess I should take this opportunity to repent my sins.

"Got it. Here it is, OK, I'll read to you from the Gospel of Saint John."

There was a man named Lazarus who had fallen ill. His home was at Bethany, the village of Mary and her sister Martha.

Kita listened, his eyes on the light coordinates shining across the bay.

The sisters sent a message to him: "Sir, you should know that your friend lies ill." When Jesus heard this he said, "This illness is not to end in death: through it God's glory is to be revealed and the Son of God glorified."

"It's a bit dark," she added. "Let's turn on the light," and she flicked the switch. The reading continued in the glow of the orange light.

On his arrival Jesus found that Lazarus had already been four days in the tomb.

Jesus said, "Your brother will rise again." "I know that he will rise again," said Martha, "at the resurrection on the last day." Jesus said, "I am the resurrection and the life. Whoever has faith in me shall live, even though he dies; and no one who lives and has faith in me shall ever die. Do you believe this?"

Shinobu seemed to be asking him the question directly. Kita spluttered. If you believed that, you'd never manage to die. For a man like him, about to die by self-execution, the words had a certain encouraging ring to them.

Having told Jesus she believed in him, Martha returned to the village and called her sister Mary. The Jews of the village followed her. Now wherever he went, Jesus was persecuted by the Jews, driven out and half killed. He was proposing a new interpretation of their laws, which they completely misunderstood. So Jesus entered the tomb of Lazarus, in front of his disciples, Lazarus' sisters, and the village Jews.

Jesus said, "Take away the stone." Martha, the dead man's sister, said to him, "Sir, by now there will be a stench; he has been there four days." Jesus said, "Did I not tell you that if you have faith you will see the glory of God?"

Then they removed the stone.

Jesus looked upwards and said, "Father, I thank you for hearing me. I know that you always hear me, but I have spoken for the sake of the people standing round, that they may believe it was you who sent me."

Then he raised his voice in a great cry: "Lazarus, come out." The dead man came out, his hands and feet bound with linen bandages, his face wrapped in a cloth. Jesus said, "Loose him; let him go."

Many of the Jews who had come to visit Mary, and had seen what Jesus did, put their faith in him.

Shinobu snapped the Bible shut. "That's all," she said. Embarrassed to look at each other, they sat together in silence for a while, staring at the lights on the water. Here they were, two people who in different ways had sold off their bodies, snuggled together in an Italian sports car reading the world's bestseller. And it wasn't in nineteenth century Petersburg, but at the end of the twentieth century in Tokyo. Was it his decision to carry out self-execution that brought about these strange twists of fate, Kita wondered?

"How could he have been resurrected after being dead for four days?" Kita turned over in his mind this old question that no one any longer seriously pondered.

"It's impossible in terms of modern medical science, isn't it? But dead people might have quite often been resurrected like that at the time."

"Maybe the dead back then were in really good shape."

"Still alive even when they were riddled with worms."

Simultaneously they both began to snicker, and soon the little car was filled to bursting with an explosion of laughter.

As the laughter wound down, Kita asked, "So was there any special reason why you purposely chose that bit to read?"

"Yes. I told you in the bar, didn't I? I used to contemplate suicide every night."

"Yes, you did say that."

"I decided to give up the idea when I read about Lazarus being brought back from the dead."

"Oh? Why's that?"

Shinobu massaged her temples, struggling for words. "I can't really express it," she began. "I decided to give up the idea because if I committed suicide now I wouldn't be resurrected. Lazarus was raised from the dead because he was loved by his sisters and the villagers and Jesus, wasn't he? But in Japan, when you die of course it's sad at the time, but after the prescribed forty-nine days are up everyone forgets about you. The only people who can be resurrected are the ones who live on in people's memories forever."

"You believe in the resurrection of the dead?"

Shinobu nodded hard, her eyes alight with firm conviction.

"It's essential to believe. I mean, if you doubt, you'll never be resurrected, will you?"

"You won't have any fleshly body to return to if you're cremated, you know."

"It's true. But the soul doesn't burn."

"I guess. The soul's not flesh, after all. But if only the soul is resurrected, it's not visible, is it? It's scary to think of coming back to life as a half-rotted body, mind you. I think what you're really talking about is memories of the dead."

Kita was just trying to help her express things, but Shinobu shook her head stubbornly. "No, it's not," she declared. "The dead really communicate with us. They appear in dreams. They speak. They grow, they progress, they love and hate. I think the souls of the dead are maybe like the trees in a forest or water in a river or air in a city. They're a part of nature. A dead soul might come creeping into this car here. If you turn on the radio you'll hear Mozart or John Lennon. Or think of our own dead, pop stars like Yukiko Okada or Yutaka Ozaki. Their voices are still echoing somewhere. Now isn't that some sign of the dead? Lazarus threw off his rotted body after his resurrection, and became a follower of Jesus, you know. Even if you die, you don't disappear. You just turn into something different. The voice of them, the sense of them, their thoughts and form when they were in the world – it's all put back together at random and something else is born from it. That's resurrection. A resurrected person doesn't have a name or a job or a self. They just *are*. People get resurrected only among folks who have the ability to feel that. But everyone believes it's the end when you die, so the poor resurrected dead get ignored. You have to have a really strong soul to be resurrected in our world."

"So are you in touch with the dead? How do you do that?"

"You need a bit of training. But it's easy really. You just have to remember that person. Just keep remembering them all the time. The dead get stronger when the living remember them. When you're desperately struggling with something, just stop and relax for a moment, look at the dandelion on the roadside, open your ears to the sound of the wind. The souls of the dead have become part of the natural world, so if you do this, you'll always get the sense that they're there."

As he listened, Kita was thinking of the mother he'd left earlier that day. She'd begun to lose her mind without his noticing. Maybe that was why she was still living with her husband, though he died four years ago. Maybe she was actually communicating with a dead soul, just as Shinobu described.

Shinobu straightened her back. "That's the end of Mass," she announced.

"I've started to feel people really do come back to life," Kita said with a laugh.

"You're weird," Shinobu murmured, as she started the engine of her little sports car.

"So in fact, Kita, you haven't told me a thing about yourself." They were back at the front lobby of the hotel, so late the bellboy was asleep. Shinobu spoke in a low, querulous voice. Kita felt he'd behaved quite honestly with her, but evidently he hadn't managed to dispel her doubts. Though maybe it was the luxury of having paid a hundred thousand yen that spared him from talking about himself.

"I'll just tell you one thing. But you have to promise me two things first. One is that you won't tell anyone. The other is that you won't ask why."

Shinobu gave a slight nod to indicate that she promised.

"I'm going to die this Friday. So fate brought us together only to part."

Kita hid the smile on his face as he spoke, but Shinobu said, "It's a joke, right?"

"I'll come and see you if I'm resurrected."

"Why are you going to die?"

"You promised not to ask."

"That was sneaky," Shinobu murmured, and she suddenly seized Kita's wrist and held it so hard she almost stopped his pulse.

"Let go."

"No. If I let go, you'll go to hell."

She'd already said Mass. Was she going to cast a spell on him now? He put his lips to her slender white hand, and whispered as if murmuring words of love, "I don't mind if I go to hell." Then he removed her hand, and got out of the car. Shinobu got out too, and tried to hold him back.

"You mustn't go to the next world! It's terrible! It's just the worst place!"

You'd have thought she'd been there on a holiday and seen it herself. Well, if it really was the worst possible place, and he couldn't face living there, he'd rely on Jesus' words and ask to be resurrected.

But in fact Kita even doubted if there was such a thing as the next world.

"Still, I have to go. You've given me fresh courage to die, Shinobu."

"But why?" Shinobu couldn't conceal her disappointment.

"I was in luck tonight. Let's meet again, eh?" Kita spoke his farewell with all the freshness of someone just out of the bath. He smiled. Shinobu released his arm, with a look that said she could see through that smile of his. She was left with nothing but an overpowering sense of futility after this fateful meeting with a man who could never appear in the Bible.

TUESDAY

The Flowers are Running!

After the Mass of the night before, when he'd found himself caught between a star and the Bible, Kita slept soundly. It was as though he'd been given a respite from some vague despair.

He woke at eight. After eating the room service breakfast in bed and taking a shower, he shaved carefully and took time to do his hair. His old girlfriend's husband left their house every morning at eight, he knew, and set off for his workplace at Kasumigaseki. Kita's plan was to follow the opposite route, and make a direct attack on the house while the husband was absent.

He gathered that housewives usually saw off the husband and children, then did some housework till around ten, when they took a break and went out, either for shopping, or to the beauty parlour, sports gym, or to work on some hobby. If he didn't make his raid early, he might miss his only opportunity to see her; if he got lost en route, he might very well never fulfil his wish of seeing her once more in this life. Unfortunately, the day was fine. She'd probably be in the mood to head out the door for a joyride once she'd hung out the washing.

He had to catch her before she did so. He would ring the doorbell and announce the arrival of an express delivery; both the sender and the deliverer, not to mention the package, would, of course, be himself. Choosing a different deliverer might well prove more effective at catching her off her guard, but he didn't have the time to arrange it. She might also decide to refuse the delivery, consigning the unopened package to oblivion.

He left his room empty-handed just past nine. The most suitable attire for sneaking in behind the back of the Finance Ministry employee was probably a dark suit, but the shops weren't yet open, so he made do with yesterday's free fashion ensemble.

It was now the fifth day since he'd decided on his execution, and there were only three more to go. Now at last he felt he had escaped the clutches of all those people who were just after his money, the death merchants, and the professional would-be suicides, and become his own master. If Yashiro hadn't stolen his taxi last Friday, all this would never have happened. It was thanks to the men and women that that guy had introduced him to that he had wasted two nights in Atami, not to mention signing away his corneas, his organs and his life. But hey, forget all that, he thought. Let's just assume that I've been purified of everything by last night's Mass.

Once in the train on the Odakyu Line, he settled down to think. What was the best way to announce himself in order to avenge his broken heart? What was the first thing he should say to her once he'd told her over the intercom that she had a special delivery, and brought her to the door? Would she realize who he was if he said nothing? If she asked what he'd come for, he'd tell her his name, and apologize for the unexpected visit. Naturally, she'd be bound to look put out. Surely she wouldn't come straight out and demand to know what he was doing there, when she'd vowed never to see him again? If she did, he should answer unflinchingly, "Don't worry. You'll never see me again."

Or, since he already knew he wouldn't be welcome, perhaps he should say, "I'll pay you a hundred thousand yen if you let me have tea with you at home here." And if she didn't get the joke, too bad. He should either just walk right in, or drag her out. Still, if he did that she'd take a strong stand and start treating her old lover like an abductor. It was a peaceful neighbourhood, so the police were bound to come running.

For some reason, his imagination kept tending toward negative scenarios. Surely it was possible that she'd exclaim, "Well, well, great to see you again. How are you?" the moment she saw him, and invite him in as if he were one of her many friends just dropped by. She may be indebted to him, after all, but she shouldn't bear him any grudge.

At this point Kita left off pondering the question, and instead drew a piece of paper from his pocket and checked her address and phone number.

TUESDAY

Her name had changed to Mizuho Higashi now she was married, but Kita hadn't taken this on board. It was still Mizuho Nishi who came to him in dreams, transformed herself into a soft pillow, and accepted his embraces. Naturally, she was as she had been during their short honeymoon period together. But it was all rather vague and unsatisfactory, like frolicking with the figure of a ghost. There were times when he thought he heard her voice, but as soon as he listened carefully it would fade into the dialect of passing high school girls.

He could still faintly recall what the sensation of love had been like. Back then, his sensitive nerves had registered her every word, her look, her fingers as they danced on an invisible keyboard, even the gentle breeze that brushed her cheek. Those nerves of his had been primed for her alone.

Had there been anything resembling a beginning, a development and a conclusion in her love, he wondered? The relationship had abruptly ended with the introduction of Higashi, and Kita could scarcely remember how things had begun with himself. He had a feeling he'd drawn her in a game of chance at a university party, but he also seemed to remember that things had begun with him asking her out to a concert of Beethoven's thirty-second piano sonata by an elderly Russian pianist. Or maybe that time in the park with all the cosmos in bloom had been their first date. The fact was, Kita's memory of those times had lost all sense of continuity. The passage of time and the seasons were all jumbled up in his mind.

Not that it was all so long ago his memory would naturally become moth-eaten like this. His self of that time wouldn't have been at all surprised by his present self. Nevertheless, recalling memories of Mizuho Nishi was rather like sorting through strands of memory from early infancy. For one thing, he didn't really have any memories to speak of – or perhaps he did, but couldn't really recall them. What remained clearest in his memory from childhood, he wondered?

There was the time he'd fallen from the horizontal bar in the playground, and the world had suddenly gone red. And the time he'd shoplifted that book of Dali's paintings, and run like crazy toward the river with it.

And what of his relationship with Mizuho?

There was an image of her standing on a station platform, wearing black leather boots. The time when they hadn't been able to stop laughing as they ate dinner together. The bit of fluff on her eyelash one winter afternoon, and the mosquito bite on her knee that summer evening.

He had to tell himself stories over and over till he half believed them, before he could resurrect happy memories of her. He couldn't really manage it on his own; he needed to find someone to help him. And if that was impossible, then all he could do was meekly concentrate his energies on trying to forget the bad memories. This was how the memories had come to be censored and moth-eaten to the point where all that was left was a pile of junk.

And had she ever even once been conscious of her relationship with Kita as being in love? It may well be that there'd never been a time when her nerves had tingled at his presence. In fact, those nerves of hers probably only ever really responded to Higashi, he decided.

He asked the way at the police box by the south exit, and set off. On the way, he came across a flower shop, so he got them to make up a ten thousand yen bouquet of yellow roses. He wouldn't announce an express delivery, he decided, he'd announce that he was delivering some flowers.

He sniffed at the roses as he walked. They smelt to him like the scent of Mizuho's body.

"Come along Kazuki, hurry up. What're you doing?"

A woman in a dark blue suit was calling to her son in a low, authoritative voice. The little Kazuki, dressed likewise in dark blue shorts and a white open-necked shirt, was in his own fantasy world, running a toy car along the guard rail and telling himself how the Ferrari hit a camel and exploded. When Kita went by, the boy suddenly yelled, "Hey Mum, those flowers are walking!"

Sure, why shouldn't flowers walk, after all? Kita thought, and he began to run. As he ran, his spirits lifted. He would get the better of his rival from the Finance Ministry, have lunch with his wife, and at least steal a kiss, he decided.

The site Mizuho's house stood on was of average size for the neighbourhood, but the white tent-shaped building of reinforced concrete stood out glaringly, expressing its owner's taste in excruciating detail. Tiles designed like Arabian picture plates graced the entrance pillars and balcony. The tiled fence itself formed a flowerbed in which tulips bloomed. The tiles of the gate pillars were faded from the rays of the sun. The garage doors were closed, but he could faintly discern a Mercedes Benz through the semitransparent glass shutters.

Kita passed the house and walked on another fifty yards. Then he pulled himself together, and turned back. This time, he stopped in front of the gate, but then immediately set off again in the direction of the station. After ten yards, he turned again, went back to the gate, and pressed the intercom button below the sign carved with the name "Higashi." A toy car and a bicycle with practice wheels stood side by side in the entrance. Until this moment, Kita had scarcely registered that this couple had children.

Clutching his bouquet, Kita retreated. Unfortunately, just at that moment the little boy called Kazuki was coming towards him, holding his mother's hand. If they were here to visit Mizuho, Kita would lose his chance. He and Kazuki caught each other's eye. Clutching his toy car, Kazuki pointed at the flowers. "Hey Mum, those flowers are standing there."

Pretending he'd mistaken the house, Kita moved on, then he began to trot, trying to create more distance between himself and the mother and child. It was the kind of press-the-doorbell-and-run game he hadn't done for twenty years or more.

"Look! The flowers are running!" Kazuki cried.

This was why he hated kids, Kita thought as he executed another detour. He'd been wandering the neighbourhood for around half an hour by now, and it was past ten thirty. He decided he should find out whether she was at home and whether her children were with her before deciding on his next course of action. He'd telephone. Would she agree to meet him then and there when he asked her to? It couldn't happen in front of her children. Judging from the toy car and bicycle by the entrance, she may have two kids. Or perhaps there was only one. At any rate, one was clearly a boy, maybe around Kazuki's age. If she'd had a child soon after marrying, he'd be five or six by now.

He was going to be saying farewell to everything on Friday, yet here he was still unable to make up his mind. He mustn't be scared of a child. These flowers had business to attend to with Mizuho. He mustn't be put off. He'd go back to the shining gateway, and press that button.

But there was no need. Mizuho Nishi was standing there in front of the Higashi home. There was no sign of a child. If he kept walking, he'd run straight into her, so Kita paused and appeared to be tying his shoelace in the shade of a tree, while he looked at her.

She hadn't come out to meet anyone, she was going out in the white Mercedes. From this distance, all he could make out was that she was wearing a black dress, and had short hair. He must hail a taxi right away. The prospect of a taxi in this residential area seemed hopeless, but luckily several soon cruised by on the lookout for department store shoppers. Sinking into one, Kita told the driver, "Follow that Mercedes."

He took a deep breath, and said to himself with a little smile, "OK, the chase is on."

Picnic at the Neurology Clinic

The white Mercedes went along Setagaya Street, on through Sangenjaya, and pulled up in the parking lot of a general hospital. Kita had leapt to the conclusion that she was setting off for the heart of the city to have a pleasant lunch chatting with some elegant friend, and the discovery that her destination was a hospital threw him into confusion. He'd have a hard time finding a vantage point from which to watch her and work out whether she was there to visit someone, or to see a doctor.

Luckily, he was still carrying the bouquet. If he walked down the hospital corridor with it pretending he was there on a visit, he wouldn't look suspicious. He set off at a run clutching the flowers, planning to arrive before her and hide in wait behind a pillar in the lobby.

Eyes hidden behind sunglasses, Mizuho Nishi headed straight for the reception desk. Kita watched her from three yards away as she went past. Her face was so drained of life that she might have been wearing a porcelain mask. She had grown considerably thinner in the last six years, but her arms and back emanated a languid sexiness that she hadn't had in her mid-twenties. Her listless movements were reminiscent of slowly shaken silk.

"Mizuho Nishi! Mizuho Nishi!" Kita silently chanted to himself as he watched, trying to identify the lover from whom he'd parted six years earlier with the wife before his eyes. At any rate, Mizuho Nishi was obviously alive. Kita felt gratitude to some higher force for this.

She collected a form from the reception desk, turned away from him and walked off, but then paused as if at a sudden thought. She turned, her hand went to the back of her head in a gesture that seemed to brush away the sensation of something clinging there. Kita averted his eyes, his heart racing uncomfortably. Then she turned back, and walked off toward the elevator, her heels clicking loudly as she went.

Kita checked the name above the reception desk where she had received her form, and saw that it belonged to the Neurology Outpatient section. He couldn't imagine what illness this could be. Having no urge to go up to the relevant waiting room, he decided to hang about on a sofa in the lobby sipping oolong tea until her consultation was over.

Hospitals are perennially crowded places. There are patients who commute from home, as well as those who are hospitalized for months, and some who are brought in against their will. The population rises and falls from one day to the next. No one would come in the hope of dying, of course, but it takes a certain amount of courage to place your life in the hands of others by coming here. Having sold his organs, Kita would inevitably end up in a hospital, he realized, whether he wanted to die there or not. This thought prompted him to look around, checking out the sort of place where he'd be brought as soon as he'd died.

The corpse would come in an ambulance and be offloaded at the ambulance depot, then they'd probably take it straight to some empty operating theatre.

Following the diagram of the hospital layout, Kita headed for the surgical department. Bandaged patients were moving about in the corridor on crutches or in a wheelchair. Others, either awaiting or just out of surgery, were going around with a drip stand attached to a tube in their belly.

Once removed, Kita's organs would be frozen and delivered to their various recipients, his belly would be closed up, and what remained of him wiped clean, put in a case with dry ice, and conveyed to the underground morgue.

He went back to check the diagram and see where the morgue was located, but it wasn't listed. "Are you visiting someone, or looking for a ward?" asked a passing nurse.

"I'm going to the Neurology Section," he replied.

"Third floor up on the elevator and turn right."

Kita bowed briefly in thanks for this simple explanation. Giving up his search for the morgue, he returned to the sofa in the lobby, and sank into a daze. This area also served as the waiting room for the Internal Medicine outpatients, and it was thronged with waiting people. It suddenly occurred to Kita that he may be in the way here, so he walked some distance away and found an empty seat near the lift, where he settled down to wait for Mizuho to emerge.

He observed a middle-aged man in pyjamas, sitting in front of an old man, knees touching. They were deep in conversation.

"Nah, these patients're all too weak to be able to do away with themselves. Folks what commit suicide are generally hale and hearty. Take jumping out of a window, now. How're y'gonna get yer body to make the leap if it won't do as it's told, eh? Your body's still good 'n heavy, the splat'd be spectacular I'd say, but as for me, I'm all dried up and light as a leaf. Any passing breeze blows me half off me feet. If I was to come tumblin' to earth, I'd make no more sound than the tap as a bamboo broom falls over. You've got no problem. You'd make a fine thud. Hangin' yerself's tough, too. There's that hook in the ceiling for hangin' the drips from, but whaddya do about a rope? The nurse ain't gonna bring one for you, is she now?"

"All we can do is wait for the doctors to kill us."

"You'd imagine there's all kindsa ways of dyin', wouldn't yer, but there's not that many y'know. Still, I'd say someone who's spent a lotta time thinkin' through various options would die well."

"I'd like to live a bit longer, personally. I haven't eaten all I want yet. I'd like to wave good riddance to this hospital food as soon as I can, and make a real glutton of myself with delicious food."

"True enough, hospital food's horrible stuff. How do they manage to make it so awful, eh? It's a crime to feed that rubbish to old folks who don't have much longer to live. They oughta be ashamed of themselves. The hospital food down in Kansai's a bit better, ya know."

"I'd love to eat a good filling bowl of ramen noodles."

"Sure thing. Wouldn't it be good to kill yerself with ten bowls of the very best noodles tucked away in yer belly, eh?"

"I'd also have grilled eel, whole boiled shark's fin, stewed abalone, smoked and pickled radish, Korean herb-stuffed chicken, and oysters on the shell."

"Y've really got a thing about food, haven't ya. I'm full of awe."

"If you don't die of cancer, how would you like to die, Dr Matsui?"

"I'd die over a woman."

"If you take that medicine you'd probably manage it."

"Sure thing. Pop some Viagra and die makin' a nurse gasp, eh?"

"But it doesn't last past the grave, does it? Just like joking about how to kill yourself."

"True enough. Once yer dead you don't think. You can't complain then. So be as selfish as yer want, I say. That's livin', that is."

"I saw a war documentary once long ago, with a scene of an Australian prisoner of war having his head cut off. Just as the sword was about to come down on him, he flinched and pulled his neck in. He knew he was about to die, and flinched because he imagined the pain to come. It made me feel really strange somehow, to see that."

"Hmm. Yeah. I'd say the guy who jumps from a building probably grimaces as he's about to hit the pavement too. It's gonna hurt like hell, but the next instant yer dead, aren't ya."

"That's right. I saw the same thing in a media photo from the Vietnam War. A spy who's about to be shot, kneeling there with the pistol at his temple, his face all twisted. The bullet's going to strike him straight in the head, so he wouldn't actually feel any pain."

"He might feel pain for zero point something seconds."

"Isn't there any way of dying that doesn't involve any pain, Dr Matsui?"

"My field's archeology. I don't have a clue about such things. But I hear they put monkeys on the lab table in biology and do studies, kill 'em in various ways and gather the data from their nerve responses.

Lookin' for the least painful method. Those studies apparently help in developing new means of execution, and surgical operations."

"They torture monkeys for that?"

"Someone at the research centre told me you can hear the screams of their death throes every day."

"Monkeys are killed so that people can die more easily? I hate pain, but I could put up with a little needle prick to start the process. They just use an injection for executions in the States these days, isn't that so?"

"Yeah, when it comes down to it, that's proof you're alive. You can only say 'ouch' while yer living, can't ya? Nothing hurts once yer dead." At this point, the old man with the Kansai accent noticed Kita sitting there listening to their conversation in fascination, and addressed him. "You've been eavesdroppin' on our odd conversation about death and pain and so on, haven't you? Are you here to visit someone?"

Kita gave a nod, and replied that an acquaintance of his was in the Neurology ward.

"Neurology ward, eh? What's his problem?" asked the fat middle-aged man.

"I don't really know."

"I think Neurology's for patients with things like autonomic dystonia, or headaches, or neuroses," said the old man.

"Not necessarily. You also get patients with serious problems like Parkinson's, or progressive muscular dystrophy, and things like that."

Kita glared at the pyjama-clad man, outraged. It made him mad that this guy was trying to label Mizuho as a patient with some serious disease.

"You don't have anything wrong with you yourself?" asked the old man.

"I'm about to die," Kita replied.

"Eh?" said the old man, but he ignored this and went on, "What problems do you both have?"

"I've got cancer. They took it out of the oesophagus, but now it's gone into the lymph glands. I'm finished."

The other man let the old man finish his announcement, then he said, "I've got diabetes and cirrhosis of the liver. How do you know you're about to die?"

"I've decided on it."

The two looked at each other, the unspoken question "Why?" frozen on their faces. Just at this moment, the elevator door opened, and Mizuho Nishi appeared.

"Good luck," Kita said to them, and set off after her. As she was stepping out of the hospital entrance, he spoke.

"Mizuho-san."

Though her name had been called, she didn't turn immediately. She walked on three paces, then slowly turned to face him. Even once her eyes behind their sunglasses had fixed on him, she didn't react.

"You're Mizuho Nishi, aren't you?" Kita asked a little anxiously.

"Yes," she answered, her voice pitched high.

"I'm Yoshio Kita."

There was a moment's pause, then Mizuho raised her voice in a little cry that could have been either a scream or a cry of delight. Then she stood still, lost for words. At least she hadn't forgotten him, apparently.

"Could we have a bit of time to talk? I won't be a nuisance," Kita began, but at this she seemed to return to her senses.

"Why are you here?" she asked accusingly.

"I'm sorry. I followed you by taxi from your house. I wanted to meet you one more time before I die."

"I can't do anything for you. Please go home."

"I didn't have any other way to meet you. I've only got a little time left."

"Goodbye. I'm sorry."

Mizuho hid her face with her left hand, and turned to escape in the direction of the parking lot. She walked with a somehow unnatural rhythm to her step. Kita ran quickly up behind her, slipped around in front of her, and continued his pleas.

"Wait. Please. Just hear me out for five minutes. I won't ever come to you again, I promise. I don't want to destroy the life you've made for yourself. Believe me. At least please take these flowers. Show me some pity, I won't be here any more after this Friday. Just five minutes please."

Kita blurted out his stream of imprecations, but Mizuho seemed not to hear a word. Kita couldn't fathom why she was being so cold.

They arrived at the white Mercedes. Kita redoubled his pleas.

"Why are you so scared? I won't do anything. I was wrong to just show up out of the blue like that. I can see why you were surprised. I just suddenly thought of doing this. I thought I have to see Mizuho. Just five minutes! Come and have tea with me. I beg you on my life."

Mizuho put the key into the door, then turned to Kita. "I'm not afraid of anything," she declared. "It's just that the worst possible thing has already happened."

Mizuho seemed so stern and cold it was as if she was keeping her distance from the very air around her, let alone Kita's words and bouquet. She looked as if at the slightest touch she would murder him. Her face was like a demon's mask. Kita put the flowers on the bonnet of the car, and stood back in silence, waiting for her to leave.

Mizuho ignored the flowers, and got into the car. "Good riddance, and I hope you have an accident," Kita thought vindictively as he watched her through the window. But then the lock on the passenger door clicked open, and she was beckoning him to get in. Clueless about what was going on in her mind, Kita picked up the bouquet again, and gingerly climbed into the passenger seat.

There was nothing of the Mizuho he knew. He could only guess that some dreadful thing must have happened that had put her so on edge. But he still didn't have the courage to ask what it was. Mizuho started the engine, and took Route 246 out in the direction of Aoyama.

It was she who finally broke the painful silence.

"Thanks for the flowers."

A Poem in Mourning for a Lost Child

"Why did you decide to visit me? You were saying something rather odd just now."

"Forget it."

"You won't be here after Friday, you say?"

"Certain circumstances mean I can't be in this country any more. I'm leaving on Friday. Thank you so much for changing your mind. I'm so happy we can talk like this."

"I'm sorry about how I was just now. I just couldn't control my emotions. I'm impressed you recognised me. I'm a different person from six years ago, aren't I? That person's quite invisible now."

"Are you ill?"

"I have nerve pain all over my face, and palpitations. I was having fainting fits earlier, but that's subsided now. I've been forbidden to drive, in fact, but I don't want to see anyone, so I need to use the car. I have to be able to control my emotions while I'm driving, so it's actually quite a good form of rehabilitation."

Mizuho wasn't the sort to openly express emotions as far as Kita could recall. Her feelings were always well hidden under her skin. Kita knew. He'd been so thoroughly taken in by her straight face that he'd let the Finance Ministry man get under his guard, after all.

"Your marriage must be good I guess. You live in a house that would even stand up to an earthquake, and I'll bet your kid is cute, too."

"You don't know anything, do you?" Mizuho moaned softly. She stopped the Mercedes on a side road that led to the Outer Gardens of Meiji Shrine, and turned off the engine. A wood shielded the area from the noise of the city beyond. There was nothing but a single restaurant and a wedding parlour on the quiet street. Mizuho rested her cheek on the steering wheel and closed her eyes, trying to control the emotion that rose in waves through her body. It was as if she was resisting a wave of nausea and swallowing down the urge to vomit. She gave a sigh, cast him a sidelong glance, and suddenly murmured, "He died. My child died."

Kita was dumbfounded. He had simply had the image of a happy family life in a plush part of town. Now at last it was all clear to him – the urge not to see anyone, and the nervous problems.

"I've finally got to the point where I can talk about it. If you want to know, I'll tell you. If you don't, I'll go back home now."

"Tell me," said Kita. He knew there was nothing he could do for her, but he hoped he could at least atone for the mistaken assumptions he'd made about her and the grudges he'd held against her all this time.

He was a child of four, named Shingo. One day he'd suddenly developed a fever of forty degrees, and lost consciousness. Antibiotics failed to work, and after ten days of battling the mystery virus, he had succumbed. He had been at his most delightful. He was learning to ride a bicycle. He'd named his bike "The Dinosaur Tank," and was always riding off on it to play with his little friend Takuya nearby, a toy car in the basket. He was in the infants grade at kindergarten, and he went happily along there each day. He was good at playing up to adults, and he would constantly snuggle up on his teacher's knee, and never do any harm to his friends.

He was a child who was gentle both with people and with things. He had a pet goldfish, but when he came back from a trip to find it dead, he was inconsolable. They made a grave for it together, and when she said "Let's pray that he can swim around happily in the next world," he'd asked her innocently what "the next world" was. It's another world where dead people go, she replied. What kind of people are there? he asked. Your granddad from Kagoshima, and fine people from the past, and Charlie Chaplin, she said. And then he'd said, "I'd like to go too, then." He loved Chaplin movies, and used to imitate the way he walked. There's a scene in the film called *Circus* where Chaplin walks along a tightrope, and a lot of monkeys come along and get in his way. Shingo laughed uproariously at that. The monkeys swarm over Chaplin's face and bite his nose, and Shingo imitated it in bed that night, trying to bite his mother's nose.

He had slept with his mother since the first week after his birth. It was hot in summer, but in winter she held him close, his warm body like sleeping with a hot water bottle. How many times a day had she kissed those smooth cheeks? And now, suddenly she found herself lying there without him, unable to sleep. He smelt of saliva, and of urine. Sometimes he'd kick her in the stomach, or climb onto her face, but now that she couldn't hear his sleeping breath she felt she never slept. It was more than a year since he'd died, but still her hands went out to find him in bed. Then she'd realize he wasn't there, an empty sorrow would overcome her, and she'd weep into the pillow. Night and day she thought about him. It was just as if she'd lost her own arm or leg. Like reaching out as usual to turn off the alarm, and finding she didn't have an arm. And though the arm was gone, it was still part of her consciousness. That's how it felt. He was dead, but she felt as if he was simply hiding around some corner. Even now it felt as if she could turn around and find Shingo sitting there. When she was in the house and heard a sound, she'd find herself going to check. Maybe he's playing alone in the playroom, she'd think, maybe he's suddenly come back from the dead. She often heard things. Mummy, I've finished, she'd hear him say – he'd always announced this loudly when he'd finished on the potty. Mummy, I want some milk; Mummy, please read to me; Mummy, I want some potato; Where are you Mummy? His voice would suddenly come to her. Whenever the intercom sounded, she'd hear his footsteps running down the corridor. "Super hyper bomber kick!" or "Squeak squeak said the samurai rat," he'd call.

Shingo was part of his mother's body – he'd been inside it once, after all. Since the day he died, she'd been only half alive. Her life was paired with his as a single entity. They had slept and woken together, she'd eaten with him, laughed with him, cried with him. Shingo loved pork cutlets, and they often went to the Bodaiju Restaurant in Futako Tamagawa for a fillet set course. He'd devour an adult serving, then eat his mother's ice cream as well. He refused to eat a balanced diet. Usually all he'd eat was white rice and fruit. The only fish he'd eat was raw tuna and sake-dried mackerel. He also like fermented soybeans, with lots of seaweed flakes sprinkled over it, so that his face became coated in bits of seaweed when he ate it. He'd looked forward to learning piano when he turned five, but this was never to be. His father had promised to take him to Okinawa on his fifth birthday.

She wanted to go back to the days when Shingo was alive. She felt she must have been too happy then, that's why it had happened. Those five years since she'd parted from Kita were probably the happiest in her whole life. Her husband was kind. He didn't try to hold her back, he let her come and go as she wanted, and he left the decorating of their new house and the designing of the garden up to her. She'd got catalogues from Italy and England, and chosen wallpaper and curtains and tiles to suit her own taste, and taken her time to create the home. His family put up all the money for it. Since Shingo was born, her husband's mother had come every day and helped with the housework, so it had all been quite easy. There was no friction between them. Her husband was good about cooking and cleaning up, he loved his wife, he was always getting back from work past midnight but it didn't bother her. If a man has to deal with children, his maternal instincts come out. Her husband was good at teaching Shingo words and numbers. He'd tug at his own ears and say playfully "I'm Mr Spock," or put on glasses and wrap a yellow scarf around himself like a robe and say "I'm the Dalai Lama." If you asked what time it was he'd look at the clock and think, then say things like "It's seventy three minutes past three."

What would Shingo have become when he grew up? she wondered.

He'd said he wanted to be a conductor. When some orchestral music began on the television or video, he'd stand on the sofa and conduct. There had been so many possible futures, if he'd just lived. He'd have started elementary school next April. She'd always have similar thoughts whenever a new phase in his life would have begun, she knew. If he was alive now, he'd have reached this or that stage in his piano training, she'd think; or, I wish I'd taken him to view autumn leaves while he was alive; or, he'd be coming back all caked in mud from a football match. But she also thought that perhaps unspeakable things would have happened in his future, so maybe it was better that he wasn't alive. There was bullying when you reached adolescence, and maybe he would have got depressed and committed suicide. The world was less and less safe, and he couldn't have hoped to live the luxurious life of an earlier era. He'd escaped all that unhappiness, so perhaps he'd gained something by dying so young. After all, everyone dies, don't they? The only difference is whether it happens early or late.

Put that way it sounded harsh, she knew. But she couldn't bear to say it any other way. Since Shingo's death, problems had arisen between her and her husband. The two of them had been united as a couple because of their son. Her husband seemed to be seeing some other woman. She could tell. He was smart, so he was careful to get rid of all the evidence before he came home, but his constant brightness and carefree air was because he was having a relationship with someone healthy. She herself had developed this nervous disorder since Shingo's death, and could no longer smile. He never made the slightest attempt to look at her. If she left home, he'd doubtless go right on working as usual, and calling in on this other woman. But she wasn't going to divorce. Why should she do him that favour? This house belonged to Shingo and his mummy. And Shingo wouldn't want daddy not to be there. He loved his daddy. As for his daddy, he was a typical bureaucrat. He'd dealt with the pain early on, and simply said now that all the grieving in the world wasn't going to bring the boy back. You had to forget the painful things as soon as possible or it would affect your work, he said. Try your hardest to consider how best to distribute the nation's tax. You can change your mood by doing money calculations. But she couldn't do that. Her job had been to bring up Shingo. She'd lost both him and her job. No, it was truer to say that she was still carefully looking after him. Inside her that's what she was doing. He continued to grow inside her mind. She often dreamed of him. The Shingo of her dreams spoke with a strangely adult voice. Don't be too sad, mummy, he said, you'll make me want to cry too. Just recently she'd dreamed he walked in the door as a young man, announcing he'd come home. Where've you been? she asked. I've been worrying about you. I've been travelling round the world, he announced. I've seen the Iguazú Falls, and Niagara, and I've walked in the Sahara. When she wept in her dream to see he was alive, he comforted her. I'm sorry, he said, I didn't want to die either, but I had to go, God had some business with me. I'll come back now and then, so please have a pork cutlet cooked waiting for me. These dreams were very painful for her. She felt he must feel most at home when he was in her dream. It was only his mother or father who could dream of him like this. And his father's head was full of money and another woman, so it was her responsibility. If she didn't welcome him back in her dreams, he'd have nowhere in this world to exist any more. That would be too sad for him, so she'd decided to keep on living despite the pain.

Mizuho paused at this point, took a handkerchief from her handbag, and wiped the tears that flowed from her eyes beneath the sunglasses. Then she handed Kita a snapshot in a plastic cover, of her son as he had once been. He was a long-lashed boy. He was eating an ice cream, a white creamy moustache around his mouth. He didn't strike Kita as some unknown child. He was the child of Kita's former lover, and when Kita told himself this boy was no longer in this world, he felt an urge to at least look after the boy in the next. He also wished he could do something for this mother who had grieved so much this past year. Could he help in some way? he asked her. She shook her head silently.

"We won't meet again, but please go on looking after Shingo. I'm sorry I made you tell such a painful story."

He sought her hand to shake it, but she gripped his feebly in return. "Where are you going?" she asked.

"Somewhere far away," was all he replied.

"You're not going to kill yourself, surely?"

Her perspicacity startled him, but he dissembled with a smile. He planned to leave without giving vent to any desire for revenge over lost love.

"I wanted to die too, so I know, you see. You've lost all hope, haven't you? Haven't you, Kita?"

"Goodbye. I have to go."

Kita opened the car door, and set off walking down the main road, without turning to look back. Mizuho's voice followed him.

"You mustn't do it! Don't die!"

Her voice came to him as faintly as if it were a hallucination.

Fleeing Together

The boy had died, but he still managed to live on in his mother's memory. He was even now travelling, eating pork cutlets, learning piano, and speaking in a grown-up voice, but if his mother's attention was suddenly distracted by something else, he'd vanish. She'd have to reassemble him, all of him, from his face and voice to his limbs.

That child had once lived in this world, walked its streets, played with shining and moving things in woods, by rivers, in parks or in his playroom, and been affected by emotions at every moment. But the child his mother was looking after now was not that child. He was just like him, but he was a phantom, made of an entirely different substance. She cared for him in the full knowledge that he was a phantom. One can still feel pain in a limb that's been severed, so it's only natural to go on loving a child who's died. It doesn't matter if it's a phantom, as long as you can maintain the illusion that the child is still alive.

After he'd achieved his wish to meet his old lover, and had learned of her loss, Kita Yoshio sat alone in his hotel room weeping. It wasn't his own child, and he'd never met the boy. The child who had been born between the woman who'd slighted him and the Finance Ministry bureaucrat was no more to Kita than a tree in the wood. What did it matter whether the tree lived or died? Still, his tears continued to flow.

Given that he was due to die on Friday, Kita thought to himself, would he continue to live like that boy in someone's memory? Was there anyone who'd look after him in his phantom form?

That boy had no past to speak of, it was true. He'd only lived for four years. Those four years were a golden time for his mother. She had to hang onto the memory of his short time on earth in order to retrieve for herself those four lost golden years.

Kita, on the other hand, had a past of more than thirty years, but they were only there to be forgotten. As death approached, his consciousness should naturally slip into remembering mode, and he should begin to lament all that he would miss. But there was no sign of this happening. Death was weightless, of course, but his own death seemed as light as a sigh.

This thought didn't make him particularly sad. In fact, it felt more like a little joke if anything. It was funny that a man who was about to die should be crying for a boy who'd died, and pitying his ex-lover who lived with the boy's phantom.

It was already past four on Tuesday afternoon.

Alone like this in the hushed room, another self appeared, one who was exactly like him but made of a completely different substance. This was the fellow who'd decided to die on Friday. Before he knew it, Kita had started doing what this fellow told him to. The fellow had a very persuasive way about him – that was what had led to this.

To everyone there comes a moment when your life blazes at its finest.

Well, thought Kita, he hadn't had any such moment, and it didn't look as if he was ever going to have one. At this point in his thoughts, his Other broke in.

In that case, you should die. In the last moment before death, your life will attain its great climax. Needless to say, of course, you'll need strength for this. And money. You'll leave it too late if you wait till you're over sixty and drawing your pension. Everyone dies sooner or later, they don't need any help to do it, but where's your blazing moment if you leave things to fate? Right now, you have the strength for it. You have the money. Now's your chance. The desire for death is simply part of the territory for humans, like the desire for food or sex. It's OK, you're not crazy. You're a totally normal guy. If you see a fine woman you want to sleep with her, if you're mocked you get mad. When you hear the sad tale of that poor little boy and his Mum, you weep. You have feelings that respond from moment to moment, just like they should. You're all you should be – and that's precisely why you want to die.

Ever since Kita had decided to die next Friday, his feelings had been torn this way and that. If things went on like this, he was worried he might suddenly panic when the moment to die actually arrived. He had to admit it, he was scared of death. He still had three days to go, but at this stage time felt like it was passing awfully quickly. When it came to the crunch, his urge to die might just desert him. This was Death by Choice, after all. Choice included the freedom to choose not to do it. If he chose against it, though, what was his Saturday going to feel like? The very thought made him shudder. He felt an overwhelming sense of futility, a deep melancholy and regret… and at this point, his Other spoke again.

I'll be with you. I'll make good and sure you die, don't worry. Even if you waver, the desire for death has seized your subconscious and it won't let go. It'll take a lot more than a bit of dithering to shake it off.

But he hadn't even decided how to do it yet.

Try a process of elimination. How about drowning, for instance?

He'd once come close to drowning at a beach where he shouldn't have been swimming. A wave had dumped him, and he'd been left foundering underwater. He struggled to rise to the surface, but he'd lost all sense of direction and ended up swimming sideways instead. He was sure he'd drown, but when he relaxed his face rose naturally to the surface. How delicious the air had been! He had this habit of trying to get out of dying, so it might take a bit more to achieve than he'd hoped.

How about hanging? All you need is a bit of rope.

But I haven't been condemned to be hanged. My eyeballs would pop out, I'd shit myself – no way!

OK, how about jumping in front of a train? You could time it well.

I don't want to mix my Mum up in all the compensation problems that would involve.

An electric shock to the heart? It's easy.

I'm not an electric guitar, you know.

Take potassium cyanide? That's how spies die.

I've always hated swallowing medicine.

Well then, how about you charter a helicopter or a Cessna, and jump out without a parachute? You'd feel great.

The problem is, where would I land? If I land in the sea, I drown. If I land in some town, I'll involve other people. If I land in a forest I'll be skewered on a tree.

OK then, don't make up your mind. You've still got three days. It's more important to get yourself into a state of mind where you know you have to die, than to worry about how. People can die even when they have no reason to, after all, so it's even easier if you've got one. Sad or happy, these last three days are going to be the best in your life, see. Don't just sit there shut away in your hotel room, get moving!

And so, urged on by his Other, and without any real purpose, Kita prepared to sally forth into the night streets of the capital. It wasn't a good idea to be alone. And besides, he wanted to shut that Other up.

The telephone rang – the hotel telephone, not the cell phone. The blinking light told him he had a message. He picked up the receiver, and there was Shinobu's voice.

"Kita? Where've you been? I've telephoned again and again. I couldn't get you on your cell phone – I thought you might be dead."

"No, it's still only Tuesday."

"You OK? What are you planning on doing now?"

"I haven't decided. I thought maybe I'd have a meal."

"Buy me one please. OK? I'm in the studio right now doing a shoot. I'll come round there at five."

Kita had a premonition that she was up to something.

"Yashiro and those *yakuza* guys aren't involved, are they?"

"No way. This isn't to do with business."

"Why do you want to spend time with me? It's weird."

"Don't you want to see me?"

"Of course I do."

"Well then, don't argue, just meet me."

He was only too happy to do as she told him. He was inclined to do all he could for Shinobu – after all, she'd promised him rebirth, even if it was only a joke.

Shinobu turned up in the hotel lobby unaccompanied. She was dressed casually, in jeans with ripped knees and a red yachting parka, with a bandana around her head and no make-up, giving her a completely different look from the night before. "I'd love to go somewhere far away," she said in a wheedling tone.

There was a limit to how much he was inclined to indulge her, but he asked anyway just to see what she'd say.

"A mountain hot spring resort."

Hot spring resorts again! Why did women love going to these places? At Kita's bitter smile, Shinobu's expression became pleading.

"I've just felt so empty and forlorn since last night. It's your fault, Kita. I wanted to pack everything in, work included, and run away somewhere. Let's run away together."

"You mean it?"

"I mean it."

But her eyes were laughing as she spoke. Kita stalled by inviting her to eat with him at the hotel, but she held her ground. "We're going to the mountains," she insisted. Kita couldn't guess what her plan was, but he allowed himself be sent back to his room to pack, and then checked out of the hotel. "Look at you," Shinobu said when she saw him with the backpack on his back. "You're all set for the mountains with that on."

They hopped in a taxi and set off for Tokyo Station. The only plan was to head for the mountains, they didn't have any particular destination in mind. "Let's just get on the bullet train and get out of Tokyo," Shinobu insisted. "Once we're out of the city there'll be hot springs all over the place."

They took seats in the first class carriage of the six thirty-five northbound bullet train, heading for Niigata. Before boarding

Shinobu went crazy at the station kiosk, buying chocolate-coated cracker sticks, silverberry juice, cheese paste, banana cake, vinegared squid, persimmon peas, strawberry rice-cakes and so forth, and then settled down to pig out on them. She was just trying to cheer herself up from the miseries and rage of normal life, she explained. Her hands and mouth never paused for an instant; she ate with the vigour of someone literally eating the house down. Kita noticed that she had her own particular style of getting through the food. First off she consumed five cracker sticks. Next was a mouthful of cheese paste. Then came one vinegared squid tentacle, after which she demolished a rice cake. Then she spent a while picking out the persimmon peas from the packet, after which she'd suddenly remember and take a deep swig of the silverberry juice. When the food wagon came around in the carriage, she bought beer and Oolong tea, and after slaking her thirst with these she set in on the banana cake. Finally, she returned to the crackers.

Sitting beside Shinobu with her blatantly terrible eating style, Kita contented himself with picking at the contents of a local specialty bento. He couldn't summon much of an appetite.

Once the train was past Takasaki, Shinobu's blood sugar levels seemed to have returned to normal. She heaved a sigh and said, "Let's get off at the next stop." They'd bought tickets as far as Echigo Yuzawa, but they hopped off one stop short, at Jomo Kogen.

The carriage had been nearly empty since Takasaki. Only five others besides themselves got off at Jomo Kogen. Both the station and the street in front were silent and deserted. Mountains rose in the distance, lit by the moon. Apparently this was the closest mountain hot spring resort area to Tokyo.

They made inquiries at the station about whether there was some secluded hot spring hotel in a nearby village. "A secluded hot spring hotel?" repeated the young station attendant, and thought for a while, his eyes following Shinobu as she danced around in the empty station, humming and looking at the posters on the wall.

"Hoshi Hot Springs is the best. But it's too late to get there now. The last bus has gone. You'll have to get a taxi."

"No problem," Kita said. He got the telephone number, and made the call from the public phone booth. The man from the hot springs sounded rather reluctant, but he agreed to let them stay without an evening meal.

The taxi ride into the mountains took about an hour. A little before nine, they arrived at the lone hotel building in the woods, an area reputed to provide frequent sightings of monkeys. They were shown to a room with two sets of bedding already laid out for them on the floor; the table held little dishes of boiled vegetables, grilled fish, pickles and rice balls that seemed intended as side dishes for sake. The waitress informed them that they could take a bath any time of day or night, and there were drinks in their refrigerator.

A stream flowed beneath the window, spanned by a corridor leading to a wing on the far bank. Apparently this wooden hot spring hotel was over a hundred years old, built in the early years of the Meiji era, and was closed during the winter months.

"OK if we sleep in the same room?" Kita asked.

Shinobu looked much more cheerful than she had when they were in Tokyo. "Shall I read you some more from the Bible?" she said.

"No, that's enough Bible. But is it really OK for you to be in this remote place? You must have work tomorrow, surely?"

"It's fine. I've sent those spooks packing. I want to give them a hard time, you see."

"You ran away?"

"That's what I said, isn't it?"

"I didn't think you were serious."

"I'm serious. I'm taking my revenge on the world."

"It's like I've kidnapped you or something."

"I'm the one who's kidnapped you."

"No one's going to see it that way. What do you get out of kidnapping me, after all? But if someone abducted you, everyone'd go crazy. And there'd be money in it."

"No one would pay the ransom."

"I bet they would. The production guys would."

"No way, not that stingy company boss."

"Well the politicians you've been with would then. You're in a position to cause the downfall of two members of parliament plus a top bureaucrat from the Treasury. You're a walking bomb for them."

Shinobu was sitting up on one of the beds like a little god of happiness. "Kita, would you abduct me please?" she said, gazing flirtatiously up at him as he stood by the window. In the hotel the night before, Kita had dreamed of running away with Shinobu. Needless to say, it had only been a fantasy. And yet here she was, begging him to abduct her. Maybe a whole new life had begun for him suddenly.

"I've got two things I absolutely must do before I die. One of them's a ski jump."

Professional ski jumpers looked as though they just went bouncing gaily along, but apparently they were white with fear when they first started. The beginning was like a prison sentence or death dash to escape. The criminal hurls himself from the prison down the perilous cliff face in the swirling snow, not knowing if he'll live or die, and if by pure luck he lands safely, he grasps both life and freedom. No one can believe they'll survive, that first time. Sure they'd die, and the prison guards wouldn't bother pursuing them. That "freedom or death" leap had become a competitive sport that judged participants on their form and the length of their jump.

"If I tried a ski jump it's quite possible I'd die, it seems to me."

"Kind of like committing suicide by jumping to your death, eh?"

"So the order should be to do the other thing before I try the jump, in fact."

"And what's the other thing?"

"To abduct someone."

"Kita, you've been wanting to abduct me all along! This is great!"

"The success rate for abductions is pretty low, you know."

"Don't worry. I'll help."

"OK, let's try it."

"Sure. But first, let's have a bath."

They changed into bathrobes and headed off along the squeaky wooden corridor for the bathhouse, their slippers flapping on the floor. Steam filled the dimly lit bathhouse, a room as cavernous as a temple hall. The big bath was reminiscent of a holding tank for fish. It was divided in four, with a log across the middle of each. A group of old couples, three middle-aged ladies who made no attempt to hide their breasts from sight, and an awkward-looking young man were all soaking themselves blankly. Kita and Shinobu disrobed behind the screen, then stepped together into a vacant bath. The bottom was lined with fist-sized stones.

"This feels great." Shinobu's naked body swayed palely in the soft, translucent water. Blissfully she scooped water in the palm of her hand and poured it down her back. Kita was blissful for different reasons – he was tasting the delight of seeing with his very own eyes this image of his adored idol's naked body before the photographs had hit the stands. She was no phantom, but it nevertheless seemed to him she'd disappear if he reached out to touch her. Perhaps it was the hot spring steam that made him feel this way. At any rate, that's how he chose to feel.

"She's been abducted by me. I'm in charge of that body of hers until Friday," he told himself. In order to convince himself, he'd go through the motions of the abductor, one by one. First off, he should let the production chief or the manager know he'd abducted her. An abductor always made some demand. They'd suspect him if he didn't. OK, he'd demand ransom money. What would be a suitable sum? He shouldn't go too high or too low. Maybe thirty million would be about right. He ought to make all sorts of unreasonable demands as well. Acting wilful was her responsibility.

Once out of the bath, he bought some milk in the vending machine, and as he sipped it Kita stood at the phone booth by the corridor and dialled the chief's home number.

A woman who was evidently the wife answered. "This is the Fujioka residence," she said, in a voice like a slowed-down recording. Taking his cue from her polite way of speaking, Kita began, "I'm sorry to bother you at this hour. Would your husband be in?"

"My husband is out just now. To whom am I speaking?"

"My name is Yukichi Fukuzawa," Kita said, borrowing the name of the famous early Meiji scholar whose face was on the ten thousand yen note. "Could you pass on a message for me please?"

"Mr. Fukuzawa, is it? I'll take your message."

"I have Shinobu Yoimachi. Don't inform the police. Just prepare thirty million yen. That's the message. Thanks."

"Er, could you explain?"

"This is an abduction. I'm serious. I'll phone again. Goodbye."

Shinobu stood beside him listening as she drank down a can of Pocari Sweat. "That was cool, Kita," she said admiringly. Kita grinned shyly. "Let's go back to the room and take a rest," he said. "I'd like to hear some more of that Bible."

They settled down on the bed and sipped beer while Shinobu read from the twelfth chapter of the Gospel according to Luke, where Jesus preaches to the Pharisees and lawmakers. Lightheaded from the bath, Kita felt the words of Jesus swim like water into his brain.

Think of the ravens: they have no storehouse or barn; yet God feeds them. You are worth far more than the birds!

Can anxious thought add a day to your life? If, then, you cannot do even a very little thing, why worry about the rest?

He felt as if the room had suddenly grown bright. All the strength drained from him, and he sank into sleep as if led there by some hand. When he woke again, it was two in the morning. Shinobu lay on the bed beside him. She breathed peacefully, holding Kita's arm against her breast. Her cheeks were flushed, and she didn't appear to be worrying about anything. Kita gently stroked her face.

Would those businessmen who sold Shinobu for profit be hustling around all night long to get together the money to win back their prize possession? Or would they come back at him with some ploy he couldn't imagine? Kita thought of confronting the enemy. He felt not the least concern.

Kita went back to the telephone booth and called the chief's house again. The call was answered after a single ring.

"Is that the chief?"

"It's Yukichi Fukuzawa, isn't it? You're kidding me, son, aren't you? Shinobu's not in danger, is she?"

"She's sleeping like a baby. Have you rung the police?"

"No. You're the one who said not to, ain't you?"

"If your first concern is Shinobu's safety, you'll do everything I ask."

"Put Shinobu on the line. I want to hear her voice."

"She says she has nothing to say to you."

"Don't tell me she's in on this thing with you."

"You'll find out soon enough. Get together thirty million of those Yukichi Fukuzawa faces by tomorrow noon. I'll telephone later with directions on the hand-over. OK, sleep well."

Kita noted that he felt great every time he acted the abductor like this. He went back to the empty bathhouse and plunged into the bath. He ducked under the dividing plank in the middle, then amused himself by trying to walk along it. Not long after, Shinobu turned up, having found him missing.

"Bet you thought I'd disappeared."

Shinobu looked sulky. She jumped into the bathtub, and splashed Kita's face. Her breasts floated up and down in the water. I've abducted these two lovely round boobs too, Kita told himself, as he felt a still greater sense of fulfilment wash over him.

The Art of the Fugue

In the morning, an old woman came in to fold away the bedding. Both Kita and Shinobu were naked. The memory of the embrace that had lasted through till dawn still clung languidly about their bodies. They hastily donned bathrobes, and together set off for the bathhouse again. Kita's arms, chest and neck gave off the faint lingering scent of Shinobu; the sensation of holding her still registered in the palms of his hands and on his belly. When they had first met at the hotel, she had seemed to him nothing but an intricate, life-sized wax doll, but now he knew the warmth of her flesh and the rhythm of her breath. Suddenly, he was no longer sure whether he was abducting her, or whether he was in love. Perhaps abduction was actually one form of love. After all, you do hear of cases where the kidnapper and his hostage fall for each other. And apparently, a law of nature dictates that the hostage will not condemn her kidnapper. In the beginning, she'll watch him carefully in order to protect herself, but before long an attraction begins, and both begin to care for each other. Then, when the criminal is arrested, his victim will declare that he behaved in exemplary fashion. She's the only one who can treat his crime lightly. This is why a kidnapper is wise to anticipate what will happen after he's arrested, and be as polite and hospitable as possible to his victim.

Needless to say, Kita felt absolutely no animosity towards his own "victim." He was a very lucky abductor. He had money. And he was pretty well loved by his captive.

There in the bathhouse with the morning sun streaming in, he made a bet with Shinobu on the question of whether those businessmen who sold her off would come up with the ransom money by the allotted time.

Kita put fifty thousand yen on them doing so, and Shinobu bet the same amount that they wouldn't.

"If they haven't paid those three thousand Yukichi Fukuzawas by noon, it means you'll get killed, you know."

"But I'll get fifty thousand yen, won't I? And if they do pay up on time, I may lose fifty thousand but I'll be thirty million the richer, after all. I don't stand to lose whichever way the dice rolls."

"So you plan to pocket your own ransom money, eh?"

"Let's split it. You'll be able to live in clover for a while."

"I'm going to die on Friday, remember."

"Postpone it a while."

"No way. Look, let me tell you something, honey. I'm not going to get myself caught by the police. I wouldn't be able to kill myself on Friday if I did."

"That's sly. And I've just fallen for you, too."

"That's great to hear, but this is something I've made up my mind about."

"I swear you'll change your mind if you stay with me."

"Hmm, I wonder."

"Jesus won't let you do it."

"I'm a Buddhist, so I don't care. I'm not saying I don't like Jesus, mind."

Shinobu sighed, and sank into the hot water.

After they'd eaten breakfast back in their room, Kita telephoned the boss again.

"Have you got those Yukichi Fukuzawas together?"

"Not yet. I don't have a hope of making it by noon. Where are you right now, Fukuzawa?"

"I'm at the Showa Base in the South Pole."

"Don't get smart with me. I'm assuming Shinobu's safe?"

"I've popped her in the hot water and she's boiling nicely."

"Stop the kidding. Put her on the phone."

"Sure. And in return, you put on the detective who's listening in through his headphones there beside you."

"I haven't told the cops."

"Oh yeah? So who's the guy there in your room frowning and holding his breath, hey? I can see him all the way from the South Pole. Quick, put him on."

Another man took the receiver, mumbling something. "Is that the police?" asked Kita.

"No," the other replied in a trembling voice.

"So who are you?"

The other guy seemed in agony. "No one," he said.

"Well then, go top yourself."

Kita put down the receiver. Over at the hotel shop, Shinobu was busy buying up fancy horse oil, pickled plums, and sweet rice cakes.

"I didn't get quite enough sleep," Kita announced. "Let's go sleep some more."

He urged her back to the room with him, where he flung himself down on the matting.

"It's great weather. Let's head out for a picnic in a while," said Shinobu, twining her fingers through his hair. Outside the window, the leaves on the mountainside were playing softly in the sunlight. From where they gazed at the scene, it looked as if a huge green fish was swimming through the air. Through the open window wafted a scent of mineral waters from the hot springs mixed with the aroma of plants, which ruffled the opening of Shinobu's bathrobe over her breasts, and tickled Kita's neck.

"Wouldn't it be nice if the next world was as good as this," Kita muttered with a yawn.

"All you have to do is stay here like this, you know," said Shinobu.

"I'd love to. But hey, everyone heaves themselves to their feet when the time comes, you know. Hey ho, they think, back to boring old everyday reality, eh? This is the best experience I've ever had, being here like this with you. I really believe that. And that's because I've decided to kill myself on Friday, see. I don't have to go back to boring old reality. It feels just great."

"I'm so happy for you," murmured Shinobu, sitting beside him gazing out at the landscape through half-closed eyes.

"Eh?" said Kita, surprised.

"I really envy you, going to die the day after tomorrow. Aren't you scared of dying?"

"Nope."

"Do you feel hopeless?"

"Nope."

"So why are you going to kill yourself?"

"I've come to the end of my life."

"And who says so?"

"I dunno. God, I guess."

"How do you know?"

"I don't. Why did I get the urge to die?"

"I read the Bible to you, didn't I?"

"Yeah, and thanks to you I'm not scared to die any more."

"It's cowardly to kill yourself. You're running away."

"You're right."

"You make me want to die too, Kita. I'm scared."

"There's nothing to be scared of if you die with me."

"No." Shinobu spoke firmly, and peered into Kita's relaxed face, her brow furrowed. Kita smiled benignly at her, with the air of having already severed all ties with this world. She felt she'd seen this expression somewhere before. Yes that was it – it was just like the face of the dead Yutaka Ozaki.

She got abruptly to her feet, and heaved a deep sigh. This was worrying, really worrying. She really did feel the urge to die with him. What would happen if instead of convincing him not to kill himself, she was lured into the trap herself?

Just past noon, Kita and Shinobu called a cab and left the hotel for the nearest town. They left their bags in the relatively deserted restaurant of the little hot springs town, and Kita made his fourth threatening phone call from the telephone box outside. It was not the boss but some other man who came on the line this time.

"Have you got those three thousand Yukichi Fukuzawas ready now?"

"Thirty million's a big ask. We've got seventeen million. Wouldn't this do?"

"You're tryin' to talk me down?"

"We're just a small business. This is all we can manage. Shinobu's a precious star, she supports our office. Send her back unharmed, we beg you. Her mother's in hospital from the shock. We want to set her mind at rest as soon as possible. Come on, let's compromise. Make it seventeen million."

"Shinobu'd be pretty sad if she knew you guys were tryin' to beat down her price. If that's what you want, I have a plan."

"Don't hurt her please. Her fans all over Japan would be devastated."

"I'm loath to kill her myself. There's heaps of others I'd rather kill than her. No, I was anticipating that you mightn't come up with the ransom money, see, so I've got another plan. Shinobu's had some experience providing 'comfort' to some pretty famous politicians and high level bureaucrats. I'll get her to tell the story in public. Here, listen to what she's got to say."

Kita beckoned Shinobu to the telephone box, and handed her the receiver. Watching Kita's face, she began to talk in an unhappy voice.

"Help me please! I don't want to die yet! Don't make him angry."

"Shinobu, have you spilled the beans about your relationship with those Congressmen?"

"I had to. He had a knife to my face, and he ordered me to tell everything, so I talked about it all. He's got it on tape, and he's going to send it to the television stations!"

"Shinobu, where are you right now?"

"He'll cut my ears off if I tell you."

"Goddamn the guy for causing all this trouble! Put him back on."

The man on the other end of the line clicked his tongue in vexation, then his voice turned intimidating as he said to Kita, "I'm onto you, buster. You're the guy who paid a hundred thousand to have a drink with Shinobu that night. I recognize your goddamn stupid voice. You've made a big mistake, you bastard. I hope you know what you've let yourself in for."

Kita was strangely calm in the face of this exposure of his identity. He answered with the same calm tone he'd spoken with till now.

"Congratulations. You uncovered me, you crook. I'm not Yukichi Fukuzawa after all. I'm Ono no Imoko," he went on, giving the name of a famous bureaucrat in the court of ancient Japan.

"Whaddaya mean, you're Imoko? Hey Kita, don't mess with us buster. You'll be dead tomorrow."

"No, it's the day after I'm going to die. If you want to kill me you'd better hurry."

"Don't push your luck!"

"Pay up that thirty million. Get those stupid Congressmen to foot some of it. That should bring it up to twenty-eight million or so. You can borrow the remaining couple of million from a loan shark."

"OK. We'll get the full amount ready. Come and get it."

"There's no time to go do that. Donate the lot to the International Red Cross for helping poor sick kids."

"What?"

"The International Red Cross, you idiot. Donate thirty million to them in the name of Shinobu Yoimachi. I'll check whether you've really done it or not."

"What crazy nonsense is this? Are you in your right mind?"

"I'll let the newspapers and television stations know. You don't need to keep this thing a secret any longer."

Kita put down the receiver and left the telephone box in high spirits. Now this abduction was really getting into gear at last.

Shinobu stared hard at him. She looked scared.

"They're going to pay the ransom. So I win the bet." Kita smiled at her, but she still seemed dazed.

They went back to the restaurant and ordered beer, grilled fish, and slices of raw devil's tongue, while he plotted their next move. For some reason, Shinobu seemed displeased. She sat there with lips pursed, chin propped on hands, looking sulky.

"You really hate losing the bet that much?" Kita said teasingly. But at this, her eyes filmed with tears. "What's up? This is weird."

"Yeah, it sure is. Why do I have to get killed?"

"What're you talking about?" said Kita, grabbing her hand. "I'm not really going to kill you!"

She squeezed his hand tight. "No, no, not you. They're the ones who'll kill me. I know exactly what they're thinking," she went on. "There's no way they're really going to pay that money. It won't matter a damn to them if I die. They actually want you to kill me, Kita."

"But why?"

"They want to shut me up, that's why. They'll be running round frantically working on the press right now, making sure that even if I spill the beans about the politicians it won't get in the news. I know too much, see. It's better if I'm out of the way. They'll be bringing in the gangsters, who'll finish me off and set it up so it looks like I've been killed by my abductor."

"Hmm, I wonder. Anyway, let's do what we can. We can't quit now in the middle of the job, after all. I've been a plain old Mr Nice Guy till now, you know. The only thing I was good at was sacrificing myself for others, just like my old man. I've only got two days more to live. The final gesture I want to make is to act completely willful in some way. It's asking a lot to want to involve you in this too, but please stick with me just a bit longer Shinobu."

"I was the one who asked you to abduct me as a joke, but I never thought you'd throw yourself into it quite like this..."

"You've gotta promise to keep it an absolute secret. Don't ever tell anyone I did it for fun, will you. This was a forced abduction, right? It wasn't a put-up job. Don't tell the truth to a soul. Promise me."

Shinobu nodded, overwhelmed by the earnest tone of entreaty in Kita's voice.

"You won't get killed, don't worry. I've been planning how to make sure you're safe ever since last night. Just leave things to me."

Shinobu nodded over and over, wiping her eyes with the napkin.

"You're on the stage, aren't you?" said the old woman who brought them their plate of devil's tongue. Her gaze shifted from Shinobu to Kita and back again. Maybe their conversation had the look or sound of a play to her.

"Would there be a bank near here?" asked Kita.

The old lady drew a map on the table with her finger. "You turn left at the second set of lights, there's a *pachinko* parlour here, and the bank's right next door." She added the observation that it was maybe not the best idea having the bank so close to the *pachinko* parlour.

Kita needed to withdraw the getaway money, but before he did so he stepped into the phone box with the plan of giving the news-starved media the information about the abduction of a star. He dialled Information for the number that would put him onto the press section head of one of the television stations. Then he rang and left a message.

"I've abducted Shinobu Yoimachi, and told her production company they have to donate the thirty million yen ransom money to the International Red Cross. Put this on your afternoon gossip show and the seven o'clock news. I'll make a public announcement at three this afternoon."

The person on the other end was evidently a professional, trained to deal with whatever message came through in the same businesslike way. "An abduction, right?" he said perfectly coolly, repeating to check facts. "Shinobu Yoimachi, you say?" "Thirty million yen." "Three pm." Well the message seemed to have got through, at least.

This was Kita's plan. If he made the abduction public through the media, it would at any rate mean that those gangster businessmen wouldn't so easily be able to shut Shinobu up. On the other hand, of course, it would make the abductor's escape extremely difficult. For a start, the victim was a star known and loved in living rooms throughout the nation. If she was seized from the living room screens and seen walking about in the street, a patrol car would be onto her right away. Their only hope was to hole up somewhere where no one would see them. Kita had the vague idea of moving on to Niigata. He didn't have any particular hiding place in mind, but he'd been there two years earlier, so he had a sense of the place. All he needed was not to get caught before Friday. On Friday he'd free Shinobu and let her loose on the media reporters. Then she could stand there live in front of the cameras and spill the beans about how she'd had to keep the wicked doings of the Congressmen a secret to save her own skin. This would then provide a chance for this star on the way out to leave her old identity behind and reinvent herself as the much-lauded heroine who pitted herself against social evils.

"Right, I'll get our getaway money out of the bank and then we're off to Niigata." They left the restaurant, Kita's arm around her shoulder, and called in at the bank.

"I need to buy some clothes and disguise myself," Shinobu announced. Kita's bank balance should by now hold the money he was owed for selling his organs. But when he slipped his cash card into the machine, he was confronted with something unexpected. The machine refused to accept his card. Even if the organ money wasn't there, he should still have five hundred thousand left in his account.

"How much have you got, Shinobu?"

"About five thousand I think."

"Any credit card? Any cash card?"

"All I've brought is the Bible. I left everything in the car. What's the problem? Isn't there any money?"

Kita had the gut feeling that this was the doing of Heita Yashiro. He knew Kita's bank account number, so he could fix things so the cash card was invalid. He didn't want Kita getting away, that was it. Yashiro had dealings with those gangster businessmen, and he'd probably already sent someone to finish Kita off. After all, he'd boasted that he could arrange things with an assassin for five hundred thousand yen, hadn't he?

Surgeon on the Side

A professional would consider a mere five hundred thousand an insult. In fact, Yashiro was driving a hard deal.

"You haven't notched up a real murder yet, so this is all you're worth. It includes expenses, by the way."

Yashiro didn't have a high opinion of the guy. He tossed him an envelope with a down payment of two hundred fifty thousand. The man tucked it away in the pocket of his dark blue suit, and launched into a complaint about the paradoxical ways of the world.

"In this profession, no sooner do you get a name for doing the job than you're finished." It wasn't worth the game, he declared. He'd probably end up spending his retirement quietly awaiting execution. And if he made a hash of things, he'd die on the job.

"You just do it for a bit of extra on the side, though. I wouldn't normally even bother asking an assassin who'd never killed anyone, you know."

"Every assassin's had a first assignment. Every job's got to start somewhere. But I've spent years studying the art, and gaining knowledge and skill."

"So all you're lacking is experience, eh? That's too bad. Oh well, you can have all the pride you want, just so long as you're cheap."

There was a few seconds silence while the contract killer simply stood gaping, then he closed his eyes and started to laugh. Yashiro laughed with him, watching him carefully as he did so. Finally the killer sighed and grew quiet. He drew a deep breath through his nose, and declared shrilly, "This money's way too little, whatever you say. Too little to buy my skills, too little to buy the other guy's life."

"Don't you worry about the other guy. Kita's life is already paid for. And things are fixed so he pays you your reward as well."

The killer looked unhappy. "Does this guy want to get himself killed or something?"

"Well he wants to die, let's put it that way. This Friday, actually. Don't ask me why."

"You don't need a reason to kill yourself," said the killer. Still, he didn't quite get it. Why should he have to kill a guy who'd do the job himself? He could throw in the job he'd undertaken and save the fellow, but it wasn't the task of an assassin to save someone who wanted to kill himself.

"So my client's going to get me to do something pointless, eh?"

"Just forget about the client, OK?" Yashiro said softly, his voice low and threatening. "It's not just a matter of killing him. You seem to have a wide repertoire in the field. That's why I'm employing you. Well in Kita's case I want an accident, right? He mustn't be allowed to kill himself, and he mustn't die in anything crime-related. You got set it up so it's clearly an accident, get it? And an accident that leaves his corneas and organs intact. Can you do that?"

A smile hovered on the killer's face as he replied, "If the guy cooperates, I can extract his organs and deliver them, sure, but it'll cost more."

"Oh yeah, that reminds me, didn't you work in a hospital or something? Surgery, wasn't it?"

"That's right. I still do."

"So your regular occupation's saving lives, and on the side you're in the business of taking them, eh? I guess it comes down to a way of balancing things out for yourself."

The killer seemed dazed and remained silent for a moment, then he recovered with a laugh. "It's all the same in the end," he said.

Yashiro had been introduced to this killer through a gangster associate he played golf with. Apparently a younger member of the gang hadn't had the guts to lop off the tip of his little finger for a misdemeanour as the rules required, so he'd gone along to the hospital and asked the surgeon if there was a way he could get the job done with anaesthetic so it wouldn't hurt. The surgeon was only too happy to oblige, and promptly did the job that day in his lunch hour. He popped the severed piece of finger into a plastic bag in a saline salt solution, and handed it over to the young gangster like a goldfish in a bag, and even gave him a prescription for painkillers. The gangster froze the piece of finger and took it along and proffered to his boss together with his apology, and there he assumed the matter would end. But word got out that he'd actually had a surgeon do the job for him, and he was ordered to go off and do it all over again. Back he went to the surgeon with his bit of finger, and asked to have it put back on again. The surgeon didn't so much as blink. He set to and performed a swift and meticulous operation, and there was the fingertip, beautifully reunited with its finger.

But the boss ordered the young gangster to sever his finger again while the stitches were still in the wound. When the man turned up at the surgery for the third time to get his finger stub attended to, the surgeon exploded. He demanded to know the name and address of the boss who'd put him to all this trouble for nothing, then he went right round there personally and gave him a piece of his mind.

"You got complaints about my surgical skills? You'd better learn more respect for the medical profession or else, my friend. I could come along and steal your organs in the night while you're sleeping, you know!"

The surgeon stared down the gangster boss, gimlet-eyed. His underlings began to move in to eject this insolent fellow, but the boss had other ideas. A flash of intuition had told him that he could use this man. He soothed him with a polite apology about the severed finger episode, and added a hefty payment for all the fruitless trouble he'd been put to.

There was a fuss at the hospital over the fact that the surgeon had helped a gangster fulfil his obligations. The result was that he was removed from his post for unprofessional behaviour, and that was the end of his medical career. But the gangster boss had taken a fancy to him. He found him a new place in another hospital, and in effect he was kept under the wing of the gang as its pet surgeon. Most of his work these days was in the line of extracting bullets and looking after wounded patients who couldn't reveal their identities in public.

Yashiro was aware of all this, but he hadn't heard why this surgeon had added part-time murderer to his profession. It just takes a slight rerouting of the neurons for a surgeon to become a killer, of course, but the patients at their hospital have no idea. This man at least had conscience enough to perform the job outside the hospital.

To cut a long story short, the surgeon took on the job of assassinating Kita for five hundred thousand yen. Even if he did get the remaining half of his pay after Kita had met his accident according to instructions, plus an extra hundred thousand, it would still not be enough in his opinion. Sure, it was the going rate for a professional Filipino killer, but this guy came with a guarantee from Yashiro's gangster friend, so he could be trusted. Yashiro calculated that if Kita could have an accident that didn't involve much physical damage, he'd get a tidy thirteen million in his own pocket: a million commission for selling the cornea and organ set to a waiting transplant patient, plus twelve million for being Kita's insurance beneficiary. He'd done a deal with Miss Koikawa behind Kita's back, which made Kita a paper employee of his company with the company head as beneficiary, and made thirty per cent of proceeds payable to the insurance agent (Miss Koikawa). Yashiro was taking meticulous care that Kita's death should not go unrewarded.

Kita was apparently of the same opinion. Therefore, when Yashiro had heard from the studio boss that Shinobu had been kidnapped, he'd decided he had to hasten matters with the killer. Once the police got mixed up in the story, the killer would have a harder job, his plans for the insurance money would go awry, and the price of the victim's organs would go down. Whatever Kita's motives for this abduction might be, Yashiro wasn't going to sit back quietly and watch his own profits go up in smoke.

In order to limit Kita's movements, Yashiro cancelled his cash card and credit card. Meanwhile, the studio boss planned to use the abduction to give Yoimachi all the publicity he could. He also used his connections with the Finance Minister who'd paid for use of Shinobu, and thereby managed to get onto the bank's online records and find out where he'd been trying to withdraw money. Then he set about controlling things by hastily selling the story of the abduction to the media, arranging to provide them with video footage and photographs from her debut as a star until now, and even gathered comments from family and friends.

Impelled not so much by the half a million yen reward as by an inextricable combination of Yashiro, who was intent on making a profit from Kita's death, and the studio boss, who was intent on wringing money out of Shinobu's abduction, the killer found himself to his own bewilderment mingling with the passengers on the northbound bullet train. At his feet lay a Boston bag containing the seven essential tools of his trade. Kita and Shinobu were apparently headed for Niigata. He knew that Kita had tried to withdraw money from a regional bank in a hot springs town in Gunma, and that he was hoping to escape somewhere and cover his tracks. The killer put in a telephone call to the station nearest the bank, and asked if anyone had seen Yoimachi Shinobu. Yes, one of the young station employees at Jomo Kogen had seen the nationally famous star apparently as happy as could be. Few people passed through the station, so the fellow's memory would be reliable. Apparently the man with her had on a backpack, and was humming some unfamiliar tune. The two had taken the northbound bullet train.

Terrorist for Justice

Kita and Shinobu arrived at Niigata Station at two in the afternoon. After buying a change of clothes and a pair of sunglasses for Shinobu in the shopping mall of the station building, and some stomach and eye medicine for himself, Kita had only thirty thousand yen left in his wallet. Once they'd run through it, that would be that. But since all was due to be over on Friday anyway, things were going to plan. There was nothing to be scared of.

Shinobu emerged from the changing room in a shiny dress printed with tiny carnations, and crossed her white ankles in a pretty pose for him. "How do I look?" The faint brown birthmark on the outside of her left calf was clearly visible. Kita had discovered it the night before, and felt it added something new to Shinobu's list of charms. This short black dress with its carnation print would be more photogenic than the torn jeans and shirt that revealed her belly button, he thought. He had Shinobu promise to reveal to the media that her abductor had bought her this dress. Shinobu said the round yellow sunglasses were to hide her tears.

At three, they boarded the bus for Niigata Port. Shinobu had declared she wanted to look at the sea.

Kita had been on the same bus two years earlier, but the ride felt quite different this time. Back then he'd been a travelling salesman in the health field, intent on cultivating his outlets, an expression on his face that was quite unrelated to his feelings and the same words constantly in his mouth. Sure, that had been one way of sustaining life, but he hadn't felt there was much life in him to sustain. The company had a motto to the effect that an employee who was selling health had to be healthy himself, but in fact Kita was a burned out wreck at the end of every day. That had been back when health products actually sold. Egg oil, turtle extract, royal jelly, chlorophyll juice, immune system boosters, multivitamins, slimming oils, seaweed soap – this all-purpose health product company had handled them all. Health was no exception to the rules of season and fashion. The company employees were the monitors of early signs of trends; they anticipated what was going to be next, and went around promoting its health benefits to the public.

Two years ago, Kita had been in Niigata Port trying to sell turtle extract and multi-vitamins to the fishermen and crew of a Russian boat, but they weren't having any of it. As long as they lived on the sea, they were plenty healthy enough, they told him. So Kita gave up selling health, with the result that his spirits markedly improved, and he regained his own health.

They arrived at the bus terminal. The sunlight bouncing off the white concrete was dazzling. They set off along the quayside, a warm salty breeze playing on their cheeks. Soon it would be time for Kita to telephone the television station again and make his announcement. They went into the ferry terminus, and located a public telephone. The ferry wouldn't be in for quite a while, and there were only a couple of people in the waiting room. The ticket office was closed.

"I'd love to go there," Shinobu said, pointing to a poster for Sado Island, but it seemed to Kita that they shouldn't try an island. There'd be nowhere to go if they were cornered. He shook his head.

"I want to be on a boat," Shinobu said in response. "Even a fishing boat's OK."

"I guess we won't get a good night's sleep tonight even if we're on land," he said.

"So let's run away to sea."

"Would there be a boat that would take us on board? I mean, you're a star and I'm a kidnapper. We'd have to make sure it all went according to plan."

Kita winked at Shinobu, picked up the receiver, and dialled the number of the television station. "I'm Shinobu Yoimachi's abductor," he said. "Put me onto the head of the news section."

"S-s-s-sure, one moment," mumbled the receptionist. *Please hold, someone will be with you shortly,* a recorded female voice repeated, before being replaced by a resonant baritone.

"Hullo, this is Yamanouchi from the SM television News Section. We received your message. You're with Shinobu Yoimachi now, right?"

"Correct."

"Why did you kidnap her?"

"I want to help children suffering from serious illnesses."

"You say you've demanded that the thirty million in ransom money be donated to the International Red Cross, right?"

"That's right. I have a few other demands as well, actually. Here goes, OK? Get rid of the American military bases in Okinawa, and scrap the Japan–U.S. Security Treaty. Resignation of all Cabinet members. An end to the death penalty. A mandatory retirement system for all members of the National Diet. A ban on those "golden parachutes" for retired government officials in private sector employment. Support Tibetan independence. And drop those stupid variety programs and gossip shows on TV." Kita was reeling the list off the top of his head as he went on. His idea was to estimate Shinobu's life at the highest possible value, though the effect was a little like praying at one of those shrines that offer lots of benefits for a mere coin or two at the altar.

You could hear the wry smile behind the voice as Yamanouchi replied, "These are demands to the Japanese government, are they? I have to tell you there's no one in this country who could possibly fulfil them. What are you going to do about it?"

"I'm not expecting them to be fulfilled. But I want you to at least report the kidnapper's demands verbatim to your listeners. If you don't want to see her killed, you must report them all fully. All will be revealed on Friday. Shinobu will tell you herself, if she's still alive then. I want you guys in the news media to put pressure on her studio manager to pay up that thirty million to the Red Cross. And while you're at it, you must give a lesson to all those useless politicians. You'll not only be saving Shinobu Yoimachi, but for once in your life you'll be doing something for the sake of the world. This abduction is my own way of calling for justice. What I'm hoping is that it will set off a wave of Justice Terrorism. I want people to come clean about the secrets of the business or office they work in, and make a clean breast of all their nefarious doings. Terrorists of conscience throughout the nation, now is your hour! Here ends the declaration of Shinobu Yoimachi's abductor."

Kita put down the receiver, took a deep breath, and turned his mind to discussing with Shinobu where they should go to hole up.

"You sure made a lot of demands there. You're a real pro, Kita."

Kita had never received such praise in his life; in fact he'd been told the exact opposite when he worked as a salesman. Seemed like people really could change if they wanted to. Of course the level of responsibility was different when you were selling a life than when you were just selling health products. His working life had been devoid of responsibility until now, so it was only natural that he'd never improved. He'd been skilled at shutting up and listening to others, with the result that another of his skills was passively conforming to others' expectations of him. Now he realized this old self had suddenly evolved. It felt pretty good.

"I'd say they know we're in Niigata by now. That saleswoman in the shop where you bought the dress realized who you were."

"Am I a millstone for you? Do I stand out?"

"That's why we've got to hide somewhere, see. The police may already be on the move."

"Well maybe, but this town feels pretty sleepy. It just doesn't seem like the sort of place where anything would happen."

"We're the ones who'd be the event. If a patrol car sees us, we're done for."

"Really? It's making me drowsy."

The port had a lethargic air. The sound of a distant steam whistle drifted in like a yawn, while the two wandered along indecisively. Shinobu peeped into the deserted kiosk, and began idly looking for chocolate nibbles to buy. Kita bought himself a sports paper and a can of barley tea, put some eye drops in his eyes, and settled down on a bench with the idea of waiting for a good idea to present itself.

"Couldn't we escape onto some boat?" Shinobu was perched on Kita's knee, chewing gum.

A hotel would make them too visible. Abductors often holed up in a vacant house or some derelict building, but that was in the movies. They had no time to go searching around for the perfect ruin. They could just keep on the move, but they didn't have the money for that. Finally, they settled on hiding on a boat. What kind? wondered Kita, and the moment he did so he recalled the face of the Russian he'd tried to sell health products to a few years earlier.

If they could get refuge on a Russian ship in port, he thought, neither the police nor the gangsters would get to them before Friday. The only problem was, would the ship take them? He'd heard the Russian Embassy was surprisingly unhelpful to refugees. Luckily, though, a Russian ship was not an embassy. It would all work out if they negotiated with the ship's captain, he decided.

He approached two Russians as they got off the bus, huge paper bags clutched in both hands, and addressed them in English. Were they going back to their ship? *Da, da*, they nodded. Two faces, one like a grotesque kewpie doll and the other with great blubbery lips, ogled Shinobu as they spoke. Kita smiled back. He'd like to speak to the captain, so would they mind introducing him? *Captain?* The one with the gleaming lips pointed at the grumpy kewpie. Ah, you're the captain? Kita asked. *Da. Ya. Captain* replied the kewpie. It seemed his English wasn't too good. The thick-lipped one translated for him, rolling his r's, while Kita dedicated himself to the task of negotiating, mouthing his English syllables with a heavy Japanese accent.

"My name is Minami. I'm a director of a television station. This is Mizuho, a reporter. We are making a travel program about Niigata. We would like to include your ship in our footage. Therefore, could you please show us your ship?"

The two had a few exchanges in Russian together, while Kita waited, wondering if his request had got through. Then the thick-lipped one turned to him and said *How much can you pay?* Sure enough, it was going to need money. How much do you want? he asked. *Fifty thousand*, came the outrageous answer. Kita looked resigned, shook his head, and turned as if to go.

OK, said Lips, *forty plus a can of caviar*. Forget it, muttered Kita. Lips came down another ten thousand. If you put us up on board for tonight, we'll make it thirty thousand, Kita offered. *You want to stay?* Lips winced and looked dubious.

"You see, we want to cover the everyday life of Russian sailors," Kita laboriously explained. "We want to know how you spend time while you're in port, what you eat, what you talk about."

Lips nodded to each thing Kita said, but he looked as if he couldn't fathom just why they wanted to do this. He asked if the woman would come too. Yes, said Kita, she was eager to spend time on the ship as well. At this, Kewpie grinned broadly. *Khorosho,* he said, and reached for Kita's hand to shake on the deal. It seemed negotiations had reached a happy conclusion.

They were taken on board the five hundred ton freighter *Pugachov*. On the deck they found two second-hand Japanese cars, tied up with wire rather like Gulliver in Lilliput. There was also a pile of second-hand refrigerators, television sets, and the kind of bicycles that could have been abandoned at railway stations. It looked like a street on special trash-collection day.

They were introduced to each crew member in turn. Nicolai, Sasha, Misha, Alyosha, Kosta…it was quite an array of faces. Each was passing the time in his own chosen way. Some were playing chess, some exchanging cups of vodka, others reading, playing the guitar or sleeping. Shinobu smiled sweetly at them all in a rather bewildered fashion.

Then they were shown into the captain's cabin, where they raised welcoming vodka glasses with Kewpie, and ate the proffered fatty salted pork on black bread.

They were given two empty bunks, one above the other. A young crewman brought them some damp sheets and mouldy-smelling blankets, and informed them that dinner was at six.

"We've managed to find a hidey-hole, haven't we?" murmured Shinobu, gazing out at the sea through the round porthole in their room.

"Mind you, we're not absolutely safe even here."

"Let's hope all goes well."

"I'll go off into the town after dinner and take a look at things," Kita said. "I won't stand out if I'm alone."

Yawning irrepressibly, Kita lay down on the narrow bunk. Shinobu snuggled in beside him. She poked a finger into his nose and chin, and murmured sulkily, "You're going to leave me on this ship all alone? What will you do if I get raped?" She rolled up his shirt and began to stroke his ribs.

"Stop it, that tickles."

"What'll you do, Kita? If the ship leaves while you're away, I really will be kidnapped."

"Don't worry. I don't think Captain Kewpie's a bad fellow."

"How do you know? He might be part of a mafia gang for all we know. All the crew look like mafia members, don't you think?"

"Do the mafia collect junk like that?"

"They'd be carrying guns. Tokarevs or Kalashnikovs, I'd say."

"You want one? Shall I inquire for you?"

"I don't want to kill and I don't want to get killed."

"What if you had to choose?"

"I'd kill. What about you?"

"I'd die."

"Not fair!"

"Look, I promise I'll be back, right? All I'm going to do is just check that the abduction's been reported in the media, and see if the money's gone to the Red Cross yet."

Shinobu pouted, and nodded unwillingly.

Six o'clock came, and the entire crew gathered in the ship's dining room. Shinobu was somewhat relieved to discover that there were two Russian women among the crew. She and Kita were invited to the captain's table as the evening's guests, where they were re-introduced to the other members, and raised vodka glasses together.

For dinner, they were given a tomato and cucumber salad with hamburgers. There were also canapés of salmon roe on buttered black bread. As they sat there surrounded by a sea of Russian language, laughter, and hummed song, the two of them amused themselves by coming up with nicknames for each of the crew. The captain was "Valkewpin." The translator was "Lipsikov." A man who sang in a hoarse voice became "Tomwaitsky," while the woman who served the meal was "Chubbinya." The man who'd been working on one of the rescued refrigerators was "Siberian Electrics," the glitzy six-foot woman was "Glitzerina," a huge two hundred twenty-pound man called Misha became "Fatsikov," and so on. Every time one of them came up with another name they'd laugh, and after a while a young crewman who spoke English asked with undisguised curiosity what they were talking about.

"We were wondering whether you have any Tokarevs or Kalashnikovs," joked Kita, emboldened by the vodka.

"*Yakuza?*" somebody asked.

"We're not *yakuza*. We fight the *yakuza*."

"*Polis?*"

"No, we're not the police either."

"So what are you?" Fatsikov asked.

In his rudimentary English, Kita spelled it out. "I love her. She loves me." This proved a hit. *Gorika!* cried Tomwaitsky, and everyone sang out the same word in response. *Kiss!* Lipsikov commanded. Apparently *gorika* meant "bitter," and lovers had to kiss in order to make the vodka sweet. Not really following all this, the two were made to blushingly kiss.

Siberian Electrics came over to Kita and earnestly began to explain that Tokarevs were no good. "Makarovs are much better. Tokarevs are made in China so they're cheap, but most of them are poorly made. Kalashnikovs also depend on whether they're made in Russia or China. The Russian ones use fat bullets and are very destructive. If you want to buy a gun, buy a Makarov. Makarovs aim well."

"How much does one cost?" asked Kita, and was told fifty thousand yen. But you could get one for five thousand in Vladivostok. A Tokarev cost one thousand.

A pistol suicide wasn't a bad idea, Kita thought. It was nice and straightforward. But he didn't have the money.

When darkness had descended, Kita left the ship to go take a look at the town. Shinobu asked him to bring her back an ice cream.

Kita took a taxi into the central shopping district, where he found a closed electric goods shop that had left the televisions running in the window. Every set, large and small, was tuned to the baseball. Two other men paused in the middle of the arcade as Kita had done, and stood with heads twisted, watching the match. A little girl just learning to walk came tottering out onto the pavement, pursued by her worried father. Kita felt he'd seen the same thing happen somewhere before. No doubt this little scene had also been played out yesterday and would be played out tomorrow, in other shopping arcades in other towns, repeated again and again without anyone ever noticing.

The little girl about a year old looked up into Kita's face. Kita smiled back, with a sudden sense that he'd come across this particular child before. This man's going to die the day after tomorrow, Kita told her silently. You're going to go right on living for a long time. You live well, won't you? Even if one day here or there doesn't make much difference to you, with your long life to come. Then he walked off.

He stepped into a telephone booth, and called the merchant of death. "Hey man, where are you?" Yashiro said casually when he heard Kita's voice.

"Give me back my money. I'm in a fix."

"You want some money? I'll send it through. You're in Niigata, right? Where are you hiding out? Is Shinobu OK? You've finally stuck your neck out, haven't you? It's do or die. I admire you. Have you seen the TV news? You're a fantastic promoter. You've made Shinobu a star overnight."

"That doesn't benefit me one bit."

"Shinobu's got the main part tonight. No one knows you're the kidnapper yet. I'll bet you're holed up somewhere out of sight with her, eh? You won't be out wandering the streets together, that's for sure."

"Her production manager sussed that it was me."

"Don't you worry. That guy's tight-lipped. He won't breathe a word to the media or the police. The abductor's a mystery man. No one knows the name Yoshio Kita. As long as you're alone, you're just another passerby to everyone. I may call it an abduction, but to everyone else it's just some drunk's joke."

"Give me back my money. And keep your nose out of my business from now on."

"I haven't stolen your money. There'd be trouble if you escaped abroad, see, so I've put a hold on your bank account, that's all. I know a doctor who lives in Niigata, so I'll send money to him. I'll give you his number and you can contact him. You'll be OK with two hundred thousand, won't you?"

Yashiro dictated the doctor's cell phone number. Kita wrote it on his hand, and asked his name. Yashiro gave him the name of a gangster boss he knew well.

"Give him a call in half an hour. He won't just help with the money, he'll be able to do other things for you too."

Kita's ball pen added the name Kiyoshi Okochi to his palm.

Kidnap the Kidnapper!

A little after three in the afternoon, the image of Shinobu Yoimachi had appeared via terrestrial broadcast signal in the living rooms of the nation. Even her suicide wouldn't have brought her such quality attention – once it's over, the only thing left is to sigh and move on, after all. But in this case there was the cliffhanger over whether she'd be rescued or killed, and the thrilled audience was on tenterhooks.

The woman who appeared on the screen at the same time every afternoon spoke to the audience with the same expression as always.

"The singer Shinobu Yoimachi has been kidnapped by an unidentified man, and her whereabouts are unknown. At a little after eleven last night, the head of Ms Yoimachi's production studio received a telephone call at his home from a man purporting to be the kidnapper, demanding payment of thirty million yen ransom. The man demanded that the money be paid in the form of a donation to the International Red Cross, and that details of the kidnapping be broadcast on all key stations. The production manager has complied with the demand and donated the money as requested, out of fears for the safety of Ms Yoimachi. The kidnapper has also contacted SM Television and announced other demands directed at the government, including the abolition of United States military bases on Okinawa, mass resignation of Cabinet members, and abolition of the death penalty."

At this point, the recording of Kita's conversation with the head of the SM News Section was aired. A forensic psychologist had been invited onto the program, and he now set about attempting a plausible psychoanalysis of the kidnapper's motives, based on the slender evidence available.

"We know that abduction has a low success rate. This is because of the considerable risk to the kidnapper at the time of handover of the ransom money. Police involved with the case consider the safety of the victim to be paramount and ask for media restraint in reporting the incident, but in this case media reports are being made on the demand of the kidnapper. He admits that his demands to the government are unlikely to be met, but has chosen to voice them regardless. I believe his demand that the ransom be donated rather than given to him is a form of 'crime for kicks,' with the aim of taking his revenge against society. There may well be a perverted idolization of Ms Yoimachi behind his actions as well. One thing's certain, this is a form of abduction never seen before."

His expression remained stern, as if to fend off any difficult questions from his audience. He was followed by a slideshow of Shinobu back in her heyday. There she was as a new star not long after her debut; then she was singing her hit song 'Italian George'; she ran along a beach in a bikini, her breasts swinging seductively; she appeared in the movie *Tetsuko's Room*; "Oh I'm just so into the Bible these days," she announced radiantly... the star that everyone had begun to forget was reborn before their eyes from the array of images.

Being now in the red having been forced to donate thirty million yen, the production manager was desperately trying to recoup his losses by selling Shinobu as hard as he could. As luck would have it, it was a slow news day – nothing big had happened, and no one famous had died. They had the audience's full attention.

Both the name and whereabouts of the abductor were in fact known, but they were being suppressed in an attempt to deprive him of the kicks he was assumed to be seeking. The doctor who'd been set up to kill Kita had decided he must first separate him from Shinobu before his name became known to the world – in other words, his task was to kidnap the kidnapper. As for Shinobu, no doubt someone else would take care of her. Whether she was dead or alive was immaterial.

But the assassin had just received a call from Yashiro informing him that he was about to be saved the trouble of kidnapping Kita after all. It seemed that Kita was now strapped for cash, and making his way right now towards where the killer was waiting. Could Kita possibly have some inkling of what was going on? Surely this was some kind of trap – it seemed too good to be true. Yashiro wasn't to be trusted, no matter how much money he was paying out. The assassin found himself feeling almost sorry for Kita's good-natured trust in others.

Five minutes before the appointed hour, Kita appeared in the hotel lobby. He cast a quick glance around from under his brows, spied the doctor, and approached him, hunched and tentative. "Are you Mr Okochi?" he asked.

The doctor was already familiar with Kita's face from a Polaroid photograph. "Do sit down," he said, indicating the nearby sofa. He checked the face carefully again.

"I do apologize for the trouble you've been put to, doctor. I can't use my cash card, you see." Sweat dripped down Kita's nose. It was the sort of face that would leave absolutely no impression at first glance, thought the doctor. They were a good match for each other in being utterly unmemorable. These days, you saw this kind of face everywhere. It was only natural that Americans and Europeans should think of the Japanese as clones. Anyone not used to seeing the Japanese could well mistake Kita and himself for each other.

"You're in Niigata on business?" asked the doctor, in the tone he reserved for chatting to patients.

"Yes, I sell health products." Kita planned to stick to lies that were unlikely to be exposed.

"You've seen the news?" The doctor wanted to have a bit of fun by watching Kita's reaction. But Kita didn't blink.

"The abduction? I'm a fan of Shinobu Yoimachi's, you know."

"What can the guy be thinking, to do a thing like that?"

"He's probably not thinking at all." Kita spoke with a careful smile in response to the doctor's shifting strategy.

"Where d'you think they are?"

"Somewhere out of sight, I guess. Some flat in the suburbs maybe."

"Or on a park bench." The doctor tried to gauge Kita's expression as he spoke, but Kita managed to maintain a straight face.

"You're on the kidnapper's side?" Kita asked.

"I'd like to rescue the guy."

Kita gave two short laughs at this. Only someone who didn't want to be rescued would laugh like that. Patients who laughed before they were taken in for surgery often died, he found. The doctor glanced at Kita's face again, and told himself that this fellow was set on dying.

He put the two hundred thousand yen from the down payment for his assassination job into an envelope and held it out for Kita. "Thank you, you've saved my bacon," Kita said, head bowed. Then he let out a deep breath.

"Where are you off to now?"

Kita replied that he was going to buy an ice cream and head back to where he was staying, and out he went. The doctor picked up his heavy Boston bag and set off, taking care not to be noticed as he kept his eyes on Kita's back.

A light rain had begun to fall, dulling the evening street lights to grey, blurring the buildings, neon signs and passersby, dimming the sight of everything. Kita strode quickly through the shopping arcade, then dropped in to a convenience store and bought two ice creams and a mountain of cup noodles. He must be on his way to the hiding place where Shinobu was waiting. He hailed a taxi. So did the doctor.

Kita was headed towards a Russian ship. He showed no signs of noticing what was behind him. Then, when he belatedly noticed the doctor emerging from the taxi, he executed a ninety-degree turn and began to walk away from the ship in the direction of the ferry terminal. The doctor strolled casually along in the same direction. Kita made to go into the terminal building, but then realized it was dark and locked. The doctor silently approached.

He came to a halt when he was close enough for them to see each other's faces.

"What do you want?" Kita's voice trembled, and his Adam's apple jumped in his throat from the tension. The doctor kept his eyes on it like a shark.

"Nothing," he muttered.

"You followed me here, didn't you? What else would you be doing in a place like this?"

The doctor lowered his Boston bag to the concrete terrace, and drew a deep breath through his nose. Kita braced himself and raised both arms to protect himself from the anticipated blow, but the doctor simply stood there blankly in front of him. After a long silence, he spoke.

"Your ice creams will melt."

"I got them to pack them in dry ice, so they'll survive for a bit. Well, since there's nothing you want, I guess I'll be going. "

"You'd be wise not to go back to the ship."

The tone was full of certainty. Kita gulped, unable to move. So the guy knew that he and Shinobu were holed up on the Russian ship?

"Yashiro sent you after me, didn't he. What did he tell you to do with me?"

"He said to save you."

"So what are you going to do, Mr Okochi?"

"My name isn't Okochi."

"Well, then who are you? Why are you here?"

The doctor made no reply, and Kita found himself drawn into the silence, unable to figure it out. He had the feeling something unfortunate would happen if he ignored the doctor and tried to go back to the ship. And he was worried about what was in that Boston bag. The doctor was attuned to Kita's eyes as they flickered over the bag.

"Want to see inside?" He picked the bag up, and slowly unzipped it.

One look at the bag's contents and it would become clear who this fellow was, thought Kita. Maybe it contained some horribly cruel instruments of torture. He felt a sudden thrill of terror.

"You bought that ice cream for Shinobu Yoimachi?" the doctor whispered.

A shocking thought occurred to Kita. "Have you killed Shinobu?"

The doctor took from the bag a long, thin metal rod, put one end to his mouth, and blew into it. The next moment, Kita felt a sudden pain in his calf, as though a needle had pierced it.

"Did you think I had Shinobu's head in this bag?"

A needle with a capsule attached had pierced Kita's leg. The doctor packed the blowgun back into his bag. "Just the right size for a head," he murmured. Then he hoisted the bag again, and set off towards the Russian ship.

Astonished, Kita now at last understood that this man was a killer. He pulled the needle out and held it. "What have you done?" he yelled.

"I think you know," the killer responded. "You'll be able to die the day after tomorrow. If you don't like the idea, though, come with me. I'll give you an injection to reverse the poison. I'll be waiting right here, so you go on back to the ship now, give Shinobu the ice cream, and say your goodbyes. This is the end of the abduction story. I'll inform the police. You'll oblige me by disappearing."

"Why is this happening?"

"Because you trusted that fellow Yashiro. Whatever happens, you get to die. The only difference is, whose rules do you die by?"

Purulent Streptococcus

Kita would have liked nothing better than to be able to turn the clock back to last Friday again. He didn't recall having opened Pandora's box. His idea had simply been to have some modest fun with his desires, then die quietly and anonymously. Pandora's box had sprung open quite unasked, unleashing merchants of death into a feeding frenzy on some poor fellow who only wanted to die by choice. All they wanted was to make money out of some fool prepared to sell his life over to them. The day of his death was almost upon him. Kita longed to have just one day of complete freedom before he died.

Did he have no choice but to submit to the doctor's coercions? Or should he play out the abduction act to the end? The doctor was right. Whichever choice he made, he'd end up dead. The fact was, the only freedom of choice available to him now was his method of dying.

At any rate, he'd deliver the ice cream. He set off toward the waiting ship, and summoned the crew with a cry of "Hey, Bolshoi Ballet!" The gangplank was up, so he couldn't get back on board unaided. A few moments later, a torch shone down onto his face. Dark figures moved about, and the gangplank was lowered. When Kita arrived on deck, Siberian Electrics was there to greet him, grinning from ear to ear. He immediately began to press Kita to buy a Makarov. Kita shook his head.

"I saw on TV. You need Makarov, of course. Fifty thousand!" said Siberian Electric, and out came a hand like a baseball mitt. Well, thought Kita, it might be wise to have a pistol, just to stop the doctor having his way. There was nothing to prevent him shooting himself, after all. OK, he thought, I'll buy it, and he tapped Siberian Electric on the shoulder.

Siberian Electric beamed with pleasure, and gripped his hand to shake on the deal. "Yes, yes. The Captain say he want a word with you. Your lover's in his room. I bring Makarov later." So saying, he took Kita by the arm and led him to the captain's cabin.

Shinobu was playing poker with Valkewpin and Lipsikov. She looked up and saw Kita and the ice creams. "Welcome back," she said, then added with innocent pride, "I've won ten thousand! Isn't that great?"

"Sounds like these guys have discovered about the abduction," said Kita. "I don't like the look of things. Look at Valkewpin's face there. He's grinning away even though he's lost. I'd say he plans to make money out of us."

Sure enough, Valkewpin began to negotiate a deal. They'd had no idea they were sheltering a kidnapper. They were in a quandary. They had to maintain good relations with the police, for the sake of Russia's trade with Japan. But they understood his position too, of course. Both parties should be able to profit from the situation. The question was, should they report him, or protect him? They couldn't make up their minds. What was his opinion?

"I didn't think you Russians would watch Japanese television," Kita sighed, while beside him Shinobu spat out, "They're despicable! Let's get off this ship right now." She tugged at Kita's sleeve. But they were faced with a gang of people who didn't seem likely to let them get away so generously.

"What's your proposal for protecting us?" Kita asked.

Well, replied Valkewpin, the ship was due to leave tomorrow, so they couldn't shelter them much longer. Why not just pretend they'd never met? Of course, they would need some hush money... Kita waited for him to continue. They'd had to pay these guys thirty thousand to come on board. How much would it cost to get off again? The answer was a shocking one hundred fifty thousand yen!

"No way," Kita shot back. "This is pointless. Look, just go ahead and tell the police."

The price immediately came down to a hundred thousand.

In the end they agreed on one hundred fifty to cover the hush money as well as the cost of their board, plus a Makarov and three hundred grams of caviar. A loaf of black bread and three bottles of vodka were thrown in free of charge. They divided the goods between Kita's backpack and a carrier bag, and climbed off the ship together, licking their ice creams.

The doctor was waiting in the darkness of the wharf, hands clasped behind his back. "You said those goodbyes?" he asked.

Shinobu cowered behind Kita. "Who's this?" she asked, warily sizing him up.

"This is where we have to part, Shinobu. This man's a killer, and he's injected me with poison. If I don't do as he says, he'll kill me any way he likes. So this is the end of our kidnap act. Go back to Tokyo now and leave me here."

Shinobu glared up at him. "I'm coming with you," she declared. Kita wavered. It would be next to impossible to escape, and whatever they did from now on the killer would be with them. If they didn't part now, they were doomed to a much more difficult parting later. But he wouldn't be around by then, he decided, so there was nothing to lose by giving in to the impulse of the moment and going with his instincts. Besides, he'd just got himself a very handy little instrument.

"Right. We'll go it together." Kita put his arm around her shoulders, and they set off walking towards the streetlights in the distance. Behind them trudged the killer, lugging his heavy bag.

"Kita, that guy still seems to want us," Shinobu said worriedly.

Kita quickened his pace. "Ignore him. He'll disappear before long."

The killer seemed upset at being spurned like this. He addressed Kita's back. "You'll die if I don't inject you with an antidote to that poison, you know."

"Fine by me. I'm sick of worrying about it all. Just leave me alone."

The killer drew a deep breath through his nose, squatted down, and began to remove something from his bag. A round box emerged. Kita drew out the pistol from the bag that had contained the ice creams, and pointed it at the doctor, who froze for a moment still half-squatting, then went on rummaging in his bag, his eyes on Kita.

"Give the bag here," said Kita.

"You wouldn't know which of these is the antidote," the doctor muttered.

"Just give me the bag."

"I'm afraid I must refuse. I have an obligation to save your life."

"Make up your mind. Are you a murderer, or a doctor?"

"Both. I may have been a murderer just now, but right now I'm a doctor. You two can't get away, you realize. As soon as you get out into the light, everyone'll be after you. You're on stage wherever you go now."

Kita wavered again. Everything the doctor said was true, and it was getting on his nerves.

"Go on Kita, kill him. This guy's shot you full of poison, after all. Why not get your own back by shooting him full of lead?"

There was no way for either of them to know if the pistol Kita was holding was real. He couldn't trust Siberian Electrics and Valkewpin, Kita told himself. It could well be a toy, for all he knew. Meanwhile, the doctor looked perfectly happy to have a bullet put through him.

"I didn't have a chance to test this thing," said Kita, shifting his aim to the Boston bag and putting his finger on the trigger.

The doctor put his hands in the air. "It doesn't have a silencer," he argued lamely. "There'll be a big bang that'll bring the police running. Don't do it."

OK, thought Kita, I'll use that dense loaf of black Russian bread for silencing it. He pulled out the bread and held it to the end of the gun.

"You're really going to kill him, Kita? Wow! You're going to kill a killer! Don't do it. OK, I tried to stop you. I give up."

"Fine. Killers need to get a taste of what it's like to be on the receiving end."

The doctor was kneeling on the ground, his mouth half open, gazing at Kita.

"How does it feel, eh?"

The doctor didn't answer, but simply gazed out to sea. He may have been betting on Kita not pulling the trigger, and simply waiting to see which way things went. Or he may have been recalling a previous experience like this.

"Got any final words?"

The doctor seemed to have grown tired of kneeling, for he sank to the ground and crossed his legs. Then he drew a breath in through his nose, closed his eyes, and began to chuckle.

"Come on, then, shoot. I've already killed you, so now it's your turn." He sounded utterly calm – his voice didn't so much as quiver.

"I'm not dead yet."

"I may be the first to die, but you were the first to get killed. Do you know a guy called George Markov? He was a Bulgarian exile who was assassinated with the tip of an umbrella used as a bacterial syringe. He died twenty-four hours after his thigh was injected by the umbrella tip at a railway station. Well, you've got a germ called purulent streptococcus in your bloodstream. You're going to die of septicaemia like Markov did. You're as good as dead, see. But there's a way to save you. There's still time."

"I don't believe this talk about germs. I bet that was just Vitamin C you injected me with. If you want to save yourself you'd better come clean."

"You're the one who needs to save yourself. Mind you, I can understand why you're not inclined to trust doctors. We could be friends, you and me. We're in the same boat."

161

"What? You're saying you want to die too?"

"I just have a vague yearning to die. Just like all the others out there, except you."

"I have the same yearning, you know."

"But you're being impelled by something you can't control, aren't you? There's nothing like that in my case. That's why I go on living like this. But I'm beginning to change my mind because of you. I'd like you to hang around. Just in case you happen to decide not to die, if nothing else."

Shinobu tugged at Kita's sleeve. "What's this freak going on about?" she said, glaring at the doctor with undisguised disgust.

"Oh well, I'll just have to kidnap him too," Kita announced. Shinobu shrieked in horror. She had still been planning on continuing her one-on-one date with Kita. The doctor seemed to concur with Kita's plan, however, for he held out his heavy Boston bag. Kita put his pistol into it, handed Shinobu the carrier bag containing the caviar, vodka and bread, and together they set off to hail a taxi. The doctor followed a few paces behind, avoiding treading on their shadows.

"Let's take the taxi straight to my hotel and pick up my rented car," he said. "After that you can go wherever the fancy takes you."

They took the doctor's suggestion, and all three piled into the rented car. The first thing Kita did was accept an injection of the antidote, which brought to a halt the proliferation of the streptococcus in his system.

Kita couldn't detect any recent physical change. If anything, he felt better than usual. Perhaps that "streptococcus" really had been vitamin C, he thought. They decided to head back to Tokyo. The doctor drove, while Shinobu and Kita sat in the back seat, taking it in turns to doze. They enjoyed a round of Russian-style vodka toasts celebrating the success of the abduction, with the caviar and black bread as side dish. Still, it was a little difficult to decide who was the abductor and who the victim at this point. The TV news had claimed that the kidnapper's identity was still unknown, and there was much talk of desperate fears for the safety of the victim. What liars the media were!

"What it comes down to, Kita, is that you've kidnapped me and a killer." Shinobu was toying with the pistol, shifting it from hand to hand to feel its weight, in a way that made both the killer and Kita nervous. In this situation, whoever held the pistol got to be the kidnapper. As for the assassin, he could only be seen as having blown it big-time – far from kidnapping the kidnapper, he'd actually saved the life of the man he should have murdered.

"Don't let that thing off in here," he said. "The bullet will ricochet and could hit anyone." He was a cautious man. She only had to start feeling a bit high from the vodka and she could get very trigger-happy, he thought. Even Shinobu, who had no desire to die, could just idly pull the trigger the way she might flip the 'on' switch on the karaoke mike. If the bullet hit the driver in the back of the head, the car would crash and in seconds the three of them would be caviar-smeared corpses. She was the last person who should be holding the gun.

Kita felt the same way, and the stress of it kept him awake and alert till dawn. He could feel a pleasant tingling sensation in his thighs. He wouldn't mind if he dropped dead the next minute right there on the highway, he thought, and with this the tingle grew. The car could burst apart, his guts could be ripped open and his bones pulverized, but it seemed to him he wouldn't register any pain. The only sensation that would remain would be this tingle in his thighs.

"Go faster!" he ordered, though the speedometer was already registering eighty miles an hour.

"You suddenly remembered an urgent appointment, or something?"

"Do people feel a tingling when they're about to die?"

"I've no idea." The doctor was concentrating on driving, now ten miles an hour faster. Actually, Kita thought, your whole body feels kind of tingly when you're driving at high speeds like this. It was the same when you jumped from someplace high. Speed and falling… both were natural associates of death.

Kita had a sudden urge to experiment. He asked Shinobu to press the mouth of the pistol against his temple. The tingle in his thighs responded slightly to the touch of the barrel, warm from Shinobu's hands.

"Put your finger on the trigger."

"This is dangerous."

"Go on, just do it."

Shinobu's pale finger slipped through the ring that circled the trigger. The tingling sensation spread from his thighs up his back, then spread slowly to between his legs. This must be the pleasant feeling that accompanies death, he thought. Eureka!

"Dr Killer, you ought to write a paper on this. Do some research on the link between death and tingling."

"You really feel it that much, huh?"

"You bet I do."

"You're bringing me out in a cold sweat," said Shinobu, slipping the Makarov back into the carrier bag.

Only twenty-four hours remained until the decreed time of Kita's death.

As they passed the "Tokyo Thirty Miles" sign, Kita recalled the face of Yashiro, the first to have leapt out of the Pandora's box. Suddenly he was filled with hatred for this man who'd dogged his footsteps this past week, meddled continually, and tried to buy his life. The nausea in his belly wasn't all due to the caviar and vodka, he thought. Yashiro was also to blame. OK, he decided, he'd follow the *yakuza* rule. It was payback time.

"Dr Killer, it was Yashiro who sent you after me, wasn't it? How much did he give you for the job?"

"Five hundred thousand."

"That's pretty cheap. If I pay you the same, would you undertake to kill him?"

"OK."

"And could you make it straightforward, please? No bringing him back to life after you've killed him."

There was a short pause before the doctor spoke. "One must commit sin to atone for sin."

At this, Shinobu swallowed a yawn and remarked, "Seems to me this guy goes about things in a pretty funny way. He's a doctor but he kills people. There's a contradiction here."

"No, it's Yashiro who's full of contradictions. Kita would've died just the same if I'd left him alone. But that would make my duty as killer meaningless, see? That's why I killed you. I fulfilled my duty, then my duty as doctor took over, and I saved you. There's no contradiction in that. I've atoned for my sin."

"OK. If that's how you do things, that's fine by me. But there's no contradiction in what I'm asking you to do, is there? All I'm asking is that you kill Yashiro."

"If that is what you wish…"

Kita's idea was that if Yashiro was dead, he could at least get back to the way he felt last Friday. Right, he decided, for this one day I'm going to live free.

"I might get you to do something for me too," Shinobu mused. With a wink to Kita, she asked the killer for his cell phone number. Business was suddenly booming for him, it seemed.

THURSDAY

Organs Please

Yashiro woke from a truly horrible dream, in which he'd been blindfolded, bound to a chair, had his mouth forced open, and been made to swallow salted and fermented squid. The slimy taste still lingered on his tongue. He needed water. But when he tried to sit up from where he lay on the sofa, he tumbled to the floor. His arms and legs had been bound with rope, he realized. For a moment he thought he was still in the dream, but the pain in his back and this raging thirst were most definitely real.

"Good morning." The doctor's face gazed down at him.

"What're you doing here? Do you know what you're doing?"

"Sure. I've been sent by Kita to kill you."

"Stop messing around. Did you kill him? Shinobu's safe, isn't she?"

"You'd do better to worry about yourself." The doctor rummaged around in his Boston bag and brought out a tennis ball and a phial of medicine.

"What did you eat last night?"

"You're not serious about this, are you?"

"I never lie to my patients."

"I never said I wanted to die. Are you planning on killing a patient who doesn't want to die?"

"My duty as doctor is to save patients who want to die. And my job as killer is to kill people whose death will benefit the world."

"What have you got against me? Tell me!"

"Nothing. I'm just helping the world become a better place."

"Whaddya mean, 'a better place'? You're sick!"

"You're sick, and so's Kita. He's going to die without any help from me. I'll put an end to myself sooner or later too. But not you. You don't want to die, so it has to be execution."

"What the hell are you on about? You're saying you've got a license to kill?"

The doctor wiped an area of the tennis ball with a fluid, and put it to Yashiro's mouth. "Open your mouth," he instructed. Yashiro locked his jaws together and glared up at the killer. Yashiro could see the plan. The crushed ball would be pushed into his mouth, where it would swell until it couldn't be removed. The emetic on it would soon begin to work, and he'd vomit up last night's food. The ball would block the vomit and send it down his windpipe, and he'd choke to death. Yashiro clamped his mouth shut – but this prevented him from begging for his life. The killer pressed the lethal gag down harder. Yashiro drew his lips into his mouth, and twisted his face away.

"You're scared of dying?" The doctor waited patiently for an answer. But Yashiro just lay there rigid as stone, suffering the extremity of his situation. The doctor tried again. "You're scared of dying?" Yashiro, his mouth still clenched tight, gave a little cough in response. The doctor persisted. "Is that a yes or a no?" This time, Yashiro coughed twice.

The nightmare was all too real, in fact. He'd woken too late. Who'd have thought that not locking the office door before he lay down for a snooze would cost him so dear? But no, his luck had run out when he had trusted this guy in the first place.

The doctor was rummaging in his bag again. Had he given up on the idea of choking him to death, and decided on some other way to kill him? He had to free himself from this rope as quickly as possible, and run out the door for help. Or better still, shout for help… But it wouldn't do to startle the killer, he'd be sure to choose the quickest means to kill him off if he did. OK then, talk him out of it. Brute intimidation wouldn't work. But what about money?

The doctor was preparing to leave. He zipped up his bag, and bowed deeply. "Please accept my apologies for being so rough with you," he said, then added, "But you needed to be shown just how it feels to be murdered."

"What the hell're you on about?" The guy must be stark raving mad, thought Yashiro. Only someone in a dream could be as absurd as this. This guy shouldn't be left to roam free in the world. He was dangerous. Get out of my sight, and make it quick! Yashiro prayed.

"How much do you want? Name your price." What should have been a yell came out as a hoarse whisper. What wouldn't he give for a glass of water!

"You want to buy your life back? No, my friend, you can have it for free. I'll make sure Kita gives me back the two hundred thousand I fronted him, plus the two hundred fifty you still owe me. Right, I'm off."

The doctor leaned close to Yashiro where he lay on the floor, gave a couple of derisive snorts through his nose, and left. Was the nightmare over at last? But if so, this was the worst waking Yashiro had ever had. It took him fifteen minutes to free himself from the rope, heaping curses all the while on this bumbling killer. Then he rushed to the refrigerator and gulped down a bottle of chilled Mt. Fuji spring water. Now he remembered why he was so thirsty. Last night's meal. He'd dropped in to the Korean grilled meat joint next door and had salted tongue and grilled rib meat on the bone, plus two helpings of *kimchi* and a bottle of *soju*. But that alone couldn't account for the thirst. Quite likely people's throats went dry when faced with death. He'd been soundly beaten. How could he have let the guy sneak up and tie him up while he lay there asleep? And how could he have gone snoring on, believing it was a dream?

Yashiro couldn't stand it any longer. He had to ring the *yakuza* boss who'd put him onto the doctor in the first place, and tell him the story.

"He'll murder you in your sleep if you let him! Take my advice and rub him out ASAP, for your own safety."

The boss was an early riser. "What's this? He tried to kill you, eh?" His tone was mocking.

"The guy's crazy. He was trying to throttle me!"

"Hmm. How's your back? No pain there?"

Suddenly, Yashiro felt a sharp, pincer-like pain shoot from his side around to his back. Pain also stabbed his stomach. He'd been so focused on not getting himself killed that hadn't been aware of the pain until this moment.

"I seem to have strained my back."

"Really? Take a look at your back in the mirror. Check if there's any sign of stitches there.

Still not comprehending, Yashiro put his hand to his left side. "Nope, just the usual flab there. What's this about stitches?"

"Seems you're lucky. That guy can steal your kidney while you're asleep. But sounds like you're OK."

"Man, the guy's got no scruples!"

"That's a killer for you."

After the phone call, Yashiro drank more water. His body felt so heavy he could barely stand, so he sank back onto the sofa again. His stomach churned, and his head swam. Surely the guy couldn't have stolen a kidney while he slept? Surely the pain would have made him leap to his feet! But what if he'd put him under? Yashiro glanced at the time. Two o'clock. Was his watch mad as well? But the wall clock gave the same time. It'd been about four in the morning when he'd settled down for a doze. Surely he couldn't have slept for ten hours.

With an effort he heaved himself from the sofa, and went and stood in front of the mirror. A grey-faced old man stared back at him with bloodshot eyes. That couldn't be him! Had the killer poisoned him, or something? He rolled up his shirt and turned to check his back. There along his right side, the side he hadn't checked before, he saw seven staples buried in the flesh.

"He got me!" he thought. Instantly the energy drained from his body and his head swam scarlet.

Yashiro had no memory of selling his own kidney. All he'd done was arrange for Kita to sell his organs. What kind of crazy mistake had this bastard made? It had to be just a continuation of the nightmare. He'd go back to sleep, he decided. When he woke up again, his usual plump red face would be restored, and he'd go off and have himself a breaded pork cutlet on rice for breakfast. There was just no way all this could be real.

The Grave of Yoshio Kita

Once back in Tokyo, Kita chose to return to the hotel where last Friday he had revelled in his first feast with Mitsuyo and Zombie, the place with the private pool and karaoke bar. It had an automatic check-in system and room service, the perfect set-up for a kidnapper and his victim to hide away in. Here he would spend his final hours with Shinobu. The moment he left this hotel would mark the end of the kidnapping escapade, and their final parting. They both knew it, and neither felt the need to speak of it. Tired out from the long drive with the killer at the wheel, they took a hot shower, then lay on the bed, and after necking a little, sank into a light sleep.

Kita dreamed that he was walking alone through an empty desert at dusk. There he came upon a little gourd-shaped mound of sand. In it was stuck a long, thin board reminiscent of a broken grave marker, with the name YOSHIO KITA written there in a child's clumsy hand. So this is my grave, here of all places, thought Yoshio, clasping his hands before him. Then there was a cry of "Kitaaa!" and when he turned to look he saw in the distance Mizuho Nishi with a little boy. She was clad in a bikini, and smiling shyly. The child held her hand, while in his other hand he carried a little fish scoop. He ran up to Yoshio. "Papa!" he cried.

At this, Kita awoke. Perhaps he'd overindulged in the caviar or vodka, for his throat was terribly dry, and his breath rasped. He gulped down a can of Oolong tea. "Me too," murmured Shinobu, holding out a naked arm. He propped her in his arms and fed the tea to her.

They turned on the television. Immediately, an image of Shinobu against a background shot of Niigata Port leapt from the screen. It seemed the police and the press had swarmed to Niigata on the evidence of an eyewitness there, and were busy scouring the place for them. They must have passed them going the other way on the expressway as they'd headed back to Tokyo. There was also a shot of the Russian ship where they'd hidden for a few hours the evening before. It felt like ages since they'd gone on board and negotiated with the captain. It was only three days ago that Shinobu had read the Bible to him, but the memory had receded like some distant event in the past. Everything was coming to an end.

"It's twelve. I'll leave here in another hour," Kita said.

"And what will become of me I wonder?"

"You'll have heaps to talk about, that's for sure. Use your tongue as your shield. Don't let things prey on your mind. Jesus is with you."

"That's true, but still..." Shinobu looked unhappy. She buried her face in the pillow. Kita took a handful of her hair to his nose, wanting to remember the scent of it. If this scent filled his nostrils at the moment of death, he'd die happy, he was sure of it.

"I don't want to go anywhere," Shinobu's muffled voice emerged from the pillow.

"You have to. The show must go on, but it can't unless you go out onto that stage, you know."

"OK, I'll retire then."

"You don't have to do a thing. Just go out into the crowd with your Bible in your hand."

"What about you, Kita?"

"I'm leaving the crowd behind."

Shinobu abruptly sat up and hugged him. Let me not forget the feel of these breasts either, thought Kita. He felt again that tingling he'd experienced as Shinobu held the pistol to his head while the killer drove. He longed to drown in the softness of her breasts and the scent of her hair.

"Hold me. Hard. This is the last time you'll embrace a woman. Sear this feeling into me, as proof that I lived. Hurt me if you like. You can bite me if you want to. My body will be your grave, Kita." Tears trickled from the corners of Shinobu's eyes. Kita licked them gently with his tongue, took her two arms inside his and squeezed. He sucked at her neck, her nipples, then slipped into her. Shinobu was half sobbing, half moaning with pleasure, and shaking her head as if desperately resisting something.

The face Kita saw before him was one he'd never seen before, not on television or in photographs, nor in the four days they'd been together. She might be in pain, or trying to dispel her fear, or about to burst out laughing. Her eyebrows were drawn down either side, her brow was wrinkled, and her lips curled.

"Let's die together." The heat of sex was over and the sweat-soaked bed was beginning to grow chilly when Shinobu suddenly spoke. Her tone was casual.

"No," Kita said flatly.

"Why not? You're going to die, aren't you? Why should you care whether I want to die too? I've got a pistol right here, after all."

"Don't you dare. Your parents would be devastated."

"And what about yours?"

"My father died four years ago. My mother's gone senile."

"Well I'll be sad if you die, Kita. I'll be so sad I'll die too. So come on, let's die together.

"You'd regret it."

"There's no such thing as regret once you're dead."

"I'm saying this for your own good, so please just live a bit longer. Another ten years or so. If you do that, you'll find you've changed your mind."

"Don't you understand, Kita? I love you. How can I just stand by and watch the man I love die?"

"It's sheer fancy. Just watch this man go, and you'll be sure to find another fine guy out there in the crowd. Once you've fallen in love with him, you'll forget me in no time."

"I'll never forget you," she muttered. Then she crawled out of bed, and pulled the Makarov out of the carrier bag.

Kita leapt to his feet. "Give me that," he said, his hand extended, but Shinobu placed the butt between her breasts and glared at him. Maybe he should just get Shinobu to shoot him right now, Kita thought. It would save him a lot of trouble. And Shinobu's sudden urge to die was really just because she didn't want to face going out into the crowd again.

"You can kill me, but don't kill yourself," he told her. "If you die too, who's going to remember me? Who can I visit in dreams?"

"Well stay alive, if that's what worries you."

"OK, say we die together. How do we do it? What's your plan?"

"You lie on top of me, then I shoot you through the back. That way the bullet will get us both."

"You're the heroine of a tragedy right now, but this is going to be a joke later, you know. Come on, get dressed. I'm going out to bring this thing to an end."

But for all his urging, Shinobu stayed put on the bed clutching the pistol, her finger poised over the trigger. Kita put out his hand and attempted to lift it from her grasp as if seizing a butterfly, but she continued to glare at him, and pointed the gun at her jaw. Her finger was still on the trigger.

"If you're going to die, do it next Friday. You've still got lots more things you've got to do in this world. It won't matter if you give yourself an extra week to do them. There must be things you'd love to do before you die. I'm into my seventh day here, and I've satisfied all my desires. But you haven't yet."

Shinobu heaved a deep sigh, took the barrel of the gun, and held it out to Kita. Then the corners of her mouth turned down and she fled weeping to the bathroom to take a shower.

Shinobu emerged in a better mood, with a smile ready for Kita, but he was no longer there. She searched under the bed, in the toilet, and out in the pool, but there was no sign of him. She stamped with vexation. Here she'd just decided to live a bit longer, and look what he'd gone and done! Fancy running off while she was in the shower! "I hate you Yoshio Kita!" she yelled, and began to throw whatever was to hand – pillow, towel, coffee cup. She came to her senses abruptly when the glass table shattered. Perhaps she would still be in time catch him, she thought. She flung on her clothes and rushed out of the room, her hair still wet. The moment the elevator doors opened onto street level, she dashed out into a street teeming with businessmen and office girls sauntering back from lunch.

People turned to watch, tittering as Shinobu flew along the street, drops flying from her hair and breasts flopping. Hadn't they seen that face somewhere? Then a cry went up: "It's her!"

Shinobu ran on. Kita had disappeared into the anonymous crowd. Still she ran. Her nipples rubbed painfully against her blouse. Her throat was so dry she felt it would split. She paused to buy a grapefruit juice from a drinks machine, tossed it down, then wiped her sweat with her sleeve and plumped herself down on a bench in front of a convenience store.

Three young men stood around her, eyeing her from a distance. They'd been on the lookout for a woman to chat up when they spotted her sitting there. A discussion followed. Now they stared blatantly, whispering her name among themselves, and to escape them Shinobu set off at a run once more. The men followed. As she ran, Shinobu remembered that she'd left her Bible in the hotel room. How could she have forgotten her protective talisman? She had to go back and get it! But she'd turned right and left and run up and down so many slopes in pursuit of Kita that she no longer had any idea where she was.

She dashed into a department store. The eyes of the girls at the cosmetics counter bored into her. Gasping for breath, she went up in the elevator. Now at last the effects of the vodka were beginning to hit her.

"Where do you sell Bibles?" she asked a lady shop assistant in the uniforms section.

"Bibles? You'll find them in the bookstore on the fifth floor. Excuse me, er, are you the one who was kidna—"

"No. I'm free again." Shinobu pushed the middle-aged woman out of the way and raced to the fifth floor. The sales floor heaved like a ship in a high sea. They were all looking. Gazes pierced her from everywhere, and she felt pursued by the whisper of her name. *That's Shinobu Yoimachi running past! She's alive! What's she doing in Shibuya? Is the kidnapper somewhere nearby? She should go straight to the police – was she raped by the kidnapper? Was she really abducted? Let's save Shinobu Yoimachi! Chase her! What fun…* Inaudible words echoed around her head. Help me, Kita! They're trying to kidnap me!

"A Bible, please," she said to the shop assistant.

"You want the New Testament? The Old Testament?"

"The one that has Jesus' words in it," Shinobu retorted irritably.

"They're both on the Religion shelf," the shop assistant said in a stupid voice.

Maybe, just maybe, she'd find Kita there browsing the Bible, she thought. But instead she found a close-cropped young man, turning the pages of a book with the ridiculous title *Ten Steps to Happiness*. Shinobu picked up a Bible with a yellow cover, and hurried back to the counter. Once more, everyone was looking at her. She had the urge to vomit. Bible clutched to her side, she fled to the toilet, rushed into the large Disabled Toilet, turned the lock, and vomited up a bitter black fluid.

If Kita were here he'd rub her back for her, he'd read the Bible to her, she thought. But here she was, alone once more. And all she had was a Bible. She idly opened it, and voicelessly spoke the words that met her eyes. These were the words from The Revelation of John that she read:

Written on her forehead was a name with a secret meaning: "Babylon the great, the mother of whores and of every obscenity on earth."

Well if Tokyo was Babylon it could go up in flames for all she cared, thought Shinobu. Along with me, and all the men I've slept with. It wasn't Tokyo's fault, but that of its tainted people. No one spoke the truth. All were equally dyed deep with evil and corruption. That was why we needed God; a God who could make us all humble and ashamed of our sinfulness. But such a God could never appear on Earth in human form. If He did, all our envy and hatred would be hurled at Him.

Ah, she thought, I wish I could see Kita again. I don't want to let him die. Even if we can't meet again in this life, I just want to believe that there can exist on this Earth a man free of envy and hatred, like Jesus in the Bible.

A sudden thought flashed into her mind. That killer – she still had his cell phone number! She rushed out of the toilet and straight to a public telephone box. He answered on the fourth ring.

"Hi, it's Shinobu. I've got something to ask of you. You can save people's lives too, can't you? If so, please stop Kita from killing himself. He absolutely mustn't be allowed to die. I'll pay you a million yen."

"Right."

"You can?"

"I'll see what I can do. I was just about to come and get my fee for killing Yashiro, actually. Is Kita still with you? Oh, he's escaped, has he? I see. But no need to worry. I'll find him, have no fear. I put a transmitter in his backpack, see, so I can tell pretty much exactly where he is."

And so Yoshio Kita was once again a followed man.

Frankenstein from Middle School

Kita intended to quit the capital again. He hadn't fixed on where he should kill himself, but he could see that it would be useless to hang around the city with its high ratio of police.

Hot on Kita's trail aided by the transmitter in his backpack, the doctor caught sight of him going into Tower Records. The doctor stood just beyond the periphery of Kita's vision, watching his feet to see where they'd take him next. Kita walked past the Opera section three times and finally left without buying anything. Outside, he hailed a taxi.

His destination was the airport out on reclaimed land in the bay. With what must be close to the last of his money, Kita bought a ticket at the counter, and proceeded to check in for the flight to Sapporo. The doctor followed suit, allowing a two-minute interval. There were still forty minutes before boarding. Still wearing his backpack, Kita went into the bathroom, and didn't emerge for some time. Maybe he was having trouble getting rid of the pistol, mused the doctor. Or busy plastering down his hair. Or did he want to be alone for a bit? Then the worrying thought flashed through his mind that Kita might actually commit suicide in there behind closed doors. He was just setting off to check when Kita emerged, looking cheerful. He went straight to the hand luggage inspection point, and passed through without any check being made of his backpack. Evidently he was no longer carrying the pistol. Well, that meant that at least he wouldn't be able to shoot himself, and also that the doctor needn't worry about being kidnapped again.

The doctor let five others pass ahead of him before he went through the hand luggage check. But then he was taken aside while his bag was inspected, and had to explain the presence of the syringes, medicine, and clinical examination equipment. In the end his bag was handed to one of the stewardesses to carry on board. The reputation of doctors must have taken a dive in recent times.

Kita wandered about the shops, but didn't buy anything. Then he went in a snack bar and ordered a curry rice. Watching at a distance, the doctor tutted at the sight of Kita standing there at the counter hunched over his food. If his planned suicide was pointless, eating curry was even more horribly pointless. No man about to die should be eating curry, and no man eating curry should be set on suicide. The doctor felt he was spying on some illicit scene. For some reason, he was suddenly consumed with anger. Nevertheless, he continued to stare until Kita had run his spoon around the edge of the plate and licked up the last morsel, like some starving student. The fellow was still brimming with life, it seemed. Perhaps there was one more thing he was planning to do. Still, this kind of energy wasn't necessarily just self-sustaining. It could easily shift to something destructive – of himself, or of others as well.

The doctor boarded ahead of Kita and settled down to doze as soon as he was seated. But his nerves were still tingling from all the running around of the last couple of days, and he was in no fit state to sleep. Before long, a recording of the three o'clock news began on the screen in front of him. The newscaster announced that at two that afternoon Shinobu Yoimachi had been found alive and well in a Shibuya department store. Her abductor was still on the run, and the police were on his trail. Shinobu was refusing to give any information about him, either his name or distinguishing features. In an interview with the press, she had said, "The man who kidnapped me is not a bad person. I want to save him. He's taken our illness upon himself."

What would the viewers make of this? Not knowing what had actually happened, and seeing her looking as fervent as her words, at best they'd probably assume she'd fallen in love with her kidnapper, or even that the whole story had been a fiction. But perhaps there'd be a tendency to try to see some logic in what she said after all. It was true, the kidnapper wasn't a bad person. That in itself would probably elicit some public sympathy. Personally, the doctor was unmoved by Kita's apparent goodness, but somehow he felt a tremendous pity for him nevertheless. He was surely wasting his time by shadowing Kita all the way to Hokkaido like this, but he had an urge to meddle in his fate.

Once the plane was airborne, the doctor suddenly recalled someone who somehow reminded him of Kita. He'd forgotten the guy's name, but he'd known him at middle school. They'd been in the same class in the second grade for a mere three months. Rumour had it that the boy had lost his parents in an accident, and his grandparents were taking care of him. He had a hook-shaped scar on his head, and in class he was constantly either snivelling like something coming to the boil, or chuckling to himself. In the first week everyone avoided him and kept their distance. In the second week, someone came up with the nickname "Frankenstein," and from that moment on he'd been tormented. He was the perfect target for the violence of his fellow students. He made no effort to resist, so even people who were physically weaker felt safe to hurl the name at him. He also had a habit that the others couldn't understand. As he lay there snivelling while he was beaten and kicked, he would murmur to himself, a little smile on his face. You could never really catch what he was saying. When a bully asked him to say it again, he'd simply turn away with a little chuckle. This would incense the bully, of course. He'd register a momentary unease at not knowing what his victim was thinking, and he'd have to inflict a bit more pain on Frankenstein to dispel it.

The doctor had wanted to stay out of the gang who made this boy a scapegoat, but one day he began to feel he'd like to see the guy dead. The boy was silent in class, but all the time he spent alone seemed to have induced him to think things through and develop his own philosophy, which he seemed to long to share with someone. On the way home from school one day, the boy stopped him and told him something like, "The world's forsaken me. But what this means is that I've been chosen by God. I must battle alone against the world. I'll probably be defeated. In order to win, I must become the incarnation of the world's evils. When I do this, the world will find it needs me."

The doctor had forgotten his name, but he clearly remembered these words. It could just be that the guy had been a genius – there are countless unlucky geniuses like that in the world. But hearing these words back then by the bridge in middle school, the doctor had been just one more of those with common sense who side with the world.

About a month after he'd begun to wish this incomprehensible possible genius dead, the guy was transferred to another school. If he was still alive today, what would he be doing? There was no way to know whether he'd died or possibly even been killed in his teens. This was why the boy haunted him. Even all these years later, that face would pop into his head several times a year, and always it would leave him brooding over whether he should have just killed him back then, or become his friend, or whether he should employ a detective and search him out, or whether the fellow still hated him. He even dreamed sometimes that the guy could now be a doctor with a side job in killing. Every time he recalled him in the past twenty years or so, the doctor thought to himself now, he'd talked himself into believing he had nothing in common with the guy.

But now that he'd come across the peculiar make-up of this fellow Yoshio Kita, it struck the doctor that the middle-aged Frankenstein would undoubtedly decide to condemn himself to death, just like Kita. The point is, the doctor tried telling himself, these folk who wage a losing battle with the world set up some grand suicidal scheme really for the sake of their own little egos. Nevertheless, he still felt disturbed.

His brain was spinning along at terrific speed, but his tired eyes and body couldn't keep up, and he felt oppressed by dizziness. The doctor closed his eyes and attempted to simply wait quietly for the plane to land. It was smoothly losing momentum now, but his dizziness made it feel as if it was going into a tail spin. He felt ill. It was always at such moments that images of bloody human organs came floating past under his closed lids. If only the damn plane would just go down, he thought, bury its nose in the middle of some hapless town below and burst into flames – anything rather than this.

Kita disembarked ahead of him. The doctor retrieved his bag from the stewardess and stepped briskly after him. He gained ground on the departing backpack, thinking that he could safely hail Kita now without risking him running off. Just then Kita turned suddenly right and ran into the toilet. The doctor was obliged to follow him, and he placed himself at the next urinal. Even this failed to alert Kita, however.

"I'd ask you not to go eating curry at airports," the doctor said.

Kita turned to look at him with an expression of distaste, and heaved a deep sigh. "God, how unlucky can I get!"

In a few more hours, Friday would begin. Why should a guy who was due to die tomorrow have any need for luck?

"No need to worry. I'm not planning to get in your way." The doctor smiled at him in friendly fashion, but Kita frowned.

"So what the hell're you up to then?" he demanded fiercely, and turned to wash his hands.

The doctor held out his handkerchief for Kita to wipe his hands on. "I have something I'd like to discuss, you see."

"How did you know I was going to Hokkaido?"

"Oh, sheer coincidence. I was after a holiday in Hokkaido myself."

"That's a lie."

"You're right, it is."

"You've been asked to follow me, haven't you?"

"No. I'm accompanying you out of mere personal curiosity."

"I'm not some kind of exhibit, you know."

"And I'm not here as audience, I assure you. If there's anything I can do, I'd be glad to help."

Kita drew a deep breath, then suddenly took off at a run. The doctor ran beside him. At the taxi stand, Kita turned to face him. "Stop meddling in other people's business! Get lost!" he gasped desperately.

"I understand," the doctor nodded expressionlessly.

"You! I'm talking about YOU!" yelled Kita, leaning threateningly over the doctor, but the doctor merely continued talking in a soothing tone.

"I've followed your instructions, and dispatched that man who tried to take advantage of you. You're now quite free to be your own man. I won't meddle, don't you worry. But you know the saying, 'Companions on the road.' Just allow me to have dinner with you, that's all I ask. I was wanting to discuss methods of payment with you. You'll be setting off on a long journey tomorrow, Kita. Tonight's the last time you'll have a business conversation, you know."

"Oh yeah, I forgot. I'm so sorry."

"You're headed for the city centre? I don't know when you plan to die tomorrow, of course, but tonight's your last night, isn't it? I was wondering if you'd care to have a sympathetic ear for any last words you may have."

The doctor was clever not only with his hands but with his tongue. Kita couldn't very well turn him down, since he'd come for his promised payment, so he meekly followed the doctor's beckoning hand and got into the taxi with him.

This last week felt like an endless series of changing vehicles. How many taxis had he taken by now, he wondered? Looked like it took a lot of changes to get you to the next world. Maybe in New York or Rio de Janeiro you could get a taxi that would take you straight there.

"So what are your plans for tonight? You must be rather weary," the doctor said.

"Kidnapping's an exhausting business. Is it all sorted now?"

"I'd guess Shinobu is being mobbed by the press right about now. It's the rebirth of a star."

"Did I do the right thing, then?"

"You did, I'm sure. And you got away without being caught, what's more."

"True. By the way, Mr Killer, you mentioned back there that you'd dispatched Yashiro. You actually killed him?"

"He's still alive. But I've shortened his life considerably. He'll go another three years at the outside, could be six months, then he'll die."

"What did you do?"

"I stole a kidney. You can't sell a life if you steal it, after all, but you can get some money for a kidney."

"And how is he?"

"I couldn't really say. We exchanged greetings after the surgery, that's all. I imagine he's probably in hospital by now. I had to perform the surgery in that filthy office of his, so I'd guess quite a few bacteria got in. How he gets along will rather depend on how good his immune system is, but you can be sure he'll be befriended by quite a variety of illnesses from now on, and forced to spend his days contemplating approaching death." The doctor sounded positively gleeful.

"Does this count as murder?"

"I wonder. I could maybe be convicted of robbery and grievous bodily harm. Maybe negligence leading to death. Although it wasn't negligence, it was intentional. The question comes down to whether there was any intent to kill. You ordered me to kill him, so I guess the answer is yes, but I didn't in fact kill him at the time, so it would be hard to prove intent to kill. You're going to die tomorrow, so you won't be in a position to bear witness. Therefore, I can only conclude it can't count as murder."

"So what did you really want to do?"

"I couldn't say. I simply chose the most rational approach."

"You weren't sure whether to kill him or save him, so you stole his kidney, is that it?"

"That's what it amounts to, yes."

"In that case, you can't claim to have killed him, so I'm not obliged to pay you."

"Ah, I see. That's what you're driving at. Never mind. I got a decent sum from selling his kidney on the black market."

The taxi was stopped at a red light, and the driver was eyeing his two passengers in the rear view mirror. He met the doctor's eye, hastily averted his gaze, and turned up the radio.

"We're practicing our parts for a play," the doctor informed him drolly.

"Truth is, I've got no money." Kita opened his wallet and showed the doctor. He had less than three thousand yen there. There was money enough in the bank, of course, but no way of getting it out.

"OK then, we'll have to steal some. You borrowed two hundred thousand from me, Kita. I still haven't been paid the outstanding two hundred fifty thousand from Yashiro either, so something has to be done about that as well."

"I'll pay you with my organs. Organ extraction's your specialty, after all."

"I guess that's all we can do then. I'll need to accompany you to your execution ground. Will you permit me?" The doctor spoke as if he was reading from a score he already knew.

Kita pulled at his hair in despair. "Why the hell should it cost me all this money to die!" he cried.

"That's capitalism for you," murmured the doctor.

"Oh shut up," said Kita crossly.

The Connoisseur Food Eccentric

It seemed the doctor really was upset that Kita had eaten that curry. He was still harping on about it even once they were settled at the table for Kita's last supper.

"Do you have something against curry, is that it?" asked Kita. "So what could I have eaten that would make you happy, eh?"

But the doctor only came back with the same thing, over and again. "Curry's just the pits."

"So I should confine myself to sashimi and crab, or something?"

"Well that's better than curry, at any rate," muttered the doctor. He stripped the shell from the horse crab that had just been delivered to their table, flipped it over, and set in on the ovaries and crab butter. Both suddenly grew taciturn as they settled down to commune with their crab. But neither had much of an appetite in fact. The doctor tipped some warm sake into his crab shell, mixed in some orange crab butter, and sat there sipping. Kita imitated him. This was called "crab shell sake," he learned. "I've never come across it before," he remarked. At this, the doctor launched into an enthusiastic lecture. Had he ever tried charfish bone sake? Or blowfish roe sake? You could also mix sake with salted sea-cucumber entrails... on he went.

"You're some sort of gourmand, I see," remarked Kita, sounding bored.

"You can't have eaten any decent food in your whole life," the doctor retorted firmly.

"I always had strong likes and dislikes as a kid."

"Me too. Up until I was about twenty-seven."

"So you turned around and became a gourmet at twenty-seven?"

"That's right. My physical make-up changed with the death of someone I knew. He was a doctor, my teacher actually. The immediate cause of death was rupture of the heart, but his body was in such a bad way he could easily have died of any damn thing. Diabetes, cirrhosis of the liver, hypertension, bowel cancer, he had the lot. And how did he get that way? Overeating, nothing more nothing less. In the hospital he'd be handing out warnings on diet to the patients, but he exempted himself from his own rules."

"You're pretty weird yourself, but so was your teacher, eh?"

"Let me just finish. Patients generally come to hospital wanting to regain their health, right? But there's no need for the doctors to be healthy. He was out to commit slow suicide, that's my view. People who eat things they're not supposed to eat, they're shortening their life through a crime of conscience. That's right, you can die by eating, you know."

All along the doctor had acted like butter wouldn't melt in his mouth, but suddenly all that changed and he now spoke in deadly earnest.

"He had an eating disorder, that's what it comes down to. He recognized it himself, and he once told me it was related to his experience as an infant during the war. That fear of starvation never left him even in adulthood. He felt anxious and restless unless there was food nearby. As a result, there was always food in the refrigerator and cupboard. But once or twice a year, it would happen that stocks ran out. When he discovered this, he'd immediately go out and fill his belly somewhere or buy stuff in, no matter if it was past midnight, or in the middle of a typhoon. These days, of course, you've got twenty-four-hour convenience stores to take care of the anxiety of such people, but back then there were no convenient local food outlets. He'd have to get a taxi into the city centre to find one of those late-night shops.

"He used to play the gourmet and pretend it was an epicurean affectation that made him walk the streets in search of food. He defended a huge territory, and he was au fait with all manner of international foods and cuisine. When he travelled to conferences he'd make a point of hunting out the specialties and delicacies of the region, and astonish everyone with his appetite. He'd eat at least two dozen raw crabs, then demolish enough bouillabaisse for three. He could consume a two-pound T-bone steak, rare. He'd spend a long time at a sushi counter, ordering two rounds of everything they had on the menu.

"But all this is no more than you'd expect of your average glutton. He passed himself off as a suave, big-eating gastronome in company, but in fact he was the worst type of food eccentric. There's nothing esoteric about being a food eccentric, no arcane knowledge or anything like that. He'd eat whatever he could get his hands on. Weird eating was his greatest pleasure in life. And one aspect of this discipline of his was food perversion.

"My teacher adored pigs' ears. Now pigs' ears are a staple item in Okinawa and Taiwan, where they eat them vinegared or jellied. Their gelatinous marrow and skin gives the dish a fabulous texture to the bite. You can turn a woman on by licking her ears, of course, but it's not on to actually eat them. So you ease your frustration by eating pigs' ears. My teacher never ate a single woman's ear till the day he died, but he chewed up and digested the ears of no less than three hundred pigs to make up for it.

"He also had a passion for internal organs, brain and liver and kidneys, and so on, and he was a constant customer at the street stalls that specialized in offal dishes.

"Now freshness is everything when it comes to offal. He'd go to these places in Shinjuku in search of the organs of cattle killed that same day, and order up dishes of raw liver, heart, brains, and what have you. Raw brains have a richer taste than cod's roe but they're not as strong, and you can get quite addicted to the particular crisp texture of pink brainstem. Cattle have small brains relative to their overall bulk, so raw beef brain is quite costly. But that didn't stop him. He'd order up three plates of it, until I found myself wishing I had four stomachs like a cow to hold it all. But this was just the hors d'oeuvres. The main course was beef offal stew. This went well with a heavy Bordeaux red, so he'd take a case along when he went. Offal may be a stamina food, the guy behind the counter would warn him, but it's packed full of cholesterol remember. I'm a doctor, he'd say with a shrug, I know what I'm doing, and he'd order a second helping of stew.

"He was also a sucker for animal fat. Take thick noodles in a soup of back fat of pork, for instance. Or Chinese dumplings with a creamy stuffing made with heapings of that lard you use for heavy fry-ups. We're still in the realm of fat that might be enjoyed by many people on a regular basis here, of course. But my teacher had what you might call a literal weakness for the stuff.

"Now we Japanese as a rule don't go for fat, with the result that we have excellent longevity. You don't die young just from eating the kind of fat you get in noodle soup or Chinese dumplings, for one thing. Let me just mention here that lard is a healthier kind of fat than butter or beef fat. Okinawans are long-lived, and Okinawa's a lard paradise. Mind you, their impressive average life span is actually thanks to other causes. They have a balanced diet, and the climate and air are conducive to a long life. They're not addicted to fat like some races.

"But as for my teacher, well he was on familiar terms with butter, beef fat, lard, you name it. Seal fat, duck fat, sheep's fat, camel fat… The Provence region of France prides itself on a dish called cassoulet.

You cook fatty duck in an earthenware casserole dish with white beans and sausage, so the beans absorb the duck fat, and the soup's heavy with it. Apparently even the French have heartburn the day after they eat this dish. My teacher ate it three days running. He didn't just eat it, he soaked up every last bit of fat at the bottom of the casserole dish with bread. I'd guess he shortened his life by about a week at each meal.

"Whenever he ate fat, he knew one thing for sure. Whether it was salted pork sirloin or chunks of beef fat in sukiyaki or stewed camel's hump, or goose fat foie gras, he knew it was going to put pressure on his circulatory system, increase the adipose tissue around his liver, add wear and tear to his heart, diminish his vigour, and as a result take him one step closer to death.

"He would go into raptures over spicy and salty things. Now fat, of course, disguises much of the taste of hot or salty food. If you put salt on your tongue, you register the salty taste, and if you bite a chilli your tongue burns, but fat not only lessens the heat and the saltiness, it tames it right down. So of course his fat-soaked tongue craved food that was hotter and hotter, saltier and saltier.

"He kept the refrigerator permanently stocked with a number of salted and fermented foods. Sweet miso with fermentation starter, high-grade stuff with lime added, fermented cuttlefish blackened with its ink, he had the lot. He'd put salted fish innards and roe or salted sea-cucumber entrails in sake and drink it, he'd soak octopus or blowfish stomach or salt pickled sea squirt in green tea, or put salt-pickled baby rabbitfish on tofu, and he'd eat anchovies neat. He was a great fan of salt itself in all its guises. He'd of course use rock salt on meat dishes, and natural sea salt with fish, but he'd also blend different regional salts to create compounds for his personal delectation. This became a passion in his final years, the reason being that his body couldn't cope with anything more than salt and water by this stage.

"Well if you're a connoisseur of salt, you'll also be a connoisseur of miso, soy sauce, and fish sauce. This man would serve himself dollops of finest Hatcho and Nishikyo miso washed down with sake, and slake the resultant thirst with drafts of Calpis. His pursuit of saltiness led him to start gulping down pure mineral spring water.

His daily consumption of salts and sugars leapt, while his taste buds dulled. He craved ever stronger taste sensations. He took to having chilli, Tabasco sauce, or Chinese chilli paste with everything, which of course ate its way through not only his tongue and stomach but also his intestines."

"You and your teacher make a fine perverted pair, I must say." Just listening to him was giving Kita heartburn and a dreadful thirst. He ordered water.

"I'm just saying this is one more way of committing suicide. It takes a while, mind. Obviously, I'm not suggesting you try it yourself. I mean, you're a man who'll eat curry for almost his last meal, after all."

"Just drop it, OK? You're saying I should've eaten noodles? I don't want to eat another thing."

"Curry! Noodles! You're a man with a sorry stomach, you are."

"Don't judge a man by his stomach."

"Oh but I do. I hate Americans, for instance. This world isn't such a simple place that you can conquer it with goddamn hamburgers."

"Just what're you trying to tell me?"

"I'm speaking of the sorrows of the flesh. That explosive appetite of this teacher of mine did its work and sure enough his organs fell apart. Food eccentricity is a kind of terrorism, when it comes down to it. But it was also the only way my teacher could slake his desires.

"We're all starved of love, and tormented by the fear of losing love. From time to time we have to ease our fears and cravings by a bout of overeating. We search out food to replace the love we can't chew and swallow – or in some cases we do the opposite, despair of finding love and thus cease to desire food. At any rate, love and food are fatally interconnected.

"I cannot live without love. Yet love evades me. This is our dilemma, and we've constructed two ways to ease the pain. One is fervent eating. The other is refusing to eat anything at all. Being starved of love both stimulates the appetite and removes it. Both these responses are destructive impulses that derive from a sense of love's absence. The one leads to overeating, the other to anorexia. Either way, too much or too little, we die. We humans survive by maintaining a balance between the two, but overeating and anorexia don't hurt others, so no one interferes. Of course your lover or your family might try to save you, but this involves love of some sort, and the result may well be that your destructive impulses subside. Anyone threatened with death through over- or undereating is actually in a crisis of love. Yet this is where someone who has no dealings with love steps in – the doctor. Where destructive impulses are directed at others the police and the legal profession step in, but they're not in a position to interfere with self-harm. All that can be done is for a doctor to treat the problem as best he can. You may find a good one, and with luck you'll survive.

"My teacher was lucky in that he himself was a doctor, but in some ways it was his downfall as well. At any rate, just before his sixtieth birthday he collapsed and died from overeating. It was a hideous death, but not a tragic one. His close family no doubt felt sorry for him, but those around him had no sympathy. In their astonishment they laughed rather than grieved, and at length the ironic smiles gave way to real reverence.

"What a lucky guy to die from overeating, one of his colleagues said. Meanwhile his students gossiped that he must have been aiming to get his name in the Guinness Book of Records with the readings on his cholesterol, gamma GTP, blood sugars and so on, all measures of his various ailments.

"The poor man could barely eat anything in his last years. He'd sit there lost in thought before a dish of plain broiled fatty eel and foie gras sauté, finally manage to carry a morsel to his mouth, then reach a trembling hand to a glass of water to wash it down. His flesh sagged and spilled out between his shirt and the top of his trousers. He'd developed a thick layer of fat everywhere beneath the skin, and a marbling of adipose tissue covered his muscles and organs. His breath stank and sweat constantly poured from him in all temperatures.

"At this point, he made up his mind and prepared for his last supper. The table was laid with an array of dishes devised over long years of eccentric eating. A beef brain and pork saddle fat salad, a jellied broth of pigs' ears and fig, foie gras and Chinese chilli sauce ice cream, ravioli of fermented bonito intestine and washed cheese, green chilli stuffed with caviar, tuna eyeballs in champagne. He assembled a row of his favourite wines – Romanée-Conti, Château

Latour, Tokay and so forth. It took him five hours to polish it all off, sieving off the fatty juices and injecting them into his system. He collapsed on the spot, was rushed to hospital in an ambulance, and died of a heart attack en route."

"Why on earth would he go to that extreme? He must've been pretty desperate," muttered Kita.

The doctor drew a deep breath through his nose, and gazed steadily at him. "That's exactly how my teacher would breathe sometimes, flaring his nostrils. Like he found the world despicable."

"This teacher of yours wouldn't be your old man, by any chance?"

Still holding his gaze, the doctor raised his lip in a lopsided wry smile. "You're pretty smart. I am the son of this eccentric eater, you're right."

"And are you one too?"

"I'm no match for my father when it comes to appetite. I hated even eating while he was alive. I despised people who were addicted to food. I virtually lived on thin air. I didn't eat red meat or fish. I'd occasionally snack on a leaf of lettuce or cabbage, or eat a piece of unbuttered toast. When it came to meals, it was a bowl of white rice and some miso soup. I ate what you might call the absolute minimum to survive."

"Your own form of rebellion against your father, eh?"

"I imagine so, yes. I was twenty-seven when he died. After that, my physical constitution changed radically. My repressed appetite was liberated, and I started eating meat and fish. On the anniversary of his death I went off to one of those offal specialty restaurants and had beef brain, and when I went to France I made a point of visiting Provence to have cassoulet. But I must admit my stomach isn't as strong as his was."

"You inherited his appetite, but not his stomach?"

"That's right. But I did inherit his despair. He expressed his destructive impulses through perverse eating, but I—"

"Murder people?"

"No, I haven't murdered anyone yet. I try to, but I end up saving them. I'm still caught between killing and rescuing. I chose to become a doctor in order to render my murderous impulses harmless. I hoped the urge to destroy could be satisfied by cutting people open and messing about with their organs. But I was wrong. Pa's eating problems worsened with age, and it seems my destructive impulses are doing the same thing."

Why had the doctor chosen him to confess to? Kita wondered. Was it because he thought Kita would understand the despair of this gluttonous father and his murderous son? The doctor had analysed himself, but now what?

"You're sick. Go and see a doctor." Kita was trying to throw him off with a casually dismissive remark.

"I'm asking you to stand in for a doctor here," the doctor replied.

Kita smiled wryly. "This is turning out to be some last supper," he muttered.

"Kita, why do you want to die?"

Everyone he met asked him the same question, and he didn't have an answer. He simply made up some witty response on the spur of the moment to get the other person off his back.

Now he said the first thing that came to him. "A kind of self-sacrifice, I guess."

"So you think your death is going to help the world?"

"Not really, no."

"OK, why die then?"

"My instincts are telling me to. Just like your instincts tell you to kill people and then to save them."

"I get the feeling we've got something in common, you and me. We can't explain our impulses."

"Why don't you want to kill yourself? You can save someone else by dying yourself, you know."

"No, being alive allows me to save you. But in any case, the world doesn't give a damn whether I live or die, it doesn't suffer either way. Even if nothing much happens in the world on any given day, a lot of people still die. And we're both going to join the anonymous dead sooner or later. The world at large doesn't have anything to do with each and every person who dies, now, does it? We're part of the world, but once we go the gap's soon filled. My, what a cold hard world it is, how easily it forgets! How many of the dead do we each personally remember, hey? Family, close friends, important people we've respected, famous artists – probably no more than ten or so, right? But just think of the millions who die during our lifetime."

"What're you trying to say?"

"The world will abandon you."

"So?"

"So haven't you felt that before you die you'd like to do something that would lodge you in people's memory somehow?"

"Not really, no. I don't give a damn whether I'm forgotten or not."

"Do you believe in the next world?"

"There's no such thing. What was it Shinobu said? The next world is just the worst place, or something."

"Even so you want to die?"

"Yes, I do."

"You have no regrets? Nothing to tie you to life?"

"Nothing."

"You have some grudge against the world perhaps?"

"When I die, my world will disappear. I can't destroy the world. No matter how many people you kill, the world will still keep going. Mao Tse-tung, Stalin, Hitler – they all massacred vast numbers, but the world kept going. So you see, you should give up murder and kill yourself instead. That way you can at least get rid of the world you personally live in."

"You say this, Kita, but surely you've struggled with the world? You're actually a hero in disguise. The fight begins now."

"You have a strong will to live. That's why you kill others instead of yourself. You must be motivated deep down by hatred and malice, even if you can't really comprehend yourself, I think. This will of yours to live'll get the better of you one day, and you'll die. Just like your father died from over-eating."

Kita yawned and stood up.

"Where are you going?" cried the doctor, leaping hastily to his feet.

Kita smiled at him. "My father died a bland, kindly man. He was used by others all his life, he had no friends, he was abandoned by the world, and he died quietly alone. No one remembers him now. My mother's lost her marbles, his son's about to die. All that will be left is his grave. But most people in the world live like him, and die like him. Mao Tse-tung and Stalin and Hitler killed anonymous millions just like him. They killed some famous folk too, of course, but they were in the minority. So at least where dying's concerned, I'm one up on my Dad. I managed to get a bit of my own back on the world, and I met the woman of my dreams."

Kita put on his coat, shouldered his backpack, and disappeared into the crowded streets of Susukino. The doctor in turn picked up his heavy bag and set off after him, maintaining a steady distance.

All that remained by now in Kita's wallet was two thousand five hundred ninety yen. Whatever he did now, his range of choices would be pretty limited – a nap in some sauna, for instance, or a couple of cheap drinks in a bar. Perhaps he should set himself up to sleep the night in a park or doss down between a couple of high-rises. No doubt he could dip into the doctor's pocket for expenses, of course, but it felt somehow right to spend his last night on earth sleeping out in the open. It was time to gaze up into the sky in this northern city, ask the doctor to keep his mouth shut, and make some final decisions about how to carry out his imminent execution.

He walked slowly north from Susukino along Minami Shijo, heading for Odori Koen. The benches around the fountain were all occupied by couples, but along the street under the trees was emptier. He chose a spot between two trees, and the two of them spread out some newspaper salvaged from a garbage bin, and settled down for the night. Kita closed his eyes and concentrated on the question of how to kill himself, dimly aware of the distant cacophony from passersby in the park and its surrounding streets. Then it suddenly struck him that he wanted to try ski jumping just once before he died. Well how about throwing himself off the Okurayama ski jump where Sasatani had performed his feats back in the Sapporo Olympics? With luck, he'd smash himself up badly enough to die. As luck would have it, though, he might manage a successful jump. Either way, it was worth a try. How about tossing back the remaining bottle of vodka from the Russian sailors and then speeding down the ski slope on a bicycle? Even his internal organs would squirm with excitement, for sure.

As Kita lay there grinning to himself, the doctor suddenly sat up. "Sorry, but there's something I forgot," he said. "As I understand it, Shinobu's in love with you."

What was the use of hearing this now? Kita had lost his love four hours before he flew to Sapporo. "I'm grateful to her. She's managed to make my suicide into a kind of art."

The doctor drew a deep breath through his nose. "An art, eh?" he said softly. "I finally get it, Kita. You, my father, even me – we're all death artists."

The Death Artist

Kita lay there breathing in the fragrance of the damp stone in the night air. He took a swig from his last bottle of vodka, then got to his feet. "Well then," he said to the doctor. "Shall we be off?"

"Where to?" asked the doctor, but Kita didn't reply. He simply walked off through the park, as if carried on the wind. This park felt too comfortable. He wasn't inclined to fall for the temptation of settling in to live here on the streets. Why not leave his backpack here for someone else to use? He only had a few more hours of life left, after all. He needed to get on with finding his execution ground and setting things up.

He tried vaguely to picture the place he was after. Somewhere completely undistinguished, he decided. Somewhere wild and natural. There'd be birds flying about in the clouds overhead, and no sign of anyone about; his scream would vanish in the wind, his corpse would be hidden in the deep grass. He'd set off in search of just such a place, and when he got there, he'd find a flat rock just the right size to lay himself down on. It would serve very nicely as an operating table.

The doctor followed him wordlessly, but his left shoe rubbed, and the limp slowed his pace. The fifteen-pound bag dragging on his shoulder felt more like thirty pounds. He wished he could have a good long soak in a bath and settle his exhausted body between some freshly starched sheets. Why oh why should it be so tiring to save someone's life, while the guy he was saving could follow his every whim? It was one thing to save someone lying meekly on the operating table, but there wasn't much he could do with this particular patient when he kept moving restlessly about, stubbornly intent on dying. He was only a surgeon, not a professional counsellor who could talk Kita out of suicide; the only thing left for him to do under the circumstances was to watch him kill himself, perform a swift operation to remove his organs, and deliver them to the organ market. Good grief, he thought, let me have a quick rest before we get on with it.

What kind of organ thief was he right now, anyhow? He had no desire to get himself caught, but exhaustion compounded his fear, and made him desperate. He was also a murderer, and there's nothing scarier than a desperate killer. Yet Kita was using him as his manager, for Heaven's sake.

Kita was headed for Sapporo station. As he walked, he eyed the cars parked along the road. Having scrutinized the makes, number plates, and interiors of each car he passed, he came to a halt in front of a BMW with a Tokyo license plate, and put his hand on the door. Needless to say, it wouldn't open. He walked another ten yards, and tried a Nissan Skyline with a local Sapporo plate. No luck.

"You're trying to steal a car?" the doctor asked irritably.

"They're all locked," muttered Kita. Well of course. Yet he doggedly went on trying one after another. He was sick of walking.

The doctor got ahead of him and paused at a Chevy Camaro with an Osaka plate. He beckoned Kita. "This one has 'Please make free use of this vehicle' written all over it. Let's take it." He took from his bag what looked like a metal ruler, inserted it between the doorframe and the window, and began to pump it gently up and down. Immediately there was the shriek of an alarm piercing enough to tear the flesh from one's temples. The doctor frowned, but didn't pause in his work. The lock broken, he slid into the car, opened the hood, briefly fiddled with the electronics, and the alarm stopped. He started the engine.

Kita had been standing there with his hands to his ears. The doctor motioned him into the driver's seat, settled down beside him, put on his seat belt, and tutted in vexation.

"Come on, what're you hanging around for? Get this car moving."

Kita took a short breath. Then he wheeled the white Camaro around and set off in search of his execution ground.

The doctor didn't ask where they were going. He settled back and closed his eyes, letting things take their course. He woke from his nap with the nasty feeling that Kita was clumsily up to something again.

The roads decided where the white Camaro went. It raced straight along whatever road it happened to be on until it had to turn, and then alternated right and left at each new junction. There'd be no going back from this journey.

Kita was pretty impressed with the doctor's car thieving skills. It wasn't just organs that the guy could steal, it seemed. In this man's hands, his corpse would be quickly dispatched. Kita looked at the sleeping doctor with renewed awe and fear.

It was a fabulous car for speeding. It seemed almost made to be crashed. "Thanks for such a great gift," whispered Kita, but the doctor pretended he hadn't heard.

Now and then the road was momentarily illuminated by the stark light of a gas station or convenience store or drinks machine. It seemed so insubstantial it might disappear at the merest puff of breath. And sliding along it the white Camaro seemed it might melt into thin air if he closed his eyes for a moment, Kita thought. The steering wheel and accelerator were amazingly light to the touch, and his own body too could have been made of styrene foam it felt so weightless. Bearing down on this feather-light accelerator, he felt a thrill run right from his temples down his back. He pushed the speed up a bit further, past seventy-five miles per hour, and the thrill ran down over his knees. If he really put his foot down, the thrill would reach his heart and penetrate his pores and blood vessels, and he'd crash to instant death, laughing till he drooled. The white Camaro would be his coffin. And if a spark ignited the gas in the tank, that would deal with the cremation at the same time.

The speedometer now registered over ninety, and the street lights sped by like fighter planes. There were only a few inches separating him from death. Within his narrow field of vision, a stark white high-rise sprang up like a gravestone. Narrowing his eyes, he made out the word "Hospital." He slammed on the brakes, and in the same instant his pulse started throbbing violently and the weight returned to his body.

Held firmly by his seat belt, the doctor gave a low groan. The tires squealed around a gentle curve in the road. The thrill that had been rushing through Kita's body now subsided, replaced now by a stirring and hardening between his legs.

"You were going to take me with you there, weren't you?" the doctor muttered hoarsely.

"I wouldn't have minded just crashing the car back there, but then I saw that hospital." Kita glanced sideways at the doctor, who was wiping the sweat from his hands, hollow-eyed.

"Goddamn hospitals everywhere you go," the doctor spat.

"You don't like hospitals?"

"They make my heart ache."

Kita gave a laugh like a cough. Fancy that, this man who could dispose of people and bring them back to life as casually as he'd move chess pieces around a board actually had a heart. "You look done in," he said sympathetically. "Don't worry, you can rest easy. I don't plan on killing you too."

The doctor raised his hands, spread his fingers and yawned, trying to get his circulation going again. It was all very well to be told he could rest, but how could he possibly doze in this hearse with someone bent on dying at the wheel? Besides, the law stipulated there should be only one corpse per hearse.

Perhaps it was having just passed a hospital that had given the doctor his nightmare. He had been in a high-ceilinged hall, full of dazzling light. Around fifty people sat in the audience holding their breath, their eyes fixed on him. He was in the midst of a performance of heart massage. He climbed on top of the patient on the operating table and sat there, both hands to the inert heart, leaning his weight into the task of pumping it at varied rhythms and tempos. He was a percussionist, and the audience was appreciating his concert.

He went on massaging, working up a great sweat as he pumped. The muscles in his arms were jelly, and pain and exhaustion gripped his back. He wiped the drops of sweat from his brow with his white sleeve, and glanced at the audience. Some were dozing. Others were rising to leave. Still the doctor couldn't end his performance. There would be no rest for him until the heart began to beat of its own accord again. But even that rest would be only brief, before he had to begin work on the next patient. More and more patients in cardiac arrest were being brought into the hall.

Even if he failed to resuscitate someone, the doctor thought, he wasn't directly responsible for his death. It was now around two hours since the heart had stopped. The situation was hopeless. Continuing the heart massage was a mere formality.

He was tired. He longed to stop. There was no way the patient would revive. Yet the audience was poised to applaud the very moment the patient was resuscitated. If he got down from the table now, they'd not only boo him, they'd lynch him. A thought came to him: what if he fainted right now?

The next instant, the prone patient opened his eyes, and gave him a leer that seemed to see through to his very soul. The doctor felt his own heart squeeze tight, and at that moment the dream bumped him back into reality.

"Could you please go someplace where there isn't a hospital?" he asked Kita confidingly.

"I don't suppose you've been dreaming of all the patients you killed getting their own back on you, have you?"

The doctor sighed in response, and said, "Heart massage is a nightmare. I've had it up to here."

"It really does make your heart ache, eh?"

The doctor could remember heart massages that had gone on for four hours straight. If there's no response within thirty minutes, you can generally assume brain death, but the patient's family still hadn't shown up so he had to keep going. You have to show the relatives that you're massaging the heart. The doctor will go on trying until he's too exhausted to pump any more, so that the relatives will acknowledge that he's done all he could. The family will use the doctor's sweat as surety for the fact of their relative's death. That's the custom in hospitals.

"So what does it feel like to massage a corpse?" Kita suddenly asked.

"You have to like corpses. If you think it's pointless, you can't get your arms and back working strongly enough. You have to tell yourself it's for humanity and the world as you press."

"How do you do it?"

"You get on the corpse, shake your head around wildly, yell 'Don't die, you crazy fool!' and go like this." The doctor placed his hands against the dashboard and leaned into it, breathing heavily. The car swayed slightly.

"I guess it would feel pretty good to the guy being massaged."

The doctor drew a deep breath through his nose, and irritably tutted again. The next time he makes a bad joke, he thought, I'll give him a shot to put him to sleep.

He closed his eyes again, but he didn't want to return to the dream, so he imagined music. The prelude to Mozart's *Don Giovanni*. He used to listen to this opera a lot in his student days, so he thought he could remember most of the melody, but it began to repeat itself half way through and he couldn't move it on. Oh well. To cheer himself up, he taunted Kita, "By the way, maybe it's natural to get an erection when you're close to death." He'd apparently noted the shape of Kita's pants of the corner of his eye. "I think it's a normal reaction," he went on, red-faced.

"It felt like having sex with a car back there. Literally car sex."

"A car accident is sex with a car, you know. You don't need a man and a woman for that. All you need to do is step on the accelerator. You reach climax in no time."

It was four in the morning. Kita had no idea where he was going. There wasn't a building to be seen along the roadsides. No hospitals, no graveyards. The road simply stretched ahead to carry them along. Kita pressed harder on the accelerator again. His forehead grew hot, and a thrill ran down to his thighs.

The doctor chuckled reminiscently, and murmured, "You know, after a car accident you sometimes find people with a blissful expression on their face. Just like they've come through wild sex."

That young hot-rodder had been like that. He'd been playing tag with a motorcycle cop, failed to take a corner, and piled into a noodle shop. That was the first time the doctor had seen that ecstatic look. The accident happened right near the hospital where he worked, and the patrol car had taken him to the site. Three broken ribs appeared to have pierced his stomach. The helmet was smashed, but his head was unhurt, and he was conscious. When he was carried into the operating room, he was drooling and grinning, his eyes glazed. When they removed the bloody clothes and set about dealing with his injuries, they found his pants were wet with semen.

He'd apparently ejaculated at the moment of impact. His penis was still engorged.

The boy had seized the nurse's arm and said, "Suck me off." She was appalled. He went on, "One more time, one more time before I die!"

"Pull yourself together!" the nurse scolded him. She took hold of his penis.

"Thank you," he said, and lost consciousness.

It must have felt really good, for he developed a taste for it. He managed to crash his motorbike not once but three times, and get himself brought back to the same hospital. Each time, he had the blissful expression of Saint Sebastian. The third time he came in, however, the back of his brain had been gouged out, and he died three hours later.

"By the way, what happens to your penis if you die with an erection?"

"I'd say you'd lose it," the doctor replied curtly.

"Wouldn't it stay for a while?"

"Who knows. Why do you ask?"

"It'd be pretty amazing to have an erection when you're already dead. How was it with that Saint Sebastian fellow?"

The doctor shook his head. "It didn't work for him that third time," he told Kita. "The guy's brains had spilled out, after all. There wasn't even any point in massaging his heart."

After a brief silence, Kita announced, "I've decided how I'm going to kill myself."

"In a crash?" The doctor frowned, and scratched his head. "You'd already made that decision when you stole the car, hadn't you?"

"That thrill just drives me wild. I'm going to commit love suicide with my car, like your Saint Sebastian."

"But dying in a crash won't be good for your internal organs, you know. We can't use a liver or kidney that's been pierced by a rib."

The doctor was still after his organs, it seemed. "I'll make sure it's OK," Kita promised, but the doctor gazed steadily at him.

"Are you really sure you'll succeed first time? It's a question of probabilities, see."

"You're saying I might not die?"

"I once saved a young man's life even though his heart was cut open. He was struck by a truck and brought in unconscious with dreadfully heavy bleeding. I was sure he was done for, but I opened his chest up then and there, without anaesthetic, pinched the wound in his heart together and stopped the flow of blood, and spent a long time sewing him up. Six months later he left hospital and went back to work."

"Now you're boasting. You're saying if I get a hole in my heart, I should stick my finger in it and wait quietly for help? No way."

"I also saved a man who tried to kill himself by sticking a pistol in his mouth. The bullet pierced his upper jaw, travelled up beside his nose, destroyed his right eye, and came to rest in the cerebrum. His face was a mess, but there wasn't much damage to the brain, so his life was saved."

"Goddamn stupid thing to do."

"Well, in his case you might be right. As soon as he was back on his feet he took himself up to the roof of the hospital and jumped off. He landed head first in a flowerbed. Died instantly."

"There's nothing a doctor can do about instant death. I'm planning on having one myself. It'd be terrible not to quite manage the job. I've run through my money, see, and I've got no desire to go back into the world again. Come on, doc, promise me you won't try and save me."

The doctor was silent. It seemed pretty clear Kita was up to something really tricky again. Sure he could let him die, but he needed to be sure those pre-sold organs stayed unharmed. He might have to put his skills to work repairing any organ that happened to get damaged, then wait until Kita was well again and make sure he was there for his next suicide attempt.

"Is there some way I can do a thorough job when I crash the car, do you know? Tell me."

"I've no experience there I'm afraid. I suggest you give up the idea. It's pretty painful, you know."

"No, I've made up my mind."

"You'll burn to death if the car bursts into flames. And in that case, your organs—"

"Would be roasted entrails, I should think," Kita finished for him.

"We'd have to remove the gasoline so you don't burn. I'll get you a cremation later."

Kita remarked that he didn't mind the thought of cremation, but he quite fancied being left out for the birds to pick clean. Now it was finally Friday morning, he was having a few final wishes.

"There aren't any vultures in Hokkaido. If you want a sky burial, you should go somewhere like Tibet. Have you ever heard of the Japanese who was given a sky burial? He didn't actually want one, it's just that he happened to die in a hospital way up in the mountains in Tibet so his burial followed the local custom. They don't have the wood to fuel any furnaces for cremation in Tibet, see. But they do have vultures. There are specialists in sky burial funerals, you know. They have the body carried down into the valley and placed on a large flat rock, where they cut up the flesh and break the bones. They use a rock to smash it all up, cranium, knees, the lot, so the birds can feast on the brain and marrow as well."

"I wonder how the guy felt. Maybe he felt all tingly when the birds were eating him."

"Well he'd be dead, so he wouldn't feel anything. But I wouldn't like a sky burial myself."

Kita looked at the doctor in surprise. "You got some special reason why you don't like the idea? I had you down for the type of guy who didn't care what happened after death," he said.

"I just don't like birds," the doctor replied shortly.

"There's that northern fox here in Hokkaido, isn't there? I wonder if we could manage a fox burial. Would they eat me, do you think?"

"I doubt it."

"How about I give it a try? Whatever happens, you'll cut me up to take out the organs, won't you? So how about dismembering my remains then like they do in sky burials so foxes can eat the rest?"

The doctor coldly rejected this proposal. "I'm not a funeral director or a butcher, you know. I'm a doctor."

The guy dug in his heels over the oddest things. And here he was, harming his medical profession by turning killer and treating human life in this high-handed fashion, and he turns out to be afraid of birds!

"I'll bet your father would've liked a sky burial, you know," Kita remarked jokingly.

"Hmm, yes," the doctor said, nodding thoughtfully. "He would have made a wonderfully nutritious corpse," he added quietly.

Don't Tickle my Corpse

Five in the morning. A sense of the sea somewhere nearby. There was light all around by now, but the sky was like poured concrete.

Kita pulled the car over to the side of the road and got out, leaving the engine running. Outside, the air was cold and grass-scented. Before him stretched a gently undulating plain. If he couldn't get himself eaten by vultures or foxes, at least he might be able to disintegrate into particles in the wide-open spaces someplace like this, and turn to fertilizer. A spare and simple burial of this sort would suit him perfectly, thought Kita.

The doctor had laid back his seat and was sound asleep. Kita set off into the plain, making his way among the tufts of tall grasses and plants he'd never seen before. The muddy red earth stuck to the soles of his sneakers as he walked along in search of a flat rock to lay himself down on. The chill morning air enveloped him. Suddenly seized with a need to piss, he found a suitable place and relieved himself. I'll do this maybe twice more before I die, he thought. And I'd better make sure there's nothing left inside me to emerge when I do die. Also, I'd really like to take a bath. And get some new clothes. And a haircut.

Behind him he heard the sound of someone pushing through the grass. He turned to see the doctor making his way towards him, out of breath. As always, his face was expressionless, but the exhaustion of the last few days showed in the stubble on his chin and in his sunken eyes.

"I wasn't trying to escape," Kita explained.

The doctor stared resentfully at him, breathing hard. He held a handful of plants in each hand. There were no flowers, and each limp, drooping leaf had five fingers, like a baby's hands. "I'd heard about this growing here, but I never really believed it," he said proudly.

"What is it?" Kita asked.

"Marijuana," the doctor replied.

"You know about plants too, eh?" Kita said casually, turning away.

"It relaxes you, see. You need to relax before the big event," the doctor said, like a sports coach. Kita felt a bit like an athlete before an important race.

They went back to the car, and the doctor laid the freshly picked marijuana on the hot hood. He launched into another unasked-for sermon.

"You dry it like this, then roll it into a cigarette to smoke it. That way you'll die happy."

"Is there a town nearby? I feel like a change of mood. There's still a little time before the event."

"There's one about ten miles on from here I think."

"Where are we?"

"I'd say we're somewhere in the Yufutsu Plain."

The sound of this name brought it home to Kita that there was no going back to Tokyo. He shouldn't feel any more attachment to the place. There was no need to walk those familiar streets or climb those steep hills ever again. He'd never be back there in the crowds flowing past Shibuya Station or through the Shinjuku underground passages.

"The town will still be asleep, so we should take a bit of a rest too." The doctor yawned, and with the fresh outdoor air in his lungs, immediately went back to sleep. Kita followed his lead, but once his eyes closed images from the past few days began to flit through his head. The face of Shinobu reading the Bible, and of Mizuho, whose days were spent with the phantom of her dead child, wafted through his brain like drifting smoke. His mother, whose mind had slipped back twenty years into the past, rose like steam before his eyes. And then he shifted into reminiscence mode.

"So I'm going to be leaving Mum and Mizuho and Shinobu behind," he thought, and instantly his pulse quickened, and he opened his eyes. To shake himself out of it, he turned on the car radio. Good grief, there was a voice just like Yashiro's, giving some Buddhist sermon! He hastily turned it off again.

Unable to stand this feeling of limbo any longer, Kita got out and collected the dried marijuana, got back in, slipped the car into Drive, and took off. This time, the doctor was soundly asleep.

At the first sign of human life in three hours, Kita came to a halt and asked through the window where he was. But there was no response. The old lady kept her mouth clamped firmly shut. Was there a hotel nearby? he asked. Still she remained silent, and only stared at him cross-eyed.

Giving up, he nodded to her and took off again.

In another fifteen minutes, he could feel he was very close to the sea. He turned off onto a side road, and drove along until the sea suddenly spread before his eyes. Realizing that he was almost out of gas, he turned off the engine. There was a lone farmhouse not far away.

"You want something there?" The doctor's sleep had been interrupted for the third time.

"I'll just go check it out," Kita said, getting out. He was sure at least that the little tiled house wasn't empty. There was a small farm truck parked in the garden, and a crouching dog warned him off with glowering eyes. He wasn't much of a guard dog, though. Perhaps he was the shy, retiring kind, for he merely gave a couple of low barks.

One of the aluminium-frame windows slid open a little, and someone peered out. Before Kita could say "Good morning" the window slammed shut again, and there was the sound of running feet inside. Kita waited. Next, the window opened rather wider, and a middle-aged woman's voice said, "What do you want, so early in the morning?"

"I'm gathering material for a radio show," Kita replied.

There was a short pause. Then, "Who might you be?" the voice asked.

"My name is Kita. From the Tokyo radio station. I just managed to make it here on time." He wasn't thinking at all, but he sounded quite convincing. He knew he'd be asked what sort of material he was after. "That's funny," he muttered, looking at the name by the door. "This *is* the home of the Kikuis, isn't it? I had an arrangement to come along early this morning for a personal interview."

The door opened, and a middle-aged woman in an apron appeared. A girl in her mid-teens stared curiously out at Kita from behind her.

"Is your husband here?" Kita asked.

"He's gone to Sapporo."

"Oh dear, so I've missed him. That's a shame. He must have forgotten. You didn't know? We'd fixed it for me and a Tokyo doctor to come here and spend the day with you to see how you lived, for our program."

"Ah."

"We've driven right through the night to get here so we're rather tired, and the doctor's not feeling well. Would it be too much trouble to beg a place where we could rest a little? I do apologize for making such a request."

Mrs. Kikui couldn't disguise her bewilderment at being faced with this stranger, but she found herself unable to refuse the persuasive request that slipped so smoothly from Kita's ex-salesman lips. "Well, if you don't mind a place like this," she said. It seemed there was no need hereabouts to lock the door even at night or while people were away. Where would her husband, who knew no one in Tokyo, have had the chance to become acquainted with Kita or the doctor? But around here, even a stranger was accepted once you'd met him, so Kita's off-the-cuff request met with no resistance.

He called the doctor over, and they both went in to the living room. Mrs. Kikui was in the middle of preparing breakfast. Her daughter didn't have school that day, but she too was up bright and early.

Kita and the doctor drank down the miso soup with tofu and spring onion that Mrs. Kikui made for them, and tucked into fermented beans and seaweed in soy. They downed two bowls of rice each. Finally, as they sipped their tea, she ventured a question. Just what kind of personal interview was it that her husband had agreed to? she asked, searching their faces.

"The theme of the program is How to Enjoy Life," Kita explained. "I should confess that I myself am at the end of life. I'm going to die this afternoon. The plan was to consult with your husband about how to make the most out of one's final time on earth."

"He's going to give the advice?"

"That's right. I'm the one who's going to die, see."

In the airless silence that followed, Mrs. Kikui stiffened. It was her daughter who gathered the courage to remark that Kita looked pretty healthy, and didn't seem like someone about to die. Indeed mother and daughter were looking a lot paler than him by now.

"Well, people can die or kill for no reason, you know," Kita said in a low voice.

Mother and daughter swung round to stare at him. "There's no money in the house," the mother said, her voice trembling as she pulled her daughter to her.

"I'm pretty low myself. I've only got two thousand five hundred ninety. Mind you, I have a feeling the doctor there has quite a bit."

The daughter gazed quizzically at Kita, face to face. "What are you here for?" she demanded. The doctor, meanwhile, was taking out his wallet. He produced twenty thousand yen, and laid it on the table.

"Thanks for the excellent food," Kita said. Then he rolled over on the floor where he sat, settled himself in a prone position, and became engrossed in the television. A singer was playing reporter, chatting to the local fishermen in some seaside village.

The doctor finally opened his mouth. "Don't worry about us, we're just normal guys."

But the mother and daughter looked incredulous. These two men in front of them were surely anything but normal. Whatever they were up to, robbery or sexual assault, the two women felt a definite danger in the air.

"We'd very much appreciate being able to take a bath and catch some sleep, if that's okay with you."

Mrs. Kikui's worried face forced itself into a polite smile. "Well, we're not a B&B, I'm afraid," she said.

"I'm aware of that," the doctor replied coldly. "We'll pay ten thousand each," he added.

"You're going to, er, stay the night?" Desperate to protect herself and her daughter, she'd decided to do her awkward best not to aggravate these men.

"I'm just asking you to provide some rest for this gentleman before he dies. All we need is for you to draw us a bath, lay out some bedding, and keep quiet. We'll be gone this afternoon."

Mother and daughter looked at each other, seeming to read each other's minds. The mother set about clearing up the breakfast dishes, while the daughter went off to run the bath.

While Kita was in the bath, the doctor apologized to the Kikuis for the sudden visit, and explained that he was there to try to talk Kita out of committing suicide. He had no intention of causing any harm to them, he explained. After all, they had nothing to do with Kita and his problems. Still, this was a man facing his own imminent death, and he was unpredictable. If they could help to soothe his nerves, he may calm down enough to see the folly of his suicide plans. Kita had no doubt come into the house on impulse, but his motive was surely a desire to spend a few last peaceful hours before he died. They didn't need to do anything really, just let him rest. "I'll guarantee your safety," he finished.

Mother and daughter nodded as they listened, then laid out bedding in the guest room, plus some beer and two jerseys. The doctor asked the daughter if she could lend him either a Bible or a dictionary. She hesitated over the choice, then brought in a Bible, having decided this would work best to calm the heart of the intruder. The doctor proceeded to find a page of psalms that had a substantial margin of white page around the print, then tore it out and cut it into four. On each piece he laid some of the marijuana leaf that he'd picked back there on the plain and dried on the car hood, and these he deftly rolled into four joints. His idea was that a good bath, a drink of beer and a hit of marijuana would soothe and relax Kita physically and mentally, and inevitably lead to a weakening of the suicidal impulse. Then, when the moment was right, he'd telephone Shinobu and get her to talk Kita out of the whole thing. It was sheer chance that he'd found that marijuana, and that Kita had rocked up to the Kikuis' home, but the doctor was following the ninja rule of seizing the opportunity as it arose.

After the bath, the two sipped beer, and drew on their biblical joints.

Next thing they knew, their eyes were drooping. A warmth invaded them, and their face muscles relaxed. The rays of the sun shining in through the window crept slowly towards them. Kita breathed in, and suddenly the room flashed bright. He felt he was in a noonday pool of sunlight. The doctor's eyes were unfocussed. The corners of his eyelids were deeply creased.

Whenever Kita tried to move, his nerves twanged. His limbs felt like spaghetti cooked *al dente*. His torso felt fine, but his legs and arms flopped carelessly about. He stretched out his hand, but it seemed to move in a slowed down skip-frame motion. His brain felt as soft and wobbly as tofu in his skull. Any sudden change in the position of his face caused his grey matter to hit the side of his skull with a shudder. His mouth was dry, and the membrane clung to his tongue and upper jaw like cling film. Even a swill of beer didn't unstick it.

It seemed to Kita as though his whole body had been plugged with sensors that responded vividly to the slightest stimulus of sound, colour and light. Each tick of the clock beat against his temples. His arms and feet responded to this steady rhythm, so that even though he was sitting cross-legged on the bedding, he felt as if he was dancing. Each time he poured a glass of beer, he was astonished at the huge sound it made. He began to hallucinate a waterfall close by.

The doctor turned on the radio, and the room filled with the sound of a Bach unaccompanied cello suite. The deep notes reverberated in every corner of Kita's gut. He could even hear the slight friction of the bow as it came down to bite the string before a note. Soon the melody began to insinuate itself about the little room like a cat. Then before he was aware, Kita was chasing the cat, dancing a kind of Kita-style gavotte or saraband as the air tossed him gaily about.

The doctor had smoked the same amount of Yufutsu Plain dope, but he didn't start dancing. Instead he sat jiggling his leg in time to the dance music, watching Kita's antics with a big grin.

"Boy, this Yufutsu Gold sure does work," he remarked to the daughter, whose white face peered in at them from the living room.

"It doesn't for me," she muttered grumpily.

The doctor roared with laughter. "You smoke a lot of this stuff?" he asked.

"We're not allowed it at school, but it grows round the house, so I can have it any time I want."

Kita too erupted into laughter at this. "I'd love to tell the kids back in Tokyo," he exclaimed.

"So how is it? Does it make you happy?" The doctor's grin was frozen on his face.

"This is great medicine, doctor. You look pretty happy too. I'm happy, the dog's happy, Mum's happy." Kita burst into fresh laughter at his own words.

"I'm not," said the daughter.

"You're pissed off with things, eh?'

"Not especially."

"Got a boyfriend?"

"No way. This is the country."

"What sort of things do you like?"

"Taking photos."

"What do you photograph?"

"Scenery and people and dogs and cows and stuff."

"Would you take one of us, for the record?"

No sooner had Kita spoken than the daughter disappeared into her room and came back with an old Nikon single-lens reflex camera. The doctor tightened up his already grinning face, and Kita beamed blissfully. Click! went the camera. This would be the last photo of him, Kita told himself.

"What's your name?"

"Aki."

"What do you want to do in life?"

"I want to be a stewardess."

At this, both men burst into fresh gales of laughter. Aki tutted in annoyance. "I don't care what really, just so long as I get out of here," she said.

"You want to travel?"

"Sure I do."

"Would you like to be a star?"

"I couldn't even make a hit singing folk songs, the way I look."

For some reason, these blunt answers of hers were absolutely hilarious.

"You ever heard of Shinobu Yoimachi?"

"Yep. She's the one who got kidnapped, isn't she."

"Did they get the guy?"

"Not yet. Like, she won't say who it was, will she. I bet she fell for him."

"Kita." The doctor leaned over to him. "I'll give her a ring right now. Would you like to talk to her?"

"No thanks. That kidnapping's long in the past now. Hey Aki, it was me who kidnapped her, you know. That's pretty cool, eh?"

"No way," Aki said uncertainly, checking the doctor's expression.

The doctor couldn't keep the grin from his face. "It's true," he said.

Aki still couldn't quite believe it, but a look of amazement came over her face, and she looked at Kita with evident awe. "Why did you donate the money to the Red Cross?"

Lying there holding a pillow, Kita replied, "A guy who's about to die isn't going to be able to use all that money," and he burst into fresh laughter. "How would you use thirty million yen, Aki?"

Aki lowered her eyes and thought for a moment. "I'd give half to my parents, and go to Europe with the other half," she replied.

"Why Europe? You should go somewhere warm. How about Tokyo?"

"I've never been outside Hokkaido. But a friend who went to Tokyo said that Sapporo's got more going for it. And anyway, I don't want to go south."

The doctor mumbled that there were a lot of suicides in Europe. She glared at him with an expression that said, so what?

"Mr Kita, are you really going to die soon?"

"I sure am. Some way that feels good."

"Why do you look so happy?"

"There's no point being sad about death. What I'm saying is, there can be happy deaths."

"Have you ever tried to kill yourself before?"

"No, this is my first time. It's so exciting."

"How are you going do it?"

"I'm going crash the white coffin I'm driving."

"I think you should give up the idea."

Kita rolled about, beside himself with laughter. Aki found herself grinning too.

"Yep, you should give up the idea," the doctor, said, nodding vigorously. "The best way is to put an electric shock through the heart. Why not use an electric socket right here and do the job? You're feeling really good right now, after all."

Mrs Kikui had been listening in from the kitchen. Now she put her head round the door, kitchen knife in hand, and cried fervently, "Oh please don't do that! Don't commit suicide in this house, I beg you!"

She looked so desperate that both men were astonished for a moment, but they were quickly overcome with laughter again.

Knife still gripped in her hand, Mrs Kikui began to lecture Kita.

"You've no right to go throwing away the precious life your parents gave you, young man. I don't know what's happened to make you like this, all I know is suicide is stupid. Look at me, stuck here in this backwoods place, long years of poverty, tired out. I shouldn't say it in front of my daughter, but there are times I'd like to die. But then I look at the sea, and I forget about it again. You should go look at the sea, you know. Go and throw all your pains and sorrows into the sea. If you stay alive, you'll have all sorts of joys in your life. You'll be able to eat all sorts of wonderful food. Pain and sorrow doesn't last. Tell me now, what's your favourite food?"

"Curry," Kita murmured.

"Curry, eh? Right, I'll make you some right now. A special curry with potatoes and venison. You'll feel great again if you eat this. Don't you give in. Crawl back out of that big black hole, and make your life a success. I won't go telling the police or anyone else. Just make it through today, see in tomorrow, make it through tomorrow, and stay alive for the day after. I guarantee that day something good will come your way. Just do as I tell you, make it through the days. If you start wanting to die again, eat a big meal, look at yourself in the mirror, and give yourself a great big smile. If you want any more of those leaves there's lots growing out in the garden here, I'll send it down to you. You want some more beer? Or maybe you'd rather have sake? How are your shoulders, a bit tight? Aki, go give him a massage."

Aki barely blinked. She did as told, and started massaging Kita's shoulders with her thumbs. The ticklish sensation made Kita guffaw with laughter, at which Mrs Kikui, worked up by her own sermon, brandished the knife and yelled, "This is no laughing matter! You'll pay for it if you kill yourself, you mark my words!"

This made the doctor choke with laughter. "You planning to kill a guy who's just killed himself? You'll fillet him with that knife of yours if you're not careful. Watch out. I'm having this fellow's organs, you know."

"Don't be so ridiculous!" she grumbled, as she retreated to the kitchen.

"Right, let's get a bit of shut-eye." Both Kita and the doctor had laughed themselves into a state of exhaustion. They couldn't fight their drooping eyelids a moment longer.

Kita awoke to the smell of curry. For a moment, he wondered where he was. In the living room, Mrs Kikui was watching television, still in her apron. Kita spent a while in the toilet seeing to his needs, then combed his hair in front of the mirror. The doctor was still sound asleep. Mrs Kikui was about to speak, but Kita signalled for her to be silent, and sat down at the dining table. Hearing his stomach rumbling, she disappeared into the kitchen without a word.

She emerged with a curry containing whole potatoes and a slab of venison as big as a steak. Kita wolfed it all down. The marijuana seemed to have stimulated his appetite. The taste brought back happy curry memories for him. Ever since he was a boy, whenever he was feeling really low he'd always tucked into a bowl of curry, he remembered. The instant curry his Mum used to make always tasted exactly the same, and over the years, the taste had come to embody his own youthful disappointment with life. After he left home at eighteen, he'd gone on eating curries – curries piled high on plastic plates in student and later company cafeterias, in front of railway stations, in underground shopping malls. Everywhere and at all times, he'd swallowed down his own explosive emotions with a bowl of curry, and gone on obediently doing what the world wanted. Now at last, he didn't need curry any more.

Kita changed out of the casual jersey he'd borrowed, back into his own personal clothing style again, whispered his thanks to Mrs Kikui for the great food and the useful consultation, and attempted to tiptoe out leaving the sleeping doctor behind.

"You've changed your mind, haven't you now?" urged Mrs. Kikui, seeing him off to the doorway. Kita had slept off the marijuana high and returned to normal. He smiled at her, and replied that he was off to the sea to get rid of everything.

"You're sure you shouldn't take the doctor along? He's your personal physician, isn't he? After all, he came along with you to save you, didn't he?"

"We're parting ways. I'll be fine on my own now. Where's Aki?"

"She's around somewhere. You take good care, now. Oh, wait a moment." She disappeared into the kitchen and quickly re-emerged with something wrapped in cling film, which she handed to Kita. "Please take it. This came from the garden."

It was a ball of freshly picked marijuana leaves. Boy, thought Kita, this was his lucky day. What kindness he'd received from this house he'd dropped in on out of the blue. His luck would surely hold this afternoon.

When he got back to the white Camaro, there was Aki in the passenger seat, holding her camera.

The doctor wiped his sweat, breathing heavily. He'd only just managed to escape from a dream in which the white Camaro came racing straight at his bed. Seeing no sign of Kita, he got up and went outside to search. Where was he? he asked Mrs Kikui, who was busy at her make-up. What? He'd headed off towards the sea?

Kita had gotten the better of him. Still in his borrowed jersey, the doctor hurried out, clutching his fifteen-pound bag. There was no sign of the white Camaro. How had Kita managed to turn on the engine? Hastily, the doctor arranged to borrow the family's pick-up truck. Even if he couldn't prevent Kita's suicide, he must somehow manage to extend someone else's life by transplanting those organs. A grim determination seized him.

Kita reluctantly agreed to take Aki as far as the town. But when they got there she remained stubbornly glued to her seat.

"Your Mum will be worried," he told her, but she shrugged this off. "I'll get pretty excited when I'm about to die, you know. You could get raped," he tried, but she responded to this threat with a bluff, "That doesn't scare me." Was she prepared to lay her body on the line to prevent him from killing himself? Why were all these messengers cropping up to stand in his way? His problems all began with Heita Yashiro, then there was the ex-porn star, the four times failed suicide, the driver with the nihilist fixation, the old couple off on their journey to die on the wayside, and the Koikawa brother and sister who sold life insurance and body parts. When he'd gone to see his Mum he'd found her senile, and his old sweetheart Mizuho Nishi had lost her darling son and was in mental anguish. True, Shinobu's Mass had soothed his heart, but then he'd somehow gone and abducted her, and thereby inflicted that doctor-turned-killer on himself. Then he'd had a lecture from the lady of the house he happened to drop in on, and now here was the daughter, firmly stuck to him.

Shinobu would say, "These are all messengers from God, you know. God has decreed that this man mustn't be killed. These messengers are all using whatever means they can to massage your heart back to normal, and draw you away from the temptation of death."

Right, thought Kita, I'll send her a farewell message. He got out of the car and headed for a phone booth, with Aki shadowing him, clicking away with her camera. Maybe she was planning to record the last thoughts of someone condemned to Death by Choice.

No sooner had he dialled than Shinobu came on the line, as if she'd been sitting there waiting.

"Kita? Is that you? Where are you? Are you far away? Come back as soon as you can." She sounded dispirited. He guessed that as soon as he'd gone those vultures had gathered around again to peck and harass her. "What's the matter? Say something!"

"You OK?"

"No, I'm feeling absolutely lousy. Come back and abduct me again, Kita."

"Sorry, honey, that's not on. I have to tell you goodbye."

"Don't! I want to see you again! What reason have you got to die? What have you ever done that could justify this?"

"It's recompense for my sins."

"What sins? Abduction? No one's blaming you for anything, Kita."

"I stole a car."

"So? Just give it back."

"I ordered that Yashiro be killed."

"The guy who killed him's to blame for that. Not you."

"I've done stuff you don't know about. No one does, except me."

"God will forgive you."

"God may, but I don't forgive myself."

"What did you do? Tell me."

"I killed a child."

"When? Where?"

"When I was five."

"Who did you kill?"

"I drowned my kid brother."

"It must've been an accident."

"No. My parents thought it was too, but it was me that killed him. No one blamed me. That's why I believed that it really was an accident. I haven't once told myself in all these thirty years that I killed my own brother. I'd forgotten my own sin. But then one day I saw two little brothers quarrelling on a riverbank and it all came back to me. It was no accident. At the time, I definitely wanted my little brother to drown. When I understood this, I just couldn't stop crying. Thirty years later is too late to remember something like that. No one's going to punish me now. A little boy's life was ended at the age of three by his big brother. And his big brother lived on for thirty years and never paid the price. I was crushed at the thought. I went down to Kyushu in order to at least confess at my father's grave. That's where I made the decision to condemn myself to death. I decided to go and tell my mother, but when I got there I found she'd gone senile in the four months since I'd last seen her. So neither of my parents will ever know what I did. You once said the next world is a horrible place, didn't you? But if such a place exists, that's where I have to go. I want to find my kid brother and beg his forgiveness, and look after him. He was only in this world for three short years. He never got to taste the pleasures of this life. I want to tell him all about this world of ours. That's why I gave myself a week's grace, so I could taste some of its pleasures myself."

"Your little brother has forgiven you, I'm sure of it. He'll be wanting his big brother to go on living."

"He died without knowing why. That really wrenches my heart. My own death is a different matter – it's willed, and it's justified.

Neither Yashiro nor the doctor know the reason. They both think you can commit suicide without needing to have a reason. But I wanted to tell you. You refuse to accept that I could die for no reason, see."

"Couldn't you go on living, for my sake? Why did you turn your back on me when I suggested we should die together?"

"The time for love is past."

"You can atone for your kid brother's death even if you stay alive, you know. You can commune with the dead without having to die yourself. You just have to think about him. You'd forgotten till now, but from now on you can remember. Please, come back."

"I've told you this already, but if I'm resurrected, I'll come and see you. Thank you. Goodbye."

Aki was there beside him as he headed back to the car, but he managed to trip her up and leap in before she recovered. He gave her a merry wave and took off, leaving her standing there disgruntled, snapping her last photographs of the rapidly retreating rear end of the white coffin. For some reason she'd found it quite elating to discover that this way of living, or rather dying, was possible. She'd hopped in to the car in the hope that he might abduct her too, but it hadn't worked out that way. Still, it had given her a certain courage. Maybe I'll just go ahead and leave home, she thought.

He'd better crash the car before the gasoline in the spare tank ran out, Kita decided. He'd find a bit of coastline just right for plunging the car into, and give himself a sea burial. After all, his kid brother had drowned. Where was he now? How far would wind-blown Cape Erimo be from here? That would be a good place to drive off a cliff. But at this rate, he was likely to grow old worrying over irrelevant questions. Better be quick. He'd had a pretty good last week. It was great to have thrown everything to the wind for once. He'd put up with too much in his boring life, God knows. This person called "Yoshio Kita" was a pretty bankrupt specimen. But this last week he'd been on a really good roll, so let's say it had been a good life. He had loved. He'd had lots of great sex. He'd eaten his fill of seafood and curry. He'd donated lots of money to the Red Cross. He'd almost been poisoned to death. He'd gone to two hot springs, and smoked dope. The memory of this reminded him what a weird guy that doctor was. He hadn't ever learned his real name. The guy would probably die a lousy death. He despised life, after all. Why should there be room in this crowded world for people like that? True, the world had turned out to be a crazier place than Kita had assumed. By average standards, Kita was a pretty regular guy after all. Well then, he should die the death of a normal citizen. Spur of the moment, and no second chance. Just slam the foot down on the accelerator. If he took off from the cliff edge at about a hundred thirty miles an hour, he'd probably achieve about the same distance as a ski jump. But maybe he should just take a peep over the edge before he went. There was an ideal curve right there. And – a lucky break – no hospital in sight.

Kita got out and looked over the cliff edge. It was about fifty feet high. Down below, foaming waves washed up over the black rocks. If he smashed through the guardrail and went over, he'd have to be pretty unlucky not to die. He'd probably need a run-up of no more than three hundred yards or so.

Right, was there anything else he needed to do before he took off? Not really, but why not pause and look at the sea? This was the sea that would be his grave, after all. That weedy stuff floating over there beyond the rocks where the waves were breaking must be kelp. It looked somehow like it was beckoning him with its long slippery arms. He'd soon be taking his eternal sleep cradled in those arms like a sea otter. A seaweed burial, eh? Not a bad thing, after all.

The only worry was how hard it might be to crash through the guardrail. It didn't look all that solid, so he guessed he'd get through without any problem if he hit it at around a hundred thirty miles an hour. What did professional ski jumpers think about before a jump, he wondered? They always looked as though they were mourning lost love, but that was surely due to the tension. They were probably imagining the parabola of a perfect jump.

Why not take a piss? There wouldn't be any public toilets on the banks of the Styx where he was going, after all. But for that matter, there were none here either. OK, his last piss by the side of a street. His last meal had been curry. His last companion in life had been Shinobu. The last person he'd shaken off in life was Aki. His last lover was Shinobu. His last love was Shinobu. The last thing he'd read in life was… the Bible, right? This looked a bit *too* good. OK, how about singing a last song? The old Shinichi Mori number 'Nothing happens in the spring at Erimo.' I guess nothing happens in summer there either. And Fall? Winter? Right, he'd taken his last piss. Now was the time for his last drive. No, hang on there. He hadn't stood on his head for the last time yet. Why not try it? He hadn't stood on his hands in quite a while. He checked left and right in case a car was coming, then put his hands down in the middle of the road.

He twisted his back as he went up, but he still managed to walk a few steps on his hands. In the old days he used to make it to fifteen steps. He'd aged. OK, exactly how long had he lived now? Let's count up. Today was Friday the 13th. His birthday was also the thirteenth, so that made him exactly thirty-five years and six months old. What would he be doing tomorrow, if he were still alive?

Enough! Thinking about this on the day of your execution just made you sad. It was important to enjoy this Death By Choice. Yoshio Kita was going to go out with an erection and a blissful expression, like Saint Sebastian. Although he was feeling a little tense. Right, let's try a bit of muscle relaxation. His last loosening-up exercises.

The sun peeped out from between the clouds. Come to bless him, eh? This needed some kind of fanfare. Shame the only audience was himself.

Right, that had the ol' death hormones pumping now. Turn on the radio. They'd just set in on the prelude to *Carmen*. Fabulous timing. He was fired up and ready to go. Energy flooded him.

Turn the car around and back up five hundred yards. Another U-turn. Check the clock. Fourteen eleven. That would mean he died at around two fifteen on the thirteenth. That's if the car's clock was set right. OK Mr Yoshio Kita, you ready boy? The prelude was reaching its crescendo. Wait, he hadn't written a will. Oh well, what the heck. He'd told his last wishes to Shinobu. Sorry doc, but my organs are going to be fish food.

Full throttle! Tyres screaming. There's that tingle, really pumping. Ooh, here comes the erection. Man, this is almost too much. OK, here goes. Bye!

The guardrail leaped towards him. One good solid punch to the jaw and he was through. Suddenly there was something pressing hard against his chest. The air bag. The Camaro was airborne. Now it was falling. Up comes the sea. My God, what a force. Just like an ejaculation.

And then, a shock that went straight through his bone marrow. Can't breathe. Something pressing against his stomach. Something sticking into his shin. Pain. Was he in the sea? The car was sinking. *Carmen* still playing. This some kind of aquarium? Why didn't the water come in? Goddamn, I'm still alive. Didn't it work? Maybe I can't die unless the water comes in. Maybe the glass'll break if I just wait. Or should I break it? Intense cello music. And some sound like water poured onto a hot fry pan. Water! The water's beginning to come in. This is going to take a while. Got to break the glass to lessen this pain.

Kick it. And again. What about the power window? Nope, broken. Head-butt it. The head's the hardest part of the body.

The glass broke. Kita was swallowed by the sea.

Through the band of light above him, he could see a stream of bubbles rising. Fish had already come flocking around the Camaro where it lay on the sea floor, sounding it out. Kita had escaped the car and was floating in the water, bent over. Ah, it's me, he thought. He felt he'd forgotten something in the car, so turned back to check. There was a child playing there, ducking in and out of the trunk. "Hey, what're you doing? You'll drown!" Kita called. "I drowned long ago," the child replied.

"Are you my little brother?"

"Never laid eyes on you before." This kid was only three, but he was sassy. Around him was a belt of kelp, covered with minuscule writing. Do you hate me, kid? I pushed you into the river. You must have suffered. I'm sorry. I wanted to see you again. To apologize… But the child had disappeared, leaving the kelp floating empty.

Kita was in a familiar child's room. On the wall were the letters "WXY," carved in the wood with a knife. In Kita's mind when he was a child, this had signified the body of a woman having sex. These letters began to move, and shifted to the figure of his mother washing her hair in the bathroom. His kid brother was crying in the bathtub. *Yoshio! Yoshio!* came a cry. His father was digging a hole. *I'm putting a pole up here for the koinobori carp streamers.* Ah, I'm way back in the past. Looking up at the sky. I've seen this blue sky full of scaly clouds before somewhere. *Sorry, Kita, I just can't go on being with you any* – Stop it, don't apologize! You'll kill my love. Now a child yelling, *Papa! Papa!* I'm not your Dad. Who are you? Is that Shingo? Do you recognize me? *Yeah, you used to love Mummy, didn't you?* That's right. You might've lived if I'd married your Mum, you know. *No, you're wrong. I've never been born.* Shingo goes skating off into the distance. And now here comes Shinobu, riding in an Alfa Romeo. *Kita! Come to the hospital with me.* No, I hate hospitals. *No no, don't say that. I think I'm pregnant, see.* My kid? *Of course. So come on, quick, come to the hospital.* But hang on there, I've just committed Death By Choice. *Oh, everyone these days wants to die. Kids, middle aged folks… Did you know, my friend Jesus had a time when he wanted to die, when he was just past thirty. But before that he'd had a life and death battle with the world. He chose to lose the battle, and he won. You're just like Jesus. Come on, quick! You're going to be reborn.*

I'm being sucked down a narrow tube. Am I off to the other world at last? My body's being drawn out like a piece of spaghetti. This hurts. I can't breathe. I can see a hole. A small hole. All I can do is try and escape through it. The other world must lie beyond it. A brilliant light is shining in. An unbearable tingle! Who's doing this to me? Is this a sign I've arrived?

Solitude by Choice

Some time before night fell, the doctor discovered the broken guardrail on a curve of Route 336 between Ogifushi and Sakaimachi, where the road ran along a cliff above the sea. He informed the local police and requested an investigation, and early Saturday morning the diving team arrived, donned aqualungs, and dived to the bottom. There they discovered the white Camaro, but the body of the driver wasn't in it. A three-hour search was conducted with two boats and a crew of six divers, but there was no sign of the body. The most convincing theory was that it had been washed far out to sea. If he had by any chance managed to survive he would surely have sought help from a passing car or someone living nearby, but no one had seen him, and there was no way of confirming the death.

The doctor returned to the capital. There was nothing more he could do.

He was deeply exhausted. No sooner was he flat on his back at last than the ceiling began to spin. He shut his eyes and pressed his fingers to them, then looked at the ceiling again. The window, the wall, the door, the chair, all looked like spinning fragments of crystal. It was as if he was gazing down a kaleidoscope.

Could this be some message from his brain telling him to stop staring at things? Now he came to think of it, these eyes had spent too much time recently looking at bloodied organs, corpses that had just breathed their last, and flat ECGs on a screen.

He held his eyes tightly shut, but now it was his own body that was beginning to spin on the bed. He'd spent the last few days hurtling from place to place, playing both doctor and killer, he told himself. If he didn't rest, he'd burn out, but the impetus from all this frenetic activity kept his body spinning even after he'd hit the bed.

He swallowed a sleeping pill to force the spin to a halt, and slept the sleep of the dead. He planned to dream away these last few days of utterly futile effort, then to proceed to forget all about the dream and get back to good ol' lazy, uneventful everyday life again.

He was woken by the sound of the telephone.

A woman's voice informed him it was checkout time. He had no memory of having slept so long, but the clock told him it was noon. What? he thought. He suddenly couldn't believe that he'd been wandering in the realm of dreams for thirteen solid hours. What day is it? he asked her.

"It's Sunday."

Oh yeah, Easter Sunday, Resurrection day. Yesterday was Saturday, and the day before was Friday thirteenth.

The doctor booked himself in for another day, ordered up a room service brunch, and ran the water for a bath.

As the hot water began to soak into his parched skin, a heartfelt sigh escaped him. His blood vessels expanded, a sweat broke out on his forehead – and then suddenly the bathtub he was lying in began to spin down a whirling hole.

Here we go again, thought the doctor. He tried ducking his head under water and massaging his temples, but things went on spinning. He felt seasick, as if he was in a boat on rough seas. This just didn't make sense. He jumped out of the bath, grabbed his bathrobe, and began to pace the room.

As long as he was moving, he discovered, he didn't feel dizzy, but as soon as he lay down it was back again. Maybe a good stiff drink would improve things a little. He tossed back a beer from the minibar and tried a few warm-up exercises. Soon after, his room service clubhouse sandwiches arrived, so he set to and sated his appetite in hopes that would work. But once he leaned back on the sofa it wasn't long before the room began to heave up and down and tilt from side to side on a rough sea, and then it was back spinning again. He drank another beer, then emptied two mini bottles of whisky, but the goddamn spinning just went on. He felt he would vomit unless he got up and started pacing the room again.

This was all Kita's fault!

There was no question. It was Yoshio Kita, the man who'd disappeared into the North Pacific on Friday, who was behind this dizziness. The doctor had no idea if he'd really died or not, since he hadn't personally managed to check the corpse. This was what was getting to him, and making his middle ear act so strangely.

As a general rule, if someone smashes through a guardrail and plunges fifty feet into the sea inside his car, he'd have an eighty percent chance of dying. What's more, since this particular man chose to do this as an act of suicide, the odds would surely be higher than usual. But no body had been found. The doctor had failed to lay his hands on the cornea and organs he'd paid for. He had been ejected from the story without a chance to ascertain anything for himself, and there was nothing he could do about it. Except somehow get through this dizziness.

Rest was denied him. He was forced to keep on going, round and round, pointlessly. He was being ordered to keep going, keep trying, or else he'd just spin in place. And who was doing the ordering?

The doctor pulled back a few days. Just who was it that had given him his orders and involved him in this chain of events? Heita Yashiro, that's who. But he'd settled things with that guy already. If you made your living dealing in other people's lives, you could only say it served you right to have a kidney stolen. And it was a safe bet that Yashiro, though he was probably still alive for a while yet, wouldn't want to lay eyes on the doctor again. It was too late to get that kidney back now. It was tucked away inside someone else's belly, busy filtering out the poisons. Yashiro had done quite a bit to poison the world, but at least his kidney would be helping someone else get rid of some. Meantime, some of his own poisonous dealings had caught up with him and shortened his life considerably.

So who had ordered the doctor to try to save Kita, then? Shinobu, of course. He had no idea whether he'd managed to do as she'd asked or not, in the end. Still, he felt he had to report in to his employer. He picked up the phone and rang her. He found on his cell phone a message from her, almost a prayer for Kita's safety.

They hadn't found Kita's body, he informed her. She wanted to meet right away, she said. She added, however, that wherever she went she was inevitably trailed by gangsters, gawkers, and cops.

Could he come to her place, in the guise of a consulting doctor? And make sure to dress the part as obviously as possible, please.

Well at any rate, now that he'd been given the task of making his final report he was at least freed from his dizziness for a while.

He shaved, carefully parted his hair, put on a tie, picked up the Boston bag of medical equipment he'd been carting everywhere, and hailed a taxi. Upon arrival, he swept ostentatiously into the flat, white coat fluttering, before the eyes of the doubtless lurking onlookers crouched in their cars or hidden in the shadows.

Shinobu had undergone a change in the last two or three days. She had a new poise and dignity about her. Yet there was also an air of unswerving determination, quite unlike the single-minded devotion of those few days. Could it be that this over-the-hill idol was suddenly drawing fresh breath now that the eyes of the world were on her again?

"You've changed," the doctor observed bluntly.

"I've lost three kilos in the last five days," she replied, gazing at him levelly. The doctor flinched a little before the strength in her eyes. This was not the look of a girly idol who flirts and fawns.

"I imagine they've grilled you to death over it all. You're the only one who knows the details of the abduction, after all."

"The cops have kept the pressure up. They're trying to claim the abductor and I were in cahoots, and it was all a put-up job. I spent another five hours being questioned yesterday. And once the cops were done, it was the turn of the reporters. I'm worn out, let me tell you. Then the production manager's been fleeced of all that money, so he's going to use me to the hilt to make up for his losses. I have a half-day off today, then tomorrow I'm back on the treadmill again – magazine interviews, appearance on a talk show, recording discussions, discussions about appearing in some TV drama. In the next few months I have to decide about my future, so I'm being as nice as I can to everyone."

"You sure no one's eavesdropping?" the doctor murmured nervously.

"No, we're fine in here. This is Daddy's flat. I can't go back to my own, it's too dangerous. But they'll be turning their attention to this place, too, before long."

She wouldn't be sleeping properly, he guessed. There was no way she could call a halt to this show-in-a-million she'd set in motion. She'd have to keep up the lies till the day she died. If they ever learned the truth about that abduction, they'd arrest her as an accessory to fraud. If she ever did get the urge to confess, the safest way would be to use a public broadcast. She'd be arrested, true, but at least she'd be free of the harassments of the production manager and the gangsters and politicians. They were bound to smell something fishy about this whole abduction story. And if they started following up their hunch, all they had to do was ask at the inn at that hot springs resort where the two had stayed, and the answer would be clear. Then it would be only a matter of time before they figured out that it was Shinobu herself who was behind all their problems. They'd wipe her career, for sure. Mind you, God knows what kind of career she had to look forward to anyway.

The cops weren't completely satisfied that she was a victim, yet there was no way they could really set her up as an accomplice either. How could they find a motive that would stick? The only theory that would hold water was that she had been driven by her ambition to get back into the public eye. The mass media were playing up the claim that this former idol was using her misfortune to her own advantage. Meanwhile, the public was on the side of Shinobu and her unknown abductor. Many were saying that even if the whole story proved a farce, they should be let off lightly because, after all, they had helped sick children. Some sympathizers were even saying that thirty million yen was cheap at the price, while fans claimed Shinobu had grown up thanks to her abduction, and cynics spoke of "the starlet whose comeback cost a bomb."

The names of the production manager, the gangsters, and the politicians who'd put up the ransom money had been publicized. They'd been made to squirm by being asked to explain themselves and clarify whether they intended to recover their money. In response, they had been forced to unanimously declare that Shinobu Yoimachi had their unwavering support and that they were delighted that she had come back safe and sound. This being the case, they were happy to have been able to help those unfortunate children with their donation.

They'd been forced to act charitably, and it made them hopping mad.

"Do you plan on keeping up the lie, then?" the doctor asked, just to remind her.

"Sure, no problem," she replied. "Just so long as I can keep the money flowing. Those guys are just dogs that will follow along wherever the money runs. If they rubbed me out now, it would be their loss."

"But sooner or later everyone'll forget this thing, you know."

"Sure. And I have lots to do before that happens. The battle's just begun." Her eyes held neither uncertainty nor loneliness.

Kita had looked just this way on Friday, the doctor thought. Though he made bad jokes, though he got giggly and stoned on marijuana, the determination in his eyes never wavered. Like her, he had had the will to fight.

Meeting Kita had changed Shinobu. What was it that had brought them together? That's right, he'd been a fan of hers. He'd paid a hundred thousand yen to meet her, thus fulfilling one of his last wishes before he died. Shinobu must have sensed something at that meeting. She must have understood that within this man dwelled a proud and noble will.

When Kita had decided to end his life on Friday, his feelings must have been those of a soldier headed for the front – a tangle of tension, elation, and an exalted sense of purity. Shinobu's keen senses would have picked up on this. And it was Kita, yes Kita, who had coaxed her from her cocoon and encouraged her to spread her wings. And Kita who had sent the doctor his dizzy spell.

"Just what is it you plan to battle, Shinobu?"

Neither she nor Kita would really have a clear enemy they needed to fight, after all. Surely there was an element of random willfulness in all this. The doctor couldn't imagine a battle without an enemy in any terms other than as sheer hard work. But Shinobu had her reply ready.

"It's simple. Kita and I fight freedom."

"Freedom? You mean you're a slave and you're fighting to be free?"

"No, no. It's just that I can't any longer believe in sham freedom. Everyone keeps using the word, but all it amounts to is some limited freedom they're grateful for being given by someone. Everyone's 'free' on someone else's terms. Freedom of expression, freedom of occupation, freedom of religion, freedom of living, freedom of movement – it's all just about the rules of society really, not something I personally have won for myself, see? Look at it this way. No one's going to give you the freedom to kill others, or to steal, or to commit arson, or to dispose of a corpse, or dig a grave wherever you want, or live on the street. So you may as well stop wanting to do any of those things. No one can actually be 'free' without being given the nod to do it. No one can even understand what freedom is. I get the feeling I've been deceived into thinking I was free all this time. So from now on, I intend to fight the lie of freedom."

The doctor listened entranced. He could never have imagined that such an argument could have come from the mouth of this pouty-lipped star with fabulous breasts.

Maybe this realization of hers was due to the experience of having abducted herself along with the kidnapper, and given her own ransom money to sick kids instead of using it in some way connected with herself. It was the old Shinobu, the one who hadn't yet met Kita, who'd sulked about how she was just a means for other people to make money. But having been abducted from her former self, she had learned the value and use of treating herself as property.

And so – eureka! Shinobu had discovered that she could change in all sorts of ways depending on who used her for what. And that she could change herself, any way she wanted.

She'd arrived at pretty much the same place that Kita had after his week-long travels – hadn't she? Kita had thrown everything to the winds, and she'd taken on his colors and changed too. Or so it seemed.

"I guess you're not afraid of dying now, eh?"

Shinobu snorted at this. "By the way, what's become of my friend? If no one's found his corpse, that would mean he's still alive somewhere, surely?"

How was he to answer this? Kita appeared to have killed himself. The doctor had personally witnessed the wreckage. He hadn't managed to prevent it, so he couldn't claim payment from her. Miraculously, however, the suicide attempt might have failed. Perhaps Kita hadn't died. The rest was groundless speculation, but he guessed Kita may have stubbornly tried to kill himself again, by some other means. Or perhaps he'd forgiven himself, given up on the suicide, and was back to his everyday life again?

"If he were alive now, what do you think he'd be doing?"

Shinobu thought for a while. Then she lowered her eyes to the floor, for all the world like a rejected child, and murmured, "I don't think there'd be anything he could do."

The doctor agreed. After all, there was nothing he could do himself, and he was beset by dizziness.

"I'd guess he'd be much more miserable to be in the world than he was before he tried to kill himself," Shinobu continued.

"True enough. After all, if he's still alive he'll be wanted for abduction, theft, attempted murder, drug offences, and fraud. He'd be an overnight sensation, like you. I'm an accomplice, after all, so I know what I'm talking about…"

"No," she broke in, "that's not what I'm saying." Then she went on, twisting her fingers as if to weave together into a coherent whole the words that floated insubstantially in her mind. "What I mean is… Kita, well he rejected all the lies about freedom. All he did was plan to kill himself without anyone ordering him about or meddling. But then all these people gathered like flies and tried to use him. Even suicide isn't a free act. But I think that Kita ended up confronting society without ever intending to; he just let things take their course. It's just that when he encountered an enemy bent on obstructing his freedom, he could only turn and fight. It's backbreaking work, maintaining real freedom. If his suicide attempt really did fail, he'd be left living a life that was a hundred times as cruel as his old one. And he'd really and truly be alone this time. No one who's had a near-death experience can ever return to a world and a life of lies, see."

It was as if someone from some other existence were borrowing Shinobu's voice to speak.

"Freedom is lonely. Jesus Christ has taught me that. If you want to be truly free, you have to resist all the temptations of money and fame and nation and society. As long as all you want is your own happiness and the pleasure of the moment, you'll remain a slave, whoever you are. Christ cut himself off from the world for the sake of those who'd come after him. I want to follow him. If Kita really is alive, I want to be a comfort for his loneliness. I believe that if people who've discovered what real freedom is can join hands and work to create the future, the evils of the world will slowly improve. If I didn't believe that, I could never survive this cruel present."

This meant that Yoshio Kita had in effect given Shinobu the courage to live in true freedom, didn't it? He'd shown her that even when there's nothing more you can do, you have to bear it. The doctor wasn't inclined to hear any more of her religious confession. She could choose to become her own version of a saint or Joan of Arc if she wished. He guessed she wanted to save her soul from the depressing reality she lived in. But as for the doctor, he'd never had any truck with Freedom, or The Future, or The Soul. He'd lived his life simply in terms of biological life and death. He'd been too busy cutting up others' bodies, putting them back together again, and sewing them up, to spare a moment's thought for such deep questions. From Shinobu's point of view, he'd be classed among the people who go about madly conning and deceiving others.

"I doubt we'll meet again," he said, and put out his hand.

She took it in a weak grip. "What will you do?" she asked.

What indeed? He wasn't cut out either for doctoring or for killing, but he'd realized this a bit late. Yet he too had been given a kind of cruel freedom, and he had to bear the painful reality of it. "I think I might try working in a convenience store." For some reason, it seemed to him that this would be what he was most suited for. A bright, white space that somewhat resembled a hospital ward, providing "convenience" to a series of transient, anonymous clients. A quick word of thanks directed at their departing backs. A presence neither hated nor loved, merely considered convenient... could it be that he'd spent all these years unconsciously wishing to fulfil just such a role? If only his path had crossed with Kita's and Yashiro's and Shinobu's simply through the fleeting exchange of employee and customers, he'd have been spared all the hassle and misdeeds of this past week. At this thought, the doctor suddenly found himself imagining the expressionless convenience store employee as a kind of priest of infinite wisdom, quietly living his life in accordance with the laws of nature.

"If you really do plan on working in a convenience store, we may meet again in fact."

The doctor nodded. Then he bowed, and left the room almost certainly never to come back. Why not head straight for a convenience store? he thought. But three steps on, he had a sudden thought. Just possibly, if Kita hadn't died, he'd suddenly turn up there wanting a packet of instant curry.

The Cruelty of Freedom

The sky was a pale pink. He'd never seen such a sky. There ought to be sea below it, but everything was dyed such a pink that there was no distinguishing one from the other.

His skin was so goose-pimpled with cold that you could have grated cheese on it. The cold was fierce, but there was no point in worrying over it. His body didn't register the cold.

He wished someone would explain to him what he was doing here. Why was he lying here sodden, on this rocky beach? Why was he so horribly thirsty? Why was blood running from his hairline? Was there any reason why he wasn't wearing shoes?

When he drew in a breath, his chest wheezed like an ocarina, and he coughed and spluttered. No one was there, yet he felt as if someone was gently patting his back. Trying to tell him to stop? Someone was beside him, but he couldn't see anyone. Or was it a rock? A rock that bore a strong resemblance to his mother. When had his mother become a rock? But when he looked more carefully, it looked rather like the grumpy face of that killer, who shared his mother's Alzheimerish puzzled look about where and who he was. Kita had forgotten whether the killer had died or was still alive. And what had happened to his mother after she lost her memory?

It was cold. He wanted to go somewhere a bit warmer. If he prayed for it, no doubt he'd find he was lying on a paradisiacal summer beach. Here goes – one, two, three.

There must be some mistake here. He couldn't remember how things were supposed to be. Before he'd got here... yes, he could remember swimming. Underwater, in his clothes, through the swaying seaweed, deep down in the salty water with bubbles racing upward. While someone was making him tingle.

Had he been dreaming? And if so, did that mean that this gooseflesh and his sodden trousers and socks were part of the same dream? Was blood red in dreams just like in real life? Maybe the sky and sea were this pink colour because it was a dream. There was a certain special way to behave in dreams. He didn't need to do anything. The dream would do it all for him. But whose dream was this? The stone's dream? The sea's?

How he longed to get into a good hot bath. OK, let's try a bath dream. And he'd love to eat some noodles or curry. Right, let's have a curry dream while he was at it.

The sky had turned a dark brown. The sea was dark red. Time was constantly slipping forward somewhere at the edges of his consciousness. The blood on his forehead had apparently dried now, and his clothes were barely damp. Well at any rate, he thought, let's chase time.

He set off to walk along the water's edge, picking up a driftwood stick to use as a crutch. He must have walked for close to an hour, his easy tempo following the rhythm of the waves, yet still time seemed to be racing ahead of him. His toe had been cut up on shell fragments, and he could walk no further. But when he sat down, he found himself looking at a shoe like a weather-beaten old fisherman's face, washed up on the shore. He put his wounded foot into this and walked on some way further, and then he came across a sneaker that looked like some fat kid just woken from sleep. With two shoes, he could now walk at a pace that kept up with the passage of time – but now the wind had changed direction and was blowing in from the sea, catching him like wind in a sail and pushing him up towards the mountains.

He listened attentively. Sometimes the wind sounded like the cry of a bird, sometimes like the moan of a discontented woman, and then again like an electronic hum, or like clothing being ripped. It paused for a second, and then he found himself enclosed by trees with brown, scaly trunks, far from the sound of the sea. Softly, a muddy darkness began to descend over the wood. His nostrils drew in the scent of pine resin and night dampness.

He curled up in a hollow made by the roots of a great pine, snuggled down like a bagworm under a layer of leafy branches and grass he'd gathered, and closed his eyes.

His eyes were prized open by a shaft of light shining down through the branches. "Wake up!" someone seemed to be saying. He looked about him. A skylark was singing madly, and to his ears it seemed to be shouting hysterically "Die! Die!" But another skylark that shot across the tree above him from a different direction was wailing "Free!"

He'd spent the night in his curled position, and now pain like a needle shot through his back. And with the pain, his consciousness of himself returned.

What the hell am I doing here? Kita shivered. A combination of cold and fear raced along his dulled and frazzled nerves into every corner of his body.

Sure enough, the thing he most feared had become reality. His plan to reach the other world had somehow misfired, and he'd been denied entry. Had he chosen the wrong method? Was death itself turning its back on him? Or was it that the other world was actually much more distant than he'd imagined, and he had to cross endless mountains, rivers, valleys and seas to reach it?

He'd assumed humans died more easily than this, but this had obviously been a fatal error. Here he was, it turned out, unable to become a corpse, dragging around this useless garbage of a body. Did he have to recycle himself, was that it? If only he'd managed to transform himself neatly into a drowned corpse, this self and its shame, memories, words, and despair would all long since have evaporated, and he'd be floating gracefully upon the waves, with everything given over to nature's hands. But no, it seemed becoming a corpse wasn't anything like so easy. That's what someone was trying to tell him.

Think of all the men and women who'd tried to stand in the way of his suicide. There was no question they'd all been sent as messengers from beyond that mysterious curtain. They'd appeared because, from the moment Kita had decided to commit Death by Choice and kill himself the following Friday, he'd been minutely observed from beyond this inhuman curtain of death. He'd had the death part of his sentence excised and been left simply with the choice, the freedom. In other words, he'd been ordered to be free even from death.

But what on earth could he do? How was he supposed to use this freedom? It was precisely because there was nothing else he could do that he'd given his stupid laugh and decided to die. But his play had been parried. And now here he was, unable to act again. He was back to where he'd started eight days ago.

Still, that Friday eight days ago he'd still had things to do – the visit to his Dad's grave, the feasting, abducting an idol, donating to the Red Cross, seeing his old lover again. He'd had a certain amount of money, not to mention physical strength, and the urge to act. A short life and a merry death, that's how it should have gone. But look at him now. The two thousand yen in notes he'd had in his pocket had apparently gone as an offering to the sea, and all that remained in his pocket was forty yen. His physical and mental strength were both at an all-time low, and he was left gaping at this apparently endless nightmare unfolding around him.

What would happen if he simply waited and did nothing now? Kita summoned what little imaginative powers remained to him, and tried to think.

He'd spent too much effort in fruitless resistance of one sort or another, that was the trouble. That's why he'd been left hanging onto life like this. Enough. No more resisting. He was as good as through the door into the other world, after all, so why not simply accept whatever may happen now? Everything except meddling from other people, that was. Luckily, there was no sign of a soul around here. Still, you never knew when some curious hiker might come striding along, or someone out after wild herbs, so he'd be better off hiding deeper in the forest. He should look for some sheltered spot out of the rain, make himself enough space to lie down, and gather some wild coltsfoot leaves for a roof. This would be his grave. If he stuck it out for two weeks or so, surely he'd manage to turn into a mummy as he lay there.

It took him half a day to climb the narrow mountain track, cross a stream, push his way through thickets of dwarf bamboo, and walk around till he found a suitable gravesite, a cave between two great rocks. He set about stamping down the dwarf bamboo on the floor, then he laid down the coltsfoot leaves he'd picked along the way, and plugged the gaps in the walls with wet clay. By the time he'd made himself the kind of den where a bear would happily settle in to hibernate, the woods were growing dark. He'd worked hard.

It was quite a pleasant coffin to lie in. The coltsfoot and bamboo blanket kept up a constant rustle, but they held the warmth. Strangely free of hunger, he slept deeply. The silence of the forest at night was so complete that his ears rang and his heart beat loudly, but the soft rustle of the bamboo leaves helped calm his fears.

He dreamed of eating curry. With each mouthful he found more curry on the plate, till it had grown to a small mountain before his eyes, which spilled over and engulfed him.

When he woke, he was seized with a fierce thirst and a desire to vomit. He struggled out of his coffin and made his way through the dwarf bamboo in search of the stream. It seemed he'd be making this thirty-minute trip there and back every day from now on. The nausea subsided once he'd drunk, but it was now replaced by fierce stomach cramps. At last, around noon, he managed to shit.

The nausea and headache were a little better while the sun was shining, but as soon as night came on the darkness clamped painfully around his stomach and his head. There seemed to be a kind of tidal rhythm to the pain.

As he lay there in the darkness, he felt the boundary between life and death grow blurred. His body would eventually return to the soil, but he felt that his consciousness too was shifting, and growing more intimate with the earth. The only problem was, the suffering got in the way.

You're still alive. The pain is the proof of it.

He decided to pick up a small stone every time he went for water, and make a pile in front of his grave.

He was growing more sensitive to pain and fear. The enemy was obviously urging him to become increasingly aware of approaching death. Well then, he'd make himself insensitive, he decided. But though he managed to do this to some extent, time stretched out and drove him mad. It was easiest to sleep, but he was terrified of being seized by insomnia when night came, so he lay there with his eyes open while it was light, looking at the trees and shrubs and clouds, and listening to the sounds of the forest. There was a shrub nearby that, like a trompe l'oeil, became now a plump woman's face, now a malicious-looking rabbit face, now the backside of a squatting sumo wrestler. And then there were the endless, meaningful whisperings of the forest.

Groaning, he rolled about in his rock shelter, sweating profusely, his stomach stabbed by fierce pains like a sword piercing his guts. It was literally a battle with death. Even if he admitted defeat and surrendered, though, his merciless ordeal would continue. Why such pains in his stomach, when he'd eaten nothing? He'd had no idea until this moment just what suffering was involved in not eating. It seemed he had chosen the very opposite of an easy death.

Not only his stomach but his head was wracked with pain, and now the pains cycled more and more swiftly through him. Almost like the pangs of childbirth. There was pain in the birth of new life and the relinquishing of old life alike.

Even when the agony weakened a little, he now knew to anticipate the cycle, and was braced against its next onslaught. Then, just a little later than he'd anticipated, fresh pain would surge through him.

Today, it took twice as long to make his way down to drink water and return. He had all the time in the world, but how much longer would his strength hold? When all that was left was his bones, time would still flow gently along in the stream and forest.

His cheeks were sunken, his trousers were loose on his frame. The loss of flesh meant that the cold penetrated more fiercely. He sought out the sunlight as much as he could, and lay curled in it.

It was terrible not to sleep at night. The darkness and the silence doubled his suffering. The only tiny salvation was in the soft burr of the crickets. It sounded in his ears like music, like song. Then a cicada began, its rhythmic rasping call seeming to say "eat and sleep, eat and sleep," or "life or death, life or death."

For the insects, what lay here was a huge and marvellous lump of potential prey. They must be gathering round to check him out. After all, it would be their job to return him to the earth.

Rain fell. He settled his head so that his open mouth could catch the drops, and lay there for a while. This allowed him to forego the exhausting business of making his way down to the stream and back.

The rain brought a faint scent of herbs. Forest tea, he thought as he drank. He feverishly counted the drops that entered his mouth – a total of 5,411.

It must be poor circulation that made him feel so cold. But his body was frail now, and walking was a huge effort. His legs in particular felt terribly weak. Once he could no longer go for water, death would no doubt come quite swiftly.

He began to suffer fierce palpitations. His heart was racing uncontrollably, pumping blood around the body, desperately trying to keep his body temperature up. Kita was doing his best to die, but his heart was bravely trying to keep him alive. This pain that flowed into every corner of his body must be his organs and nerves rising up in protest at his death. But he was by now less than half alive.

His skin was parched, and flaking off in raised scales. Smelly pus oozed from the wound in his forehead.

Hey, worms, be glad and rejoice! You'll soon be served a lovely big lump of meat jerky.

The pebbles he piled up one by one even on the days he didn't go for a drink had now reached more than twenty. By now, his body no longer responded to orders. And yet he wanted water.

The torment went on, in a blur of day and night. He managed to piss a tiny trickle of urine once a day, but each time with more pain.

He thought perhaps an escape into the world of dreams would lessen the suffering a little, but the dreams were never pleasant. He was tired of dreaming. He wanted to become a figure in someone else's dream for a change. That way he'd feel neither pain nor cold, even if he were beaten, abused, even killed.

This was horrible. All he was doing was not eating, so why should he be suffering such pain and cold?

Christ underwent a fast of forty days in the wilderness in his thirtieth year. Buddha attained enlightenment after a forty-day fast, and Moses was given the Ten Commandments after fasting forty days. So all the great religious founders had undergone this horrible suffering. They must have had exceptional powers of endurance.

More than likely, though, these saints were either extreme masochists, or people with an exceptional physical make-up.

He hadn't had the slightest intention of getting pally with the saints, or of understanding how they'd felt. He'd only wanted to die a light-hearted death. If he'd realized what a cruel ordeal those men had been through, he'd have bowed in heartfelt reverence before both God and the Buddha.

The saintly hermits of old would have tasted the extremes of loneliness, hallucination, and suffering as they underwent their experiences of life and death, light and dark, good and evil, freedom and restraint. Those fierce oppositions would have registered along their nerves as aching head, aching stomach, cold, nausea, paralysis, dream, hallucination, and fear. Half dead, their thoughts came with the half-life left to them. They saw no one, ate nothing, made no attempt to escape or hide; they relinquished the self, and existed simply in this in-between state. The unbearable pain of fasting would have driven them again and again to almost yield to the temptation to flee to either life or death. Life up till now wasn't all that bad, they'd have thought. Now that I've withstood all this suffering, the old life will feel wonderfully easy after this. They may have felt that it was better after all to resign yourself to the constraints of normal life rather than endure this brutal freedom. Or maybe they felt more inclined to give up trying to think with the life that remained to them, and instead simply hasten their death.

Yet they resisted. They stood firm in this limbo state, learned the art of enduring the cruel extremes of freedom, and in the end walked back among the people again. No doubt what awaited them there were misunderstandings and oppression by the authorities. No one would be able to think like them, or have the strength to endure as they had. They had nothing more to fear. It was the people and the authorities that now feared them.

And he had mistakenly entered that same limbo, where misunderstanding, persuasion, discrimination, and persecution meant nothing.

Having understood so late in the day, Kita felt the urge to pray to something. He had defiled holy ground, and he feared that still crueller torments awaited him. And now, for the first time since chasing himself into this forest, he felt that it would be better to escape.

This was the worst day so far. Pain stabbed at him constantly, and he was assailed by a nausea so strong it threatened to turn his guts inside out. Twisting his now useless body about he struggled to endure, lost consciousness when the pain became too great, regained it again to continue his suffering.

He had forfeited all chance of escape now. In a few more days he'd surely be dead.

Rain fell, and for the first time in three days water touched his mouth. The clouds were bringing water for the dying.

If he had a phone handy, he'd like to get onto the god of death and say *Quick, kill me! I'm waiting!*

He wasn't fasting. No, it's just that there wasn't any food, nor any appetite. The thought made him want to laugh. Food has escaped me. And there's no way I can escape.

He no longer knew whether he felt pain, or cold, or indeed anything.

He'd grown very thin and light. Shrivelled as a slice of dried squid. Put him over a flame and he'd curl.

Water, he wanted water. Once the messenger of death came for him, he'd be taken to the River Styx. Then he could drink his fill.

Rain. He'd thought he'd be dead by morning, but there was still some life in him after all. Lots of rain today. He'd drunk a bit too much. Pissing was painful. Once he'd managed to piss, his body was attacked by sharp pains like being packed in needles of ice. Maybe he'd die of cold before he died of starvation.

If only the forest would burst into flames, he prayed. It would release him from this cold, and give him a cremation.

A beautiful day. Same pain, but less excruciating if he stopped focusing on it. Come what may, he'd try going for water today he decided. His legs had completely given in by now, but he could roll down the slope, and crawling was still possible. But he wouldn't be able to get back to the cave, would he? He didn't have the strength to make himself a new bed sheltered from the rain and wind. Well, he was nine tenths dead by now, so what did it matter? He could choose to stay in this coffin till he shrivelled to a mummy, or return to earth somewhere out there among the dwarf bamboo, or set off to meet the River Styx halfway – at any rate, he'd die faster by moving.

So out he crawled. OK, he thought, let's see if I can walk. He tried standing with the support of the rock face. His legs no longer had anything to do with him. His will set off to walk, but his legs refused to do as they were told. He staggered three steps, his body carried unwillingly along above the tottering legs, then collapsed.

He tried again and again, crawling along on all fours in short bursts, but he'd only gone barely thirty yards from the cave when his strength gave out.

He rolled over and looked at the sky. The clouds were laughing. Ah, he thought with a sigh, how stupid I've been to struggle, and he made his way back to the cave with the same repetition of crawl and stagger. He'd finally given in now. It was just that it was such a beautiful day he couldn't bear to stay still.

He'd now become part of this nameless forest.

His cells were cannibalizing each other, it seemed to him. The law of strong eats weak was being displayed right here in his own body. And cannibalism hurt.

Still being dismembered? Not over yet?

He really should have drowned. Compared to starvation, all those other deaths – drowning, hanging, electrocution, falling off a cliff, poisoning, shock – were just a roller-coaster ride.

Still not dead? Oh come on, stop joking.

I'll be there soon. Just have to cut the thread.

Even after all this, still dreaming. Still a bit left in the battery, eh? The doctor was serving in a convenience store, and he complained when Kita turned up to buy a packet of instant curry.

"I'm supposed to get your organs when you die, you know." Good God, he was still on about that. Forget the organs, just remove the pain in here, will you?

He really should be dead by now, but the pain was still there.

What's that? A helicopter? Has a war begun, maybe?

Hey, looks like someone's out there. Come to fetch me across the river at last, is that it?

Nausea. Come on, spew me out onto the far shore for God's sake.

Where am I? Still in limbo, it seems…

WHAT IS "DEATH BY CHOICE"?

How are you?

I'm so-so, myself. Bored, as usual. One life cycle completed and into extra time, pottering about in my tiny patch of garden like an Englishman intent on finding his pleasures among the mediocrities of existence, tending cucumbers and scallions, and cutting lengths of bamboo from the local grove to make little bamboo trinkets. Younger friends remark that age seems to be catching up with me these days, and I guess it's true, I've reached that time of life. And now, in my dotage, I've come up with this kind of desperate novel, in which I've given myself free rein to portray a decadence in keeping with this *fin de siècle* moment, and preparations for what's to come. Those who read this book will be a step ahead of everyone else by getting a sneak preview of life and opinions at the beginning of the twenty-first century.

Actually, I have to say I've already published quite a few novels that accurately predicted the future. I flatter myself that I haven't just done what a journalist does, tagging along in the wake of alarming events with an analysis of their social pathologies – I've been consistently aware of historical trends, and tried to grasp what lies beneath the superficial currents of the age. You could call me the last canary that's taken into the coal mine. But the canary is rather like the boy who cried wolf. I love that boy, and I never could believe he was lying. I choose to think that he was simply more highly-strung and sensitive than anyone else in the village.

You don't have to be a depressive – everyone who's lived twenty or thirty years has once or twice felt the seductive urge towards suicide. My own thoughts have turned that way repeatedly ever since adolescence. I've managed to survive thanks to the fact that I was never really all that serious about it, but I know you don't necessarily need some strong motivation or hell of despair for suicide. Other people, the ones left behind, assume that you must have been driven to it by some dreadful anguish, but the person who dies doesn't consider it in such complicated terms. This is the case with Zombie (alias Izumi Mizusawa) in the novel. On the contrary, I'd guess that if you were in a state of mind that allowed you to pause and really think about why you needed to kill yourself, there'd be a pretty good chance you'd give up on the idea.

We can't pop over to the other world and ask the people who've committed suicide about this, so their real motives for suicide must remain a mystery. Actually, there may well be such complex reasons and motivations behind the act that even they themselves aren't aware of them. You can't find all the factors behind a suicide in the personal consciousness and situation of the person involved. It's perfectly possible to have suicides produced by social situations, or being swept along by mass psychology, or even resulting from fashion. Think of the people who kill themselves as a sacrifice to some popular idol, or as a result of the Internet circulating suicide manuals or offering cyanide for sale.

I don't feel any urge to recreate some outmoded suicide manual from a passing fad. I don't see anything wrong with the existence of manuals like this – they're pretty much like those for conducting love affairs, or cooking, or wandering the world. The important thing is to find out whether things really happen the way they say they do in these manuals. After all, that kind of advice is just simplified generalization. Even if people follow precedent exactly, the process and the result will differ completely from one person to the next. I'm a novelist, so all I can do is doggedly pursue the tale of one suicide.

After adolescence, the period that is most closely connected with suicide is one's forties, when it's the leading cause of death. This has some relevance to me, since I've only got a couple of years to go before I turn forty. So I feel the need to work through the question of suicide till I've grown sick of the subject, in order to get my head around how to deal with my coming middle-aged male crisis. This impulse is what lies behind *Death by Choice*, a detailed look at the last week in the life of a man who's decided to kill himself the following Friday.

Just suppose you had a million or so yen in the bank and knew you only had one week before departing this world – how would you spend your remaining time?

This may be a tired old theme, but I don't imagine many have actually thought the question through to the bitter end. I'd guess everyone's first thoughts would turn to the pleasures of the flesh. How about, for instance, a dish of boiled shark's fin plus abalone steak plus underbelly of bluefin tuna, all you can eat, followed by sleeping with three rabidly sexy ladies and a champagne bath to top it off? But the pleasures of the flesh can get pretty wearying. Next morning you're in the grip of heartburn and a hangover, not to mention a sore groin. OK, why not go take a break at a hot spring resort? And meet up again with an old lover before you die, maybe kidnap the star you're crazy about, and since you're going to die anyway you could donate your organs to someone who wants them, and do something remarkable that will make good and sure your life in this world will be remembered? You just have to set your mind to it for a moment and you'll uncover a tangle of all manner of desires, impulses good and bad, and vanities. People don't usually give a thought to what happens after they die, but when death is finally approaching, your mind can suddenly rush frantically to the question of that future time when you're no longer around. People in their forties contemplating suicide will think of the family they'd be leaving behind, and take out some insurance. If more than a year has elapsed since you signed the form, the insurance company will pay out in the event of suicide – and apparently there are quite a few cases where someone does kill themselves after the year is up. How to imagine the world you'll leave behind you – this is the real ethical question. It's wrong to decide that you can get away with anything since you'll soon be dead anyhow. We have the freedom to choose to die, but this freedom of choice is a cruel thing. Understand this, and you'll feel increasingly inclined to put off the actual deed once you've had your fill of the pleasures of the flesh.

To be honest, when I began this novel my plan was to write up the theme of suicide in a kind of muscular comedy form à la Chaplin, Lloyd, or Keaton. The idea was to address those youths who mystify suicide in their pallid novels, and say to them Come on guys, enough. It's really just a comedy, you know. At any rate, that was the plan until I got as far as THURSDAY.

When I launched into FRIDAY, things took a new direction. Then I put off the publication deadline, and added another chapter called SOMEDAY.

Once the Friday deadline is passed, what Yoshio Kita confronts is death itself.

If I can claim to have understood anything in the process of writing this novel, it's that there's another kind of urge besides the urge to eat, the sex urge, and the urge to know – and that's the urge to die. Freud was right.

Masahiko Shimada